FIRST SHIFT

AF091686

THE WOLVES OF ROCK FALLS
BOOK ONE

FIRST SHIFT

Quill & Flame
EmberLight

AJ SKELLY

Quill & Flame
PUBLISHING HOUSE

First Shift

Copyright ©2021 by April J. Skelly

Second Edition Copyright ©2026 by April J. Skelly

Published by Quill & Flame Publishing House, an imprint of Book Bash Media, LLC.

www.quillandflame.com

All rights reserved.

No part of this publication may be reproduced, digitally stored, or transmitted in any form without written permission from the publisher, except as permitted by U.S. copyright law.

This is a work of fiction. Names, characters, and incidents are products of the author's imagination or are used fictitiously. Any similarity to actual people, living or dead, organizations, business establishments, and/or events is purely coincidental.

NO AI TRAINING: Without any limitation on the author or Quill & Flame's exclusive copyright rights, any use of this publication to train generative artificial intelligence is expressly prohibited.

Hoc autem scripsi ad me.
And for my AV kids. They know who they are.

BOOKS BY AJ SKELLY

First Shift
Rogue Shift
Sworn Shift
Pack Shift
Lost Shift

Of Flame & Frost

Murder at Mistlethwaite Manor

An Alliance of Ash and Jade

The Rat King

AS APRIL J. SKELLY

A Lethal Engagement

Chapter 1

Sam

October, Friday night football game. Rock Falls, Delaware

Megan snagged a cheese-laden chip from the plastic container on my lap. With a saucy smile and a mischievous twinkle in her eye, she popped it in her mouth. My eyes lingered longer than they should have as she licked cheese off her finger, oblivious to the way she twisted up my insides.

The football stadium speakers boomed into the chilly night air, and I sighed. I shouldn't want her. But when her big hazel eyes sparkled with excitement from the football game, kissing her was all I could think about.

Brody Harrington sauntered by, and Wolf growled inside me.

"Megan!" He wedged himself onto the metal bleachers between Megan and the girl next to her and slung an arm around her shoulders, trapping her long caramel-colored hair underneath.

"Hey, Brody." Did she lean into him? I wanted to rip his arms off.

"Come to winter formal with me."

I stopped myself from growling outright.

Megan laughed, and some of the tension riding in my shoulders receded. "Are you serious?"

Brody's eyebrows drew together. "Of course, I'm serious." He winked as his hand slid to her upper arm. "So is that a yes?" He tightened his arm around her, drawing her closer. So help me, I would tear his face off if he tried to kiss her.

Wolf stirred within me, reminding me of my limitations. Never mind that I'd been in love with Meg half of forever. Pack rules were pack rules. Unfortunately, they didn't prevent Brody from kissing her. Stupid human.

"I'll think about it." Megan put her hand on his chest and pushed away. I exhaled. Brody turned his eyes to me.

"Help me out here, Wolfe. Convince her to go with me."

"Megan's a big girl. She can make up her own mind." Megan flashed me a smile as she ran a hand through her hair. My turn to wink at her.

"Let me know, Meg." Brody squeezed her shoulder again and mercifully hopped up and bounded down the stairs.

"Aren't you going to go with him?" Shelby Atwood sat one row behind us where she'd been digging her knee into my back half the game.

Megan turned to Shelby, her leg brushing against mine and sending sparks up my thigh. "I don't know. I can't tell if he's serious or just being a flirt."

"Are you kidding? He's totally serious. You should go catch him and tell him you'll go with him." Shelby's eyes glittered.

I resisted the urge to glare at Shelby. In the two years since Shelby had moved to Rock Falls, I'd never entirely been able to figure her out. She raised Wolf's hackles.

I swallowed hard and turned my attention back to the white-striped turf. It was the last quarter, and we were up by three. Nacho cheese and hot dog remains littered the bleachers in front of me. A cold wind made me shiver until Megan inched closer, and my blood ignited. Why could I not get this girl out of my head?

Noise pounded all around us. Lights flashed, the crowd cheered, someone two rows over dropped their coffee. Cheerleaders waved their pom-poms down on the track while our team thundered down the field.

Adrenaline raced through my veins, maybe from the game. More likely from Megan's arm pressed against mine.

With three seconds on the clock, we were in possession on the twenty-yard line and down by one. Half the town of Rock Falls was in the stands, surrounding the student section. We were on our feet, yelling loud enough to drown out the cheerleaders, jumping and wildly waving our arms in the churning noise. Energy poured from the crowd into the night skies as our quarterback was a streak of lightning on the field. Megan jumped beside me and squeaked as she slipped on someone's spilled soda. With the wolf's natural grace evident in my movements, I snatched her around her middle and brought her close. Big mistake. Her sunshine and roses scent shot straight to my head.

Her eyes twinkled from the rush. Her hand rested on my chest, right over my thundering heart.

She's off limits. You can't have her. My brain chanted.

Her breath was warm on my face. I wanted to scent her. Drag my nose up the side of her neck. I swallowed.

One kiss. Could it hurt? Yes. It could.

My eyes still flitted to her lips, full and so close to mine. My other hand found her waist, and her eyes widened in surprise and her lips parted. Her hand pressed into my jacket.

Wolf whined inside me, wanting to taste her lips, too, but wary because she wasn't our kind.

But when she stilled and didn't pull away, my fingers curled around her. Her chest rose and fell against mine.

With the crowd shouting around us, my resolve weakened. My head tipped without my permission, bringing my lips achingly closer to hers.

She didn't move, and the rest of the world fell away. Wolf picked up her accelerated heartbeat over the din of the crowd.

Her head angled, and fireworks exploded inside me. Wolf nudged me hard, and terror seized me. What was I doing? I opened my mouth to say something—anything—to break the tension I'd created between us when a hard shove between my shoulder blades rocketed me into Megan. My face throbbed where our heads knocked together.

Straightening, my arms still around Megan, I froze.

Wolf surged inside me. The tang of her blood and the bitter aftertaste of my toxins mixed on my tongue. Fear roiled through me. Wolf howled inside.

Jerking back in horror, I felt my stomach fall to the gravel below the bleachers.

"Ow." Megan rubbed her forehead.

"You're bleeding." Shelby's voice held as much horror as I felt. I shrugged off Shelby's hand still between my shoulders. She'd tripped.

Meg gingerly dabbed her forehead, her finger coming away bloody. I riveted on that tiny drop of blood on her finger. Light flared around the corners of my vision, and I thought for a second that my heart was literally going to explode.

I bit her. *I bit her.*

Panic burst in my chest. For a second, I couldn't even breathe.

"Meg, I'm so sorry." My strangled words were lost in the crash of people flocking to the parking lot.

"Wow, Sam, you've got a hard head and sharp teeth," she stammered. Her face flushed red as a blood moon.

Shelby stormed off without an apology.

A popular fantasy theme song blasted from Megan's pocket and broke the mounting tension.

She swiped the rest of the blood from her forehead and fished her phone out of her pocket.

"Rachel?"

I couldn't move. I was rooted to the spot. The ramifications of what I'd done were astronomical.

I bit Meg. While I was human. I'd never heard of anyone being turned unless they'd been bitten by the wolf, not the human. Of course, no one from our pack had bitten anyone in over two hundred years—in either form. Maybe this wasn't as bad as it seemed. *Please, let this not be as bad as it seemed!*

"Oh. How much longer do you need?" Megan swayed, and the barest hint of perspiration shone on her forehead.

Guilt and terror warred in my chest. This was definitely as bad as I thought. I had to get Megan out of there.

Chapter 2

Megan

"Sorry, Meg," Rachel said. "I didn't expect play practice to take this long, or for Luke to knock over the can of red paint onto the stage." My best friend's frustrated sigh echoed in my ear. "It's almost cleaned up, and then I can come get you." Rachel was my ride, which wouldn't have been a big deal normally. I glanced at Sam, his blue eyes piercing me with their intensity, then looked away as awkward anxiety slithered up my spine.

"No problem. Just keep me posted. I'll make my way back over to the school and meet you in the gym."

I stole one more glance at Sam, who hadn't moved, before putting my phone back in my pocket.

He'd wanted to kiss me. A part of me was secretly relieved that Shelby had ruined that, even though part of me had always wondered what it would be like to kiss Sam Wolfe. We'd been good friends since sixth grade. A kiss would mess that up.

But now we had almost-but-not-really kissed. And my head hurt. And it was getting awkward. I blinked as a wave of nausea swept over me. Worry twisted my belly.

All the anxiety must be getting to me. Cramps hurtled through my middle, and I flinched. Sweat beaded my forehead, and I chilled as a night breeze rushed over the dispersing crowd. Was I coming down with the flu?

Sam cleared his throat. "Are you going home with Rachel?"

"That's the plan. But it's taking longer than she expected." I swallowed down another roll of nausea. Although, with the way my stomach was rebelling, maybe I should go home.

Of all the days not to drive myself to school.

"Are you okay?" Sam watched me carefully; his fingers grazed my arm. And just like that, we were back on friendly footing. It was the touch of my concerned friend, not the impassioned touch of the blond-haired Adonis he might have been a few minutes ago.

"No. Actually, I'm not feeling good at all. I hope it wasn't your nachos and cheese." I attempted humor to cover how bad my body ached.

"Call Rachel and tell her I'll run you home."

"My house is out of your way." I didn't want to inconvenience him, and the thought of being alone with him in the car brought back the uncertainty of the did-we-almost-kiss that still simmered under my skin. I rubbed my head.

The breath left me in a rush as my intestines tied themselves in knots.

"Let me help you," Sam said softly. I glanced up at him. Another stab of lightning jolted through me. The salty stale smell of leftover concession-stand food littered on the bleachers around us made my already-queasy stomach revolt. I swallowed, the bile staying in my stomach for now. Something was definitely wrong with me.

"You sure you don't mind?"

His smile looked more like a grimace. "I'm sure."

Maybe he was afraid I was going to puke on his shoes. I hoped I didn't.

Chapter 3

Sam

Megan did not look good as I slid into the driver's side of my car. Her skin had a greenish cast, and her forehead was beaded with perspiration. I had to hand it to her. If what I feared was happening, she was in agony and not saying a word.

I, however, was in the fast lane toward full-blown panic. I broke one of the sacred rules. Never bite a human.

My father was going to kill me. That paled in comparison to what I'd done to Meg. Her whole life, her whole world, would no longer be what she thought it was. And I had ensured that any feelings of security, her understanding of what was real and what was fantasy, would be ripped from her with mind-altering force. *If* she changed.

The moon was full—it would be tomorrow, too—illuminating the road and giving the approaching meadows and encroaching forests an ethereal beauty.

I glanced at Megan. We'd been quiet for about five minutes, lost in private thoughts. Or private pain for Meg. I sighed. I'd made a fine mess of things. Guilt squirmed in my gut. If I'd been allowed to date her—beautiful, perfect human that she was—knocking heads and accidentally biting her wouldn't have been my chosen method to express my interest. "How you doing?"

"Actually, I feel a little better. My stomach just hurts still. I appreciate you taking me home. Thank you." Taking her home was the least I could do after I bit her. I glanced at the tiny cut on her forehead. Dread cramped my gut.

I caught a whiff of Brody Harrington's smell still lingering on her. I squeezed the steering wheel, Wolf curling his lips back, remembering the way his gaze had devoured her. Shoving thoughts of Brody aside, I focused on the positive. She was feeling better. Excellent. I hadn't seen the telltale signs of the shift. Could it be possible that it was some random fluke? Could we both be that lucky? After all, I'd been human when I bit her...did that matter?

Hundreds of years of untarnished pack history and I might have just destroyed it. I swallowed thickly.

"Glad you're feeling better. And it's no problem to run you home. How's your head?"

She chuckled and then winced and ran a finger over where we'd collided. "I'll live." She forced a smile.

My gut unclenched a fraction of an inch. Her belly hurt. First shift was insanely intense. I tried to convince myself that maybe she got a bite of bad nachos. My hands released their white-knuckle grip on the steering wheel. I was about to breathe again when I saw it.

Her shoulders heaved.

We were in the middle of nowhere on the back roads between school and the other side of town. Open meadows hugged the road, flanked by forest.

A strangled noise choked in her throat. We were out of time and out of luck.

I slammed the brakes and skidded to a stop on the gravel shoulder of the road.

"Sam, I'm going to be sick." She fumbled for the latch.

"It's a lot more than that," I muttered, racing around to her side of the car.

I opened her door as blood spewed from her mouth and she fell out of her seat. I caught her and eased her out of the car, her shoulders convulsing, her pulse pounding beneath my hands.

"No, no, no!" I whispered, wanting to let my wolf loose. I didn't know if I could stand to watch the pain Meg would go through—pain caused entirely at my own fangs.

I steered us into a lightly wooded patch, far enough from the road that nobody would see what was about to happen.

She moaned, low, harsh. Her breathing was labored.

"I...think...dying," she whispered brokenly, her breath hitching. She buckled in over herself.

Whipping my hand through my hair, I tugged at it, as if pulling my hair could distract me from what was happening to Megan. "Megan, listen to me," I tried. My voice squeaked, while Wolf lunged inside me. I forced him back down. "Listen to me," I tried again. "I know what you're feeling. It hurts. A lot. I'm *so* sorry!" Something that sounded like a sob echoed inside my head. I think maybe I was crying. "You're going through *first shift*. You're going to turn into a wolf."

She turned tortured eyes on me, and I could feel her anguish, terror, and confusion. Wolf begged for release. I wanted to phase, be a wolf, let the animal lead, to run and run for miles and think of nothing but the fragrance of the forest and the wind in my fur.

Meg screamed, and I about lost it.

Her skin started to crack open, the seams of her body coming unhinged. Blood gushed from her mouth again, and it sprayed the ground in front of her. Her back quivered as her shoulders rolled backward into her spine. Her backbone lengthened, and her shirt split as caramel-colored fur rippled through her skin. Her legs drew up and her feet pushed out of her shoes, claws appearing at the end of paws and footpads. With a mighty shake and a sound more roar than howl, she stood before me on all fours. A beautiful auburn wolf in a clearing, the full moon shining down on her in all her glory.

Every cell in my body honed in on Megan. Wolf demanded that I shift and claim her. She was my mate. There was no denying it. I took a deep breath to calm the shock. I couldn't let my wolf out now, though I had never felt the urge so strongly before. I clenched my hands into fists and took a calming breath to still the tremors that rocked my arms. I had to think and act in my human skin. Megan didn't need to be scared more than she already was. Regaining control of myself, I crouched down at eye-level with Megan-the-wolf. I couldn't stop myself from ever so slowly reaching my hands out and stroking her head.

Wolf howled inside me that Megan was my mate. The only one I'd ever want. The only one I'd ever love. I gulped.

"Hey," I said softly. "Your wolf is beautiful." I stroked her ears, and she let out the most guilt-inducing whine I'd ever heard.

Chapter 4

Megan

The pain had subsided. But I was unbelievably disoriented. My brain seemed fuzzy, and I felt, not quite bloated, but stretched—like I didn't fit into my own skin anymore.

Sam was in front of me, awe on his face as he gently stroked my hair. Was he trying to put it behind my ears? Was he going to try to kiss me again? Why was he touching me like this? It felt incredible. Brody had been flirting with me for weeks, but it had never felt this genuine. Heat pooled in my belly, and I was about to lean into him so he could reach me better when he spoke.

"Your wolf is beautiful."

My wolf. In one second, violent images and flashes of bone on bone and sinews snapping filled my brain. I thought I'd lost my mind. An echo of Sam's voice ricocheted inside my head. *You're going to turn into a wolf now.*

A wolf. I looked at my hands but saw giant paws with curving claws instead. I started brutally, jerking at the shock, my teeth clicking together with the force. Sam's hand softly stroked my head.

A sob choked its way out of my throat—at least, I tried to sob. It came out as a pitiful whine.

Terrified and confused, I shook my head out of Sam's hands and tried to back away from him. What had he done to me? I tripped on something. My *tail*? With an undignified *thump*, I landed on my rear.

"Easy, Megan," Sam said. His voice was soothing. The wolf creature—*thing*—that I was, immediately warmed to it. But I—at least what I assumed was left of the human me—wanted to escape. What else would or could he do to me? My jaws snapped at him, but the wolf recoiled, and all I accomplished was to bite my own tongue. Helplessness, anger, fear, and bewilderment roiled through my gut.

I whined again. Tears, or whatever the wolf equivalent was, pricked at my eyes. Slumping to the ground I covered my head with my paws in defeat and whimpered.

"It's going to be all right. You're not going to stay a wolf. You'll change back in a few minutes."

My head came up. I tried to convey my jumbled thoughts—I needed answers.

What am I? my brain shouted.

Sam jerked like I'd slapped him. He took a deep breath. "I'm a werewolf. You're...you're a werewolf now. When I, when we collided." He took a deep breath. "When I bit you, my wolf toxins must have infected you, too. I hoped maybe it was just a bad nacho. I was human when I bit you. I wasn't sure if it would change you or not. Obviously, it did. I'm so sorry." His eyes told me he was undeniably sincere.

Werewolf? Werewolves were *real*?

The tingling started at the base of my *tail* and shivered up my spine before I could formulate my next thought.

I whimpered, afraid of the pain that would certainly follow.

"Don't fight it," Sam instructed gently. "Let the shift come and feel your shape going back to your human form. Imagine your arms and your legs and your fingers and toes."

I did my best to follow his directions. In fact, I became so focused on the sound of his voice that the creaking, groaning, and cracking were dull noises in the background until the fire that started in my gut became a raging inferno. Every inch of me felt enflamed. A howl escaped my lips, and I was vaguely aware when it turned into a scream.

The scream stopped, and I lay on the grass panting, utterly worn. And then I felt cold wind on my sweaty skin.

Oh. My. Word.

I was naked. In *skin*! But totally, completely, naked-as-the-day-I-was-born, naked in front of Sam Wolfe.

I felt him drape his jacket around my shoulders, and I gripped it around me, covering as much of my exposed self as possible. My humiliation was complete even as my brain was spinning.

"Turn around," I rasped.

"What? Are you okay?" He sounded totally baffled.

"No! I am definitely *not* okay! I am *naked*!"

"Meg?" He trailed off.

I took a huge gulp of air and rolled the thoughts through my aching head. Blood. Fur. Claws. Skin. I felt a nudge inside me—the *creature* was still there.

Werewolf. They—I—were *real* and not the product of over-active imaginations. I choked back the horror. Okay. Focus on what I could control. Process the insanity later.

"Did you see anything?" I croaked. "As little as possible," he replied.

I knew full well he must have gotten quite an eyeful. At least he was attempting to be chivalrous and reduce the confusion, insecurity, and mortification swirling inside me. The rational part of my brain knew it was stupid to be worrying about my nakedness when my body had just defied the laws of physics. But nakedness I felt I could control. Turning into a wolf? Not so much. I grappled with reality and fiction and felt I was teetering on the brink of both.

A sob started building in my chest but before it could escape, a hard fist of irrational anger surged to the front. I sucked in a breath through my teeth, barely containing my wild emotions.

"Are you okay right here for a minute? I've got some extra clothes in my trunk."

I sniffed and nodded. "Meg?"

I forgot he had turned as I'd asked him and hadn't seen me nod. "Yes."

Wrapping my arms and the sleeves of his jacket around me, I watched him jog to his car. I shivered. It was cold. I was naked. I was in pain. And I'd just turned into a wolf.

Laugh? Cry? Commit myself to a mental institution? All three? I hardly knew what to think. I prided myself on being a relatively rational, logical sort of person. But rationality and logic were utterly failing me now. My emotions were ratcheting around inside me, and I was sure I was going to explode any minute. I closed my eyes and took a deep breath. I pictured Grandma Elsie's face, all warm and wrinkled and round, with a dusting of flour on her cheek that she often had when we'd baked together. Another breath. Anger still simmered below the surface while tears leaked without my permission from the corners of my eyes. I gripped Sam's jacket around me like a lifeline.

Leaves crunched as Sam returned with a wad of clothes.

"I'll leave them here and turn around again." He briefly met my eyes as he put the clothes on the ground beside me, and to his credit, his eyes didn't drift anywhere else.

I tried to scramble for the clothes, but it felt like I had to unlock each joint and focus each muscle to make it move. I'd never been this clumsy—like I was numb but completely on fire while trying to wade through chest-deep gelatin.

"The stiffness is normal. It'll pass after a while, and you won't be sore at all after shifts," Sam tried to encourage me, apparently hearing my awkward attempts to get dressed. I silently seethed at him and couldn't quite help the sob that escaped as I tugged the gray sweatshirt over my head. I hurt all over, and I did not want to be a…I couldn't even think the word. My brain refused to process what had just happened to me. *Werewolf.* I forced my mind into submission. The internal presence nudged me again, and I flinched.

"All right." My voice was rusty.

He turned. His face contorted in distress. Some—but not much—of my panicked anger faded at his miserable expression.

"Meg, I don't even know where to start. Let's get you back in the car where at least it's warm."

He held out an arm to help me, but I ignored it. At that moment, I wanted nothing to do with Sam Wolfe. The thing inside me lurched happily toward Sam's outstretched hand, and I stumbled as I resisted the beast's movements. Pride and anger won out over the creature's sudden fondness for the boy with the shaggy blond hair and blue eyes. My eyes landed on my shoe. What was left of it. The leopard spotted ballet flat was ripped apart where presumably, my *paw* had gone through it.

"Those were my favorite shoes," I said wistfully.

One more casualty to add to the list tonight. "I'm so sorry," Sam whispered.

I blundered over a fallen branch in my bare feet but still refused the arm Sam offered.

Chapter 5

Sam

I blasted the heater and aimed all the vents at Meg, who sat shivering in my sweats on the passenger side. Man, she looked good in my clothes. I shook my head. She may be my wolf's mate—a rare enough phenomenon in itself—but clearly, she was not reciprocating any warm fuzzies. Which was puzzling, since I was the one who bit her. Apparently, it didn't go both ways. I wasn't quite sure what was going on, but I did know I was in way over my head and that I'd be in a whole pile of crap once my dad found out.

She pulled her knees up to her chest, clutching my jacket over her. I'd tried to be quiet and let her process. The silence was deafening.

Finally, unable to stand the stillness, I slowly reached my hand out to her.

"Mm-nn. Don't touch me."

I jerked my hand back, Wolf whining inside at the terror in her voice. "What can I say, Meg?"

"Is this permanent? No chance of cure?"

"It's always permanent when you're bitten by a wolf, but since I was fully human at the time, and you didn't change right away...it would be something to double check with my dad."

"Your parents know?" She somehow seemed both hopeful and scandalized at the thought.

I nodded. "My dad is the leader of our pack." She blinked twice.

"Your pack. How many is the...pack?"

"There are fifty-three of us. We're a fairly large pack."

"Fifty-four," she muttered.

I had no idea what to say. After another minute of silence, she spoke softly. "I want to go home."

I'd been dreading this unavoidable topic. My stomach lurched while my wolf crawled back into the dark recesses, leaving the human me to deal with this alone. *Wimp*, I silently chided my wolf.

"You can't go home."

Despair settled over her face. "What do you mean, *I can't go home*?" Her voice broke on the word home.

I sighed. "You're unstable. For at least the next few days and probably the next few weeks at night, you won't be able to totally control your phasing. You'll shift randomly as you and your wolf adjust to each other. You could hurt anyone in the vicinity, not to mention scaring them half to death, and you'd reveal the existence of werewolves." I tried to be gentle, but firm. This was so much for her to take in but going home wasn't an option for her right now. She needed the pack—she needed me—whether or not she realized it or wanted it.

She was silent for a long minute. Her jaw clenched. "Screw you, Sam." Her voice cracked, and she furiously swiped a tear that trailed down her cheek.

A slap across the face would have hurt less. Wolf cringed at her anger and desolation, wanting to comfort, completely unable to.

I took a deep breath. "I'm sorry, Megan. I don't know what else to do. You need to come home with me and let my dad and the pack help you. They may know something I don't." Dread filled me, and Wolf whined as I thought of explaining this to my father. Being the son of the Alpha wasn't easy. There were expectations, and no matter how hard I tried, I always felt like I came up short. Tonight's events would plunge my father's opinion of me to uncharted depths.

"Fine." She frowned, resigned. She got her phone out of her purse from the floorboard.

"Who are you calling?"

She stared at me. "My grandpa needs to know not to expect me home tonight then, don't you think?"

I nodded, guilt swamping me. George Carmichael was the only family she had left. They loved each other fiercely in a way that I envied. I had the pack, and I had my parents, but things with my dad, especially, weren't perfect. Sometimes I wished we could just be a regular father and son, without being an Alpha and Beta.

I pulled the car away from the curb, thankful that no one had happened upon the whole first-human-into-wolf experience.

"Hi, Grandpa," Meg said in a forced light tone. "I'm going to stay at Rachel's tonight if that's okay. She's having some boy trouble and could use the moral support." It was a good excuse. Megan and Rachel had been inseparable since first grade.

"Okay," she said after a pause on the other end. "Love you, too." She hung up, sniffed, and wiped the back of her hand across her eyes.

I started to apologize again, but she cut me off, her voice weary.

"It's not that. I've never lied to my grandpa before."

We had to pull over one more time for Meg to shift before we got to my house. Unfortunately, the sweatshirt I'd loaned her didn't make it. We arrived in my driveway both half-dressed—Megan in my shirt, sweatpants, and jacket, me in my jeans and my shoes. This wasn't exactly how I'd envisioned bringing my mate home to meet my parents.

I slowly took the key out of the ignition, avoiding the coming confrontation as long as possible. "Meg," I began hesitantly. I swallowed. "My parents are likely to be almost as shocked by this as you are. They may say things they don't really mean. Whatever comes, I promise I won't let anything else happen to you. Okay?"

Her eyes, dark and large in her pale face, stared at me for a full minute, sizing me up. "Promise you won't let me...shift in front of them?"

I nodded. "Promise."

Discreetly, she brushed a tear from her cheek. I wished she'd let me do that. This would be easier for me if she'd let me at least try to comfort her.

The night air was cold on my bare chest as I walked to Meg's door and opened it. Her face tightened up as she slowly got out, refusing my help once again. The sidewalk to the front porch seemed to stretch for a thousand miles. It was both the shortest and longest walk of my life.

Chapter 6
Megan

Sam led me to the front door of a large brick house in a secluded neighborhood surrounded by forest.

Fear of the unknown twisted in my gut. Were werewolves safe?

I shook my head and then winced as my muscles protested the simple movement. I'd known Sam for years. Granted, I'd never known he was a werewolf. As scared and confused as I was, I tried to keep hold of the fact that Sam hadn't bitten me on purpose. It wasn't like he'd kidnapped me and changed me against my will. Although, he had technically changed me against my will and might as well have kidnapped me. I swallowed the resentment down as it flared back up.

We were at the door. I gulped. I felt the animal pacing inside, threatening to erupt again.

"Sam," I whispered shakily. His eyes trailed over my face, and he took my hand before I could refuse. I thought it might have been as much for his benefit as for mine. He'd never been anything but kind to me, was even voted the most responsible guy in our senior class. He wasn't a figurative monster.

Please don't let me burst into fur and then be naked in front of his parents!

Sam squeezed my hand as though sensing my thoughts. I tried to tug my hand from his grasp but was strangely relieved when he held it firmly.

He opened the door, and my world shifted on its axis for the second time that night.

"Rev?" I blurted unceremoniously as my eyes focused on the three people in the room. Sam's parents jerked to their feet. The third adult was none other than my grandpa's closest friend and army buddy, Reverend Daniel Butterfield.

Rev took one glance at me, sniffed the air as if for confirmation, and his eyes nearly popped out of his head.

Mr. Wolfe stood heavily, nostrils flaring, shock widening his eyes as anger turned his face red. A vein pulsed in his forehead. "Samuel." It was a thunderous statement that had my bones knocking together and the animal inside me cowering. Sam flinched beside me as his hand tightened around mine. My worry kicked up another notch as Sam subtly angled himself in front of me.

Was I in danger? Too many thoughts swirled in my brain, and I felt dizzy.

Chapter 7

Sam

Dad's voice echoed around my head. He was even angrier than I'd anticipated. I instinctively angled Meg behind me, not that she was in any real danger, but it was a natural instinct—protect your mate at all costs.

The vein in Dad's forehead throbbed. Another stood out along the side of his neck. "What. Is. This."

It wasn't a question—it was a condemnation. Not only from a father to his son but from an Alpha to a subordinate.

I swallowed and tried not to wither on the spot. "It was actually an accident," I answered, thankful there was no tremor in my voice.

"An *accident*?" Disbelief colored in his words. He jolted forward, intent on searching Megan's neck for the bite.

I was quicker and pulled her fully behind me, shielding her from my father's angry face, but bringing me straight into the inferno of my father's wrath.

"How do you *accidentally bite* someone, Samuel? You've put the entire pack in disgrace! Have you no respect for the law? Show me the bite." Steam seemed to rise off him as his rage was barely contained behind his clenched teeth.

My feet rooted to the spot, planting me firmly between Megan and my leader.

"Move aside." I felt the words to my core. It was an Alpha's command. I fought it for a few seconds and then felt my feet move against my will. I still gripped Megan's left hand but now stood beside her instead of in front of her. I felt weak. Shame tasted bitter in my mouth.

Dad stalked one step closer, his face inches from Megan. Slight tremors shook her hand, but I knew it wasn't her wolf trying to come forward. Her wolf was probably cowered in abject terror in her first meeting with an angry Alpha.

My throat was dry as I tried to swallow. Meg stared at my father, fear clearly in her eyes, but her back was straight. She was amazing.

Dad searched each side of her neck and then hunted up and down her throat. "Where is the bite?" His frustration was palpable.

Megan glared at him and raised her finger right in front of his face and pointed to the tiny slit already starting to heal on her forehead.

My dad blinked and stopped short. He'd never looked so perplexed as the rage simmered down to a slow boil.

"Perhaps I should take Megan to a different room while we discuss this a bit more privately," Rev cut in smoothly.

Without waiting for my dad's permission—a statement in itself—Rev gently put an arm around Meg's shoulders. She flinched but didn't pull away. Her eyes found mine as her fingers squeezed my hand. My heart slammed in my chest, which was embarrassing because I knew the other three wolves in the room could hear it.

"Are you okay for a few minutes?"

She gulped. She was not okay, but if Alpha Dad wanted me to stay and talk, I couldn't go with her. She nodded. I let her fingers slide through mine, and Rev led her to the stairs.

I turned to face the wrathful judgment of my father.

Chapter 8
Megan

"Rev, what are you doing here, of all places?" I demanded as he led me upstairs to a bedroom that I briefly processed as Sam's.

"There's a lot of things you don't know, Meggie-Girl," he replied slowly.

I scowled at the use of my grandpa's nickname for me. "Are you one of them?" I had to clench my teeth to keep from snarling the words as betrayal churned in my belly.

He ran a dark hand through his frizzy gray hair. "Yes."

The bluntness of his words shocked me more than his admission. I sagged onto the bed as raised voices carried up from downstairs.

"If you think you'll be all right alone for a few minutes, I should go back to...mediate."

What if I shifted again? I cringed at the sinew-snapping thought. But the overwhelming desire to have a moment alone in the middle of this crazy had me waving my arm stiffly at him to go.

His deep brown eyes locked onto mine. "You're sure you're okay? I'll stay if you'd rather."

I shook my head. The sudden desire to be alone was tremendous. I nodded. "I'll be fine," I squeaked.

Rev's eyes took me all in again and then left the room, closing the door gently behind him. I wilted to the floor the minute the door was shut. I took a few shuddering breaths and glanced around the room, a little bewildered. What was I supposed to do now? There were a surprising number of books on a floor-to-ceiling shelf against the far wall—a lot of sci-fi and histories, I noted absently. It was next to the window, but I was on the second story, so escape seemed unlikely. Besides. Where would I go and what would I do? I was stuck here. I would shift again, according to Sam, and right now, his word was all I had.

Plucking absently at the beige carpet beneath me, I desperately wanted my grandpa to tell me everything was going to be okay and have him wrap me in a hug. He had always been my rock—my fortress against the world. But I could hardly call him and tell him what had happened. The shock of it all might kill him. Crap. My phone was still in Sam's car. I felt tears threatening. This whole situation was so completely impossible.

More shouting sounded from downstairs. I wondered what kind of trouble Sam was in. And what kind of trouble *I* was in. Wrapping Sam's jacket tighter around me, I almost jumped in excitement when I felt something heavy shift in the pocket. Nearly yanking the pocket from the jacket, I snatched the phone out.

Please don't have a passcode, please don't have a passcode, please don't have a passcode, I thought as I powered it on.

It opened to the main menu screen.

I couldn't call my grandpa, and there was only one other person on the planet that I trusted with my life. I dialed Rachel's number with shaking fingers.

She picked up on the third ring. "Hello?"

"Rachel," I choked.

"Meg? What's wrong? Are you okay?"

I cleared my throat. "Listen to me. I swear on Grandma Elsie's grave what I am about to tell you is true."

"Okay—Are you hurt?"

"Yes—no—Sam is a *werewolf*, and he turned me into one, too," I whispered fiercely into the phone.

"Did he slip you something?" Anger laced her voice. "Where are you? I'm coming right now." There was clanging, and I knew she was literally getting her keys out to come get me.

"Rach, don't. No, he didn't slip me anything, he didn't even mean to—the game—we collided. His teeth and I—changed." Tears slipped down my cheeks. "Fur and claws." I had to stop talking so I didn't completely sob into the phone.

"What can I do?"

Just like that, Rachel accepted what I'd told her was the truth. I could hear it in her voice. She believed me. I breathed a little easier. "I don't know. But I...I just needed someone to know."

Sam's door slammed open, nearly coming off its hinges. There stood Mr. Wolfe, red faced, quivering with silent rage—and maybe terror—at the phone in my hand.

With two steps and a cry of animalistic fury, he stormed the room and yanked me to my feet, dragging the phone from my fingers, nearly crushing both the phone and my hand in the process.

"Meg?" Rachel was still on the line. Mr. Wolfe turned murderous eyes on me.

Before I even had time to cower, Sam, faster than humanly possible, darted through the door and around his father and planted himself right in front of me. I'd never been so grateful for anything in my life as I was for Sam standing between me and his dad in that moment.

"Who did you tell?" Mr. Wolfe ground out. His eyes bugged out from his head.

More moisture could be found in the Sahara than in my mouth while my heart beat out a rhythm far faster than was healthy. The pounding in my chest grew and the tingling started. *Crap, crap, crap!* I was petrified I was going to shift—leaving me more vulnerable than ever, right in front of this man I was certain wanted to kill me. I was losing it. In every possible way.

I felt bones creak, and then, through the haze of red covering my vision, Sam turned to me. He kissed me. Hard. His hand firmly held the back of my head as his lips locked on mine, shocking me to my core. So momentarily stunned, I didn't even register that my bones stopped creaking, that my digits quit tingling. The shift *stopped* leaving me panting, cold, and sweating, but still human.

He broke away without making eye contact and angled his body in front of mine again, taking hold of my hand.

Mr. Wolfe still shook, the veins in his neck and forehead still visible. He clenched his fists but said nothing.

"Dominic, it's done," Mrs. Wolfe said softly from the hallway. I glanced over. She and Rev stood right outside the bedroom door.

"Sam, pack up. Take her to the cabin while I figure out a way to clean up your mess." He dragged a hand through his dark hair before pointing accusingly at Sam. "You take care of that phone call. *Any means necessary.*"

The door slammed so hard the wall rattled. Sam and I were alone in the room. Tremors shook my body from head to toe, and this time when Sam offered, I let him touch me. He held his arms out, an invitation without pressure, and I willingly fell into them. He'd suddenly become a safe haven.

I had no idea what my future held, but at that moment, regardless of what else happened, I knew Sam was on my side.

"Are you all right?" he whispered. One arm was wrapped tightly around my shoulders; the other hand softly brushed down the length of my hair.

I shook my head. I was definitely not all right. The trembling slowly started to fade as Sam held me.

"I'm sorry, Meg," he whispered against my hair. I sniffed and belatedly realized my face was pressed up against his still bare, and rather nicely sculpted, chest. Despite the fact that I had turned into a wolf, Sam's dad was on the warpath after me, and that my entire life had been radically altered, my face heated at my nearness to Sam's chest. I could feel the heat blooming across my cheeks, and I quickly struggled to put some distance between me and Sam's skin. My eyes blinked rapidly a few times. Embarrassment, anger, regret, and exhaustion all battled for prominence. Anger was the easiest of the emotions to deal with, but Sam's dad in Alpha-action had sucked the energy to be angry right out of me. It left me bone-weary tired.

"Yeah," was all I could manage in reply.

"Okay. Let me grab a few things, and we'll get out of here and to the cabin before you need to shift again."

Shifting again terrified me. Adrenaline and panic suddenly replaced the fatigue. My hands gripped Sam's forearms. "Will...will you stay with me?" My voice was tiny in the stillness of the room. I didn't know if I could handle shifting on my own after everything I'd just survived, even though it hadn't seemed so bad only moments earlier.

Sam's blue eyes warmed even as his brows drew together. His hands lightly cupped my face and some of my fears stilled. "I'm not going anywhere. I promise."

The pads of his thumbs brushed over my cheeks, and the intimacy of it both kindled something in my belly and made me uncomfortable. There was a restlessness in me that quieted at his touch, basking in the attention, while another part of me wanted to jerk away.

Before I could decide how to respond, he spoke. "I'm going to throw a few things in a bag, and then we'll go."

Chapter 9

Sam

My fingers tingled where they touched Meg's face. Her fear was written plainly across her features, but some of my own anxiety lessened as she let me touch her. My wolf was desperate to be near her, touch her, protect her. One more inhale of her sunshine and roses scent, blessedly now free of Brody's lingering smell after her shifts, and I released her, relishing the last brush of her skin on my hands.

I shoved clothes in a bag haphazardly, knowing Meg didn't have long before she'd need to shift again. My kiss—that magnificent, instinctual moment—wouldn't stave off her change for long. I threw a shirt on over my head and checked on her. She hadn't moved at all, just watched me with large dark eyes.

I held my hand out, not sure if she'd want me to touch her again after everything my touch had brought her tonight. Much to my relief, I felt her cool fingers slide into my warm palm.

Rev met us in the hallway by the stairs. "I'm going to go check a historical account of a"—He cleared his throat, his eyes darting to Megan—"biting incident involving two humans, rather than the more traditional wolf biting a human." He stopped as Meg's face grew noticeably whiter. "At any rate, I'll come up to the cabin as soon as I've completed my research. We'll both be here to help you through these first difficult days, Meggie-Girl." He patted her shoulder. Her fingers gripped mine harder, and I squeezed back reassuringly.

"Rev, what, what about Grandpa? I—what am I going to tell him?" she asked. The old man's brow wrinkled heavily.

"We'll talk more when I come up to the cabin. Rest assured though. Your grandpa is one tough devil. He'll understand."

She raised a skeptical eyebrow.

Mercifully, my parents were nowhere to be found as I led us out to my car, snagging another jacket on the way out.

I opened Meg's door for her, and she crawled in stiffly. Her joints must have still been aching pretty badly. I shrugged into my jacked and zipped it up as I opened my door and slid in.

"Where are we going?"

"The cabin. It's our family's cabin out in the woods—mine, I guess. It was actually deeded to me on my last birthday. It's kind of the teen wolf hangout for the pack. We meet up there most nights for a pack run." I glanced over at her as we pulled onto a gravel drive that would take us out of the subdivision and into the woods. Her face was white, her jaw clenched. "Meg?"

"It hurts," she bit out.

I reached for her hand again, but she flinched away like my skin was acid. I swallowed and tried to ignore how bad that minor rejection stung. My wolf didn't take well to rejection, especially from his mate. I wasn't a fan either.

Taking a quick breath to calm the wolf, I tried to explain. "It might lessen the pain a little if I'm touching you."

Her left eyebrow raised. "Why?"

"Your wolf reacts to mine," I hedged. "Proximity to me should quiet your wolf for a little bit."

"Like when you kissed me?"

I winced. "Yes. Sorry to spring it on you like that." *Especially after what happened at the game.* I thought. "I didn't know any other way to keep you from shifting right there in front of my parents, and I promised you I wouldn't let that happen." I tried for a grin, but it might have come across more like a grimace. I briefly wondered if she'd let Brody kiss her.

She processed for a minute. "All right," she conceded as she put her hand palm up on the console. I slid my hand on top of hers, and she sighed softly. "Thank you."

"For what?" I was genuinely puzzled. Could she warm up to the thought of being a wolf so quickly? My heart sped up at the thought.

"For not letting me—shift—in front of your parents. And I'm sorry I snapped at you earlier."

"Oh. You're welcome." I quashed my hope and squeezed her hand again. Another sideways glance told me Meg wasn't so angry anymore—not that she was happy, but she wasn't spitting bullets. I needed to get to the next part of my orders from Alpha-Dad.

"Who did you call earlier?" I ventured, desperately hoping it wasn't Brody.

"Rachel. I had to tell someone, and I couldn't very well tell Grandpa. The shock of it all might be too much for him." Her shoulders shook as a light shudder went through her at the thought.

Squeezing her hand again as my shoulders sagged in relief, I tried to delicately phrase my next question. "Don't take this the wrong way, but did she believe you?" Rachel and I were casual acquaintances, friends, but we weren't close. I didn't know her that well.

"She did." Meg bit her lip. "That's bad, isn't it? I mean, the way your dad reacted when—" She dropped off and her eyes got huge. "Oh! I have to call Rachel back. I was mid-sentence when your dad grabbed the phone. She's going to kill me." She bent over to search for her phone in her purse. "Or march herself over here and get *herself* killed," she muttered.

Rachel picked up on the first ring. She was yelling loud enough I could hear the entire conversation. "Megan Elizabeth Carmichael! Where are you? Who do I call? The police? The National Guard? National Geographic? The Yeti Seekers? Do you have any idea how worried I've been?"

"Calm down." Meg hiccupped. "No, don't call anyone."

"Are you okay?" Rachel interrupted again.

"No, I'm not okay, not at all, but I'm...safe." She glanced at me. "For the moment."

"You're sure? You're absolutely, one-hundred-percent-sure you're safe?"

"Yes. I'm here with Sam."

"Well, isn't he the jerk-face that turned you into a werewolf in the first place?" Rachel sounded incensed. I could imagine her wild red curls bouncing around as she waved her arms in the air to explain her displeasure with my fangs. I winced.

Megan sighed, her eyes closing. She pinched the bridge of her nose. "Yes, he's the jerk-face who turned me into a werewolf, but he didn't mean to. It was an accident."

"An accident." Suspicion dripped from the other end of the phone.

"Yes. We were sitting close at the game, and Shelby knocked into Sam getting past him, and we sort of collided. My head and his teeth."

Silence. "Oh. My. Word. I can't believe it. Okay. So. Accidental werewolf nipping." Rachel blew out a big breath. "How can I help, Meggie? What do you need me to do?"

Megan glanced at me once more.

"Want me to talk to her?" I whispered, sure I'd be unleashing Rachel's wrath on me like the hounds of hell. Megan nodded. Great.

"Rach, I'm going to let Sam talk to you a sec." She passed the phone over.

"Sam Wolfe, when I get my hands on you—" Rachel started.

"Hi, Rachel," I cut in, wanting to get this over with. "Look, I don't have much time right now; Megan could need me again in a minute." As I'd hoped, that shut her up.

"Fine," Rachel snarled. "Tell me what I need to know right now, and we'll figure the rest out later."

"You can't tell anyone. I mean *anyone*. You breathe a word of this to the dog next door, and all of us are in hot water. As in, telling anyone could jeopardize our lives—particularly Megan's."

"Got it. Lips are zipped." She paused, and her voice dropped. "Sam, is Megan really going to be all right?"

"She will be. The next two or three days may be a bit uncomfortable, physically and mentally, but she's going to be fine." I smiled at Megan reassuringly. Her lips were pursed. "I'll pass you back over."

"Yep. You take care of my best friend. I haven't forgiven you yet."

"I will. All right. Here's Meg."

Rachel was calm enough now that I couldn't overhear the whole conversation over the roar of the engine in the cold night.

"I will, Rach. To the ends of the earth. I'll call you tomorrow." Meg glanced at me, and I nodded. Rachel was in the know now. No sense in keeping the two girls from talking on the phone. It might actually ease the transition for Megan. She clicked the phone off.

"I guess there is some rule against telling people werewolves exist," she said with mild sarcasm.

My thumb twitched against the wheel.

"The top two rules are No Biting and No Revealing. I kinda royally screwed them both tonight. Not the best night for the Alpha's son."

Part of me was crushed at how this whole night had gone—I'd not only ticked off my dad to epic new heights, but I'd stripped Megan of any hope of a normal human life after this. She'd always know werewolves existed after tonight. She was one of us now. The other part of me, the part that recognized Meg as my mate, couldn't bemoan this turn of events. Megan was *it* for me.

"Sam—"

Her shoulders twitched. We weren't going to make it to the cabin before Meg shifted again. I cranked the car to a screeching halt on the gravel path and raced around to the passenger door. I got her out just as her shoulders rolled back and her eyes fluttered.

Gripping the sleeves of my jacket Meg still wore, I was able to get it off before her shoulders widened, but I wasn't quick enough for the shirt or my sweats. Meg arched her back, sobs turning to whimpers as she thrashed.

"Don't fight it." I tried to sound soothing. My voice sounded like sandpaper. Megan hung onto her human form resulting in a suspended shift. Her legs and feet were changed, paws clawing at the dirt, her torso covered in fur, but her arms and hands remained human. Her face had the snout and jaw of her wolf, but her very human eyes were like frisbees. Fear radiated off her. Panic bled all over her face, whimpers turned into howls.

"Meg, listen to me." My heart constricted all over again. The first day of shifts were the most painful things I'd experienced in my lifetime, and I was born to it with full knowledge of what was going on inside me when it happened. "Listen to my voice. I'll talk you through this. You can do this. You are strong. This is perfectly normal for a werewolf."

She howled in pain and frustration, and my own wolf pushed for release. I shoved him back down. Meg still needed me in skin.

Chapter 10

Megan

It hurts, it hurts, it hurts! I don't want this! I don't want this!

Wracking sobs hitched in my chest and came out as garbled animal sounds. I was afraid of the pain. I was afraid of turning wolf. I was afraid of losing me, of turning into some creature I didn't understand and not being able to come back. I didn't know how to do this. I didn't *want* to do this. I just wanted to be me—*human me.*

"Meg, listen to my voice." Sam's voice was calm and steady. I tried to slow my frantic heartbeat and quell my panic, but the searing pain doubled me over. Hands covered in fur and paws where my feet should have been met my gaze, sending another wave of panic crashing over me. I was stuck half girl and half wolf. My mind stopped. Panic overtook me. There was nothing rational left in that moment as I thrashed on the ground, trying in vain to become one thing or the other. The creature inside me tried to take over, but my panic overrode everything else. A great fire tortured my body. Every single hair that poked through my skin was a razor cutting deep into my flesh. My bones were broken in several places as they were arrested, fused half human and half animal. My teeth were jagged, piercing my gums and a tongue that no longer fit into my mouth. Black dots danced in front of my eyes.

"Megan, you are all right. Don't fight this. Embrace the pain. I know it sounds crazy but lean into the pain, and it will be over sooner."

I screeched and wailed against the agony, but I tried to follow his instructions. Doing my best to set aside my terror, I took a heaving breath and let the pain ride up my legs and over my hips, the great fire burning hotter and hotter in my belly. I screamed, and a wolf's howl came out. My body lurched forward without me, and I crashed to the ground in a whimpering heap of matted fur and sweat.

Sam was saying something in a soothing tone. His voice was deep. It rose and fell like water over smooth stones.

Everything was in a fog. It took me a minute to orient myself, and right as I realized Sam was actually singing softly, not talking, I felt the telltale tingling pain in the base of my tail. *My tail.*

Gritting my teeth, I forced the rational part of my brain to the front and told myself I wasn't afraid of the pain and that I could do this. The flames engulfed me as I managed to keep my panic at bay. The shards of fur sliced their way back through my skin as my bones ground against each other and shattered into a thousand pieces to fit themselves back to their human shape.

Mercifully, the change back was quick but left me again, naked, in a teary, snotty, shivering ball at Sam's feet.

I'd never felt so vulnerable in all my life.

Sam covered me with his jacket again and then retrieved a large gray robe from the bag in his trunk. I shivered on the ground, sweaty, achy, exhausted beyond comprehension, but strangely alert.

"Here," he said and shook out the voluminous robe in front of me. He held it out for me to slip into as he turned his face away to give me some small measure of privacy.

"We have these specially made," he explained as I jerkily put my left arm into a billowy, though short, sleeve. "They are made so a person can shift to their wolf while wearing one of these. They're roomy enough to accommodate the change, but loose enough your wolf can wiggle out of it without opposable thumbs."

"Fabulous," I quipped, choking on the edge of hysteria creeping in. "I don't suppose they come in pink?" I asked dryly, surprising myself with my sarcasm.

Sam snorted, trying not to laugh, as surprised as I was at my retort. "I'll check on that right away." A grin tipped the corner of his mouth as he steered me back to the still-running car. For a fleeting moment, he was just a good-looking, nice guy from school. Someone I'd always had a special fondness for but who had been somehow unattainable. Something inside me gravitated to that grin while I just as forcefully shut it down. If it weren't for the uncertainty of my newly acquired furry side, I'd be long gone from Sam Wolfe.

My teeth chattered as we finished the rest of the short drive to the cabin. It had been in sight as I shifted. It was a simple but tasteful building in a small clearing surrounded by beautifully mature trees. It was bigger than I'd imagined, and in the moonlight it was charming. If only my circumstances were so lovely.

Sam shut off the car. "Are you feeling better or worse after your last shift?" His face was so sincere. The rational part of my brain knew that changing me hadn't been in his plans, but part of me still wanted to be angry and blame him.

Grandpa always said, *Anger makes a bitter brew if left to steep too long.* Expelling a gust of air, I flexed my fingers. Wiggling my toes next, I was pleased my rusty joints moved with more control and less brittleness than they had before the last shift.

"Maybe a little better," I conceded. "But everything is still sore." I ached like I was bruised black and blue. Even moving my digits had been painful.

His eyebrows knit together. "I know. I can't tell you how sorry I am, Megan. But if your muscles are a little looser, that's a good thing. Let me grab my bag, and I'll come get your door."

My head settled against the headrest as I let out a long breath. I could be angry with Sam, use up whatever mental energy I had left, or I could put it aside and let him help me through the coming pain of the next phases.

A tear escaped as I briefly contemplated my future. Things had been so rosy this morning. Everything looked pretty bleak now, overshadowed by a giant wolf somehow coexisting within me.

The door opened, and Sam held out his hand. I closed my eyes for one second, took a deep breath, and whooshed out my anger with it. Most of it, at least.

A new chapter of my life had just been forced upon me.

Chapter 11

Sam

The lock clicked as I turned the key. Ushering Meg in ahead of me, I closed and locked the door behind us. The bright tang of pine and wolf greeted me, instantly taking me back to a hundred different memories here. Coming here with my parents, having my first shift right outside these walls, meeting here to run with my pack, accepting Beta at the communal fire ring out back—one of the last times I remember my father looking proudly at me as his son.

So many wonderful memories were held within these walls. And now I'd brought my mate here—though it was nothing like I'd imagined.

Instead of bringing her here with the intent of sharing something profoundly intimate, I felt like Attila the Hun, having practically kidnapped her, carted her off to a foreign land, and forced her to be with me. *Welcome to your new home, Megan.*

"This is it," I said instead, swallowing back my desires and dreams of how I'd once thought of bringing my mate—the woman I intended to spend the rest of my life with—to this place.

I tried to take in my cabin's interior with fresh eyes as Megan might.

Directly in front of the door was the kitchen—small, but fully functional. Off to the left of that was the tiny bathroom, comprised of a shower, sink, and toilet. Jutting out from the wall beside the bathroom was a stacked washer/dryer combo.

There was a little eating nook directly to the left, and to the right was a large sectional couch that cocooned a living room/gathering space. Behind the far side of the sectional was the full-sized bed where I always slept if I stayed overnight. A small, bricked fireplace was against the back wall and on the other side of that was a queen-sized bed with a bunked sleeping space above the back half. There were two chests of drawers and a nightstand scattered between the beds and fireplace and a collapsible table leaning against the back wall.

It certainly wasn't palatial, but it was clean and homey. I glanced at Megan. I wasn't sure if she was aware enough of her surroundings to notice much or not.

"Why don't we get you comfortable on the couch, and I'll start a fire and get things warmed up." I was cold, so I knew Meg must be freezing with the alternate sweating and chills first shifts brought on.

"What is that smell?" she asked, clearly puzzled.

"Can you describe it?" It smelled the same as it always did to me, but Megan's senses were changing as my toxins altered her body.

She took another whiff. "It smells...strong. Dark. Woodsy. Part revolting and part intriguing."

"I don't know about the revolting part, but you might be smelling some of the lingering scents of pack members. We all use the cabin from time to time. There's a lot of different smells. It's probably a little confusing to your nose right now. Your sense of smell—your vision and hearing, too—will all get sharper over the next few days. Part of the werewolf package." I grimaced as she wrinkled her nose.

She sank wearily down into the couch cushions, and I grabbed the spare blanket off the edge of my bed and wrapped it around her shoulders, now curious if she'd find my scent on it—and if she'd like it. Suddenly, I wished I'd grabbed a different blanket. I'd never been self-conscious about my scent before, but I was now. If she smelled anything, she didn't let on. I was both disappointed and relieved. Her nose probably couldn't pick up individual wolves yet. I had hoped she'd find my scent attractive at the least.

With some quickly crinkled newspaper, splinters of kindling, and a few logs on top of that, a cheery crackle and popping soon filled the quiet space. Meg huddled under my blanket. I couldn't read her face, and honestly had no idea how to approach her now that we were here. Alone. Just the two of us, waiting for her next shift. I nervously cleared my throat.

"Um, are you thirsty?"

She blinked, startled. "Yeah. Actually, I'm parched."

Chapter 12

Megan

Sam got a large blue stoneware mug down from one of the honey-colored cabinets and filled it from the tap. My brain buzzed with thoughts. Fears. Images of shifting. Half-baked questions. But one thing concerned me most. My fingers trembled as Sam handed me the mug. Our fingers grazed, and I found it curiously annoying when my tremors stopped at the contact.

I licked my dry lips and took a long drink.

"I imagine you have some questions?" He sat down opposite me on the sectional, his shaggy blond hair flopping over his forehead. He steepled his fingers in front of him, elbows braced on his knees. In the firelight, I could just make out some blond stubble along his squared jaw. I felt an inward nudge again, reminding me how handsome Sam was. Was that, how did I say it? My wolf? It irritated me to have my thoughts dictated by anything other than my own mind. But that was irrelevant to my current train of thought.

"Sam, I...how? When, I mean, that is—" Nothing was coming out right. I couldn't quite wrap my brain around what I wanted to ask. Finally, I blurted, "Am I going to try to eat my grandpa's face off the next time I see him?"

"What?" His face was as shocked as I was at the words that had tumbled from my lips. "Of course not!"

"Am I going to turn into this bloodthirsty monster that craves flesh all the time?"

He appeared genuinely wounded. That probably wasn't the most tactful way I could have approached things. Oops.

"I think you might have read one too many vampire books," he said stiffly. I felt mildly chastised; though, I wasn't sure I deserved chastising after tonight's events. He blew a breath out his mouth. "Sorry, that didn't come out very sensitively." At least he realized it, too. I sighed. I hadn't been overly tactful tonight either.

"Werewolves don't eat flesh, unless it's a nice medium-rare steak. They don't drink blood, and as soon as your first shifts settle down, you'll be perfectly normal during the day. You might still be a little unstable at night, especially as the next full moon approaches."

"You mean this is, like, an everyday thing, not just during the full moon?" I was a little horrified at the thought.

"For you, it definitely will be. Most werewolves prefer to shift and have a good run nearly every day. But you won't have total control over your wolf at night until the next full moon, which is in about four weeks. During that time, it will be especially important for you to be near a more, um, powerful wolf, to make sure you're able to control it, or if not, then the other wolf can step in and help."

Maybe my eyesight was improving like Sam said it would, because I could have sworn his cheeks pinked a little as he stammered out his explanation. I wasn't really tracking with what he was saying about a more powerful wolf. I was tired and just wanted to go home to my grandpa and my own bed. Clearly that was out.

"So I get a wolfy bodyguard?"

"Not exactly."

I was about to press him for more details when there was a knock at the door, right as the wretched tingling started in my tailbone.

Rev walked in as my feet were turning once more into paws. I ignored Rev and listened as Sam coached me again. It was easier this time. And honestly, knowing I wasn't going to be totally naked, thanks to the "wolf robe," helped. My bones had some memory of what they were trying to do, and the scant knowledge of understanding what was happening helped me feel slightly more in control. I let myself surrender to the change, letting my skin sprout the fur.

"You're doing a great job, Megan. Keep letting yourself feel the little things your body is trying to do. Yes. Just like that. Good job. Let your snout come out longer. Don't hold it back. There you go. Now your ears. That's it! Push them through. Fantastic! Shake it all out."

I had to admit it, Sam was a great coach now that I was actually listening to him and letting him instruct me. And the pain had only doubled me over twice. My face swung to Rev, my wolf eyes taking him in clearly with his chocolaty skin and frizzing gray hair standing up. There was a look of awe stamped on his weathered face I would never have expected. He clutched an old book under one arm, a large thermos in the other.

The wolf only remained for a few minutes before I shifted back. I was glad about that—I was far from comfortable being a wolf, and I had about a million questions for Rev and Sam. Assuming I could stay awake long enough. I was so tired. The gray robe did its job. I was able to stay covered during the shift back, for which I was profoundly thankful. My nakedness had been observed enough for one night.

"You did so much better that time," Sam encouraged as I wrapped the robe around me tighter and let him pull the other blanket up higher on my lap.

"That was an impressive shift for one so new at this," Rev agreed.

"Um, thanks?" I stammered. How did one accept a compliment for changing to and from a wolf?

"I have found the case I wanted to check, and I have some news for both of you." He glanced seriously at Sam, and I got the feeling there was some unspoken communication going on between them. He cleared his throat. "Nearly two hundred years ago, there were two incidents of a human being bitten while the werewolf was in human form. The details of the incident are unimportant right now, but suffice to say Henry was quite the Casanova and bit Luella and Marcy while he was still human. Luella and Marcy both changed forms, much like you're doing now, Megan, but by the next full moon, Marcy stopped shifting. She remained human. Luella did not. She stayed fully werewolf. This sort of thing is so rare, it's hard to gauge what exactly is going to happen, but it stands to reason, based on these two cases, it's possible you might not stay a wolf, Megan."

My heart pounded in my chest. I could go back to just being human?

"How soon will we know if I'll stay human?" I glanced at Sam and briefly noted how drawn and pale his face had become. Maybe it was a blow to his ego that his bite wasn't strong enough to keep me wolf? I didn't really care at the moment. I was most concerned about figuring out how to stay in skin. Permanently.

Rev twiddled his fingers. "I'm sorry, but we will just have to wait until the next full moon. Unless you want to stay a wolf?"

I shook my head vehemently. "No, thank you."

Rev glanced at Sam. Sam gave his head the barest of shakes. His mouth drew down at the corners, his blue eyes dark. I wondered what was going on inside his head. Rev conveyed something else with his eyes that made Sam's brows draw down even farther. I cleared my throat.

The men snapped out of it, and Rev turned his attention back to me. The thermos clanged onto a little side table next to the couch. "Right. You want to stay human. Again, we won't know if this is the case or not for a few weeks, but in the meantime, there are a few details we should work out. I know it's late, and this is going to be a huge shock to you, but I think we should bring your grandpa over."

I gaped at him. "Tell me you are not serious? Grandpa can't see me like this. It would give his poor ninety-year-old heart an attack for sure." I couldn't believe Rev would even suggest such a stupid thing.

His brown lips pursed. "Meg." He paused for nearly a full agonizing minute. "Your grandpa has known I'm a werewolf for years."

My jaw hit the floor. Nothing in the world, not even turning into a werewolf myself, could have prepared me for this. Grandpa knew Rev was a werewolf? He knew werewolves existed? I sat, totally stupefied, staring blankly at Rev's face.

Sam moved from the seat opposite me and sank down beside me. "Meg?"

"I have no idea how to even respond to that." Betrayed. I felt totally, completely betrayed. I wanted to doubt Rev's word, to call him a liar, prove that my grandpa had no idea these creatures existed outside myths and fairy tales. To know Grandpa had lied to me my entire life by covering up something this huge was unimaginable. How could he do that? How could the man I loved and adored more than anything else let me go out alone at night, knowing *werewolves* freely roamed the area?

My breaths were coming too short, and tiny black spots quivered at the edges of my vision. Sam forced my head down between my knees. I gulped big breaths and gradually the quavering dots receded. I shook my head. How much more of this could I possibly handle before I came apart at the seams?

"Why don't you rest for a little bit. Shifting takes it out of you, and I imagine finding out so many new things is also pretty exhausting," Sam volunteered.

My head was spinning, and I had so many questions and fears floating around in my brain that the oblivion of sleep sounded more welcome by the second. I turned to Sam.

"All right." I was too tired to say anything else.

"Do you want to just lie here on the couch? Or do you want a bed?" Sam shrugged.

I glanced around. If Grandpa was coming over in a short while, I thought dozing on the couch might be the easiest option.

Without another word, I curled down into the couch, hugging my knees to my chest. Sam covered me up with the blanket and then rested his hand on top of my calf. If I hadn't been so tired, I might have objected. It somehow felt too familiar. As it was, his touch quieted the persona I was beginning to realize was the wolf. If it made her happy, then I'd put up with it. I didn't think I'd be able to relax properly, but I was deeply asleep within seconds.

I woke to the sounds of whispers around me. My senses were heightened. It wasn't one of those sleeps where you wake up totally groggy and disoriented. I remembered everything and, oddly, missed the weight of Sam's hand on my leg. Before alerting everyone else to my wakefulness, I listened.

Grandpa was here. I could make out his low gravelly voice mixed with Rev's smoother one, and though he didn't say anything, I could sense Sam standing there with them, too. "I'm not sure about this, Rev. Of course, I think it's the safest thing, but I'm not sure that it's fair," Grandpa said.

"I agree, but what's done is done, George. She needs help, and Sam is the only one in the position to give her the help she needs."

"Sam, what do you think about this? This obviously affects you, too," Grandpa said.

"It doesn't matter what I think. This is about what's best for Megan," Sam replied softly. A dull *thwap* sounded, and I assumed someone clapped him on the shoulder.

"You're a credit to men everywhere," Grandpa said solemnly. They fell silent, and I chose that moment to officially wake up.

"Hi, Meggie-Girl," Grandpa said as soon as my eyes opened. Joints protested as I shoved myself to sitting. Belying his age, Grandpa scooted himself over by me on the couch, putting an arm around my shoulders. I stiffened, still feeling utterly betrayed.

"It was safer if you didn't know, sweetheart," he whispered to me as if reading my mind. I melted against him and buried my face in his wrinkled neck. I wanted to cry, sob out all my frustrations, but I reined it in.

"How did you find out?" I asked. "About Rev?"

Grandpa glanced at his oldest friend. I did too, and for the first time, really looked at him. He was the same age as my grandpa. They'd been army buddies back in World War II. Rev hadn't aged a day over sixty-five, and Grandpa, he looked good for ninety, *really good*. But definitely a lot older than Rev.

"Do you mind if I listen, too, sir?" Sam asked Grandpa. I was grudgingly impressed with his manners.

"Of course not. It's a simple enough tale." Grandpa absently patted the seat beside him, and Rev and Sam both sat down opposite us on the sectional. I scooted up enough that I could watch Grandpa's face as he told his story, but not so far away that I was out from under his arm.

"Rev and I grew up in the area together. Went to school together, even went on a few double dates to establishments friendly to Blacks." Grandpa grinned and winked at Rev. Rev grinned back, sharing some long-ago memory. I forgot this would have all been before the Civil Rights Movement. To my knowledge, Rev had never married—so much for those double dates. "We also joined the army together. Rev is just a few months younger than I am, and he convinced me to wait and join up with him since my number hadn't been called up yet. Your Grandma Elsie and I had been courting for three years, and with our parents' blessings, we got married. Rev and I joined up in October of 1943 on his eighteenth birthday.

"Let me tell you, as keen as I was on fighting for my country, it was mighty hard to go off and leave your grandma behind. We wrote each other every week, though a lot of our letters didn't make it through. Rev and I were separated. Colored folks had their own divisions, but we kept in contact. Our divisions ended up stationed together, miraculously enough, in France. We were all engaged with the enemy when a mortar busted through and exploded. I caught a leg full of shrapnel and was bleeding out."

Grandpa paused and patted his leg. I'd never known him to even have a limp, though I had seen the long, jagged scars. "Rev wasn't willing to let me die." Grandpa paused again as he and Rev nodded at each other. "He gave me a field blood transfusion, right there in the middle of the battle. Without it I would have most certainly died. He had to let me in on the secret when I started developing some werewolf attributes. I could see and hear better than ever before. My leg completely healed in record time. I've never limped. Werewolves heal at a much faster rate than us mere humans. Of course, these things faded after a few months as I had no contact with his saliva—only his blood—but my leg was healed, and Rev had saved my life. And, of course, I was in on the secret."

I sat, completely dumbstruck. How could all of this have happened, and I never had a clue?

"Did Grandma know?"

"She knew something profound had happened between Rev and me on the field in France, but as far as she knew, it was just the sort of bond that men form when one saves the other's life. She never knew Rev's secret. Never knew werewolves existed."

I tried to digest this information that my grandpa, who still loved his wife with every molecule he possessed, had kept this monumental secret from her for their entire lives. Somehow it lessened my anger and betrayal toward Grandpa.

"So now you know, Meggie-Girl," Grandpa said softly as he soothingly stroked a hand over my tangled hair.

"But there is so much I don't know," I offered, still lost in this sea of previously unknown.

"That is true, but the good news is that you have friends that will help you. You have Rev and Sam. And you always have me. Always."

I glanced at Rev, his eyes warm and caring, and then at Sam, his face still drawn up tight, but his blue eyes pleading and...hopeful? I groaned. This was all too much at once. I needed to go back to sleep. Part of me wanted to stay awake and ask thousands of questions, but the rational part of my brain argued I'd function better and retain more, as well as have fewer hysterics, if I had some sleep and let my poor battered body rest.

The suggestion to let me sleep on it was on the tip of my tongue right as I felt the tingling and fur started poking through my feet. I whimpered and turned panicked eyes to Grandpa.

Rev grabbed his arm and helped him scoot backward away from me. "It's all right, Meggie-Girl. I will love you just the same. You go on now. Sam is here to help you."

I tried to swallow past the knot in my throat, a hot, tight ball of emotion and then the shift took over. Sam was beside me, offering encouragement and instruction through my whimpers, screams, and howls. My shifts were taking less time each phase, and it was only a few minutes before I was back in my human skin, sweating and chilled to the bone.

My eyes frantically swung to Grandpa, and my heart broke a little as he looked on me with the same steadfast love he'd always shown me, tear tracks running down his weathered cheeks. Assured that Grandpa was all right, and he wasn't going to have a heart attack, my eyelids closed of their own volition, and I sank into the dark abyss of exhausted slumber.

Chapter 13

Sam

Megan's head dropped and her eyes closed. Her breathing evened, and she was gone. Totally gone. I briefly remembered after my first shifts, I slept nearly twenty straight hours. Megan was handling this so well in spite of everything. I sighed and staggered a hand through my hair.

George Carmichael, a man I'd always admired, though I didn't know him well, patted his granddaughter's knee and then turned his eyes to me. I gulped. His was the stare of a concerned parent, not condescending, not accusing. My dad was still having a coronary, and here Mr. Carmichael sat, having witnessed Megan's shift, calm and collected.

"Well then, Sam. What are your intentions toward my granddaughter?"

His question took me so aback that I jerked. "Excuse me, sir?"

Mr. Carmichael's left eyebrow rose up his forehead. Rev intervened, and my heart's galloping pace slowed a fraction. "George, believe me, Sam's intentions are wholly honorable. I was there, and I saw his resolve. He refused an Alpha's order on Megan's behalf."

Both white eyebrows traveled up to Mr. Carmichael's hairline. "Is that so? Well then, young man, I'd like to shake your hand."

I got up and extended my hand. Mr. Carmichael's hand was like tissue paper wrapped leather. Hard, gnarled, wrinkled, tough but fragile.

"I, I want what's best for Megan, sir." I wanted her to stay a wolf, to stay with me. But above that, I wanted what was in her best interest. She obviously wanted to remain human. And based on Rev's research, that could still be an option. I wanted her to have the choice. Too many choices in my life had been taken from me because I was the Alpha's son and because certain things were expected of me. I didn't want to be the one that took Meg's choices away from her. I wanted her to love me, but I wanted her to love me on her own terms, not be stuck with me because she had no other choice. Not be stuck with me because my foolish desire to kiss her had ended in catastrophe.

"Very well. Gentlemen," Mr. Carmichael intoned, "we have some discussing to do, and I imagine your father will want to be a part of it," he finished, gazing at me.

Wolf shuddered. Neither of us wanted to face my father again so soon. I'd messed up enough for one night—for a lifetime—and had no desire to revisit the wrath of my father.

"You know, I think for now, we could do all of this via a phone call with Dominic. That might be easiest at the moment. Any objections?"

Bless you, Rev.

After a few snatched hours of sleep on the couch opposite Meg—I happily gave up my bed so Rev could have a spot to lay down that wasn't a bunk bed while Mr. Carmichael took the queen—I stretched sleepily. My eyelids fluttered open, and I found Meg's hazel eyes watching me carefully. Her body had finally given up last night, too tired for more shifts. I'd stayed awake, mostly talking with Rev and Mr. Carmichael, but also to ensure Meg wouldn't need me for another shift, for several more hours after Meg dropped off last night. My own body protested being awake, but there was a lot of ground to be covered today.

Her eyes were beautiful but unreadable, and we simply held each other's gaze for a few minutes. I could hear even breaths and knew the others were both still deeply asleep.

"How do you feel this morning?" I finally asked softly.

She cocked her head to the side—amazingly like a wolf would do when studying a new curiosity.

"I'm stiff, but my body feels fairly good otherwise. A lot better than I expected," she whispered back. "I can see the individual hairs on your jaw," she quietly marveled. "And Grandpa's heartbeat is much more regular than the doctor thought at his last check up." The right side of her mouth tipped up the tiniest bit.

I nodded. "It sounds like some of the changes are already making themselves known."

"Will I start shifting again like I did last night?" Only a hint of fear lingered in her voice.

"You will probably shift randomly a few times today, but the shifting will speed up more once the moon is up tonight."

She grimaced. "How long does the uncontrollable shifting last?"

"Usually only the first two or three days. A few days more during the nighttime hours. But it won't hurt for that long."

"Will I be able to...go out in public?" A new fear lit her eyes. "Will I be able to go back to school? I can't stay out indefinitely. My GPA needs to stay where it is."

"Calm down." I tried to sound soothing with a voice still scratchy from sleep. "We have fall break this week. We're off Monday and Tuesday. You'll be fine during the day by Wednesday. No problem. You can go back to school, and nobody will be the wiser."

"Except Rachel."

My turn to grimace. "Yes. Except Rachel."

"I need to call her soon. What if I start to shift in class?" Her eyes were wide, her mouth a grim line. There was rustling behind me. Rev would be awake soon.

"Well." I wasn't sure how to ease into this one. "I can help your wolf settle for short periods of time."

She suspiciously raised an eyebrow. "How?"

I cleared my throat. "The same way I did back at my house last night."

"Which is actually a good starting point for a few things we need to discuss today," Rev interjected from my bed behind the couch.

Megan pursed her lips, clearly not happy or satisfied with my answer—possibly Rev's intrusion. We hadn't talked about the near-kiss-that-ended-with-a-bite or the one I laid on her last night to stop her shift.

"Sam, would you call Steve Rivers and tell him I said to bring over coffee and some breakfast? They should be back from their campout by now."

I nodded, snagged my phone from the end table, and dialed their landline. Steve's daughter, Raven, picked up. "Hello?"

"Hey, Raven, it's Sam."

"Oh! Good morning. You want to talk to Cade?" Raven was a year behind me and a sweet girl. Her brother, Cade, and I had been best friends since we were babies. Their dad worked a lot with Rev and my dad on pack business when he wasn't running his own construction company. He was a decent, hard-working guy and someone I'd always liked and respected.

"I need to talk to your dad first. Is he around?"

"Just a sec."

"This is Steve."

"Hi, Steve. Sam here. We've, um, had an interesting turn of events up here at the cabin. Rev asked me to call and check if you could bring some coffee and breakfast over here."

"Sure thing. For how many?" Apparently, this wasn't the first time he'd done this sort of errand for Rev.

"Four. Actually, make it six, to be on the safe side. My parents will be coming up." I suppressed a shudder at the thought. At least the night may have cooled some of Dad's ire.

"I'll be over in half an hour, forty-five minutes tops."

"Thanks, Steve."

"Absolutely. You need Cade?"

"You know what, I'll just text him. Thanks."

"See you soon."

Rev was bustling around the table getting something laid out. Mr. Carmichael flopped an arm over his head in his sleep. Meg was still watching me, quiet, thoughtful, maybe.

"Do you want a shower?" I offered.

"Is your dad coming?"

I bit the side of my lip and glanced up at her. "I hope not," I said quietly.

"Sam, thank you. Really, thank you. For sticking up for me last night. In front of your dad." Her shoulders twitched as a shiver worked its way down her spine. I would always come between her and any possible threat. It's what I was created to do as her mate.

"You're welcome," I said instead. Her eyes darted to the colored rug on the floor, breaking the moment.

"If I'll be shifting more today, should I put this robe back on after my shower?"

"We'll get you some of your own clothes today. For now, you can use the robe, or you're welcome to anything I brought back from the house. Although I'm not sure what's in there. There's probably a spare pair of pajamas or a few T-shirts or sweats lurking in some of the drawers in here." I shrugged apologetically. "I..." I swallowed. "I can quiet your wolf for a little while if you would rather put off shifting until tonight. If you're more comfortable in regular clothes, though, it might make your shifts a little more intense later."

"Let me worry about a shower first."

In the end, she opted for a gray T-shirt with *I'm a Dog Person* scripted on the front and some black sweatpants we found in a drawer. Both probably belonged to my cousin Tammy, who probably forgot they were here. I found a red zip-up hoodie in another drawer and added it to the pile of clothes for her. I hoped this meant I'd get the chance to taste her lips again today, if only to calm her wolf.

Once the shower was running and steam was wafting out the bottom of the crack in the door, I took the opportunity to fire off a quick text to Cade.

> Hey. Wanted it to come from me. I bit Megan Carmichael last night. As a human. Totally accidental. Fill you in later. Keep it quiet.

My phone buzzed about thirty seconds later.

> Dude. You okay? Your dad totally ticked?

I snorted. Was my dad ticked? I'd never seen him so angry.

> Beyond ticked.

I hesitated and then added one more line.

> Megan is my mate.

> Congrats! Seal the deal yet?

> Complicated. Details later. Got to go.

Mr. Carmichael finally stirred as I clicked my screen off.

"Oh, these old bones don't move like they used to." He groaned as he lumbered to the table where Rev was finishing stacking his papers into neat little piles.

A knock sounded at the door, and Steve was there with coffees and a big handled brown paper bag with the logo of a local coffee shop stamped on the front. I sniffed sausage and eggs, and my mouth watered.

"Thanks," I said appreciatively.

"You got it. Anytime." That was one of the perks of pack life. We always had each other's backs. He popped his head in the door and waved at Rev.

"You need anything else, Rev?"

"Not at the moment."

The younger man nodded and turned to me. "You need anything else? Anything else I can do to help out here?"

"I appreciate it, but no. We'll call if we do. Tell Cade and Raven I said hello."

He smiled and nodded before leaving. I didn't stand on much ceremony as Beta, but the pack, all but my dad anyway, treated me with respect. My word carried a lot of weight, and as Beta, I was second in command. Even to those pack members older than me. Sometimes it made me feel awkward, like someone with more experience should be the Beta, not me. But werewolf packs followed bloodlines, not democratically elected members.

Chapter 14

Megan

A shower had never felt better. I let the water run as hot as I could stand it, nearly scalding my skin. I imagined washing off any lingering wolf, though when my thoughts strayed there, the creature inside me would rear its head, nudge me, do something to let me know she was still very much there and active.

I scowled down at my legs. I had shaved yesterday and already there was a healthy layer of stubble. I was definitely blaming that on becoming a werewolf. I made a mental note to make a list and call Rachel as soon as I could. She'd know what to bring.

A frustrated gust of air blew through my lips as I finally shut off the faucet. I wrung my long hair out, twisting it up to get the excess water out. Wet and twisted, it still came halfway to my belly button over my shoulder. It probably wouldn't hurt me to get a trim. There was a decent-sized mirror over the sink. I wiped off the fog with my towel, then wrapped up my wet hair in it. I stared at my reflection for a long time. I didn't look different. Just tired. My eyes were shadowed, but otherwise there was nothing abnormal about my body. It felt weird to stare at my reflection, knowing all my bones had broken and changed shape mere hours ago, and to find nothing out of the ordinary in the mirror. I shrugged and went to put my borrowed clothes on. Ugh. Underwear and a bra were so at the top of that list. I was suddenly very glad to have the red hoodie Sam found. Running around braless in a room full of men, even if two of them had known me all my life, was not something I was anxious to experience.

I emerged to mouth-watering aromas. I knew the sausage, egg, and cheese biscuits smelled good, but having a sharper sense of it was suddenly alarming. I could literally differentiate each ingredient. I knew it was a smoked provolone cheese, eggs sautéed in butter, pork sausage with a bit more caraway seed in it than I liked, all on sourdough biscuits. There was coffee—French roasted. I could distinguish the smells of each fruit in the fruit salad and the two types of scones. My belly rumbled. Rev and Sam grinned while Grandpa smiled his wrinkly smile.

"Better after a shower, Meggie-Girl?"

"A little bit." I turned my eyes to the food Rev and Sam were setting out. "I can smell *all* of it," I said, a little freaked out by this newest wolf revelation. My immediate world was clouded by a haze of smells.

"Your senses are developing," Rev explained. "Everything will be completely new to you right now, and your senses of hearing and smell might be a little overpowering for a day or two. They will calm back down soon, though. Only a few days or so and then you'll still have the increased abilities, but you'll adapt, and they will become normal to you."

I bit back a sarcastic retort.

Rev continued, though I'm sure he noticed the slight narrowing of my eyes as I kept a rein on my tongue. "Why don't we all sit down and eat? I believe Mary and Dominic will be up a bit later. He needed to finish some legal business first."

I tried to gauge Sam, but his face was unreadable. I moved nearer the table and was quickly reminded of my lack of underwear. This was one problem that had to be solved sooner rather than later. I refused to go commando.

"Can I call Rachel first and have her pick up some things for me? There are a few of my own things I really need."

"Of course. You can step outside for a minute, if you'd rather?" Rev offered.

"Let me show you a good spot for cell reception. It can be a little spotty," Sam suggested. I nodded, and he opened the door for me.

I stepped out into the cool, sunny morning, and my nose immediately found the prickly green scent of lightly frosted grass and the sweet, smokiness of changing leaves. Again, I was glad Sam had included the red hoodie and found a pair of house shoes. The hoodie was already zipped up, but I crossed my arms in case.

"Over here. Reception is generally pretty good in the cabin, and it's all right out here for the most part, but I thought you might want some privacy. You'll want to go at least as far as here"—he pointed as we walked toward a sunny patch about five yards from the house—"to be sure no one will overhear anything unless you're whispering."

I glanced up into his blue gaze, surprised at his thoughtfulness.

"Thank you. Um..." I hesitated. "Do you think I'll shift anytime soon?" My face screwed up a little. I couldn't tell when a shift was coming on until it was right on top of me, based on last night's schedule. I didn't want to shift with Rachel on the phone. She'd be out of her mind with worry all over again if she heard me wailing and thrashing.

"It's hard to tell. It might be in the next few minutes, or it could be another hour or two."

"This sucks." It slipped out before I could censor it, and pain momentarily flashed across Sam's face. He opened his mouth like he was going to say something and then shut it again with a quick shake of his head. I inwardly cringed at my callousness and felt the wolf inside growling at me. She didn't approve of my insensitive tone to Sam either. I was suddenly aware of her very real presence inside me—not just that the wolf was there, I could tell that—but I could sense a personality emerging. It was me but enhanced and separate at the same time. I shivered. Not from the change, but from an awareness I wasn't sure I wanted.

"Meg? You're white as a sheet."

A gasp escaped. "It's her. I mean, the wolf. Inside me. She...she has her own self separate but completely linked to me." My eyes widened, my belly queasy. I wasn't sure if it was from lack of food or something else, but the sensation wasn't pleasant.

The wolf inside me paced and then jerked violently, wanting release. I doubled over as the wolf tried forcing her way out. The ferocity, the dominance, scared me. The shift was starting, and I wasn't ready. I wanted control, not this she-devil inside me.

"Sam, she's trying to get out," I whimpered. *Not yet, not yet!*

"It's okay. You're safe here. Safe with me."

"I don't want this." My voice sounded broken to my own ears. I shook my head.

Sam touched my arm, and the heaving slowed but didn't quit. "Do you want me to quiet her?" he asked, uncertainty written all over his features.

"Yes!" I gasped desperately.

Not two seconds later, my face was cradled in Sam's hands and his lips were pressed gently against mine. The wolf settled and went back to a more dormant state immediately. Sensing the stillness, Sam drew back, his hands reluctantly falling away. I was breathing hard, but the tingling had stopped, and I could tell the wolf was momentarily satisfied.

"I don't know how you did that but thank you."

Sam's eye twitched, and he nodded stiffly. Was it that bad to kiss me? Was that what had stopped him last night at the game? Not that this was actually a kiss, per say, it was a semi-mutual meeting of lips. There was no meaning in it. Just a means to an end.

"That should keep her still enough for a little bit. Definitely long enough to make a quick phone call. I'll head back in, if you're okay? I can stay if you'd rather."

"No. It's fine. I'll come back in soon. Save me a scone?"

One side of his mouth tipped up. "You've got it."

I watched his retreating back. He tiredly dragged one hand through his dark blond hair. Once the door was closed, I frantically punched Rachel's icon on my phone. She picked up on the first ring. "Megan, how are you? Are you okay?"

"Well," I said shakily, trying not to burst into tears at the sudden emotion clogging my throat, "I survived the night." I gave her the abbreviated version of shifting and then got to the exciting part. "*But!* There may be a tiny ray of sunshine in this whole hot mess," I said, a note of excitement quivering my voice.

"Sam Wolfe owes you majorly?"

"Ha! Better—it's possible I might come out of this still human. No more wolf, no more shifting, no more pain, no more mess. Back to normal life. Rev found one documented case, I don't know, I guess in their werewolf histories or something, about two other women who were bitten by a werewolf in his human form. One of them became fully wolf, the other stayed human. So it stands to reason, I've got at least a fifty percent chance of staying human."

She squealed on the other end of the phone, echoing my internal delight. "So what happens until we find out if you get to keep your skin?"

"I don't actually know. I have to wait until the next full moon to know for sure. Everything has been so much of a jumble, and so much has happened. It's crazy. Like, right before I called you, this *thing*, the wolf, tried to get out of me—to make me shift. Sorry, I'm not explaining this very well. Anyway, Sam offered to quiet her for a little bit. This is so bizarre. He kissed me. Like, not really kissed me, but put his lips on mine. Which, I guess is technically a kiss, but it wasn't like that at all. It was a little weird. His eye twitched after, and he was all uncomfortable. Honestly. If the circumstances were any different, I'd be a little insulted." I tried to make my sentences more coherent. I realized I was rambling and probably not making a lot of sense.

"You liked it, didn't you?"

Only Rachel could possibly pick up on that from the tone of our conversation.

"It wasn't really a kiss, Rach. It was just making the wolf...go away...for a little bit."

"Why do you think the wolf reacted to Sam's kiss?"

I didn't want to explore that too closely. "I need to get back in. I'm starving, and they have a ton of food set out back in the cabin. But I need you to do something for me."

"Anything. You name it."

"Can you please go over to my house and pack up some clothes? Seriously, Rachel, I have no underwear. I am going commando. I cannot express to you the importance of having a pair of my own clean underwear. Also, I'm running around a bunch of werewolf men with no bra on. And one of them is Sam Wolfe."

"And he's probably loving every second."

"We are not going there."

She had the audacity to chuckle. "No problem. You want your brush, makeup, mousse, toothbrush, that sort of thing, too? I'll bring nail polish. Nail polish helps everything."

"You're a life saver. And for the love, bring me a razor. I swear my legs are walking carpets. And I shaved yesterday." I knew I could count on Rachel. No matter what else was going on in my life.

"We might actually be going to the ends of the earth together, *chica*." She echoed the sentiment that had come to define our friendship.

"Let's hope it ends in skin and not fur. Thanks, Rachel."

"Want me to bring them over there today?"

I bit my lip. "Um, yes, but let me double check that I'm safe for you to be around. Shifting gets pretty intense. Call you back in a bit?"

"For sure. I'm grabbing a granola bar and your spare house key as we speak. I'll get things together."

"You are the best." I hiccupped, emotion welling up within me again.

"Meg, we'll get through this. Together. Just like everything else we've ever gone through."

"Love you, Rach."

"Love you, too. To the ends of the earth. See you in a bit."

Chapter 15

Sam

I watched Megan through the back window of the cabin. The feel of her lips was imprinted on my brain. It obviously meant nothing at all to her, but it meant *everything* to me. I'd been half in love with her since she'd picked scrawny sixth grade me to be on her dodgeball team. I'd fallen even harder when she'd baked me cookies after I broke my pinky in the same dodgeball game.

I thought maybe there was mutual attraction last night at the game. But once the wolf decided she was my mate, that was it. I physically ached to touch her. I didn't want to put a chaste little kiss on her lips. I wanted to wrap my arms around her, hold her close, and really show her what I was feeling. Which was probably never going to happen. Megan made it perfectly clear she wanted no part in being a werewolf—wanted no part of being with me. My toxins killed any spark that might have been there. Wolf whined inside me. More than I wanted Megan to be my mate, I wanted it to be her choice. *I* wanted to be her choice, not her regret and not her obligation.

I wasn't sure what Dad would think of all this from a legal standpoint. There were certain wolf customs and laws that he'd insist we follow. I was happy to do that. Megan wouldn't be. Then there were human legal ramifications. Dad was a lawyer and had kept the pack under the radar and away from any legal issues the whole time he'd been Alpha. It had come in handy to have a top-notch lawyer in the pack. I cracked my knuckles as I considered possible scenarios Dad might come up with.

I'd broken his trust last night. I hadn't meant to. And our already rocky relationship was feeling pretty glacial at the moment. I didn't want to disappoint my father. Quite the contrary. I wanted him to be proud of me. Wanted him to love me as his son and respect me as his Beta. Emotions were complicated things. And I had enough emotions swirling inside to drown me if I wasn't careful.

Megan waved her free arm around as she talked on the phone, her back to the cabin. She had listened and stayed far enough away that I couldn't catch what she was saying, but she was clearly giving Rachel an earful. I wished I hadn't told her to go so far. I was curious what Meg's take on all this was—what she would tell her best friend but not say to me. A big breath I hadn't realized I'd been holding escaped my lips in a forceful gust.

"Sam, why don't you come on back here to the table," Mr. Carmichael called. I took one more glance at Meg and came over to where the old man was sitting. He patted the seat beside him, so I sat. "Sam, I realize last night was entirely an accident, and that this isn't your fault. It was just one of those unfortunate incidents. You look like you need to hear that."

Heat washed over me. It wasn't an embarrassed heat, or the heat of shame, it was something different, but it made me feel clean. Absolved me of some of my guilt. I still felt guilty, but hearing those words from this man, Megan's guardian, smoothed over some of my insecurities.

"Thank you, sir. I don't suppose you'd mind telling my father that?" My mouth tugged down in a frown, remembering Dad's rage the night before.

"I'd be happy to. In fact, if we're all going to get through this peaceably, I think we all need to realize, Megan included, that this was an accident. It doesn't change the outcome, but it changes the perception of things." His gaze met mine. "I'm on your side in this as much as I'm on Megan's side."

"Unless you break Megan's heart," Rev put in with a half smile.

"Unless you break Megan's heart," Mr. Carmichael confirmed. "And then your fur and fangs will have nothing on this old man and his cane."

I laughed. A genuine laugh. That wasn't what I was expecting, and I knew I had made an unlikely ally. His face wrinkled up in a smile, his deep-set eyes twinkling. We all glanced back when the door opened, and Meg came through.

"Is it...safe for Rachel to bring some stuff by for me today?"

Rev answered. "It should be safe enough. We'll all be here to help you through any shifts today. She'll want to be sure she comes in daylight though."

"I'll text her the details. Can we eat? I don't mean to be rude, but I'm starving."

"Definitely," Mr. Carmichael agreed.

The food was out and ready, buffet style. I handed Megan a paper plate.

"Wow. The smells kind of hit you right in the face, don't they?"

"It doesn't smell exactly like that to us," Rev explained. "We can still smell each individual component like you can, but it's not so, how did you say it? In your face."

That wrung a small smile from Megan as she put a scone and a sausage biscuit with a generous helping of fruit on her plate. Mr. Carmichael handed her a steaming coffee.

"I already put creamer and sugar in it for you," he told her.

"Mm. Just the right amount, as always," she said after a generous drink.

Chapter 16

Megan

An hour and one shift later, Mr. Wolfe was seated at the table. Possibly the most intimidating man I'd ever met. The new personality of the wolf inside quaked in fear and then scurried away into some dark recess when he entered the room. Maybe that meant I wouldn't shift again for a while. Mary, Sam's mom, sat beside him, her face serene and hands folded neatly in her lap. I envied her inner calm.

"There are some legalities that will need to be addressed," he started, his only preamble a nod and a sip of black coffee. He took out a pair of thin reading glasses from the pocket of his plaid shirt. It was such a contrast—the proper positioning of the glasses perched on the end of his nose, legal documents all drawn up neatly in a folder in front of him, the man himself dressed in rugged, worn outdoor clothes. He pursed his lips. "There are also some wolf customs that will not be ignored." He gazed over the top of his glasses, first at Sam, who gave an imperceptible shake, his mouth thinning. Mr. Wolfe's gaze grew agitated and was still black when he glanced at me. I swallowed on a cotton-dry mouth.

"Wolf law states any human bitten by a wolf belongs to that wolf."

My eyes about popped out of my head. "Excuse me?" I stammered.

"It's not like it sounds," Sam offered apologetically.

"I am not a *thing*, and I do not *belong* to anyone," I cut back, fear working its way up my spine.

"Of course not," Sam agreed.

"Once a wolf bites someone, that person is tied to them," Mary offered before shooting her husband a look.

Rev broke in. "This is the law of the pack, Megan. However, this is a special circumstance which requires a little interpretation of the laws." He entreated Mr. Wolfe who did not in any way, shape, or form, seem happy about this. Rev continued. "We have discussed this at length, and for at least the next month while your shifts are somewhat irregular, and while we determine whether or not you will remain a wolf, you will need the protection of the pack. Also, our Beta needs to be observed upholding our laws. It needs to appear like you belong to him."

Sam snorted, and his father gave him a terse glare.

Rev continued like nothing had happened. "In order to accomplish this, it would be advisable if you, Megan, appeared to be following this ordinance. If you do not stay a wolf, then at the end of the month this law will not apply to you anymore. If you do stay a wolf, then all this would mean is that you'd remain under Sam's protection." He glanced at Sam whose face remained a blank slate.

I studied Rev, suspicion lacing my gaze.

Sam held up his hands when I stabbed him with an icy glare. "No hidden agenda, I swear."

I wasn't brave enough to skewer Mr. Wolfe with a look, so my gaze moved to Grandpa instead. He nodded encouragingly like he was totally on board with all of this. I wasn't sure who was more insane—them or Grandpa.

"Megan, any wolf within several yards of you is going to know you're no longer human. We can't hide that fact. And if Sam isn't seen upholding werewolf law, it will cause problems in the pack. Big problems. It will cause political issues with other packs—packs whose support we need," Mary implored. "You don't have to do this forever, but right now, we need your cooperation as much as you need our pack."

My hands twisted in my lap.

"We need to establish the parameters of what this will look like for the next month. At least while Megan is a wolf"—Rev glanced at me.

I cringed and then shivered involuntarily. I so did not want to stay a wolf—"for this to fully uphold the pack principle, and for Megan's safety, she needs to live in close proximity to Sam."

I immediately shook my head. Rev's less than plain speaking clued me in to how touchy a subject this was. However, I was not moving out here and being neighbors with Scary Alpha.

"Megan, it's not safe for either of us if you come home with me," Grandpa broke in gently. I felt tears pricking, knowing that if I lashed out in the middle of a shift, and Grandpa was too close, I could kill him. And that would kill me. "Besides, as I understand it, Sam is the only one who can help you control your wolf aside from the direct command from Mr. Wolfe as your Alpha." Mr. Wolfe's mouth was a flat line while Rev nodded. Sam's shoulders twitched uncomfortably. Mary put a hand on Dominic's arm.

"What are you suggesting?" I hated that my voice shook.

Rev cleared his throat. He only did that when he was nervous. Not a good sign for me. "You could move into the spare bedroom at the Wolfe's residence."

"No. I won't." Terror struck me at the thought of living under the same roof as Dominic Wolfe. No, thank you.

Rev's lips puckered as he chose his next words, "The other option is to stay here. Live at the cabin for the next few weeks. With Sam."

My mouth was hanging open like a door with a broken hinge, though I couldn't force any words out.

"For the sake of the pack and our laws, it needs to be assumed that you are the Beta's...charge." Rev attempted to clarify.

"Define charge, Rev," Grandpa broke in.

The tell-tale throat clearing echoed in the quiet of the room.

"Can I speak with Megan alone for a minute?" Sam interrupted. Mr. Wolfe raised an eyebrow, his eyes conveying some secret message to his son. Sam nodded once.

"Of course," Rev said.

Sam tipped his head to the door, and I stiffly got up and followed him out into the chilly sunshine of early afternoon. He walked beside me, leading us to the back of the house and to a huge fire pit with logs and stones set up around the perimeter. He perched on a huge worn log and motioned to the seat beside him.

He stared at the pit, a faraway expression covering his face. I sat, unease curling in my stomach, wrapping tendrils around my breakfast and squeezing uncomfortably.

"Three years ago, I stood right here with my parents and the entire pack. I took the oath and became my pack's Beta. Second in command. Only my dad outranks me. I have the ability to command any member of the pack using only my words and a mental link. That's the last time my dad looked at me and I knew for certain he was proud of me."

Despite the current situation, Sam's confession tugged at me. It was plain his relationship with his father wasn't all rosy, but this just about broke my heart. I lived in a world where I was loved and adored. Grandpa was so proud of me his buttons practically popped off his shirt when he talked about me. It was embarrassing and wonderful all at the same time. To not have that with your own parent? That was awful. Part of me wanted to reach out and take his hand, but I held still, waiting for him to go on.

He took a deep breath and forged ahead. "I know you didn't want any of this. I didn't want any of this for you either. You have to know that." His eyes pleaded with me.

"I do know that. I know this was all an accident. I'm trying to work through it all still. It's a lot to believe and a lot to experience."

He nodded then cleared his throat. "Before I go on, are you and Brody Harrington..." He drifted off, and my head jerked at the subject change.

"No. He's been flirting with me for a while, but I don't think I want it to go any further than that. Why?"

He exhaled. "Okay. Good. He's a tool anyway. But that makes what I'm going to say next a little easier." He fidgeted with his shirt sleeve. Anxiety poked me in the ribs. "I'm going to ask you for one thing. It's a big thing and has several parts. But I won't ask you for anything else these next four weeks until we figure out if you'll stay human or stay wolf."

I nodded encouragement. He had my undivided attention.

"I'd like us to pretend we're dating. Pretend for the pack, pretend at school. Essentially this helps my dad save face, which in turn, keeps the pack functioning normally. If you stay human, I'll deal with the fallout then. I'm more concerned about keeping things running smoothly with the pack the next few weeks until it leaks out what I did. When that happens, I'm not sure what the ultimate verdict will be, but until we figure out the most peaceful way to explain to the pack their Beta screwed the rules, controlling the situation is the best outcome for the pack as a whole.

"Obviously, everyone is going to know you're a wolf. Like Mom said, there's no hiding that. We're going to have to tell people I bit you. But if it's perceived that it was mutual, and you are a willing participant, then it makes it easier for Dad to smooth things over, like he gave us permission. He can skirt around the issue without lying about it. The fact your grandpa has known about us for years gives the story some muscle and makes it believable. "It's also true that you'll need to be in close proximity to me. Your wolf will only react to mine or my dad's, maybe my mom's, as far as who can help you control it. I'd like to think you'd prefer me?"

My eyes were wide. "Yes. Definitely."

"That means either you're going to have to move here, or we're going to have to figure something else out so we're in the same house at night when the moon is out, and we're not around people who might get hurt."

I bit my lip and tried to quell the panic threatening to erupt. This was all so preposterous. "I will not live in the same house with your dad. He scares the crap out of me."

He nodded, blue eyes flashing in understanding. "Are you willing to live here at the cabin? With me?" Hope rushed across his face before he tempered it into an unreadable mask.

"What happens if I don't?"

His face fell a little before he recovered. "Your wolf will become more and more wild. Even once you're more acclimated to her, she may completely take over. Essentially, you'd be feral, human or wolf."

I did not like the sound of that. She was wild enough inside me now. But to completely lose myself in the animal? Again, no, thank you. "Why just you or your dad? Why does it have to be one of you?"

He sighed. "It's a little complicated, but the long and short of it is that every wolf in the pack is assigned a place. Alpha is at the top. Beta is next in line. Omega is the bottom rung. Everyone else filters into a specific spot somewhere in between—some spots are parallel to others, but everyone has a spot. Whenever a wolf shifts for the first time, they need to be in the presence of a more dominant wolf. If the new wolf is only in the presence of lesser wolves, the new wolf will assert its dominance and basically overtake the human, becoming feral. But if there is a more dominant wolf, the new wolf learns the proper boundaries. Because I'm the Beta, essentially, your wolf is a Beta equivalent and will only answer to me or to the Alpha—my dad."

I tried to process this information. It sounded like I was fundamentally going to be chained to Sam's side for the next few weeks until my body decided it was going to play nice and be human again. I rubbed my temples. A stress headache was coming on. "So I don't really have much other choice."

"I'm sorry, but no." He rubbed the crease between his eyebrows. I felt foreboding settle hard in the pit of my stomach. "There is one more thing tied to all this."

"Of course, there is." Why wouldn't there be?

Could this nightmare get any worse?

"My dad is going to insist we sign a legally binding contract of sorts."

"Why?"

He steepled his hands and studied the ground a minute before his eyes came back up. "If you stay human, there are certain laws that will apply to our situation living together that make my dad uncomfortable from a legal standpoint. He wants us to sign a marriage contract."

"He *what*?" I shrieked. Surely, I heard him wrong? Irrational anger and fear burbled below the surface where my emotions were all distorted and ready to erupt.

Sam held his hands up in surrender. "Rev said we can get an annulment easily if you claim you signed under duress."

I gaped at him like a fish trying to suck air on dry land. "I'd certainly call this *duress*." Some of the anger leaked out. "And so help me, Sam Wolfe, if this is some twisted ploy to get in my pants—"

"Whoa, whoa, whoa!" He cut me off, waving his hands in front of him to wield off my wrath and consternation. "I am so not trying to get into your pants!"

Ouch. That actually hurt a little more than it should have. Was I that much of a troll? Not that I'd let him near my pants anyway.

"I mean, yes, I'd love to be in your pants"—His face darkened to the color of raspberries and his voice cracked as he tried to backtrack—"but that's not what this is about. Not my idea."

My face was flushed now, too, although if it was from frustration or embarrassment, I'm not sure.

"I cannot believe this is happening." My head sank down to my knees and the anger seeped away, replaced by despair. The creature inside danced around at the prospect of spending so much time with Sam. She was far too chipper. And temperamental. As if she felt my control slipping with my mental distress, she took advantage, and I felt her clawing to get out again. The tingling started in my toes.

"Sam, it's happening." It was too late for him to stop it, too. My paw poked through the house shoes I had on as fur rippled down my arms, slimming the bones down to nothing and then thickening them so that the sleeves of the hoodie burst open.

The shift only took about three minutes, and as Sam had promised, the pain was lessened. It still hurt. It hurt a lot—but it was more manageable. My body was stiff and rusty but slowly remembered the intricate dance of crushing bones and snapping sinews to rearrange itself into this new pattern of the wolf. My sides heaved, and my long wolf's tongue lolled out of my mouth as I plopped in a heap beside the fire ring.

"You did a great job that time, Meg. Your shifts are getting quicker. You're learning." The wolf beamed at the praise, while the rest of me wanted to glare at him. I didn't like anything about morphing into a giant beast. I'm not sure which emotion showed, if any at all, on my wolf's face. I did not want to be a wolf, but fortunately it was now less scary when I had to shift.

"I'll go grab the robe before you shift back so you're covered."

At least he had the decency to remember I was a prude. He jumped up and ran to the front of the house and was back right as my tail was starting to shrink away. He held the robe out in front of him, covering his eyes and glancing away. I groaned when the shift was over, and I was left naked on the cold ground. I was still achy but got up as quick as I could and slipped my arms into the voluminous sleeves Sam held out for me, face still averted. My teeth were clacking together, and I was shaking with chills.

"Come on. It's a lot warmer inside. And I'm sure Rev can explain all of this to you better than I can. I...I just felt like I should be the one to tell you."

While I didn't like any of what he'd discussed, I could at least appreciate his honesty. "Thank you. For telling me yourself."

Grandpa, Rev, and Sam's parents were still sitting at the table where we'd left them.

Grandpa did a quick assessment, his gaze traveling over me, making sure I was still in one piece. I gave him a weak smile.

"Did Samuel explain how things are going to work?" Mr. Wolfe asked bluntly.

"Now, Dominic, I told you. Megan will not be forced into anything," Grandpa fired back. Mr. Wolfe's eyes narrowed. Grandpa didn't back down.

"George, did you want to speak with Megan privately?" Rev asked.

"I do, but you go ahead and stay, too, Rev. You can fill in any gaps I miss."

Mr. Wolfe seethed as he was essentially dismissed. Mary rose gracefully and put a hand on her husband's shoulder. His forehead relaxed a fraction, and he rose from the table in one fluid motion and jerked his head for Sam to follow them.

Sam smiled apologetically, nodded once to me, and walked out the door his father held open.

I sank down into one of the kitchen chairs, and Grandpa pushed a blueberry muffin in front of me.

"Grandpa, have you heard this insanity? This *plan*? I'm supposed to marry Sam Wolfe and live with him for what, a month?"

He stroked his mustache, which he only did when he was being overly thoughtful or trying to stall for time. I wasn't sure which he was doing now. "Meggie-Girl, life just got a lot more complicated for both of us, and before you get all fired up at me, I want you to listen to what I'm telling you. No one is expecting you to stay married, especially if your wolf fades. This is more of a contract that protects both you and Sam during this time of close contact. If something were to happen and you got hurt, Sam would better understand the situation and, as your husband, could sign for medical treatment for you. Your life got a lot more treacherous. He will know better what's happening to you than I will. I'd feel safer if he were allowed serious input into any medical decisions and for him to be around for your protection.

"My sweet girl, as much as we don't want to face it, it's going to be dangerous for you to be home with me other than visiting during daylight, probably with an escort. Yours is such an unusual case, no one is sure what to expect, so we're trying to cover all the bases. Besides, if your Grandma Elsie were here, she would have a conniption fit if I let you move in with a boy you weren't married to. I'd have a fit myself. Even though this is strictly a safety issue and nothing else is expected, it just looks bad."

And that was the clincher. I couldn't disappoint Grandpa, or Grandma's memory. Before she'd passed away three years ago, Grandma had dreamed of me in a white dress. I'd always wanted to be like her, saving myself for my wedding day, wearing white, Grandpa walking me down the aisle. Signing my name to a piece of paper that legally bound me to wolf-boy at seventeen wasn't exactly how I'd pictured it.

"As soon as the next full moon passes, if you are still fully human, we can have the marriage annulled quickly and painlessly. Did Sam mention the duress clause?" Rev asked.

"He did." I sighed.

"Actually, it might be better to approach annulment on grounds of mental impairment at the time of the marriage. I'd say wolf toxins definitely qualify as a drug interfering with your system. Regardless, what I'm saying, Megan, is that there are options. There are several avenues we can take, all of which will certainly end the contract," Rev said. "I will personally handle all the details myself with Dominic and will ensure nothing is left out."

This was crazy. I didn't want to marry Sam. I didn't want to marry anyone at seventeen, although admittedly, there were a lot of worse options than Sam Wolfe. I sighed and the wolf nudged me, bringing up images of other wolves. Guilt niggled away some frustration. If I didn't agree to these absurd terms, I wouldn't be the only one to potentially suffer. Sam's actions were going to affect his pack. My actions were going to affect his pack. I sighed. I needed help controlling the beast inside me. Sam was the only one I trusted to give me that help. If signing my name to a piece of paper and pretending to be his girl got me my desired outcome, I could do that. Grandpa put his stamp of approval on it. And I knew he'd never do anything he believed wasn't in my absolute best interests. He'd known about this world much longer than I had and felt this was the safest thing for me. I had very, very limited options to work with.

"You know this is completely nuts."
"I know, sweetheart."
"All right. I want to talk to Sam."

Chapter 17

Sam

Megan walked out the front door, wrapped snuggly in her robe. Dad bristled beside me. We hadn't said much while we'd been outside together.

"Mr. Wolfe, I'll do this your way. But I'd like to speak with Sam again, please," she said. Her face was resigned, her eyes sad.

"Good," was all Dad said as he took Mom's hand, and they legged it back into the cabin.

My stomach did a few flips as Megan closed the distance between us, coming to stand a few paces away. Nervous anticipation tap danced down my back and coiled my belly into knots.

"Sam, I will agree to this for one month. I will live here at the cabin with you. We will not be sharing a bed." Her eyes flashed, and I recognized the fear coming out as anger. I nodded, trying not to react at her words. "I will sign the marriage contract with the express understanding that as soon as the next full moon hits, and whether I am still human or not, it will be annulled the next business day." I swallowed, a mix of dread and elation warring within. Wolf jumped around, thrilled with this turn of events. I'd be living in the same space as Megan for the next month, at least. While that was exciting, it was also going to be a huge temptation. With the way I felt toward her, I'd have to be careful. She continued, oblivious to my internal war. "I will go along with this dating charade for the benefit of your pack."

"Our pack," I interrupted. Her eyes narrowed in a way that said, *don't push it.*

"I will pretend to be your girlfriend in front of the pack and at school. We get to drop the act at the cabin or when we're alone. However, I have non-negotiable ground rules. There will be no hands under clothing. There will be no touching skin covered by clothes. You will not touch my boobs, and you will not go near my butt. I will agree to this dating scenario for the next four weeks. After that, if I'm still human, I will walk away with no strings attached. If I'm still a wolf...we'll figure it out then. Do I make myself clear?"

I blinked at her, honestly shocked that she agreed to go along with this at all. "Megan, you have nothing to worry about from me. I respect you. Your rules are fine. I'm here to help you through the next few weeks and make them as painless as possible." Painless for her, at least.

Gravel crunched as Rachel's car came into view at the end of the drive up to the cabin. Meg's face broke out in a hopeful but tentative smile.

"Do you think I'm safe?" Meg murmured, watching Rachel's approaching car hungrily.

"Probably?" I ventured. It was so hard to tell anything with the unpredictability of first shifts. "Do you want me to stay close in case?"

She sighed, momentary sorrow clouding her face. My gut twisted. "It would probably be safest." I nodded at her words.

Rachel parked and hopped out of her car, waiting by the door, the uncertainty covering her face matching Megan's expression as she moved slowly closer to her best friend.

"Megan? You all right?" Rachel called from the driveway.

"For the moment, but I want to take things slowly, just to make sure I don't shift on you." The words came out sounding painful.

I matched Meg's slow pace until we were about ten feet from Rachel, then Rachel raced forward and wrapped her arms all the way around Megan, heedless of any possible consequences. I sucked in a breath, watching for any signs that Megan's wolf would react badly. I shouldn't have worried. Meg collapsed into Rachel's arms, sobs suddenly echoing loudly in the still air.

Wolf paced around inside me, wanting to get out, wanting me to comfort Megan, wanting me to hold her and kiss away any distress. That, however, would have been a mistake of monumental proportions, so I clenched my fists at my sides and kept a respectful distance.

"Meg, it's fine. We are going to get through this. I swear," Rachel whispered as she held onto Megan for dear life. Megan just cried harder and clung tighter.

I had no idea what to do, so I stood there like a worthless fence post, watching for any shifting activity, wishing it were me Meg was clinging to. After a few minutes of this new type of torture, Meg's tears dried up. She pulled back from Rachel and swiped at her swollen eyes.

"Sorry," she said.

Rachel glared like she couldn't believe Meg had even uttered the word.

"All right. Give me every detail. But let's go in, if you don't mind. It's getting cold out here. Let's grab your stuff," Rachel said as she clicked her key fob and popped her trunk open. She glanced at me and nodded to her trunk.

My lips thinned as I resisted the urge to roll my eyes, but I dutifully went to the trunk and retrieved not one, but two large duffels that were stuffed to capacity.

The girls walked ahead of me to the cabin. Just as they reached the door, Meg turned back to me. Her face wrinkled like she'd swallowed something sour and was embarrassed about it. I had no idea how to interpret it.

"Sam, do...do you think you could make sure the wolf...stays away for a little bit? I would like to talk to Rachel alone."

Wolf danced around, doing his version of a happy jig. She was asking me to kiss her? I looked at her face again. No, she was not asking me to kiss her, just to make the wolf leave. I bit back a sigh.

"Sure." It was the gentlemanly thing to do, anyway.

She huffed a breath and stood still, waiting, totally not participating. My insides crumbled a little bit watching her passivity. Trying not to think too much about it, I leaned down and carefully pressed my lips to hers, making sure not to put too much into it, especially in front of Rachel who watched us through slitted eyes.

"Okay," Meg said, presumably pulling back as soon as she felt her wolf quiet. She opened the door and glanced around. She came up short when she saw my dad sitting like a judge at the kitchen table. She cleared her throat. "Can we have a few minutes?"

"You think that's safe?" my dad deadpanned.

"Dom," Mom inserted softly.

"She should be fine for at least a half an hour or so," I said. Dad's eyes narrowed.

"Rev, why don't you take me down to that ice cream shop you like so well. It's only a few minutes' drive from here, isn't it?" Mr. Carmichael said, already moving for his jacket and hat. "Dominic, Mary, why don't you come with us. I'll even treat," he added, giving Dad a sugary sweet smile. George Carmichael had a pair, that was for sure.

Dad snorted but got out of his seat, waited for Mom, and then walked past us with Rev and Mr. Carmichael.

"Do you want me to stick around, just in case?" I asked Megan as the other four moved toward Rev's car. Megan bit her lip. "I don't mind," I offered. I'd stay as close as she'd let me.

"Are you sure?"

A smile tipped the corner of my mouth. "I'll go hang out by the fire pit. It's close enough I'll easily hear if someone raises their voice." I glanced at Rachel as I said the last part. "Rachel, if for some reason Meg starts to twitch or act a little funny, and she hasn't already called for me, get to the other side of the room or out the door—as far away from her as possible—and yell. I'll be there in less than a minute."

Rachel blanched a little, and Meg hung her head. I couldn't help tapping Meg's arm. "You'll be fine. She's quiet for now. Shout if you need me." How I wanted her to need me.

Chapter 18
Megan

The door shut, and it was just me and Rachel. I took a shuddering breath and plopped into a chair. Rachel followed, not quite nervous, but a little unsettled.

"Was he serious? About getting to the other side of the room and yelling for him?"

I winced. "Yes. Gah, I hope it doesn't come to that. This shifting business is pretty unreal."

"Tell me."

I smirked. "Rachel, you would want to know the gory details."

"Of course, I want to know the gory bits! It's not every day your best friend turns into a *werewolf*. Leave no gruesome detail untold."

And I didn't. On more than one occasion, Rachel caught her breath, her eyebrows drew together, and a few times indignant grunts came from her gaping mouth.

"Which brings us all to this ridiculous contract I've agreed to." I gave her the run down on the marriage contract I'd be signing at some point over the weekend.

"Wow." Rachel sat, stunned, as I finished. "If you ever get over being mad at the situation, pretend dating one of the hottest guys at school could be fun. Mrs. Wolfe has a nice ring to it," she teased.

I shot her a scathing look.

"But seriously, Meggie. This is a good thing. Not necessarily that you're getting married. That's kind of crazy. But it's safer for you to be with Sam if what they're telling you is true. And I'm guessing, based on what you've told me, you believe them."

I sighed. "I do. I'm still shocked that any of this has happened. I mean, this is something straight out of one of your fantasy novels."

"It is," she conceded, her eyes serious. "Who knows what other creatures could be out there?" Her eyes lit mischievously.

I rolled my eyes, but said nothing, because after being changed into a werewolf, who was I to argue that there might be other previously believed mythical creatures out there, roaming the streets with us? I glanced at the clock above the sink. We'd been talking for almost an hour. It had been several hours since my last shift.

As if the mere thought of a shift could bring one on, the wolf stirred.

"Rachel, go outside with Sam. Now!" I ordered as the tingling started in my toes. Wide-eyed, Rachel sprinted to the door.

"Sam," she hollered.

Fluidly, I felt the knife pricks move in a sweeping motion up my legs, my bones cracking. I bit my lip, holding in the guttural sounds choking my throat for Rachel's benefit. Sam was there then, blocking my view of everything else. "Megan, look at me."

I locked onto his bright blue eyes and held them, their depths offering focus as my back arched and my arms snapped. My eyes screwed shut as the scream I'd been trying to hold in came clawing its way out.

Once I lay panting in my fur, I glanced at Rachel. Her eyes were so large that white showed all the way around her green irises. Her mouth hung open like a door sagging on one hinge. Her whole body was frozen, one hand on the doorframe, the other on the handle of the still-open door. I whined. I wanted to tell her it was me, but I couldn't in this form.

A word I'd never heard out of Rachel's mouth dropped from her lips and hung in the air between us.

I glared accusingly at Sam. I couldn't believe he'd let her watch my shift. He swallowed, his Adam's apple bobbing.

"Sorry. My main priority was making sure you were okay and that she was out of the way," he said.

Had he just read my thoughts? I whined again, this time in concern. Sam winced, his eyes scrunching up as his face contorted.

Before he could say anything, I let out a harsh yip and felt my tail retracting back into my body.

"Rachel, she's shifting back, if you want to turn away," Sam said, though his entire focus was on me again, quietly coaching me back to my human form. Of course, Rachel did no such thing. She watched the whole thing in horrified fascination.

As soon as I had my breath back after the shift, my eyes speared Sam. "How did you know what I was thinking?" I demanded.

He ran a hand through his hair. "Remember how I told you about the Beta having a mental link to his pack members?" I nodded, my belly curdling. I glanced at Rachel. She was far more intrigued than disturbed. "That's how I knew what you were thinking."

"This is not happening," I muttered as panic tickled my gut. Hardly daring to think the question, but knowing I had to know, "How much can you hear?"

Relief washed over his face, and he held his hands up like he was surrendering to me. "I only hear what you want me to. I can't read your thoughts or pry into your secrets or anything like that. You thought your question at me, and that's how I picked it up." He hesitated. "Your thoughts will come loudly to me though, so, if you don't want me to hear, make sure you're thinking things to yourself, and not directing them to me. Make sense?"

My eyes narrowed as I nodded. "I think so. We may need to practice this. You do not need to be inside my head. Having this *wolf-thing* in here is one too many as it is."

"Is it really like a secondary personality?" Rachel asked, all interest.

"Aren't you supposed to be on my side?" I complained.

She instantly sobered. "I am. Sorry. Just curious. I didn't mean to be insensitive."

I shoved back into the chair I'd vacated when the shift started. "It's okay." I gave a mirthless chuckle. Sam cocked his head to the side at the sound. "You know, Rachel, in some ways you're probably more equipped for this wolf business than I am."

Sam glanced at her and raised an eyebrow.

"I read a lot of fantasy and paranormal fiction," she explained.

Sam grunted. "Don't believe everything you read," he replied dryly.

Sam was right. Having him hold off the wolf twice that day did make my uncontrollable night shifts more intense. While the end of my daytime shifts had been painful, they were coming more easily. Once the moon was high in the sky, I couldn't go more than forty-five minutes without a shift for the first four hours. After that, they became less frequent, and I was able to snatch a few hours of sleep between them. Sam didn't fare any better. True to his word, he helped me through each one of my shifts.

At about three in the morning, after my seventh shift of the night, I was beyond exhausted, but my body was too tightly strung to relax back into sleep. My brain buzzed with activity, humming through the events of the day.

"Do you want to try calling up your wolf?" Sam asked quietly from his spot opposite me on the couch. The two of us were alone, everyone else having left hours ago. Rachel had wanted to stay, and Grandpa would have been happy to if I'd asked, but there wasn't anything either of them could do to help the situation, so I sent them home.

"I'm not sure what that means."

"Basically, you'd be controlling the shift. You would be in charge of calling up your wolf, rather than letting her lead the parade," he explained as he rubbed a hand over his left eye. I could tell he was just as tired as I was, though he was better at hiding it. I was cranky, but I tried to put it aside. My attitude was the one thing I could control in this mess, and I had no desire to make things worse than they already were by being crabby.

"That sounds promising," I offered half-heartedly. I did want to learn to control the wolf. I *needed* to control the wolf. I was the one in charge of my body—at least I wanted to be. "What do I need to do?"

He scratched his chin. "In the wolf world, we call it asserting your dominance. You let your wolf know you are the Alpha in your pair. Once you make the effort to get to know her a little better, the two of you will become even more linked—your thoughts and actions will flow seamlessly into each other. It will help you shift at will, rather than pulling away from each other. Does that make sense?"

I thought about it for a minute. I had felt the wolf's presence all day, but I'd never thought about making her acquaintance, as Grandpa might have said. She'd only been this terrifying, wild beast inside me, contorting me and controlling me whenever she felt the urge. But if I was the dominant party, and could force the wolf to understand that, could I control it?

Closing my eyes, for the first time, I sought the wolf in my mind. I didn't have to search far. She was there, waiting for me right below the surface. She licked my face, happy that I'd come seeking her. I relaxed a fraction of an inch, and the wolf lunged. I felt the hair on my arms start to sprout and I sucked in a sharp breath.

"Don't let her control you, Meg," Sam said softly. "You control her. Show her you are the Alpha of your pair."

I didn't exactly know what that meant, but in my mind's eye, I took my hands and grasped the wolf's will.

"Your wolf is an extension of you—the wild parts of you channeled into one form," Sam encouraged.

I jerked my wolf's will back with everything I had. *I am the Alpha*, I told her. She snarled, and the hair poked farther through my skin, setting my limbs on fire as the ice-like hairs pricked through my tender skin. I snarled back. I would control her. I would not be feral and *would not* be governed by something other than my own mind.

We stared each other down for a full minute before I narrowed my eyes and squeezed my wolf's will tight between my hands. *Mine*, I told her. *Mine to control.* Slowly, my wolf raised her head, breaking eye-contact as she rolled onto her back, flashing her underbelly up at me in submission. I gasped as the fur receded from my arms and legs, as the wolf let go of her control and turned it over to me.

My eyes opened, and I sagged to the couch, bracing my forehead on the arm of the furniture. Breaths puffed in quick, shallow gasps and a cold sweat slicked my skin. *I did it.*

When I caught my breath, I looked over at Sam triumphantly. His smile was wide and oddly, pride shone in his eyes. "And that's how you assert your dominance," he said softly.

I felt a silly, sleep-deprived grin stretch across my own lips.

"Feels good, doesn't it?"

"I'd say, 'you have no idea,' but I'm pretty sure you do," I answered, the banter between us the least strained it had been since last night at the game.

"Do you want to call the shot to shift?"

"I think I need to learn, whether I want to or not."

He nodded. "It's the same principle. You call your wolf, you let her know you are the Alpha, and that *you* want to shift. *You* will let her out, and *you* will call her back in. Eventually, you'll become in sync enough that the thoughts flow without effort between the two of you, and you won't need to assert your dominance. You will be the Alpha, and she'll respond without challenge."

I took a deep breath and sat up straighter on the couch. "Okay. I can do this." Big breath in through the nose, out through the mouth.

"Yes. You can. You're doing an amazing job," Sam encouraged.

I closed my eyes again, seeking my wolf. She was there, tail wagging this time. There was no challenge in her posture, and she seemed genuinely happy at my attention.

Taking a deep breath, I let my thoughts expand to my wolf. I thought about how I wanted to shift, stay wolf for a few minutes, briefly explore being on four paws, and then I wanted to shift back.

Wolf was perfectly amiable and sat, waiting patiently for me to let her out. Shaking the rest of my trepidation off, I let go of a tendril of my control, giving it to the wolf. It was like taking apart a tightly woven braid, but instead of letting the untied cords drop, I was handing them to my wolf who was forming them into an intricate pattern on her end.

It was like the shift happened in slow motion. Each strand of the braid I handed to the wolf, she took and started changing my body. The fire of the pain was absent, too. It was still painful, but I wasn't gasping and shrieking with the effort of the shift. Once I felt the fur on my body and my bones stretching, I let the wolf have her head, and the rest of the shift just happened. It was nearly simultaneous. One moment I was inching my way from human to wolf, and the next, it was done. I was standing on four paws in front of Sam. The wolf was delighted, and she nudged us forward, her nose touching Sam's knee.

"Meg, that was beautiful." His face was still smiling, his eyes tired. He brought his hand up and hesitated before gently stroking the fur on my head and behind my ears. I wanted to back away, but wolf was lapping up the attention.

Time to move away, I told my wolf. She growled at me, and I was conscious on some level that we were growling toward Sam. He dropped his hand off, and Wolf forcefully put her head back under his hand. I gripped her will and jerked her back.

A startled yelp sounded as I sat heavily on my rump, my tail whapping against the floor. I glared at my wolf.

I am the Alpha, I reminded her. She growled and barred her teeth at me.

"Show her you're the boss in a way she will understand," Sam offered softly in the background.

At his words, something instinctive possessed me. In my mind, I took my mouth and covered her muzzle, biting down hard.

She squeaked in surprise, then rolled over and flashed me her belly again once I released her. *Time to change back*, I ordered.

She took one more glance of long-suffering at Sam and chuffed out a breath and complied. Again, the shift was almost instantaneous. And shifting back didn't hurt.

I was still breathing hard, but I was more relaxed. I had told the wolf I was in charge, and she had obeyed. That was more than I'd hoped for an hour ago.

"Your shifts should be much easier now. She knows who the boss is. You probably still won't be able to totally control them for another day or two though, and you may still have rough patches this first month. Night will still be hard when the moon pulls at the wolf." Sam smiled. "Your dominance display was pretty impressive." His smile had faded to a boyish grin, and I found myself smiling, too.

"I'm not sure she's happy about it, but this is the calmest she's been except for the times you've quieted her. Why does she react to you that way?" I was suddenly curious, though my eyelids were about to drop shut.

"I'm the one that bit you. It's a wolf thing," he said simply.

I tried to respond, but my eyes closed, and I couldn't force my mouth into the words that wanted to leave my lips. I slept. Deeply.

Sunday rolled in with golden glory over a frosted ground. Or so Grandpa told me. Mercifully, I slept through it. I woke to the sound of knocking on the door. Groggily, I glanced around and realized Sam and I were both still sprawled out on the couches. Wolf must have finally let us sleep several hours in a row.

The clock on the wall said it was ten o'clock. A groan escaped as I lifted my arms over my head and several spots in my back popped and cracked.

"What time is it?" Sam muttered, his arm still draped over his eyes.

"Ten," my voice croaked.

With more fluidity and grace than should be allowed for someone with no more sleep than he'd had, Sam rose from his couch and went to the door. I got a whiff of his scent as he moved past me, and Wolf was suddenly completely alert and awake. Snow and pine. I stopped myself just short of totally inhaling, but out of curiosity, took a tiny little sniff to confirm. He smelled *good*—in a way that made my toes curl and my gut churn.

"Morning, Rev, Mr. Carmichael. Ah, Rachel. I see the whole entourage is here. Dad? Mom? Tammy? What is everyone doing here?"

I cringed when I realized my rumpled state. I was covered in day-old dried shifting sweat, my hair was matted into a nest even rats might forego, and I was pretty sure the reek of unbathed dog was coming off my own skin. Embarrassment flushed through me, and I could feel my face heating. I sank down farther into the couch. If the bathroom hadn't been on the other side of the cabin and past the doorway where apparently all of creation had gathered, I would have made a run for it. As it was, I curled into the oversized gray robe.

Wait. Could I mentally speak with Sam? Maybe have him hold them off? It was worth a shot.

He was talking with someone at the front door, but I was prepared to interrupt. *Sam, can you ask them to wait?*

His back stiffened. "Can you guys give us a few minutes?"

There was some mumbling outside, but most of it cut off when Sam shut the door. He looked at me expectantly.

"I need a shower. And my toothbrush. I think my teeth are growing fuzz."

Sam snorted. I hadn't actually meant to say that last bit out loud. I scrubbed a hand over my face, grabbed one of the duffel bags Rachel brought over, and dashed for the shower. "Do you need to get in here before I barricade myself in for the next half hour?"

A wry smile touched his lips. "Give me two minutes."

It was rude to ignore the whole gathering of people that showed up, but I told myself it was equally rude for them to show up unannounced. I didn't mind Grandpa or Rachel, but I didn't care for anyone else to be there. I hadn't really even met Tammy. And I'd only met Sam's mom the night before last. And then there was Mr. Wolfe.

All the same, I hurried, showering off all the stink and quickly got dressed in comfortable jeans and a long-sleeved cranberry-colored Henley. With my own clean underwear and bra, thanks very much. Wolf appeared amiable for the time being, so I put on a dash of mascara and eyeliner to make myself feel more human. Wolf snorted indignantly.

Everybody was sitting around the table or on the couches when I exited with a slight cloud of steam. My wet hair was thrown up in a knot on top of my head, and I felt a drop of water trickle down my neck. Conversation stopped, and I wanted to go back into the bathroom.

"Coffee, sweetheart?" Grandpa asked, handing me a large to-go cup from my favorite coffee shop.

"Thank you," I said as I gratefully took a sip. "When do you want to start getting ready?" Mrs. Wolfe asked.

"Ready for what?"

"For the ceremony."

The hot coffee turned to ice in my throat. I had to cough to get it moving again. "Excuse me?" My eyes turned to Grandpa.

"We're the wedding party," Rachel offered drily as she scrunched her face up at me.

"Oh. I see" was all I could stammer out.

"Hi, I'm Tammy. Sam's cousin. I accidentally overheard about your change. So I'm all in the know now," blurted the girl I'd noticed around school last year—I think she graduated. Her short, black spikes of hair framed her head like a peacock's tail as she stuck her hand out. I took it automatically. She squeezed it, pumped it twice, and let go. She shrugged then took another swig from her own cup.

"Sam, why don't you and the men go ahead on back down to the house? You can get ready there, and we'll take care of everything up here." Mrs. Wolfe took charge. I glanced at Mr. Wolfe and noticed his raised eyebrow in his wife's direction. She smiled warmly at him. His expression softened but didn't change. He jerked his head toward the door, a silent command for the men to follow him out.

"Wait. I'd like to talk to my grandpa for a minute first."

"Don't take too long" was Mr. Wolfe's only comment.

Grandpa narrowed his eyes. "Now, Dominic, let's not rush this."

Mr. Wolfe grunted. Sam flashed me an unreadable expression.

You okay? echoed in my brain. My breath hitched in my throat, totally taken off guard by the same trick I'd pulled forty-five minutes before. I shook my head to clear it.

"Come here, Meggie-Girl." Grandpa led me out the front door into the chilly morning, and I followed as he walked a few paces away, his cane handy, but not used. His knees must not be giving him too much trouble today. He wrapped me up in his protective arms like he had since I was a child. "You're doing the right thing, Meggie. This will keep you safe and give your old grandpa peace of mind. Your Grandma Elsie would be pleased, too." He hesitated a moment. "Do you want to wear her ring after today?"

Tears sprung to my eyes as I pictured the beautiful gold ring that had been my grandmother's outward symbol of her marriage. It was a simple gold band set with a lustrous opal and two tiny diamond chips, one on each side. The thought of wearing it now just hurt. I didn't want to be married to Sam Wolfe—I didn't want to be married to anyone right now. Somehow the thought of wearing my grandmother's ring now seemed to taint the purity of it. Like my wearing it through this fraudulent sham of a marriage would cheapen it.

I sniffed and shook my head. "No. I do want to wear it someday. But I want to wear it when I mean it. This...this is not..." I searched for the right words.

"It's all right, sweetheart. I understand." He hugged me tighter and kissed the side of my head. Traces of his spicy aftershave and a hint of his favorite orange spice tea wrapped around me like a blanket. He smelled like home. Like comfort. I wondered if I would ever associate any smell with that again. Snow and pine drifted through my brain as the wolf raised her head. I quashed the thought.

One hour later, I had yet to shift for a first time that day. We'd eaten brunch at a leisurely pace, and Mrs. Wolfe, who insisted I call her Mary, had also insisted on giving me a pedicure with the nail polish Rachel had packed. I was impressed with her humility and wondered how a woman who appeared kind and giving had ended up with a toughened piece of leather like Dominic Wolfe.

I glanced at my toes. They shone with a beautiful opalescent polish that reminded me of a muted aurora borealis. "I won't mess up my nails when I shift, will I? I mean, will it still be the same after?"

"The more in sync you are with your wolf, the less things change," Mary explained. "I actually hadn't thought of that. It might last; it might not. Your wolf may end up with some polished nails, too. If they need to be redone, we'll redo them."

Tammy snorted. "Ever happen to you?" Rachel asked her.

"Fire engine red. I was mortified. I haven't painted my nails since."

"Tammy is a bit extreme. A lot of girls have interestingly colored nails. Especially in their early teen years. All those hormones can strain the link between wolf and woman," Mary continued with a smile. "The older and more experienced you get, the more natural going between forms becomes. It's just one of those things. It would be uncommon for a woman of my age to have her wolf's claws painted."

The conversation paused.

"Meg, I hope you don't mind, but I brought something for you for today..." Rachel drifted off as she moved to a garment bag I hadn't noticed laid out on Sam's bed.

I raised an eyebrow at her, already following where this was going. Anticipation and dread mingled with my breakfast. My wedding dress was in that bag. I really wasn't sure why we were going to all this fuss. All I needed to do was sign a piece of paper and give my word. Mary sighed wistfully as Rachel held up the bag. I stopped short of rolling my eyes and tried not to offend my soon-to-be mother-in-law.

Rachel slowly unzipped the bag, and I immediately recognized what was inside. Rachel was co-president of the drama club. She had played a major role in nearly every production the high school had put on. What was in the bag was a beautiful white satin tea-length dress. The neck was wide and scooped and was edged out to show off a little shoulder and collarbone. The bodice was fitted, and the skirt flared out gently and would hit me just above the knee, since I knew it hit Rachel just below hers. It was her dress from last year's play.

She searched my face, not sure if the offering of the dress was appropriate. It was kind of outrageously funny, but somehow fitting, that I would be marrying Sam Wolfe in a stage costume since everything else about this affair felt made up, too. But at the same time, a wistful longing twinged in my middle. Grandma would have loved this. It so reminded me of a classically elegant dress she would have worn back in the '60s if she and Grandpa had gone out for an evening.

"It's perfect," I whispered. Mary clapped her hands, delighted. Tammy did roll her eyes, and I wondered what she was thinking.

The wolf was getting a little antsy, and it was making me nervous.

"Um...I think a shift might be coming on soon," I stammered, trying not to be nervous. "Does Sam need to be here? I haven't shifted on my own."

"Oh, I can help you. You'll be fine to shift. Especially with two of us here. Tammy might not be as dominant as you, but I am," Mary offered as easily as she might have offered a glass of iced tea. "We'll wait to do your hair until after."

Rachel's eyebrows shot up to her hairline. Mary was so calm about this, so collected. Part of me wanted to scream at her that shifting was anything but calm, and the other part of me wanted Sam to be here. Wolf agreed with that part, which only irritated me more.

Sam? I called without meaning to.

Megan? His answer was immediate.

She wants to get out. I'm not sure what to do.

You can control it. Call her up and shift before she demands it.

I hated how vulnerable I felt. I wanted to ask him to come up but wanted to be able to do this on my own.

Meg? His mental voice was uncertain.

I'm fine. I gritted out between my mental teeth. I would do this on my own. I could do this. There was a forethought of tingling where my tail would come out. Crap. My clothes.

Without another thought, I tore my shirt off over my head in front of everyone and darted to the bathroom, trying to wiggle out of my jeans before I couldn't control myself.

"Megan?"

"Meg? What's wrong?"

"Stay back, Rachel."

It was a semi-mutual melding of wills. Wolf desperately wanted out; I wanted to control the shift. In the end, we both sort of got what we wanted. Wolf was out. She was happy. I hadn't entirely controlled the shift, and my wolf nails were definitely painted. We weren't on the same page.

"Let me know when you're ready, and we'll fix your hair," Mary called into the bathroom. Because that was normal.

Chapter 19

Sam

I twirled the phone around in my hands, excitement and anxiety warring for prominence. It had been several hours. We'd eaten twice. And I was still wrestling with my decision. I bit my lip. Dad probably wouldn't appreciate it—he didn't appreciate much I did without his express permission—but this was my wedding. Sort of.

I pulled up Cade's info and shot him a quick text.

> Getting married. Want you here.

> ???

> Meg. Dad's rules. Cabin.

> Finding pants. Don't start without me.

I grinned and slipped a finger between my neck and the stiff collar of my white dress shirt.

Another phone buzzed, and I glanced up as Dad answered. "Ready? About time." He clicked the phone shut and shoved it into the pocket of his navy pants. He wasn't glaring anymore, but he was still far from happy. I guess the disappointment would take a bit longer to fade. I tried to ignore the gnawing ache it set in my bones.

"It's time," Mr. Carmichael said, a genuine smile in my direction. "There is one more thing before we go. Dominic, Rev, you all go on out to the car. Sam and I will be along shortly." Dad bristled, and Rev gave me a knowing smile as he exited behind Dad. I picked up my suit coat and shrugged into it as Mr. Carmichael cleared his throat.

"Son," Mr. Carmichael began. "This is a big day for you. A big day for Meggie, too. She isn't thinking about this like you are."

I swallowed. I wasn't sure where this was going, but I really hoped I wasn't about to get a sex talk from a ninety-something-year-old man.

He went on. "You are going to make a promise in a little while. A promise I expect you to keep with your life." He had my complete attention. "When you sign that piece of paper that legally makes you Megan's husband, you take on the commitment to honor her wishes above your own." He gave me a significant look, and I felt the tips of my ears get hot. "And to protect her. I'm old. You are a young man full of promise and fully aware of the dangers of the world in which she now lives. You will be her guardian, her protector, her *man*. You see that you live up to that."

I had never felt so inadequately small or so full of pride all at once as George Carmichael dropped those heavy words on me. "And one more thing," he said, a definite twinkle in his eyes as his hand fished around in his pocket. "Meggie isn't ready for this yet. And she might never be, but if she is, you'll have this for her."

My hand closed around a tiny metal object. Opening my hand, in my palm sat a simple but elegant ring. It had Megan written all over it.

"That was my sweet Elsie's ring. She wore it for seventy years." His eyes misted, and I put a hand on the old man's arm. He blinked rapidly and cleared his throat so hard that his mustache twitched. "You'll know what to do with it if it comes to that." He clapped a hand on my shoulder. "Right then. Let's get you up to the cabin and get you hitched."

The cabin was lit up like a beacon of warm yellow light as the sun started its retreat into the purple clouds at the base of the horizon. Cade's car slid into the drive right before we did.

"Sam?" Dad's voice had a hard edge.

"He already knows anyway. I wanted him here." Rev nodded at my dad as some unreadable emotion flashed across my father's face.

"Fine," he said softly. It was the closest thing to acceptance my dad had voiced all day.

Cade stepped out of his car, nodding respectfully to my dad and Rev before coming over to me and slinging an arm around my shoulders. The sunset made his black hair appear purple. "You okay?" he asked quietly. Emotion suddenly clogged my throat. Why couldn't my dad have been the one to ask me that?

Was I okay? I was elated, terrified, in awe, and in agony. "I guess," tumbled out of my mouth. Cade squeezed my shoulders. He knew I'd been head over heels for Megan Carmichael for years.

"I hope it works out," Cade said simply. He didn't need to say anything else. Even without knowing the situation aside from the few short texts we'd sent, he knew me well enough to get an accurate read on things. Rev opened the door, and Dad and Mr. Carmichael went through. Cade gave my shoulder one last bump with his fist and then he disappeared into the warmth of the cabin, too.

I hesitated there in the cooling air. Rev waited expectantly. With a deep breath, I let go of every dream and expectation I'd ever had about my future mate. My dream was more dead than alive, and waiting for me inside the cabin.

Chapter 20

Megan

The door opened, and Grandpa shuffled in, his eyes twinkling, grin turning his mouth up under his bushy mustache. I was glad at least one of us was happy at this turn of events. My stomach rolled, sour and uneasy. The wolf pranced around, ecstatic at the prospect of being near Sam. My human frustration and apprehension were warring against the wolf's happiness and giving me a serious fit of nerves.

I stood from the chair I'd been sitting in and turned to face the door as Mr. Wolfe walked in. Mary sidled up to him, a serene smile of anticipation making her glow.

"Brides are supposed to be nervous on their wedding day," Rachel whispered so low in my ear I didn't think the others could overhear. She squeezed my hand supportively. The fabric of her light gray dress crinkled against our clasped hands.

I turned to her, fighting panic, and she squeezed my hand again. "One month. You can do this. You'll be human again before you know it." Her reminder was a balm on my frazzled nerves. My lungs filled with oxygen as I gripped her hand. Sam's friend Cade walked in, and the wolf sniffed suspiciously at the new male scent that came in with him. I'd known Cade as long as I'd known Sam. I shouldn't have been surprised to find he was a werewolf, too. Rachel's quick intake of breath confirmed she must have come to the same conclusion.

Cade turned his bright blue eyes on me, his dark head tipping in my direction. While it was a *hello* to my human half, the wolf calmed, recognizing the gesture in a primal way that acknowledged my dominance. It was a weird sensation that took my human half a second to recognize.

And then Sam came in. My heart lurched as I took in his shaggy blond head, his blue eyes, his wide shoulders in a crisp white shirt and black suit with a silver tie. A shiver whispered over me, both from nerves and appreciation at the fine figure Sam Wolfe cut. The wolf preened. I hoped her blatant ogling didn't show on my human face. I tried to shush her. She growled but calmed down. At last, I was glad for the dress and my hair that I'd decided to leave loose but curled in big waves—the way Grandma had always liked it.

His gaze met mine across the room, and he offered a half smile, unsure but widening as his eyes swept over me appreciatively. My shoulders shrugged slightly, unsure myself. I tried to keep my face neutral. I was anxious, apprehensive, but if I was totally honest with myself, part of me was a little excited.

Rev closed the door, and the tiny band of witnesses to our wedding was complete.

"Let's move this couch back. I want to have some sort of aisle to walk Meggie down." Grandpa motioned to make a walkway. Red swarmed my cheeks. I just wanted to get this over with.

Cade and Tammy both jumped in before anyone else could get to the couch and made quick work of moving the furniture. And then there was nothing left to do.

Rev stood in front of the table in the kitchen with Sam at his side. The others in the room had fanned out along the sides of the small space. Grandpa leaned down and kissed my cheek. He smiled, sadness touching the corners of his eyes. He nodded to me and propped his cane on the side of Sam's bed before looping my arm through his. There was a soft click, and I realized Rachel was taking pictures.

Our footsteps boomed in the deafening silence as he led me down the short makeshift aisle to the kitchen. Just like in the movies, Grandpa leaned down and kissed my cheek one more time before taking my hand and putting it in Sam's. Sam looked into my eyes, and I felt a slight tremor go through his hand as he clasped mine. Could he possibly be as nervous as me?

Ready? echoed in my head.

I closed my eyes. I didn't have the emotional energy to respond. I took a breath and opened my eyes, biting the inside of my lip as the wolf seemed to offer me comfort by rubbing her head against me affectionately.

Rev was saying something, but I couldn't hear the words or make the syllables into anything coherent. It was just noise as I stood there, staring at Sam, wondering how my life had suddenly taken such a drastic turn in such an unexpected direction. Sam's thumb rubbed across my skin, bringing me back to the present and exciting the wolf. She basked in his attention.

I jerked at my name.

"Megan Elizabeth Carmichael, do you take this man to be your lawfully wedded husband for as long as you both shall remain tethered by the laws of nature?"

For as long as I remained a wolf? Was that what Rev meant? It was better than the traditional "for as long as you both shall live." I couldn't give my word to that. It was probably Grandpa's doing. I snuck a peek at him, and his face was crinkled in understanding. Definitely Grandpa's doing.

The silence was pressing in around me, and my stomach lurched painfully against my ribs.

Sam's eyes were blue and hopeful, waiting for me.

He squeezed my hands softly. This was it.

"I do," squeaked from my lips and hung in the air.

"Samuel Lawson Wolfe, do you take this woman to be your lawfully wedded wife for as long as you both shall remain tethered by the laws of nature?"

"I do." No hesitation. He smiled at me.

"Then by the power vested in me—"

The tingling started—not the quiet lead up, these were full stabs that jerked my arms. No, no, no, no! Not now, not in front of these people, not right after my wedding vows. I tried to calm the wolf, but she was having none of it. She needed out *now*.

Clearly interpreting my anguish, without waiting for Rev to finish, Sam leaned forward and kissed me. Wolf immediately calmed. It might have been Sam's kiss she'd wanted all along. His lips weren't insistent. He didn't push me. Lingering only a second more than he needed to calm her, he slowly lifted his head.

"—man and wife," Rev finished.

A collective sigh of relief floated up from those gathered around us.

And just like that, I was a married woman. In name only.

Chapter 21

Sam

We were married. She'd actually gone through with it. Man, I wanted to kiss her for real. I couldn't help the smile that broke across my face. I probably looked like a grinning idiot, but I couldn't rein it in. My wolf was totally puffed up. He might as well have been a king basking in the adoration of his people. My smile faded as Megan's expression turned a little lost. I squeezed her hand again. Her eyes met mine as her shoulders sagged with a quick breath out her mouth.

"I think we should have cake," Rachel offered into the silence. That cracked Megan's face into a tiny smile. She glanced at Rachel appreciatively. I glanced at Cade. He winked back.

"Cake appears to be in order," Rev conceded, a smile hiding in the corner of his mouth.

Megan gently extracted her hands and clasped them in front of her. My heart squeezed painfully as I was reminded that she wasn't really mine for keeps.

Mom was on the move. "I'll be right back," she called as she flew out the front door.

"Why don't we sign this and get all the formalities out of the way," Rev interjected, pointing to a piece of paper on the table. Dad nodded authoritatively. The marriage license. What this whole debacle had been about. Rev motioned for Cade and Rachel to come up, too. "Will you two sign as witnesses?" Rev asked.

Cade grinned at me. There was no one's signature I'd rather have next to mine as witness to this monumental, possibly catastrophic event.

Rev handed me the pen. I signed, bold and confident. The pen shook as Megan held it. She hesitated. My insides withered a little. My lungs expanded as her trembling hand signed her name.

Rachel was next. Her eyebrows rose questioningly at Meg. Megan nodded, and Rachel signed her name, a tiny flourish on the "B" of Crumb, her last name. Cade made quick work with the pen. Last came George Carmichael. I held my breath, wondering if Megan would comment. She watched in silence, a blank expression on her face. There was time for nothing else as Mom jetted back into the cabin carrying a large box. Cake. How or when she had time to find a cake for the occasion escaped me, but one more peek at Megan said this was the distraction she needed to break up the tension between us.

We broke apart as Mom put the cake box on the table. Rachel quickly moved forward to help her. It was a small two-tiered cake done up in simple white frosting with a few elegant frosted swirls along the edges of the tiers.

Plates of cake were handed out, but before I could take a bite, Mom pushed the envelope too far. "All right you two, it's tradition to feed each other a bite of your wedding cake."

Meg's face paled. I could tell she was barely holding it together.

"I don't think we need to stand on every tradition, Mom."

Mom's face fell slightly. I didn't know why she was trying to make this such a to-do. She knew as well as anyone this was an in-name-only marriage. As much as I wanted it to be otherwise.

"Aunt Mary, this cake is awesome. Is this spice cake?" Tammy interjected around a mouthful. It was enough to start small talk up to fill the awkward emptiness.

The sun made its complete disappearance as everyone was finishing up with their dessert. My skin prickled as the chill descended, and I wondered if Meg would need to shift again soon.

"How is your wolf?" I asked her quietly, nudging her knee with mine. She'd been sitting quietly in the chair beside mine, facing toward the room as we'd eaten. She'd picked at her cake and offered nothing to the conversations around us.

"Um, still quiet for now. I imagine she'll need to get out soon though. She was pretty insistent at the altar," she quipped.

I chuckled in spite of her dry tone. I glanced at Cade, giving him a quick nod. He got the drift. "Guys, I appreciate you inviting me"—he conveniently did not encompass my father—"but it's dark, and I'll be needing to get back. Sam, Megan, congratulations." He flashed a genuine smile at us. I knew he was resisting the urge to say something suggestive about wedding night activities. One perk of my dad in attendance. I nodded and met him at the door. Meg stood politely with me.

Cade gave Megan a short hug, and Wolf snorted at their contact. I shushed him. Cade was no threat. He moved to me, and I got a hug and quick pound on the back. "Later, man." With his back to my dad, Cade raised both eyebrows suggestively.

I punched his shoulder. "Later."

Everyone else took the hint and started trailing out the door. Mom hugged us both. Hard.

"Congratulations, Sammy," she whispered. I hugged her back, glad for the support, even if it was misplaced.

"Sam," Dad said. He shook my hand firmly. Some emotion I couldn't interpret crossed his face. Sadness? Longing? It was gone before I could decide. He awkwardly patted Megan on the shoulder, saying nothing.

Tammy didn't say anything either but gave us each a hurried hug and trotted out the door. Rev's hugs were short and to the point, his smile fatherly.

Rachel gave me a quick hug before wrapping Megan in a massive bear hug. They clung to each other for a full minute or two before letting go. Rachel tipped back enough to look Meg fully in the face.

"To the ends of the earth," she said softly.

Megan blew a breath out through her mouth. "To the ends of the earth," she repeated.

"I'll call you tomorrow, yeah?" Rachel confirmed.

"Please."

Rachel's mouth pulled into a cheeky grin. "Congrats, Mrs." She winked as Meg swatted her arm.

"Twerp."

Rachel's laugh was like a silvery ball as she exited, leaving only George Carmichael in the cabin with us.

His gaze encompassed us, warmth and pride lighting his face. Without a word, he gathered both of us in his arms at once. Old Spice aftershave and something lightly orangey drifted from his skin.

"I'm proud of you, Meggie-Girl. You, too, Samuel." He pulled back. "You call me if you need anything. Either of you." He released me and gathered Megan into his arms once more. "I love you, sweetheart," he whispered.

"Love you, too, Grandpa."

He let her go, and she reluctantly dropped her arms. "You listen to Sam, Meggie-Girl. He's the man you lean on for now." Meg bit her lip but nodded. "He'll be the one doing most of the watching after you for the next few weeks." He pulled her in for one last hug and while her head was buried in the crook of his neck, George Carmichael looked me right in the eye and winked. I had no idea how to interpret that. Before I had a chance to respond, he'd kissed Meg once more on the forehead and was out the door.

We were alone.

Meg sank back down to her chair. A groan escaped her as she cradled her head in both hands, caramel-colored hair floating down like a wing to cover her face.

"I need to bake something."

"What?" I was taken totally off guard. "We still have plenty of cake?"

She sighed and shook her head, her hair swooshing back and forth. "No. When I'm stressed, I bake."

"Oh. Um...not sure what food we've got stored at the cabin." Baking? I didn't know anything about baking. "What do you need?"

"Flour, sugar, butter, salt. A lot."

I could fix this. "Okay. Make a list and we'll get it."

"Sam," she said, exasperation tinging her tone as she glanced up at me, "I can't just walk into the grocery store. I don't need to take out half of Rock Falls and the banana display with my next shift."

"Of course not. But I can go to the store for you."

"You're serious?"

"Sure. It's a grocery store. You're not asking me to climb Mount Everest. If baking will make you feel better, I'm happy to run to the store for you."

She gave me the skeptical eyebrow again.

"When was the last time you went grocery shopping?" she asked, curiosity and not judgment creeping into her voice.

"I admit, it's been awhile, but I have an excellent sense of smell. If I can't find something, I'll sniff around until I do." I grinned at her, hoping to melt off some of her doubt. She cocked her head to the side and bit her lip again. Something clicked in my brain.

"Unless you'd rather me not leave you alone that long. I have a lot of favors I can call in." I smiled again, hoping to put her at ease. Her lip tucked farther in between her teeth. Her desire to bake warred with her desire not to be left alone with her wolf. Her vulnerability made me want to scoop her up into my arms and show her I would keep her safe. I struggled with the impulse a minute before shoving my hands into my pockets.

"She is calmer with you around."

"Can I make an executive decision?"

She pursed her lips but didn't say anything.

"Let me call in a favor. I'll stay here with you. We'll work through any shifting together, maybe even work on calling up your wolf. Whatever you want to do. When the stuff gets here, you can bake to your heart's content."

"I hate to do that. It will be a long list. I don't want to inconvenience anyone."

"That's one nice thing about pack life. If one of us needs something, there is always someone there to help. In a lot of ways, we're a communal society. And I promise, once Dad puts the all-call out that we're...together, there will be wolves tripping over themselves to get into your good graces."

"Are you absolutely sure?" Her resolve weakened.

"Definitely. In fact, I know just the person."

She clenched her eyes shut. "Okay."

"Perfect. Make out your list, and I'll make the call."

After a quick run through what trays and pans were available in the kitchen, she sat back at the table with a pen and paper.

"What's your favorite cookie?" she surprised me by asking.

"Well, I'm not picky, but I've always had a soft spot for this double fudge chocolate chunk cookie my Aunt Lora used to make."

Megan actually licked her lips. I tried not to laugh. "That sounds amazing. All right. Making the list.

Um, who are you calling?"

"I think I'll try Raven. She's a good friend, and she won't mind."

"Cade's sister? We've chatted few times at school, but I don't know her well. We were in choir together last year. Do you know what her favorite dessert is?"

"No idea, but I can ask her."

"Please do." Meg went to work on a list while I dialed the Rivers' house.

"Hello?"

"Cade."

"Sam? Why are you calling? Shouldn't you be...you know..." His voice dropped to almost imperceptible levels. "Screwing your brains out?"

"I only wish."

"You really need to catch me up to speed."

"In so many ways," I conceded. "Actually, I was wondering if Raven could do me a favor. Any chance she's up for a trip to the grocery store?"

"If you need condoms, I don't think my sweet, innocent, little sister is your go-to."

Laughter burst from my throat before I could stop it. "Shut up," I quipped. "Seriously. Meg wants to bake, and her wolf is still unpredictable. I don't want to leave her alone."

"Yeah, if I'd just married a hot piece of tail, I wouldn't want to leave her alone either."

Wolf growled at Cade's slang, even knowing he wasn't being offensive.

"Uh huh." Sarcasm dripped from my tone. I sobered. "Want me to use it?" I knew Cade would understand my meaning. My dad and I, as Alpha and Beta, didn't use the werewolf link regularly—it often felt like an invasion of privacy and out of respect for our pack members, we typically used the phone unless we were in wolf form. But I didn't have a way to explain to Cade what happened without Megan overhearing, and that felt like a bad idea.

"Dude, you just got married, and I only have the sketchiest details why. Use it. Whenever you can."

"All right. I will. Raven there?"

"Sure. Let me grab her. Later then."

"Yep."

"Sam?"

"Hi, Raven. I was wondering if you could do me a favor? I'm needing someone to go to the grocery store and drop stuff off at the cabin."

"Sure, no problem at all. I was actually going to go run out for milk for my mom anyway. What do you need?"

"I've got a list. Want me to text it to you or give you a hard copy and cash?"

"I'll be over in about five minutes."

"Favorite dessert?" Megan whispered from the table.

"Oh, Raven, what's your favorite dessert?"

"My favorite dessert? I like cheesecake. Why?"

I scratched my jaw; this conversation was about to get awkward. With a breath in through my nose, I plunged on ahead. "Um, Megan Carmichael and I are *together*," I hedged, "and she's here with me at the cabin." I left things vague, unsure how much Dad wanted me to share with people. I knew Raven and Meg knew each other from school, and that Raven was fully aware that Meg was supposed to be human.

"Oh," was all her shocked voice left me with. To her credit, Raven didn't pound me with questions.

"Dad's going to put out an all-call tomorrow, so if we could keep this on the down low, that would be great."

"I got it. Cade know?"

"A little."

"Grocery store then. I'll be by for the list."

"Thanks, Raven."

"No problem. See you in a few."

I hung up the phone and stared at the screen for a second.

"Everything okay?" Megan asked softly from the table, watching me carefully. I could have sworn it was her wolf questioning through those hazel eyes.

"Yeah. Just trying to avoid letting out more details than Dad wants me to. I'm not sure how he's going to phrase things tomorrow."

Megan nodded slowly. "What's an all-call?"

"It's when the Alpha sends out information to every pack member at once. We only use it if it's big news everyone needs to know. My biting you is beyond big news. There will probably be a Gathering tomorrow night, too." I hadn't thought to bring that up until now. Too many other details vying for prominence.

Her eyebrows drew together. I sighed. She wasn't going to like this.

"A Gathering is where all available pack members get together. In this case, it will be to meet you." I gave her an apologetic smile.

She crossed her arms on the table and put her head down on them. "When does the crazy train end?"

I sat down next to her and tentatively touched her elbow. She tensed but didn't pull away.

"I'm so sorry, Meg. If it's any help, a lot of this is new to me, too. But I'll be here with you the whole time."

Her head came up, and she scrubbed her hands over her face. "What kind of dessert does Raven like?"

"Cheesecake."

She frowned at her paper and mumbled, "No spring form pan," then scribbled another few notes down. "I think I'm going to go change, if that's all right."

"Sure. I'll change after you."

She nodded and left the paper on the table as she went to rifle through the duffel bags.

Raven dropped by while Meg was still in the bathroom.

"Thanks for coming, Raven. I appreciate it." I handed her the list and a wad of bills from my wallet. She scanned it, her eyebrows raising.

"Someone really likes baking."

I gave her a tight smile. How stressed was Megan? "No worries. I'll be back in an hour or so. Nice suit." Raven smirked.

"I owe you one," I told her sincerely. "Probably more than one."

She flashed me a smile that reminded me of Cade's as she dashed back down the steps to her still-running car.

The bathroom water started running as I shut the door and figured now was as good a time as any to fill Cade in on the details.

Cade?

Lay it on me, he replied. So I did.

I was mid-story when the bathroom door opened. *Finish soon,* I thought to Cade.

"Oh crap," Meg exclaimed.

"What's wrong?"

"I only have my debit card. I don't have any cash to use for groceries."

"It's fine. I covered it."

"She was already here?"

I nodded.

She was quiet for a few seconds, her face pinching seriously. "How are we paying for things? We're going to need to eat, and I'm assuming we'll have utility bills and stuff if we're off living here by ourselves. Are our parents supporting all this? I mean, I'm used to paying for my own gas and stuff, but this is more than I'm used to."

"We'll be fine. I've got savings," I said, unsure how much detail this conversation needed. It was a huge boost to my ego to be able to tell her I could take care of us financially for the foreseeable future. Until she raised her eyebrow in a way that said she wasn't sure she believed me. Ouch.

"Do you work?" It was kind of bizarre to be having this conversation with the woman I'd just married.

"Kind of. Let me change and I'll show you what I mean." I shrugged off the lingering sting of her doubt and hurriedly filled Cade in on the rest of things as I gathered my clothes and took my turn to shimmy into sweatpants and a T-shirt.

So now I'm married to the one girl in the world that my wolf recognizes as my mate, and I can't do a single thing about it other than be polite and wait to see if she turns back into a human in a few weeks. I finished as I shrugged my tee over my head.

Dude. I'm sorry. That does suck.

Yeah. Going to go show Meg our videos. Later.

Later.

I folded my dress pants over the back of a kitchen chair and tossed my button up and undershirt in a pile by the washer.

Meg was seated on the couch with her legs curled up under her, a mug of something steaming clasped in her hands. She had red plaid pajama bottoms on and a long-sleeved black shirt. Her hair was back in a knot on top of her head. It sent a wave of longing over me. I wanted nothing more than to go curl up on the couch next to her, cuddle, and watch a movie. I didn't think she'd go for that much physical contact, so I grabbed my laptop and sat down next to her. Our legs touched, and somewhat to my surprise, she didn't immediately move away.

With the laptop opened, I quickly navigated to the internet. "Cade and I had this brilliant idea a few years ago. We had no idea it would go big."

I clicked play and watched my scrawny eleven-year-old-self stand in the middle of a meadow surrounded by forest. I had a hat on, and the camera was far enough away it was impossible to tell it was me. Suddenly, a huge black wolf charged from the woods to head straight toward me. I held up my hand and yelled, "Stop!" and the wolf obeyed. The wolf howled and snarled, gnashing its teeth—it looked half-crazed. Video-me pointed up and in a circle. The wolf took a short run at me, then leapt up in the air, spinning in a perfect backflip.

Meg gasped.

My stick arms waved in the air again, and the giant wolf got up on its forepaws in a perfect handstand. "Walk!" I shouted in the video, and the wolf staggered forward, still balanced precariously on its forepaws.

With a flash of dark fur, the wolf tumbled to the ground and in the next instant, had me pinned to the ground. I slapped the wolf's nose, and the wolf gnashed its teeth right in my face. It let me up, and it nudged me with its nose. I stood. The beast shook its great shaggy head, and I ran a few yards away then sprinted back to the wolf, used its back as a springboard, and executed a nearly perfect front flip. The wolf yawned. It stood on its hind paws and pointed its forepaws into the air.

Skinny legs whipped up into the air, and I walked on my hands in a circle around the wolf.

The video ended.

Meg's eyes were about the size of dinner plates. "I'm surprised this only has one million subscribers," she said. Her eyes met mine. "Okay. I'm impressed. Were you the guy or the wolf?"

I chuckled. "Cade was the wolf. We got in so much trouble when our parents found out what we'd done, but by then, ad money was pouring in. Cade and I split everything fifty-fifty. I work in Dad's law office during the summer, but it's nice not to have to keep a job during the school year. Too many other responsibilities being Beta and an honor student." I sighed. "Do you have a job?" I realized I had no idea if Meg worked after school or not. We were at a lot of the same school functions, and we hung around in the same circle of friends, but a lot of the day-to-day details were still unknown to me.

"Not a regular one. But one I hope I can still keep." Her face fell. "Rachel and I do a baking booth at the HarvestFest. We've done it the past three years, and so far, we've had amazing results. We're hoping to use it as a way to launch our own baking business after graduation. I guess HarvestFest this year is out though." Her shoulders slumped.

"Nonsense. It's still two weeks away. If your wolf is still irritable by then, which she shouldn't be, I'll hang around, help out if I can, or stay close to keep her in line."

"That simple?"

"More or less." I grinned at her, but unease wound its way into my belly when she didn't smile back. She was pensive, studying me.

"Why would you go to all this trouble for me, Sam?"

Why wouldn't I? And how could I answer her in a way that wouldn't send her running for the hills faster than she was already going?

I squared my jaw. "Let's just say I owe you."

She raised an eyebrow like she knew that was only half an answer but didn't push it.

Gasping, she arched her back.

"I think it's time to let her out," she panted. Before I could respond, Meg had bounded off the couch and dashed into the bathroom, leaving the door open. I didn't know if I should follow or stay where I was.

In the end, I stood waiting, halfway between the couches and the bathroom. "Megan?"

"Gah! Stay there," she yelled, the last half coming out garbled and gravelly.

Chapter 22

Megan

The bathroom was fast becoming my safe haven at the cabin.

You will not shift until I have my clothes off! I like these pajamas! I threatened the wolf. She was panting and trying her best to obey my command, but I knew a shift was imminent, and there wasn't going to be anything the wolf or I could do about it.

My shirt and pants fell to the floor in a wadded heap. Fur sprouted along my arms as I desperately lunged for the clasp on my bra. It dropped to the pile as Wolf whined, unable to control herself any longer.

Shreds of my turquoise bikini briefs littered the ground under my huge forepaws. My wolf nails definitely still had an opalescent shine.

The wolf shook herself out, and I allowed myself to join her. This was the first time I let myself really *feel* the wolf side of me. It was strange. Everything was sharper, louder, brighter. I glanced down at myself and raised a paw, marveling as the sinews and muscles contracted to obey my thoughts.

"Megan, do you need help?"

The wolf practically batted her eyes in Sam's direction.

Behave, I told her sternly. She pouted.

Together, we tentatively took a step in our wolf form. Another. We shook off the strip of silky underwear that had gotten hung up on our left hind paw. I squeezed my eyes shut and took a deep breath, releasing my iron grip on my will. There was a melding of minds. The wolf conceded my dominance, and I grudgingly accepted the wolf as a part of me. I knew I couldn't escape it, and there in the quiet of the cabin, after one of the most emotional days of my life, I came to terms with it. For at least the next few weeks, the wolf and I were going to have to work together.

I poked my head out the door of the bathroom. Sam was standing in the kitchen, and when he saw my fur, his smile nearly stretched off his face.

"Everyone happy?"

I nodded.

"Come on out. The quarters are a little close, but I think you're ready to try out your new skin for a little bit."

I felt ridiculous, but it felt good to stretch my wolf limbs, and I made a few clumsy laps around the small room. The more we paced, the more in sync we became.

After a few minutes, I stretched my back, reaching my forepaws out as far as they would go, my hind legs bunching up. Coils of muscle and sinews waited to spring into action. It was a strange sensation to have heavily muscled limbs at my disposal, waiting to launch me into the air or pad silently across the floor.

"A full body stretch feels good, doesn't it?" Sam grinned at me. He'd given suggestions of how to move to maximize the wolf's abilities my human muscles didn't have. I nodded my shaggy wolf head.

I was suddenly struck with the thought that I had no idea what I looked like in this form. Or for that matter, I had no idea what Sam looked like as a wolf either. Opening my mouth to ask him about it, a harsh bark came out. Sam cocked his head as I scowled, forgetting I couldn't talk to him. I sighed. I was ready to be back in my human skin anyway.

Trotting back to the bathroom, I couldn't be sure, but I think Sam was checking out my backside. Wolf tried to wiggle her hips, but I gave a quick yank on her will. She settled.

"You shifting back already?" Sam called as I entered the bathroom.

I yipped at him, irritated for no apparent reason. My emotions had been a roller coaster the past three days. I was ready to be human and up to my elbows in flour. Emotionally, I was completely drained, but physically, with the moon in the sky, my wolf was too excited to let me sleep. Assuming I would have to just go until exhaustion took over like it had last night, I blew a breath out. It came out sounding like I'd blown a raspberry through the wolf's muzzle. My flopping tongue had gotten in the way. I rolled my eyes and commanded wolf to shift back.

It took a minute, but then I was standing on two legs again, totally naked, my legs needing a good shave once again. Exasperation must have leaked out into my sigh.

"Megan, you all right in there? Do you, um, need help?"

"No. Just figuring out these new...wolf things."

"Wolf things?"

"I'm fine." And then I realized I had no underwear. The last pair had shredded.

Squeezing my eyes shut and pinching the bridge of my nose, I swallowed my pride. "Sam, could you please drop the blue bag right outside the bathroom door?"

There was a *plop* a minute later, and I reached around, dragged it the rest of the way into the bathroom, and shut the door. This was going to be an embarrassing month.

Chapter 23

Sam

Meg came back out of the bathroom pensive and thoughtful. I couldn't read her expression but wanted to know what was going on behind those hazel eyes.

"Did you like being more in control once you shifted?"

Her head came up. "Definitely. I like being the one in control of myself," she replied dryly with a twist of her lips. "Sam," she started. I raised my eyebrows, encouraging her to continue. "I've never actually seen your wolf."

Wolf jumped around inside me like he was on steroids. I hadn't let him out in three days, which was three days too long for him. I *needed* to let him out, but I hadn't, putting Megan's needs above my own discomfort. I hoped she was asking me to show him to her, to share this intimate piece of me.

"Do you want to?" I asked, biting back hope.

"Do you mind? I am a little curious." She smirked. "In fact, I suppose I can't even be sure you are a werewolf." She was teasing me. Sarcastically, sure, but I took this as a good sign as a smile tipped my lips. I shushed Wolf, another few minutes, and he could be free.

"I wouldn't mind at all. In fact, I need to let him out." Surprise flashed across her face, slowly coming to the realization that I'd been denying my wolf. Smiling, I took my turn in the bathroom while Meg went to sit on the couch.

I stripped, more eager than I'd been in years to let the wolf out. Without another thought, I leaned my shoulders back, letting them roll and pop as they moved back into my spine, my limbs lengthening and shortening, cording up with hard muscles. Resisting the urge to let go and howl, I pointed my nose to the ceiling and let myself have a tremendous shake. My silver-white fur rippled, and I shivered at the pleasure of feeling it and not my skin.

Anxious and proud to show myself to Megan in this form, I hesitated only a second before exiting the small room and coming into the light of the kitchen.

"Ooh," Meg breathed, her eyes like saucers, as fear, uncertainty, and...was that appreciation? lingered on her face.

She didn't say anything, and I slowly padded over to her seat on the couch. My head reached her shoulders as she sat, and with the slightest tilt of my head, we were eye to eye. Her hand raised then stopped midway. Was she going to touch me? I bobbed my head under her hand, relishing her fingers on the silky fur behind my ears. No wolf would admit it, but it was a weakness a lot of us shared. We loved having our ears scratched.

An appreciative whine came out as she scratched down a little lower.

"Aside from being terrifyingly large, you aren't that scary. I was afraid you would be."

Her face had relaxed a measure, and I was glad for it. I sat, enjoying her hand on my head for a full minute before she jerked her hand away.

"Sorry, I guess that's kind of like playing with your hair."

As if I would mind either way.

A quick knock at the door saved us any further awkwardness. It was Raven. I could smell her.

"Because this isn't going to be weird," Megan mumbled as she got up and went to the door.

"Um, hi, Raven."

"Hi, Megan," Raven replied, curiosity banked. "I've got the groceries. I'll just bring them in."

"Let me grab some shoes, and I'll help you. I can't thank you enough for doing this."

"It's no problem at all. We do stuff like this for each other all the time." Raven implied *the pack* without actually coming right out and saying, which I appreciated.

I ran back into the bathroom and shifted back regretfully, promising Wolf he could come out again soon, and threw my clothes back on.

"Hi, Sam," Raven said around an armful of groceries.

"Raven. Thanks. I'll get the rest."

"Okay, there's not a whole lot more," she answered as Meg came in behind her with a few more bags.

Her eyes were glazed. She had a one-track purpose now.

Raven didn't stay to chitchat, and within five minutes of the door closing, Meg had items laid out on the counter, plotting some demise for each of them as she grouped them together and organized her battle strategy.

"Meg?"

"Hmm?" She didn't turn around as she dug out a new set of measuring cups and spoons and put them in the sink.

"Do you mind if I let my wolf out for a little while longer? I'll stay here in the cabin in case you need me."

She paused and turned. "I don't mind." She hesitated. "Did you not shift because of me the past few days?"

I nodded, unsure how to answer her.

"I'm sorry," she said softly.

"It's fine. If it had been dire, I would have found the time. You needed me in skin." The slightest blush stained her cheeks. She nodded and went back to sorting her items on the counter.

Chapter 24

Megan

I stared at the glorious array of foodstuffs lining the counters. I could have my little piece of baker's paradise now.

Without having to think, I gathered the ingredients for double chocolate chunk cookies and set the oven to preheat. Within minutes, I was breezing through measurements. I had been baking long enough that I had a general cookie recipe down that I could modify to make all sorts of delicious treats.

I noticed when Sam came out of the bathroom, his wolf's presence taking up the space, but after a quick nod to each other, he went to the other side of the cabin and did some strange stretches, and I turned my back to him and let my mind wander. This was the way my subconscious processed best, and heaven knew I had mounds of things to work through.

The flour was soft and light as I sifted it down with the cocoa powder into the metal bowl. The whisk clicked gently and whirred as I flipped it around. The sounds and the rhythms of doing what I loved lulled me into a temporary peace. Even the wolf settled. She nudged me and without giving it a second thought, I held each new ingredient to my nose, letting the wolf get a whiff.

Everything smelled so different. There was new depth, new dimension. Smells I'd smelled a hundred times before were suddenly brand new. Cinnamon, a spice I loved, was entirely different. There was a new heat, a dark, rich spiciness that went further than the spice itself. Smelling with a wolf's nose was almost like being able to feel a color. And without realizing it, the wolf and I were working together. We were synching. More than when we walked around in fur, more than when we worked together to shift. This was my world, and *I* was including *her*, and *we* were moving and working as one.

By the time the chocolate chunk cookies were ready to come out of the oven, I had a new batch of caramel almond and praline cookies ready to go in and was finishing up the batter for mini cheesecakes to take to Raven as a thank you.

It startled me when Sam walked by me in the kitchen to go back to the bathroom, his tail fur swishing over the skin on my elbow ever so lightly. I had been in the zone. And I was feeling tons better.

Sam came out as I was dishing the first of the double chocolate chunk cookies onto cooling racks. "I've never seen anything like it," he commented.

"Aren't these similar to the ones your aunt makes?"

"Oh, yeah. The cookies look amazing. That's why I decided to shift back," he chuckled. "Chocolate doesn't taste great as a wolf. What I meant, was how you and your wolf were working together. I've never seen the human side draw the wolf in like that. It's always the other way around."

I shrugged as I processed his comments. "I can't believe I'm actually saying this, but it felt like the natural thing to do. To use these weird new senses. I didn't think about letting her in. She nudged, and I just did. Is that what it's always like?"

His eyebrows raised. "Yeah. A lot like that. You get to the point where you don't even think about it—it's the first response. She's still you. You are still her. It will settle." He grinned and wagged his eyebrows suggestively at the steaming cookies and light-fingered two of them.

He groaned and licked chocolate off the side of his mouth. "These are the best cookies I've ever eaten. Please don't tell Aunt Lora. I told her that her cookies are my favorite." He took another bite and groaned again as his eyes slid closed, drawing a tiny smile from the corner of my mouth. "But seriously. These are *so* much better than hers."

Chapter 25

Sam

It was possible I was entering a chocolate coma. I'd eaten seven of Megan's cookies before I forced myself to stop. They were *so* good. I was going to get fat with her around if she continued to be this stressed. That sobered me some.

I heard her gasp and glanced over to where she stood at the sink. Her back was arching in the familiar pattern of a shift. She gasped again as she dashed to the bathroom.

"You okay?" I called, still not sure how she'd prefer me to react to her sporadic shifting.

She grunted.

"Talk inside my head if you need to." She didn't respond, so I moseyed over to the sink and started washing up some bowls and the wiry thing she'd stirred stuff with. This was a completely foreign world to me. I didn't bake. I could grill like a boss. But baking? I could barely tell the right end of a spatula.

She came out a few minutes later, human, and completely beat. Her eyes were shadowed, and her whole face sagged. She was on the edge of exhaustion. She blinked slowly a few times, looking right through me. I wiped my hands on the towel by the sink.

"Come on. Time for you to try and get some rest." I wasn't going to be far behind her. The past few days hadn't been as shocking to me as they had to Megan, but they'd still been taxing and emotionally straining. I needed sleep.

She mumbled something incoherent and dropped like a rock as soon as I led her to the edge of the queen bed off the kitchen. Her eyes were shut even before her head found the pillow. I smiled, watching her for a second as she slept. I moved a wisp of hair and let myself indulge in a soft kiss on her forehead before I sighed. It was all the action I was going to get on my wedding night. The comforter was lax and moved up easily with a quick tug.

Moving quietly with the grace of the wolf, I finished up the dishes and fell into my own bed, needing rest. It wasn't the wedding night I'd dreamed of, or hoped for, but at least the woman of my dreams was sleeping under the same roof, if not in my bed.

Chapter 26
Megan

Sunlight slanted through the blinds at the front of the cabin. I think it had been somewhere near three a.m. when the last shift happened. I didn't remember getting into bed, but I must have slept overly hard because I could distinguish the soreness of not having moved in bed for too many hours with the soreness of shifting. It wasn't the most pleasant combination, but I'd felt worse over the past three days.

Gingerly stretching my back brought a wave of lactic acid-induced pain biting into my muscles and a noise somewhere between a grunt and a groan somersaulted up my throat.

The noise was enough to bring Sam to life on the other side of the cabin. "You alive over there?" His voice was still thick with sleep.

"I'm not sure yet. I'm not usually alive in the morning until I have caffeine." My stomach sank. "Please tell me there is coffee and a coffee pot somewhere in this cabin."

His laugh was gravelly but somehow pleasant to my ears. Wolf perked up, and I rolled my eyes.

"We have pack meetings out back. There's always coffee here for that. But unless you want an entire percolator's worth, we should probably get a regular coffee pot for the cabin."

I moved my head up far enough to glance at his across the room. He smiled and pushed himself up so he was sitting against his headboard. No one should look that good in bed head. My tongue felt thick, and I could tell my breath was bad. I swallowed. It didn't help. My head flopped back down to the pillow. Everything felt poufy and slow like I was encased in a giant marshmallow. And I was tired. So tired.

A genuine groan slipped out as I scrubbed my hands over my face, trying to snap out of it.

"What time is it?" I asked as my stomach rumbled. "Wow. It's four o'clock."

"Four in the afternoon? Are you serious?" He grinned at me as I poked my head up again.

"You had an emotional, stressful few days. I think you and your wolf have finally started coming to an understanding, and that's helping you to relax, sleep more, and sleep more deeply."

"I hope so. I need her settled so I can figure out how we're going to do school on Wednesday. Test in Kellerman's class. I can't afford to miss it."

"You'll be fine. If worse comes to worst, I can calm her between each class."

Panic must have shone on my face because his face slid into its unreadable mask. "I don't think it will come to that. You'll be fine. Especially during the day. I'll be surprised if you have more than one or two uncalled-for shifts tonight."

That was at least reassuring. While I'd made temporary peace with the wolf, I still didn't like being a wolf. I missed my uncomplicated regular skin where the worst thing I had to worry about was the odd pimple. My eyes closed again, and I massaged my temples. Also, kissing Sam was an uncomfortable topic. "I can't decide if I'm more tired or if I'm more hungry," I offered as a subject change.

"I'm starving. I vote we order pizza for tonight."

My stomach rumbled in affirmation as Wolf sent images of sausage, bacon, ham, and chicken topping a slice of pizza.

"Does your wolf send you images of what it wants to eat?" I asked, trying to keep the shudder out of my words. I liked meat, but it was weird to have the wolf sending me thoughts about it. I was still adjusting to having someone else in my head with me.

"Sometimes. Let me guess. Meat, meat, and more meat?" He chuckled at my grimace.

I forced myself to sit up and regretted it as it sent my pulse pounding through my head. I was overdue for my morning cup of coffee, and the lack of caffeine was kicking in.

"I need coffee," I croaked.

Sam lightly got to his feet and walked over to my bedside.

"Come on, let's get up, eat, and then you can sleep more if you want to." He held his hand out. I took it, hoping fervently that his nose couldn't pick up my morning—afternoon—breath.

Sam ordered pizza while I brushed my teeth and washed my face. My skin still felt too tight for my body. I didn't exactly feel bloated, but still like I was trying to wallow my way out of the giant marshmallow.

My phone was sitting on the table where I'd left it last night, and I snagged it to find fourteen texts and five missed phone calls. From Rachel. And one call from Grandpa. I smiled and punched in my pass code to skim the texts from Rachel. They were all variations on the same theme.

How was I?

Was I okay?

Did I need anything? Should she come over?

Had Sam tried anything last night?

I fired a quick text back to her.

> Sorry. Just woke up. Slept like the dead. So far so good.

She pinged back within the minute.

> Good! Keep me posted!

I sent her a smiley face.

"Here's the coffee," Sam called, holding up a giant percolator and economy-sized tub of French roast. My mouth watered. It was possible I'd drink an entire percolator's worth.

"How strong do you like your brew?"

"I tend to like it pretty strong. Are you a regular coffee drinker?"

"Sometimes. Glad we agree. Coffee is only good if the spoon stands up in it." He winked at me, and I felt my mouth curve up. It was easier to forget my anger and frustration at this situation with the easy banter between us. Maybe the whole month wouldn't be absolute torture?

A quick glance at the sink let me know Sam had done up all the dirty dishes from my baking escapade. It sent a sudden curl of warmth through my stomach.

"Sorry. Guess I kinda pooped out last night. I don't generally leave dirty dishes in the sink overnight."

"That's okay. Do you even remember getting into bed last night?"

"I really don't," I confessed.

A devilish glint lit his eyes. "You don't remember professing your undying love for me? I'm wounded."

I snagged the pillow off my bed and threw it at him. He caught it lightly and tossed it back to the bed.

"Not funny, Sam," I retorted even as I felt my cheeks flush and my mouth tip up.

He chuckled, picked the percolator up, and aimed the sink nozzle into it.

I raised my arms above my head, still trying to work out kinks; Wolf appreciated the stretch, too, though she would have preferred to be doing it in fur. Sam's phone buzzed. Grabbing it, he glanced at the screen, and his face fell. "Dad," he muttered as he swiped his finger over the screen to take the call. "Hi, Dad."

With my new senses, I could hear Mr. Wolfe's voice on the other end but still wasn't attuned enough to catch the words, but judging by the way dread was writing itself all over Sam's face, I started to get nervous.

The call wasn't long, but Sam just stood, eyeing his phone for a few seconds after it ended.

"What's wrong?" I whispered. I didn't know why I was whispering, but it felt appropriate.

Sam cleared his throat. "Um, that was Dad. Remember the Gathering I mentioned yesterday?" Snakes writhed in my belly as I nodded. "Dad told me we're having it tonight. At sundown. So about an hour and a half from now."

Shivers worked their way over my skin. Tonight? In an hour and a half? "What exactly am I supposed to do?"

He raked a hand through his already-tousled hair. "Dad will make the announcement that I bit you." He swallowed. "In the wolf world, everyone will know that means we're together. After, we'll stand out by the fire pit and everybody who is able to come will walk past us, scent you, and let you scent them. Then we'll probably go for a pack run."

I felt my eyebrows drawing together. *Scent me?* "What does that even mean?"

"It's the way we identify our own pack. When you scent someone, it's like taking a fingerprint of their unique smell. Your wolf will commit it to memory. It will probably only take one whiff for you to get everyone down. Wolves are like that with smells. It's also kind of like a pack initiation. By trading scents, it's like a wolf handshake."

"Do I have to be a wolf for this?"

"No, you'll do it as a human." His eyes were a little troubled, and I wasn't sure if it was because of the announcement that he bit me, or something else.

"How do you *scent* someone?"

He swallowed again. My stomach dropped.

He came in close. Really close. In my bubble close.

Like he was going to kiss me close. I stepped back. "What are you doing?"

"Trying to show you how you scent someone."

I arched my eyebrows. "You scent someone by leaning in to kiss them?" I tried to keep the accusation out of my voice, but I'm not sure it worked.

Sam let out a frustrated huff. "No. I wasn't trying to kiss you. Scenting is just a little personal."

It was my turn to swallow as I held still. It felt more like an act of trust with Sam standing so close, swearing he wasn't trying to kiss me. He searched my eyes for a second before slowly lowering his head to my collarbone.

Every muscle in my body went rigid as Wolf flopped onto her back, pushing me to completely surrender to whatever it was Sam wanted to do. I crushed that thought even as my heart rate picked up.

His nose skimmed my collar bone, up the side of my neck and behind my ear. Goose bumps raised all over me as I felt him inhale, then slowly exhale as he pulled back. He didn't step back though, but remained close, scrutinizing my face.

My brain was frozen, mouth hanging open. Letting Sam scent me had been somehow deeper than letting him kiss me. My mouth opened and shut, searching for words, though none came out.

"Sunshine and roses. Just like when you were human," he said then grimaced. "Sorry. That probably sounded creepy."

I chose to ignore that and focused on the technical. Scenting. My knees quavered. "I'm supposed to let how many random strangers do this to me?"

"And you'll scent them, too."

My hand clapped onto my forehead. This was too much. It felt like too much of me. Part of my brain realized all I was doing was taking a quick sniff of someone. But with the wolf side of me in full gear, it was more. A lot more. It was for sure more personal than a handshake.

"Meg?"

"I need coffee," I blurted.

Chapter 27

Sam

Meg looked rattled. I was rattled. Scenting her had been delicious. Wolf was on high alert, and the rest of me was distracted, too.

"I can finish making coffee. Since everyone will be here in an hour or so anyway, I might as well make the whole pot," I said, glad to have anything else as a diversion. Scenting had never been a turn on for me, but scenting Megan definitely was. I shook my head to clear it as I finished filling the pot to the brim. Everyone not sick or out of town would be at this Gathering.

"Um, will…will scenting be so…*personal* with everyone?"

My ears perked up. It felt personal to her, too? That was a good sign, I thought.

"I doubt it. Most of the time, scenting is similar to a handshake, but a little more up close, if you will." I paused. "How personal was it?" Dying to know her reaction, I watched her swallow and fidget as she cleared her throat.

"I think that just wasn't at all what I was expecting." Wolf sobered some. I was hoping for more. Like maybe fireworks. I nodded, not trusting my voice. She sighed, and I glanced back to find her eyes screwed shut and her mouth a thin line. She opened her eyes, met my gaze, and bit her lip. I raised an eyebrow.

"This is really awkward and embarrassing." She stopped.

I lifted my eyebrows as I put the heavy percolator onto the counter and gave her my full attention.

She stammered, "Can...do—I mean..." then all in a rush, "Can I practice scenting you?"

I laughed. I couldn't help it. Wolf was elated that she wanted to scent me. Or at least try it out. I wondered if she would find it attractive. Hopefully.

"Sure."

With the speed of a turtle, she came over to me by the sink. Gingerly standing on tiptoe, she leaned in ever so slightly and sniffed. Like she had a cold. I bit back a grin.

"Was that it?"

"Not quite." I smiled. "Let your wolf do the work. Like you did when you were baking last night."

"Hmm. That was easier. I picked up a little canister and let her sniff. I can't exactly do the same to you."

"I'm a little large for a canister. Just lean in and let her get my scent."

On tiptoes again, she leaned in, clearly still leery of getting into my space. I wanted her in my space. She inhaled a little deeper this time, though still not letting her wolf lead.

"Don't be afraid of it. It's a perfectly natural nicety in the pack." When she glanced up at me, still skeptical and uncomfortable, I lightly circled her waist and brought her in closer. Her eyes went wide, and panic momentarily flashed across her face. I swallowed back the urge to kiss her senseless and instead dropped my hands and made myself respond clinically.

"When you're scenting someone, it's okay to get closer to them than would be appropriate by human standards. You don't have to actually touch their skin with your nose, but you do need to get in close." Even though I had thoroughly enjoyed raising goose bumps on her a few minutes ago, it wasn't entirely necessary I get *that* close to her.

I held still, heart picking up as I tipped my chin back.

She was only standing an inch or two away, so she didn't have far to lean in. My eyes closed as I felt the warm rush of air leave her as she exhaled before she came a hair's breadth away from my skin and breathed deeply. Wolf nudged me to reciprocate, but I held back. She didn't immediately lean back, and I stayed still as a statue. I could sense the change in her when she let her wolf take over but was unprepared for her touch. Her hand came up and cupped the back of my neck as her nose touched behind my ear.

My knees went weak and I subtly gripped the counter.

Her wolf must have sensed something in me because her wolf faded, and she quickly stepped back.

I cleared my throat, determined not to spook her. "And the verdict is?"

"Snow and pine." Her cheeks colored lightly. "Though I think I already knew that."

I raised my eyebrows. That was news to me. I was pleased she'd already picked up my scent. "So think you can let your wolf to the surface to scent about forty-five more?"

She rolled her eyes. "Not like I have a choice."

Chapter 28

Megan

Sundown came not long after we'd finished the pizza, and people came with it.

Sam had suggested we wait out by the fire pit, and I pulled my coat tighter as much for my nerves as to ward off the chill breeze. I was thankful Cade and Raven, and I assumed, their parents, were first to arrive. Mr. and Mrs. Rivers hung back and waved to me as Cade and Raven made their way over to us. "Hey, guys," Sam said.

"Beta bro." Cade slapped Sam on the shoulder. "Beta lady," he said to me with a hint of cheek.

Sam glared. Cade grinned and shut up.

"Hi, Megan," Raven broke in, rolling her eyes at her brother's antics. "Did I get everything you needed for baking?"

"Absolutely." I was grateful to have a topic I was totally comfortable with. "Actually, I made you some mini cheesecakes as a thank-you. They're waiting for you in the fridge."

"Oh, wow. You didn't have to do that." Her smile was so genuine it helped put me at ease.

Before we could continue conversation, tires crunched the gravel and my new in-laws stepped out of a dark SUV. I felt Sam stiffen at my side and felt my own wolf tighten, instinctively anxious on his behalf, as well as nervous at being near Dominic Wolfe.

He stepped regally to the edge of the fire pit, nodding deeply to Mr. and Mrs. Rivers and then to us. "Samuel, how about we get a fire started?" he called out. His voice still carried the distinct edge of the Alpha, but for the first time, it held no traces of anger. I felt Wolf exhale, and I joined her relief.

"You good for a few minutes?" Sam said quietly. I nodded, and he and Cade went to go help stack firewood within the stone circle. Mr. Wolfe took Sam aside and whispered something in his ear. Sam shook his head, and Mr. Wolfe frowned slightly before bending down and handing Sam a stack of wood. I wondered what that exchange was all about.

"So this is your first Gathering?" Raven asked.

"Definitely. Anything I should know?" I tried to keep my voice light.

She laughed. "Nah, just the usual meet and greet." She smiled at me, but her eyes were curious. I gave her kudos for not peppering me with questions. If I had been her and my second-in-command had a newly wolfed girlfriend, which Raven had to realize by now, I wasn't sure I'd be able to remain quiet on the subject.

Mary walked over and motioned for Raven's parents to join us. She made introductions.

"Steve, Amalie, this is Megan. Megan, Steve and Amalie Rivers."

"Good to meet you," I got out.

"The pleasure is ours." Amalie smiled back. It was clear that Cade and Raven got their dark coloring from their dad. Their mom was almost white-blonde. The adults moved off a few paces after a couple minutes as other people started pouring into the back yard of the cabin.

Wolf was having a heyday with all the new smells and sounds. I was glad Raven was there while Sam and Cade were getting the fire started. Tammy came over not long after, and we made small talk together.

"So how are things?" Tammy asked, her eyes insinuating more than a casual question.

"Um, all right," I said honestly. I wasn't great, and at the moment I was a little terrified of what was coming. A distinctive twinkle shimmered in Tammy's eyes.

"I remember Sam's first Gathering as Beta. He was so nervous that he would do or say the wrong thing. He was so distracted that he didn't even realize when he set his own tail on fire." Raven snorted, and Tammy had to pause through a fit of giggles. "We've never let him live that one down."

My mouth tipped up, and I found myself laughing with them, some of the tension leaving my shoulders. Tammy had a good read on my situation, and she clearly enjoyed reliving her cousin's mishap. I appreciated the story and her efforts to make this less scary.

Sam and Cade sidled up right at that moment and Sam took one look at Tammy before rolling his eyes. "Tammy, you didn't."

"Oh, Sammy, I did," she replied with a saccharine smile.

"It was not one of my finest moments," Sam confessed to me as the glow of the growing fire lit up his face.

"Liar, liar, pants on fire," popped out of my mouth before I could stop it.

Sam processed for a second, mouth opening in shock, then burst out laughing the same time Cade did.

Grinning, Wolf nudged me, pleased at my teasing. We all sobered about ten minutes later when Dominic stood up on a three-foot section of stump as a makeshift podium. "Thank you all for coming to tonight's Gathering." His voice boomed in the hush as logs crackled and sparks flew up into the night sky. Nerves attacked my belly, and Sam reached for my hand. Much like the first time we met his parents, I wasn't sure if it was more for his benefit or for mine. Dominic continued. "We have some shocking but exciting news. As I'm sure some of you have now surmised"—he glanced at us and our joined hands—"our Beta has found himself a girl."

There was cheering and clapping as my face flushed and Sam forced a smile. His grip on my fingers tightened.

"Historically, there would have been a large celebration and a lot of fanfare with a *Changing Bite* taking place publicly—" There was a collective gasp and a few sharp intakes of breath as he enunciated the words.

"—but it was decided that this would be done more quietly and without all the elaboration for the comfort of those most intimately involved. Full approval has been given by the guardian, George Carmichael, with whom many of you are familiar, for these current circumstances. I expect this is a shock to many of you as the last time our pack was expanded by a bite was over two hundred years ago. Traditions will still be upheld. George Carmichael has known of our existence for over seventy years."

I fervently wished Grandpa was here with me now and noticed Dominic conveniently left out his lack of approval.

"Is it any wonder that his granddaughter has fallen in love with the allure of the Wolf and the charms of our Beta?" Mr. Wolfe cracked a charismatic smile, and there was foot stomping and more clapping. I wanted to melt into the ground. Sam stood resolutely beside me, clinging to my hand. His smile was friendly enough, and I tried to paste a matching one on my own face. Mr. Wolfe continued, "With that being said, please let me introduce to you our newest pack member and partner to my son, Megan."

I tried not to hyperventilate as roughly forty pairs of eyes focused on me as I now clung to Sam's hand. Mr. Wolfe's speech had not been overly long or overly approving, but it had been received well enough, and now I was the focus of everyone's curiosity.

Sam squeezed my fingers and then his voice sounded in my head. *You're doing great. Let me know if you get too overwhelmed.*

I squeezed his fingers back. Sam was more relaxed now. Dominic was saying something else, but the words were lost in the rush of blood going past my ears. Wolf rubbed her head against me for moral support, which I found both odd and comforting.

Remember to let your wolf do the scenting. Let her up to the surface, and she'll do the rest. Sam's voice echoed inside my brain. I about had a panic attack on the spot as I realized that every person there was queuing up, ready to come sniff and be sniffed.

Mr. Wolfe headed the lineup. Anyone else. Could no one else scent me first? Wolf quaked but braced herself against me, giving us both courage.

He stopped at Sam first, though they must have been as familiar with each other's scents as they were their own. Maybe this was all just formality, and it wouldn't send my knees knocking and my guts churning as it had when Sam had done it.

Once Mr. Wolfe was in front of me, he leaned down and quickly ran his nose the length of my neck, not touching me, for which I was profoundly thankful. I realized he was holding his own neck out for me, and with an encouraging squeeze of Sam's hand, I consciously called the wolf up and let her satiate her terrified curiosity of Dominic Wolfe.

Slowly I leaned in and closed my eyes. I imagined I was sniffing another spice container with the wolf. Pine and grass.

I opened my eyes. Mr. Wolfe nodded once and then Mary was there. "Congratulations, dear." She beamed.

I smiled weakly and cautiously repeated the same scene—spices. It's just like smelling spices. It was easier to do if I kept my eyes closed. Mary's scent reminded me of lilacs.

Raven, Tammy, and Cade had all managed to get to the front of the line, as if sensing my need to practice my scenting a few more times.

I soon gave myself over to the sensation of the new scents. I kept Sam's hand firmly in mine, and that helped keep the wolf under control. People were excited and nearly everyone had something nice or congratulatory to say to either one or both of us.

"Welcome to the pack!"

"I'm so glad our Beta found such a lovely girl."

"Sam, you sly old dog."

"I knew you wouldn't take the traditional route."

"You're so pretty," a tiny little girl said. I couldn't help but respond by smiling widely to her and sinking down on my knees so we were properly eye to eye.

"Thank you. I think you're pretty, too," I told the little pig-tailed child. She couldn't have been more than five.

"Can I sniff you now?"

"Darby, that's not a polite thing to ask," her mother shushed her and gave me an apologetic smile.

"Of course." I was not at all uncomfortable letting little Darby take a whiff of me, if only the rest of the pack could be so unassuming and not intimidating.

She put her sweet little nose up to my neck and inhaled deeply. "Mm. You smell good, too." I grinned, and nearly laughed when she stuck her neck out like a chicken. "Do me now!" And how could I refuse that?

I scented her, dirt and chocolate, and then I snuffled her with my human nose, tickling her and making her giggle.

"You have a natural way with children," Darby's mother cooed as she leaned down and ran her nose up my neck—touching the skin. I gave her a tight smile, resisting the urge to wipe my neck.

By the time the logs were red embers giving off little yellow sparks, I'd had enough. Wolf was keyed up with so much new sensory information that I thought I was going to explode if I didn't get some of this energy out of my system. There were two people left in the line, and they went through quickly.

As soon as it was only Sam and me standing there, I glanced around and was surprised to note that a lot of people had changed into those large gray robes. Ah. The pack run. At least maybe I'd get some energy out.

"Come on. We can go back up to the cabin, and you can change there so you're not in front of everyone."

I nodded, nearly bouncing on the soles of my feet. Never letting go of my hand, Sam walked me back up to the front of the house and held the door open for me.

"You handled that beautifully," he said as the door snicked shut.

"I imagined everyone was a large bottle of spice."

He chuckled. "Well, it must have worked."

"Um, should I go for the robe?" I was unsure how exactly the next part of the evening was going to play out. I could tell that I needed the run, although I wasn't sure how we were going to do that, since I'd never done more than pace the living room a few laps. I hoped I wouldn't fall on my face in an undignified heap of fur in front of everyone.

"You can, although you'll probably be more comfortable if you shift here and then wait to shift back once we're in the cabin again. I know you don't like, um, to be on display," he said, averting his eyes.

That was true.

"How exactly will we do this, this pack run? What if I can't keep up?" Doubts and insecurities waffled with the desire to let the wolf have her head.

"We can start out with them. I'll stay with you, and if we need to slow down, it's no problem. We can run for as long or as short a time as you want. We just need to make an appearance. This run is specifically to celebrate you joining the pack."

I grimaced. I wanted to be fully human so badly, but at least I was able to tolerate the wolf now, for the most part. She huffed at me indignantly. At least we hadn't had a sporadic shift yet. Holding Sam's hand in a vice-like grip all night probably helped.

I was able to call up the wolf without much difficulty. She was eager to get out, especially knowing I was going to attempt to let her out for the longest amount of time yet. In the cabin, Sam was gentleman enough to let me shift first in case I needed help. The change came quickly, and minutes later Sam was a wolf beside me.

My wolf took one good inhale of him and sent so many signals shooting to my brain I about fell over. My wolf was nuts about Sam. It made my head swim, drowning in the pine and snow scent of him, all musky, male, and entirely attractive. I think my tongue lolled out of my mouth before I yanked on Wolf's will and tried to shut her up. She yipped, and Sam's wolf cocked his head at me. *Is she behaving?*

No. Not particularly, I panted back. She pranced us around Sam like a little puppy, irritating me and sending my already frazzled nerves past overdrive. Wolf-Sam moved next to me, his fur brushing against mine. Wolf careened us into him. Sam skidded over a step, knocking into the table.

Enough! I growled at my wolf. She nudged me with her head—our head—and whacked it against the table. I snarled at her, and she wiggled to get closer to Sam. This was not going well.

Sam was breathing hard, but I didn't have time to worry about it. How was I ever going to control this beast long enough to coordinate a run with other wolves? If she went this crazy next to Sam's wolf, what would she do surrounded by forty others? I felt my control slipping. Wolf was taking charge and leaving me behind. I was losing myself to the animal and fear of losing myself paralyzed me.

Sam!

Wolf shook her head again, rubbing us against Sam's side. He turned, stared straight into our eyes, and put his open mouth right over our muzzle, biting down ever so gently. Wolf surrendered control at once and calm enveloped me. On some baser level, I realized something primal had happened, but I had no idea what it was. Wolf recognized Sam was in charge, and her crazy antics stopped. She sat quietly, awaiting my instructions.

I was wheezing from the emotional struggle of wills and trying to fight her for control of my own body. I stood on shaky legs, dreading going out the door to face the rest of the pack.

Wolf-Sam leaned his head down, rubbing his head against my neck, and whined softly. I felt him scent me again as he nudged me softly. It filled Wolf with heat and something like…desire? It made me uncomfortable. Like an itch I couldn't scratch. I shook my head again in frustration and tried to put one paw in front of the other. We were not perfectly synced, but Wolf was at least mostly compliant after Sam did, well, whatever it was that Sam had done.

We made it to the door, and Sam got up on his hind legs, flipped the latch with a paw, and then used his nose to open the door the rest of the way.

Moonlight streamed down onto the gravel of the drive before the house and the aromas of autumn and wolf hit me in the face with nearly as much strength as Sam's scent had. Wolf was nearly beside herself with joy as she took in the new smells. To my surprise and relief, she didn't go crazy after each new smell and, more importantly, the other wolves, like she did after her first she whiff of Wolf-Sam. Our gaze trained to the waiting pack. Fur and glowing eyes gathered around the cabin. My insecurities began creeping back up. It was worse than changing clothes for the first time in sixth grade gym class. All those half-naked bodies at various stages of development. Everyone trying not to notice anyone else and being so uncomfortable that my hands shook. It felt like that, standing in the doorway in my fur while the pack stared.

A lone howl rose up from the back, and Wolf instantly recognized it as the Alpha's call. Shock ran through me as I realized that it was that voice, that wild, throaty noise, that I would obey in an instant if ordered. I knew Dominic Wolfe was the Alpha of the pack, but until this moment, as a wolf, I hadn't felt his power over me deep in my bones. His howl compelled me forward, tripping and stuttering down the steps onto the cold grass.

Sam was right beside me, fur touching mine, warm at my side, the wind ruffling over me, bringing more new information. Sam's cold, wet nose touched my cheek. I wasn't sure if it was supposed to be affectionate or if it was to get my attention. *Ready to try out your paws?*

I gasped as Dominic howled again and started the pack moving toward the woods. The run was upon us.

Wolf took the initiative and tried to spring forward to join her pack, but my fear held me rooted, and one of my concerns materialized. Her leap and my fear hurdled us both, nose first, straight into the dirt, my feet and tail flying up over my head. Ugh.

It was cold. My paws were wet. I was muddy. There were twigs stuck all over my fur. There was so much sensory information floating around that my brain was on constant overload. I wasn't sure how much more information I could process before I blasted into a million pieces. Wolf was having the time of her life. She was running with abandon—at least as much as she could with my clumsy attempts to keep up. I was still trying to figure so many things out that we weren't as synced as we probably should have been to be running through the forest in the dark, where branches were constantly snagging my fur and roots were creeping out of the shadows to bang my shins.

After about ten minutes, I was done. I was so done. Wolf whined, not remotely finished. I was cranky, sore, and bruised. I was over it. I wanted to curl up as a human, have a cup of tea, and eat a cookie. Maybe five or six.

Sam, I need to be done.

Let's head back. Want to race?

I slit my eyes at him. He had the audacity to make some chuffing noise that I assumed meant he was laughing at me. I snipped my teeth at him. He nudged his head against me, letting me know he wasn't making fun of me and headed us back toward the cabin.

Wolf didn't want to go in, but I had no trouble asserting my dominance this time. She had been let out, she'd run outside, and she had the scents of forty-something wolves and all manner of fall noises and sights to sift through and commit to memory. She acquiesced easily, and then I stood there, naked, human, in the bathroom.

A shriek clawed up from my throat when my eyes met my reflection in the mirror.

"Megan?" Sam called.

Horror welled up as I took in my matted hair, twigs, leaves, and a particularly large stick protruding out behind my left ear. Dirt caked my nose and left streaks down the rest of my body. Mud encrusted my hands and arms to the elbows. My hairy legs sported several large dark purple bruises and more scrapes than I could count.

"Megan? What's wrong?" Sam called again. "Here, put this on." He cracked the door from the outside and shoved a gray robe at me. The sight of it was hideous, reminding me again of all things werewolf. This was going to break me. I was not going to survive becoming a wolf.

Chapter 29

Sam

There was a muffled noise of the robe moving on the floor and after a minute, I eased the door open. Megan was draped in the robe and staring at her hands, her fingers covered in drying mud.

"Hey," I said softly, not sure how to proceed. A lone tear tracked down her cheek, leaving a muddy trail. It was followed by another, and then it was like her face cracked open and sobs jerked her whole body as she crumpled to the floor.

My gut clenched, and my heart constricted. I didn't know what else to do, so I sat down on the floor next to her and pulled her onto my lap. She didn't protest. Her head found its way to my shoulder and she cried and cried. Helplessness engulfed me. The only thing I could do was sit with my arms wrapped around her as she cried herself out. Eventually, her tears ended, and her body sagged against me. I could practically feel the exhaustion bleeding off her.

She took a shuddering breath and spoke into my neck. "Sorry." She sniffed.

"For what?" I was genuinely confused. She had just had her whole world upended, turned into a wolf, gotten married, and then been forced into a Gathering and pack run without time to think anything through.

"I'm a hot mess."

"Well, you're definitely hot." I teased her gently, but truthfully. "But the dirt and sticks could go."

I felt her smile soggily against my shoulder.

"Does this happen every time you run as a wolf? My legs look like they have plums splattered all over them." She stuck one out. It was definitely streaked with dirt and I'd seen them smoother, but her bruises were already faded away to greens and yellows. She sucked in a breath. "Incredible," she breathed.

"We heal very quickly. Although I'm sorry you got so mangled in the underbrush."

"Did you get all bruised up?" She raised herself up, so we were eye level.

I shook my head. "Nope. Once you and your wolf are more on the same page, you won't either. You'll avoid the branches and the thickets and the roots without a second thought." She squinted critically at my hair.

"Seriously. You have like, one leaf stuck in your hair." She scowled. My face cracked into a grin.

"Turn around. I'll help you get the debris out."

She pulled the robe tighter around her chest and stiffly turned so that she was sitting on the floor, my legs on either side of her. It was a little hard not to be turned on, but I gathered my resolve and set to picking out the many, many leaves and sticks and twigs from Megan's hair.

Chapter 30

Megan

It took a good forty-five minutes for Sam to finish fishing out all the dead things from my hair, although he might have been playing with my hair the last few minutes, and because it felt good, I let him. But the dirt had to go. And I was going to need to buy stock in a razor company.

When I finally got up off the floor, my right leg had fallen asleep, and I leaned against the sink while the blood started circulating again. Sam brushed a final piece of leaf from my shoulder.

"You'll feel better after a shower. I'll sweep this up while you wait for blood to go back to your toes." He winked. How could he be so kind and so positive after all the crazy that had taken place over the past—was it really only two days? I angled my eyebrows. There was a literal imprint of my cheek and eye socket on his white shirt outlined perfectly in dirt wet with my tears.

"I'm sorry about your shirt." I bit my lip.

He glanced down and flicked at the dirt like one might flick a droplet of water. "Eh, it'll wash."

I smiled. A genuine smile. Sam was maybe going to be the bright spot in the next few weeks until my permanent human skin returned.

I didn't shift again Sunday night. It was well after midnight before we both fell exhausted into our beds, and we slept late again Monday. I woke before Sam, and eager to work through some of what had happened, I set to making bread. It was something I could do quietly, hopefully not disturbing Sam, and the texture of the dough as it made soft slapping noises against the counter was more soothing than sweet iced tea on a hot day.

It stretched and morphed as I kneaded, pushing my frustration and eventually the anger that resurfaced into the ball of dough. Long minutes passed as I worked. I felt my anger receding as Wolf nudged me, apologetic for her wild traipsing last night. A sort of calm stole over me, and I felt my shoulders relax, the tension ebbing down to my arms and into my hands as I repeatedly stretched and punched down the dough.

Wolf and I came to an understanding. I needed to commit to being a wolf for the next few weeks. I thought I already had, but last night's run had enunciated how clearly ill-adjusted I was for this life. It was obvious I was destined for skin, not fur, but I did need to fix my attitude, as Grandma would have said.

I wasn't happy about being here, but I was stuck here for now. And how I reacted to this situation was on me. So Wolf and I were going to act as a team for the time being. I was going to be the boss, but she was going to help me understand how to maintain the balance I needed between skin and fur. With that settled, I exhaled a big breath and folded the mass into a neat ball and set it back in the bowl to rise.

Glancing up, I startled when I noticed Sam leaning against the back of the couch. His arms were braced on the couch, legs crossed casually as he watched me. Wolf wiggled in excitement as I registered his bed head and pajama pants. I refused to admit I found him sexy.

"Good morning," he said tentatively.

"Morning," I replied absently. "How long have you been standing there?"

"A while. You were pretty intent on beating that dough to a pulp. Everything all right?"

I felt a grin tip one side of my mouth. "Yes. I think Wolf and I have come to terms with a few things. The bread was helping us work through our issues."

The rest of Monday was spent texting back and forth with Rachel and talking to Grandpa, exercising the wolf, and working on shifting on my terms. Sam and I did some laps around the cabin, letting my nose and other senses get used to the surrounding areas on a smaller scale. It was helpful and not nearly as overwhelming as the run had been.

Tuesday morning, I baked another batch of cookies and then made yeast rolls while Sam asked me questions to help prepare for the English test. He was a good study partner. With nerves mounting about school tomorrow, Sam suggested we spend most of the afternoon in fur. I was ready to try anything to avoid a massive morph at school. Wolf was behaving herself, but it was like she couldn't help it sometimes either, and she just came out. And that made me nervous.

I was up with the dawn Wednesday morning. My heart pounded, and dread pooled in my stomach. Wolf nudged me encouragingly. We had been working as a team, and she was behaving well. She promised to try her best today. I was still concerned. I lay in my bed, twisting the covers in my fists, trying not to think about the one hundred different ways I could hurt someone or expose werewolves everywhere while attempting a physiology lab. Sam must have heard my thrashing. He sat up and scrubbed a hand over his face, hiding a yawn.

"I'm not sure I can do this," tumbled out of my lips.

He got up, shuffled over, and plopped down beside me on the bed. I was momentarily distracted. I wasn't sure how I felt about Sam sitting on my bed while I was still lying in it.

"You're going to do fine," he said with a sleepy smile. "I'm not just saying it because it's what you want to hear. Your wolf knows who the leader is. And I'm one thought away. Seriously, I'll check in with you between every class."

"Promise?" I chewed my bottom lip.

"Promise." He tucked a stray piece of hair behind my ear and I shivered. "Go shower, and I'll make you coffee."

"Okay. Coffee is good. Coffee helps everything."

Thirty minutes later, I was showered, dressed, and had my makeup on. My hair was still up in a towel, but I could fix it in a bit. Sam probably wanted to shower before school, too. Red infused my cheeks as I realized what a bathroom hog I was. I wasn't used to sharing space in the mornings.

"Sorry I took so long," I called as I exited to the aroma of fresh brewed coffee.

"That's okay. I don't take long. And we've got plenty of time before we need to head out." He nodded toward the table. "Although, a package came for you while you were in the bathroom," he said with a wink.

On the table was a square shoebox with a huge red ribbon tied on top. My mouth fell open. Inside I found a brand-new pair of my favorite shoes. Replacements of the leopard ballet flats that had been ripped to shreds in the woods when my paws shot through them. Tears sprang to my eyes at the thoughtfulness behind the gesture.

"Sam." I swallowed thickly. "How did you—?"

"Rachel helped," he confessed with a smile.

I couldn't believe it. Without another thought I crossed the distance between us and gave him a hug. His hands slid around my waist as his arms encircled me. It sent shivers up my spine and prickled gooseflesh over my arms. Quickly, I stepped back.

"Thank you," I told him, meaning it down to my core.

He beamed. "You're welcome."

Not long after, we were out the door. New leopard spotted ballets completed my ensemble of skinny jeans and long black sweater. The closer we got to the school, the more my heart rate increased.

"Relax. I can smell the tension coming off you."

"This is such a bad idea. What if I change? What if she gets overwhelmed? What do I do?" My voice moved up about an octave. "What if I hurt someone?" He reached over and took my hand, giving it a quick squeeze.

"What's your wolf doing right now?"

I took a deep, calming breath. "She's sitting obediently. But probably only because you're right here." Wolf snorted. Maybe I wasn't giving her enough credit.

"Megan, you're the dominant half. You are in charge. She knows that. The moon is waning tonight. You should be fine until nightfall." He squeezed my hand again.

I blew out a breath, my gut twisting up in more tangled knots at my next words. "Will...will you calm her?"

His eyebrows raised.

"Of course. Between every class if you want." He grinned, and I could have sworn there was a mischievous twinkle hiding in his eyes. "We are supposed to be dating, after all."

"Right. We decided to start dating the night you took me home from the game. We've secretly been crushing on each other for weeks. Any other details I need to add to the cover story?"

His face tightened. "That's the gist of things. Just try to be more convincing about it. Maybe try not to look like you swallowed roadkill," he said sourly.

A nervous giggle escaped. It was the anxiety. I was so laughing inappropriately. "Sorry. I'll try to be convincing in between making sure a massive wild wolf doesn't erupt out of my skin and wipe out the senior class."

"That's the spirit," he retorted dryly.

There wasn't time for more banter as we pulled into the parking lot, and Sam whipped into his usual spot near the back of the lot. I was grateful we were at the back. It would give me longer to adjust to the new smells and sounds before actually getting into the school building. We were early enough I could take things slowly. Sam put the car in park and turned off the engine. I sat, staring straight ahead, trying to take deep breaths. *You can do this!* I told myself. Wolf nodded encouragingly. Snakes writhed in my gut.

"Meg?"

I turned to Sam, the whole whites of my eyes probably showing like those of a terrified horse. He took my face in his hands. Wolf curled up in a ball of fur and basked at his touch. "Listen to me. You are going to be fine. I will meet you after every class. I'll hold your hand in the hallway. I'll make sure she's quiet in between every period. If you need me, use the link. I will come."

"Promise?" I whispered, dazed, but mesmerized by the darker flecks of blue surrounding his irises.

"Promise. I will come. Every time."

I took a shaky breath as his eyes dipped to my lips and back to mine before he carefully dropped his head down and pressed his lips against mine. Wolf was already quiet, but I didn't mind the extra precaution. Some niggling thought at the back of my brain wondered what it would be like to really kiss Sam Wolfe. I immediately banished the rebel thought.

He pulled back, watching my face. I closed my eyes and breathed deeply through my nose, steeling my resolve. "Okay. Let's do this." I texted Rachel to let her know we were coming in. I knew having her with me would help me stay calm. She had play practice before school but promised she'd meet me when I got there.

My phone dinged. She was waiting by the doors.

Crisp air met my nose as I shut the car door and leaned against it for a minute, trying to get my sensory bearings. I could smell the food in the cafeteria, and there was a definite stink of unwashed bodies coming from the gym as the doors were opened with the entrance of students.

Sam took my hand. "Ready?"

"Nope." We walked toward the front entrance.

Eyes followed our progress across the chilly parking lot. We were early, but not so early that other students weren't coming in, too. Every eye trained to our linked hands as we shuffled to the door. I hadn't thought to check who might have witnessed Sam calming the wolf. Heat raced to my cheeks as I thought about Brody flirting with me last week. I was pretty sure he had been planning to ask me out, though I wasn't sure if I'd have said yes. Walking across the lot with my hand linked in Sam's was going to get the gossips going.

Sam was one of the *it* guys. He was gorgeous, nice, and everybody liked him. He was popular, even though he didn't do sports, and he didn't date much that I knew of. I knew a lot of girls had pined after him most of high school. My skin crawled as I felt more and more attention drawn our way. Wolf's hackles prickled, uncomfortable with all the stares. I didn't dare let go of Sam's hand. I had it gripped in a death vice.

"Relax. This is just school. You've done this your whole life."

"I hadn't counted on being the new school attraction."

"Oh." His mouth tipped up in a goofy grin. "It'll be old news by second period."

A flash of red caught my eye as Rachel bounded out the doors to us.

"Hey!" she said with far too much enthusiasm.

Having her there made me sag with relief.

First period was history. I loved history. True to his word, Sam walked me to the door of my class, but I couldn't make myself let go of his hand. I probably looked like a whiny, clingy girlfriend, but I really couldn't help it.

Before I could say anything, Sam leaned down to whisper in my ear, "You can do this." His lips grazed my ear and practically put Wolf in a stupor. He was right. I had to do this. I could do this. I *would* do this.

"Okay." Quick breath. "I'll see you after class."

"I'll be here. Let me know if you need anything."

A quick nod and I forced myself to let go of his hand and go into the classroom. Rachel followed me in and sat at our table, thumping the seat beside her.

After all she'd experienced this weekend, she appeared no worse for wear. She wasn't nearly as fazed at learning of the existence of werewolves as I was. I hesitated a moment before sinking into the chair.

The bell rang for class to start, and within the minute, Mr. Steidman was beginning his lecture of the colonization of India. Before I realized it, I was drawn into the facts and stories of the lecture, letting myself absorb the information, letting Wolf fall to the background.

When the bell rang for class to dismiss, I was surprised when I discovered that Wolf was dozing as I shoved my notebook back in my backpack. Sam was waiting by the door.

"That went much better than I imagined it would," I whispered. He smiled as he wove our fingers together. "I knew you could do it." His confidence was warming.

Rachel smirked. "You're a natural." She grinned. I rolled my eyes.

Sam had requested my schedule yesterday and steered me toward French. Rachel split at the end of the hallway on her way to Speech. She waved and gave me a thumbs-up with a wink. "To the ends of the earth!"

I nodded.

Before I realized what he was doing, Sam swung us into a blind spot behind a stand of lockers and quickly put his mouth to mine again. I nearly squeaked in protest, taken off guard, but quickly stilled. Wolf smiled lazily, raising her head from her nap. Sam pulled back, and she dropped back to sleep. He grinned down. "After French?"

I nodded, took a breath, and went into the room. Chemicals burned my nose as the synthetic sickly-sweet strawberry of Madame's air freshener slapped me in the face. I nearly gagged and started breathing through my mouth.

Once the chemical odor burned away all the hairs in my nostrils, it became a dull scent in the background. Madame ran us through some verb conjugation and some new vocabulary words. It wasn't hard work, but it was enough to keep my mind engaged.

Another class down, and I was starting to think that maybe this wasn't going to be such a disaster. If only I'd been right.

Sam met me again and walked me to Calculus. He confirmed things went well in French. "Cindy is in Calculus with you. She's not as dominant as you, but she can help." He smiled and pressed his lips to my cheek while I held perfectly still. My face went red as two freshmen girls tittered as they observed our awkward affection. I rolled my eyes and went into the classroom before I could overhear anything else.

There was a sub today, and the first new curl of unease bloomed in my belly. I took my usual seat and got out my book and notebook, studiously laying out my pencil while biting my lip. The sub took roll and then pointed to a section on the board that had our assignment for the day. I was pleased when I realized what had been assigned were problems that I'd already worked through on my own for practice to make sure I was understanding the concept.

I took out my papers and reviewed what I'd done, correcting one problem that I realized I'd messed up. But after that, the class was quiet. Since the work was done, I pulled out a novel from my backpack. I hadn't touched it in over a week with all the excitement but thought I might be able to enjoy a couple of quiet moments.

Things went well for a few minutes. Then the scratching of pencils became louder. And Anthony Perkins sat behind me. Breathing *loudly* through his mouth. I blinked hard a few times and tried to get back into my book. But it was no use. The mouth breathing sounded louder and louder, the pencils scratching on paper were a deafening drum. Wolf started pacing. We were becoming increasingly agitated together. She was holding it in, and I was holding it together, but suddenly, her limbs started shaking.

Sam! There is a mouth breather in here, and we're both about to have a fit.

Suddenly, a noise startled us from our rapid heartbeats. Cindy dramatically clutched her belly as she stood up from her desk.

"I think I need to go to the nurse," she stammered.

Wolf nudged me into action. "Here, let me help you," I offered quickly.

The sub raised an eyebrow then noted Cindy's pale face. He nodded us toward the door.

I nearly bolted the both of us from the classroom, panting in relief when the quiet of the hallway surrounded us.

Cindy stood up straight and winked at me. "You okay?"

"Much better now. Thanks. Are you okay? I'm guessing you're not actually having the mother of all stomachaches?"

"All part of helping each other out." She grinned again as we walked to the nurse's office. Sam met us halfway down the hall.

He looked me up and down, and Wolf was immediately soothed. I had to admit, I felt better having him in my sight, too. It was like he was the leader, and I was the follower, and I knew he would take care of everything, so long as he was there. Wolf and I sighed collectively.

"Mouth breather, huh?" he said, a gentle smile on his face.

"Anthony Perkins is going to have to get over his cold before I can go back to Calculus."

Sam and Cindy chuckled.

"It was kinda loud," Cindy said. "Even I was getting a little annoyed, and I've had years more practice at this than you have," she said sympathetically. I gave her a weak smile.

"Thanks."

Wolf had settled back down, trying to be obedient, and happy with Sam near us. We got Cindy to the nurse's office where she lay down until her stomachache miraculously passed. Sam claimed a headache and totally charmed the nurse.

The week progressed well. There were only a few incidents where I felt uncomfortable enough to need Sam's help. He dutifully played his boyfriend part, walking me to each class, holding my hand, quieting the wolf when she needed it. We ran each evening, and I was slowly starting to acclimate. I still didn't like most of it, but it was tolerable. Grandpa and I talked every evening, and it was a huge influence on my comfort levels about living away from home. At school, Sam and I were still a hot item. Brody had not been pleased, I could tell, but Sam had assured me that in the locker room Brody didn't speak well of the girls he dated, so maybe it was a good thing I hadn't gone out with him.

Friday at lunch we all sat down at our usual table. Our circle of friends hadn't changed much, just reorganized our table since Sam always sat beside me now.

"You guys, we need to go catch a movie tomorrow. We all said we'd go to *The Fifth Day*. It's supposed to be epic, and it's finally out," Jeremy called from down the table while his girlfriend nodded her agreement.

She asked, "Rachel, weren't you the one telling me about the new trailer they released for it?"

"Yes! The effects are supposed to be cutting edge."

"And Eric Dayton plays the jailer. Did you catch him in *Dusty Road*?" Luke chimed. He was a drama nerd along with Rachel.

Rachel's eyes glittered as the conversation continued. I knew she wanted to watch it. It was fantasy, adventure, action, and a love story all rolled into one if the trailers were to be believed. It was on my definitely-want-to-watch list, but I wasn't sure how that was going to work out with the need to burst into fur. A little sigh escaped. Rachel's expression fell. She wouldn't go without me, and that made guilt slosh in my belly.

A chorus of agreement circled the table. Sam squeezed my hand, his eyebrow raised. I widened my eyes at him. Had he lost his mind? I couldn't go to the movies Saturday night or any night. "Do you want to go?"

"Don't we, um, have plans Saturday *night*?"

His blue eyes twinkled at me, and I tamped down the urge to glare at him. "Sure, but what about a matinee?" I raised my eyebrows. I hadn't thought about that. Would it be done early enough that I could survive without alerting all of Rock Falls to the wolves that lived there? I glanced at Rachel. Her face lit up, all hopeful. I gave Sam an unsure shrug.

"Hey, Megan and I have plans tomorrow night. Can we do an early matinee?"

Since it came from Sam, it was well received, and before lunch was over, the whole group of us had plans to meet at the theater for the three o'clock matinee of *The Fifth Day*. Rachel was ecstatic. "This is going to be awesome." She grinned at me, grabbing my hand as she trotted out of the lunchroom. "Maybe we can sneak away for a few minutes, and you can finally let me know what's really going on. This is so unfair." She rolled her eyes for dramatic flair. "Sam would have to have supersonic ears."

I laughed a little, but uneasiness still wriggled in my middle.

It was a relief when the week ended, and Saturday morning passed uneventfully. I worked on my English essay, and we did some calculus together. Sam was a whiz at numbers. I wasn't any slouch at it, but I had to confess that it was nice to work on it together. We had settled into a rhythm by the end of the week, and it was gratifying that our first "normal" Saturday together since I became a werewolf wasn't awkward or too weird without school to keep us on our semi-established routine.

The washer dinged, and I got up from the table to change the laundry.

"Do you want to go for a quick run before we go to the theater today?" Sam offered as I tried not to blush when a pair of my lacy underwear fell from the washer on its way to the dryer.

"Probably. I'm still a little nervous about going anywhere this close to dark."

"I know. You'll be fine. I'll be there right with you. Besides, going for a quick run now should help *wear* her out." Sam gently teased, not missing the fallen underwear. Mercifully, he said nothing else.

"What time do you want to leave for the movie?" I squeaked as I flung the offending garment into the dryer.

"Probably about two. Movie starts at three, that gives us time to get there and get settled and whatever." I appreciated that Sam was always punctual. It reminded me of Grandpa. Shaking my head, I stopped that line of thought. Comparing Sam to Grandpa and finding more things they had in common was not going to help my staying-human cause.

"Do you have any other laundry you're planning to do?"

"No, I'm good after this."

"All right. Why don't I throw some of my stuff in and then we can go for a run. Sound good?"

"Sounds good."

I watched as Sam crammed whites, darks, and a few colors into the washer and wondered if he'd have anything that remained the same color by the time it came out.

We took a few miles at a good clip, and though part of me didn't want to enjoy it, the other part of me, and the wolf, relished the cool air brushing over my fur. It was invigorating and refreshing. It felt so good to stretch my muscles. It was like they'd been cramped for ages and getting out and running was exactly what I needed. The wolf tossed her head and raced forward, passing Sam. With a playful bark, Sam chased after me. He nipped teasingly at my heels. Wolf sprung ahead as the human part of me smiled, realizing that Sam was flirting with me. I narrowed my eyes as I conferred with Wolf, letting her know the plan. As one, we stopped and wheeled around to the side. Sam lunged past us and barked in surprise when he missed me. I laughed, the sound coming out like a chuffing noise. Wolf urged us forward again, going after Sam's heels. But instead of catching his heels, Sam anticipated and moved slightly to the side. I had overestimated the distance between us, and instead of missing him completely, my teeth caught the side of his flank. Essentially, I bit him in the butt.

Sam yelped and spun around, totally surprised. I was utterly mortified.

There was a startled minute between us, then Sam flopped onto his back with snorting, huffing noises coming from his mouth, tongue lolling out of his mouth. He was laughing. At me. He was laughing so hard that he couldn't even roll over. He just lay there wheezing like a dying goat. I was still too stunned to do anything. Sam reached a paw out and looped it around my head, dragging me down to his side. His other paw awkwardly patted my head, all the while, he was trying to stop laughing.

It was a little funny.

Wolf cracked a smile and before long, Sam and I were both lying there in a heap in the grass, a pair of snorting wolves.

Eventually we made it back to the cabin, both a little rubber-legged from all the laughing that had released some pent-up tension from the week. I was certain Sam was never going to let me live that one down. He let me have the bathroom first, and as I was getting ready to put my red sweater on over my head, I caught my reflection in the mirror.

My cheeks were flushed, and my eyes were twinkling. I knew that look. Unease slithered down my spine. It seemed to confirm what I refused to think about. Wolf smirked. Shaking my head, I pulled my sweater down over my black skinny jeans and slipped on my socks to go with the boots. I had intended to wear my leopard flats that Sam had replaced. But after watching my expression in the mirror, I thought better of it. Wolf nudged me, unhappy with my thoughts. I swallowed. I had to keep myself in check.

Sam put the car in park. We were here.

Nerves flapped in my stomach, and Wolf pranced around even as Sam opened the car door for me. I left my coat and snagged my purse.

"Sam," I whispered, "she's still all jittery. I don't like this."

"Relax," he replied softly. He took my hand as we crossed the parking lot and Wolf settled a little. I squeezed his hand.

"You sure I can handle this? It will be close to dark when we're done."

"You've done fine at school. You'll do fine here. Besides, your wolf definitely had some action this afternoon." He smiled and bit back a chuckle, his blue eyes light.

I snorted. Definitely never living that one down.

Wolf was jumpy, and the human part of me was trying to ignore the tingles going up my arm as Sam held my hand. Pretending to be dating at school was one thing. But an actual date in public was a bit different. I gave myself a mental shake. I'd been on dates. For mercy's sake, I could be on a date with Sam Wolfe.

Sam bought our tickets, and we met the rest of our group in the lobby. We were the last ones there.

As soon as we reached the rest of the group, Rachel grabbed my hand and dragged me toward the bathroom. "We'll be back in a sec. Save seats for us," she called over her shoulder. I glanced back and met Sam's eyes. His mouth tipped up at one corner. He was ridiculously handsome in his navy-blue sweater.

"Okay, spill!" Rachel squealed once we were in the bathroom and she'd done a quick scan for feet. We were alone.

"Spill what?" I felt my cheeks flush. Her face said, *seriously?*

"I know you guys are pretending to be dating at school and stuff, but something is different today. Am I right?" she prompted.

I gulped. The wolf was restless. She was completely on edge today, was that what Rachel was noticing? Or was it that maybe the human part of me was finding Sam to be more than I'd expected?

"I think I may be crushing on the wolf boy," I confessed in a whisper.

Rachel clapped her hands once with a silly grin on her face. "I knew it!" she whispered back enthusiastically. "So has he *kissed* you yet?"

"Um, no, not like that. I mean, we're still pretending, you know? And it's only been a week. But, he has, um, quieted my wolf down a few times. But I'm not sure that counts as kissing."

Rachel smiled knowingly. "Interesting," was all she said.

I rolled my eyes. "Although—" I covered my face in mortification. "We went for a run this afternoon...and I definitely bit his butt on accident."

"You what?" she whisper-shrieked. I quickly filled her in on the details. She collapsed over the sink, laughing so hard her breathing came in gasps.

"Come on, we'll miss the movie," I complained. "Besides, if we don't go get to our seats, you won't be able to gawk at Sam and me and help me over-analyze every possible detail later."

I smiled despite myself as I dragged a still-gasping Rachel out of the bathroom and found our theater.

Our group was scattered. Sam and a handful of others were about halfway up and seated in the middle, while I noticed Tammy, Raven, and a few other friends were seated farther down, closer to the front. I smiled and waved at Tammy as I caught her eye on my way up to the seats Sam had saved for us on the end of our row. I took the one next to him, and Rachel plopped next to me on the aisle seat.

"All good?" Sam leaned in and whispered as he took my hand again. Rachel subtly elbowed my arm. I wanted to jab her back, but Wolf was getting worked up again as she noticed Shelby Atwood on the other side of Sam, practically draping herself over the side of the chair and invading Sam's space. My wolf did not like that. At all.

"So nice of you guys to finally join us," Shelby said. "Poor Sam has been sitting here all alone."

Not alone enough, I thought, eyeing her proximity.

Sam was pressing as far back into his chair as he could, attempting to distance himself from Shelby. I found the gesture gratifying. Wolf snapped at Shelby, and my hand tightened on Sam's. Something about her put Wolf on edge. Probably her blatant flirting.

"Shelby, do you want to sit in your own chair, or would you like to come sit in my lap?" Sam asked, sarcasm dripping. My wolf was crouching, ready to pounce. Sam squeezed my hand, and Wolf relaxed a fraction but kept her attention on Shelby.

"Oh, please, Sam. If you wanted me to sit on your lap, you could have said so earlier, while Megan was gone." She batted her eyelashes, returning the sarcasm but with a hint of innuendo of what might have gone on while I had been away.

My teeth clicked shut with an audible snap.

Shelby's eyes narrowed at me as incredulity stamped her face. "Did you just—"

"Oh, shut up, Shelby," Ryan interrupted. "I want to watch the movie." Clearly Ryan didn't care that his date was more interested in another guy.

Shelby huffed and slumped back into her seat. I tried to relax, but Wolf was not having it. I took a deep breath the way Sam had taught me. In through the nose, out through the mouth. Feel the air come in. Feel the air go out.

Shelby assessed Sam. I caught it out of the corner of my eye. She was totally ogling his sweater-clad bicep on the sly. That was the last straw for Wolf. She lunged, and I felt my shoulders ripple softly.

No, no, no, no, NO!

As if in tune with my temperamental wolf, even as I gripped Sam's hand hard enough to break his bones, he was in my space.

His lips softly brushed mine, lingering just long enough to quiet my wolf. Instantly the wolf settled, practically basking in the presence of Sam's lips.

The only problem was that now my wolf was calm, my human side was getting a little friendly. His lips felt so good. I knew he wasn't really kissing me, only kissing me to calm my wolf. But...I *wanted* him to kiss *me*!

Sensing that Wolf was calmed, he slowly broke away. I knew I should let him go. I did not need the complication of liking Sam Wolfe any more than I already did. Daydreaming about his lips was not going to help. At all. I was going to be human again in a few weeks, and all of this wolf business would only be a weird dream.

With that comforting thought I resolved to sit back in my chair and enjoy the movie.

I opened my eyes and saw his lips still in front of me. With no intention to do so, I leaned my head forward three inches and put my lips back on his. We were still for a full second, then his lips moved ever so softly against mine. I didn't dare pull away, even though a thousand different thoughts jammed in my brain. I forced them all away, intent on being rational about this, and then his mouth moved again.

His lips were hesitant but eager. They moved against mine again. He'd never done that while calming the wolf. My lips moved, too.

What was I doing? This was such a huge mistake... My treacherous mouth opened, inviting him in.

He moved slowly. The very tip of his tongue brushed against my bottom lip, and I about melted into the red upholstered seat. Wolf urged me on with an encouraging grunt. I might have made a similar noise because with the barest scrape of his teeth on my bottom lip, his tongue was in my mouth. His lips were soft and wanting, his tongue searching, probing. My lips and tongue were doing things on their own, but Sam must have enjoyed it because he kissed me harder, pushing my head against the back of the seat. His face pressed into mine; his lips moved over mine with single-minded purpose.

Someone cleared their throat, and I froze. Oh—my—word. We were in a movie theater filled with people. Sam must have heard it, too. We jerked apart at the same time, eyes meeting and then darting away. My face flamed hotter than a supernova. I hoped Sam's did, too.

I turned horrified eyes to Rachel, whose mouth was hanging open, her eyebrows raised halfway up her forehead.

"I'm going to grab a drink. You want one? Okay, I'll grab you one," Sam blurted as he bolted from his seat and leaped over our legs. I'd never seen him so flustered. I wasn't sure *I'd* ever been this flustered. I watched his retreating back, stunned. I so knew kissing him would be a mistake of epic proportions.

"Um, so that was *hot*," Rachel said.

I held up my hand. "I have no idea what just happened."

Rachel smirked smugly and turned to watch the movie.

A few rows down at the front, I caught Tammy scowling, her face dark. She turned her back to me. What had I done?

Chapter 31

Sam

I hit the bathroom, turning the water as cold as it would go. I doused my hands, wrists, and splashed my face. I needed cold water on other body parts but didn't think a public restroom was the best place for that.

I closed my eyes and braced my hands on the sink, head bowed.

Unbelievable. There was no other word. My wolf leaped around like a pup. This mate thing was going to be even more of a problem now. Every cell in my body was hyper-aware of her. It was bad enough after I kissed her chastely to quiet her wolf. Now that *she* had kissed *me*?

Her lips were like a drug. And when she'd opened her mouth and my tongue slid in—I groaned. I was hot all over. I took a deep breath. Then another. One more for good measure.

She kissed me. Megan kissed me.

Was it possible she could want more? I tried not to hope, but it was there. It had taken root. My heart was absolutely getting mangled before this was over.

I took one more splash of water to the face and grabbed some paper towels.

There wasn't a line at the snack counter, and I ordered two different soft drinks. I hoped Meg liked one of them. I thought about getting a bucket of popcorn but settled for chocolate instead. I knew Meg loved chocolate.

As I turned to go back into the theater, a strange scent caught my attention. It was *wolf*, but not one of ours. My wolf bristled. It wasn't unheard of for another werewolf to be in town, but as packs, we were pretty territorial. We tried to give other packs either a wide berth or a heads-up that we'd be in the vicinity but meant no offense.

My wolf scented again, solidifying the smell to memory. I'd keep an eye out. I wasn't overly concerned, but Dad wasn't wild about random wolves roaming around.

The theater was dark when I came back in, sodas in hands, chocolate wedged in my back pocket. I got to our aisle and immediately felt the tension radiating off Meg. That couldn't be good. I handed her the drinks and got the box out of my pocket before I sat down.

"Which one?" I whispered, unsure how to proceed. She handed a cup over. I didn't care what it was.

Once drinks were settled, we sat there, an awkward space between us in the dark.

I held my breath and slowly reached my hand out to her. She didn't move as I took her hand. The breath rushed out of me as I felt the tension start to slowly ebb from Meg as she twined our fingers.

Okay. Meg kissed me. I was tempted to try for number two, but her back was still pretty straight. I didn't want to push my luck and definitely wanted a repeat performance at a later date. I squeezed her hand instead.

Her eyes flashed up to mine, a shy smile on her face before she turned back to the movie.

A girl who kissed the way Megan kissed me shouldn't even be capable of looking shy. My mouth tipped into a grin. We were okay for now.

I had no idea what the movie was about by the time the credits were rolling. Meg's hand was still firmly planted in mine. I had allowed myself the liberty of tracing tiny circles on the back and palm of her hand with my thumb during the movie, and honestly, it was all I could concentrate on. I had replayed our kiss fourteen ways from Sunday and was convinced that the memory of her lips was better than anything on the big screen.

We started filing down the stairs to the exit, and I felt Meg's fingers slide through mine. Did she hesitate? Was that reluctance I felt as her fingers left mine?

Tammy caught up with us as we were entering the long hallway back to the main lobby.

"Hey. I rode over here with Jake and Cindy, but they're going out to catch a bite to eat. Can I ride back with you guys? I don't want to be a third wheel, ya know."

I bit back a retort about being a third wheel in my car, too, but swallowed it. "Sure," I said with what I hoped didn't sound like false cheerfulness. So much for a ride back alone with Megan.

Megan and Rachel were chatting ahead of us, and I stepped up and let my fingers graze the small of Megan's back. Her head came up immediately, a light blush staining her cheeks again. She was so beautiful.

"Tammy needs a ride back. Do you mind?" I wasn't sure if it was relief that flashed across her eyes or not, but I hoped it wasn't.

"That's fine. No problem. Rachel, catch you Monday?"

"You bet. Call me tomorrow if you want." Rachel winked. My own skin flushed. I had no doubt that Rachel was insinuating The Kiss that she and all humanity witnessed in the theater.

The ride home was uneventful. Tammy kept most of the conversation going, though she was cold toward Meg a few times. I'd have to ask her about it later. That wasn't like her. Something must be bugging her.

The sun was setting as we pulled into the driveway of the cabin. I glanced over at Megan. "How's the wolf?"

"Tolerable, but she's going to need out soon."

"I bet there will be a few others out back within the next twenty minutes," Tammy offered. "We can all go for a pack run together then?"

"That should be fine," Meg said.

I mentally rolled my eyes as I hopped out of the car. That meant Tammy was going to stick around the cabin until then. Which meant being alone with Megan would have to wait until after the pack run. I needed a good run. My nerves were strung so tight after our kiss that I had pent up energy coming out my ears. I wanted to talk to Meg about the kiss, but at the same time, I wanted to savor it and live in the bliss that maybe, just maybe, she wasn't only pretending?

Gravel crunched outside, and I peeked out the cabin window. Cade and Raven were here along with a few others.

I glanced back to Meg and Tammy. They were chatting about something going on at school. Tammy's shoulders were all scrunched up. She wasn't relaxed like usual. I wondered if maybe she'd had a fight with her mom. They were alike in nearly every way and butted heads frequently.

I opened the door for the new arrivals as they came to the porch.

"Hey!" Raven called out.

Meg smiled back. There was a potential friendship between them. I waved everyone else in but Cade.

He got to the door, and I grabbed his arm, jerking my head back into the darkening night. "Be back in a sec," I called into the room and shut the door without waiting for a reply, dragging Cade with me.

We went a respectable distance from the house so we wouldn't be overheard, but I kept my voice down, in case others were coming on foot for the nightly run. "Cade, she kissed me. She *kissed* me." I hissed the words. My hand fisted into his shirt as I dragged his face closer to mine. "Seriously, I am never going to recover."

Cade laughed. "Dude. That's awesome." I rolled my eyes. "So—it was decent?"

I snorted. "Only mind-blowing. I had no idea a mate bond could be this intense. And we're not even...you know. I mean, she has no idea!"

Footsteps approached then, so further conversation would have to wait.

Cade clapped me on the back. "You may get her after all."

I hoped so, but I wasn't holding my breath.

We ran as a pack that night, Meg beside me. The wind was cold, almost biting. It was glorious. We covered about ten miles, running wild, free, uninhibited. Once we were back at the cabin, people slowly dispersed. I was still antsy. Wolf was still keyed up about the kiss and even the long run in the wild wasn't enough to completely calm him.

Based on how I felt about Megan, the more tired I was, the better. I'd have less energy to act on my desires.

Chapter 32

Megan

"I've still got some energy to get out. I'm going to go for another run. Two legs this time." Sam grinned. "Wanna come?" We were standing right inside the cabin door after the last pack member had gone.

Neither of us had said a word about our kiss that afternoon, and I really wanted some alone time to process it. Besides, I was beat after such an emotional day and then my time as a wolf.

"No, I'm pretty tired. I think I'm going to go grab a shower and then maybe read for a bit." I smiled up at him, so he'd know it wasn't a rejection. Even if I did plan on doing more over-analyzing than reading.

"Okay." He smiled back and touched the small of my back briefly. "I'll probably be about a half hour or so. You okay for that long?"

"Of course. I think even my wolf is worn out after today." I willed myself to keep from blushing.

With another smile he was out the door. I grabbed my pajamas and sports bra and headed to the bathroom. The hot water never felt better than it did beating down on my recently exercised muscles. I was lightly pinked by the time I shut off the water and got out. I had just finished wrapping the towel around my head when there was a knock at the door.

"Just a minute," I called. I grabbed my purple robe from the bed, but then threw it over the back of a chair when Tammy's face peeked through the window.

"Hey, Tammy," I said as I opened the door. She brushed past me into the kitchen. "What's up?"

"Is Sam here?"

"No. He went for another run. Is everything okay?"

She whirled on me, her black hair fanning around her head. "No, everything is *not* okay. Do you plan on staying a wolf?" She bit the words out.

"Um, no," I stammered, taken aback by her question and her attitude.

She ran both her hands through her short hair making the tufts spike up even more. "Then what are you doing kissing him?" she thundered.

I blinked. Was wanting to kiss Sam such a bad thing?

"You're his mate," she continued without a breath as I tried to catch up and process.

Mate?

"Do you have any idea how much you're screwing with his head? Bad enough biting you was an accident—but then to find out you're his *mate*? For life! That's the way *wolves* do things. We aren't fickle like humans. Like *you*. You have been given the ultimate gift, and you're trashing it. But before you reject perfection, you're going to make this a thousand times harder for Sam by kissing him?

"You ungrateful idiot! You keep making the mate bond stronger with no thought of what it's going to do to him when you leave on two legs. It'll be all fine, well, and good for you on your happy little human way, but Sam will never be the same after you leave. For sure, he'll never be able to forget you. You selfish stupid—"

"Did you say *mate*?" I interrupted her, my heart a cold lump in my chest. The fight suddenly left her and her face paled. We were silent for a long minute.

"You really didn't know," she whispered. She was white as a sheet, and I thought she might be sick.

Without another word, she bolted for the door. "Tammy, wait. Come back!" But she was gone.

Mate. The word rolled over and over in my mind. I needed to know exactly what that meant. With my head in a jumble, I put the kettle on and made myself a cup of tea. I was sitting at the table with my hands wrapped around the steaming mug when Sam came back through the door ten minutes later.

He took one look at me, and his muscles tensed. "What's wrong?"

I took a breath and plunged in. "Sam, am I your...mate?"

His face immediately became an unreadable mask. "Why would you ask that?"

"Tammy was here."

His face fell, and he dragged a hand through his sweat-dampened hair. "Yeah. Okay. Let me get a quick shower."

I watched him as he grabbed his stuff and went to the bathroom. Though his movements were quick, he moved stiffly like an old man. I busied myself and made Sam a cup of hot chocolate with a big marshmallow on top the way I knew he liked it.

The shower shut off, and minutes later Sam emerged wearing a light blue T-shirt and his loose-fitting gray pajama bottoms. His hair was darkened by the water and stuck out a little where he'd run the towel over it. Even in a tee and PJ bottoms, he could have been a model on the cover of any number of magazines. Why did he have to be so gorgeous?

He sat in the chair opposite my forgotten mug of tea. He sighed. I put the mug of hot chocolate in front of him, and he grabbed my hand.

"Thanks." His eyes met mine briefly as he released my hand. The chair squeaked as I sat down across from him so we could talk face to face.

"So. I'm your *mate*?" I ventured.

"Yes." The tension in my belly coiled tighter at his admission. I wasn't sure exactly what that meant, but it sounded very permanent, and Sam's reluctance to talk about it made me nervous. Strangely, the wolf inside me was quiet.

Sam took another deep breath and then turned the full force of his blue eyes on me. I bit the inside of my lip. "It's not a bad thing," he started. "It's a good thing. Really. Totally normal, though this sort of mate bond is somewhat rare. It's just a thing I didn't want you to have to deal with on top of everything else. What did Tammy say?"

"Not a lot, actually. I think she thought I knew. Something about being your mate and that kissing you at the theater made things a lot harder for you—a lot worse." Mortified, I felt tears pricking my eyes. "I'm sorry. I, I had no idea. I didn't mean to make anything more difficult."

He reached across the table and gripped both my hands in his. "Meg, none of this is your fault. There's nothing for you to feel guilty about. As for kissing me, you can do that any time you want." He smiled. It was a sad smile, but a smile that reached his eyes. I felt the tension in my belly uncoil a fraction of an inch.

"What exactly does it mean in the wolf world—that I'm your mate? Are you...my mate? How does that work if I stay human? Or if I stay wolf?"

"Well, it's a little complicated with the human-wolf factors, but I'll try to explain everything. Firstly, yes. You are my mate. When I bit you, I felt a little bit of tingling, but when you phased that first time, I *knew* you were my mate." It was a happy memory for him. His smile stretched across his face.

"Why didn't I feel anything? Besides the shift, I mean."

"This is the complicated part. When you phased, you should have felt it, too. But because I was human when I bit you, there's still a chance your body will fight off my toxins. That's the best guess I've got for it. Your wolf probably thinks of me as her mate, but obviously the human part of you doesn't. If you stay human, any of those lingering wolf feelings will fade." His eyes grew sad. "So no. I'm not your mate. If I were, you'd know."

I felt myself blush as I thought about how my wolf responded to Sam. How much she wanted him sometimes. I cleared my throat.

"Tammy said that kissing you made the mate bond stronger, and that it was making things harder for you."

His thumbs rubbed over my knuckles. He still held my hands, and I found myself wanting him to wrap his arms around all of me.

"Tammy has a big mouth, but she was at least partly right. Any physical contact you initiate with me strengthens my bond to you. When you kissed me, the mate bond definitely intensified. Don't look so worried." I was biting my lip again. His expression turned sheepish. "Although that was why I jumped up so fast. I didn't expect...I mean, I knew kissing you would be amazing. Believe me, I've thought a lot about it; I just underestimated how amazing."

My cheeks bloomed with color, and Sam chuckled. "You're not so bad yourself," I mumbled, my face flushing even darker.

"I hear practice makes perfect." He winked. I smiled, embarrassed but flattered, then sobered. "Tammy said I was messing with your head. Leading you on is the last thing I want to do." I bit the inside of my cheek as I remembered how *I* kissed *him* at the theater. "I...we agreed this would only be for show..." I drifted off then cleared my throat. "I mean, I still want to be human." Wolf snorted at me, and I swallowed hard.

He was thoughtful for a minute and let go one of my hands to take a drink of his hot chocolate. "Unless you stay wolf, this is going to suck for me one way or the other. I'm not saying that to make you feel bad. I'm just trying to get it all out there. But I think I'd rather enjoy my time with you, however long or short that might be, and however much you're comfortable with, instead of trying to deny this. What I feel for you. Obviously, you feel at least a little something, too."

We were quiet a minute, staring into each other's eyes—searching.

"What do you feel, Sam?" I whispered.

His answering smile was gentle. "I fell for you a long time before my wolf did."

My mouth made a silent O, but he moved on without waiting for me to respond. I couldn't decide if I was relieved about that or not. I had no idea what I actually felt for Sam Wolfe.

"Do you understand what a mate bond is?" I shook my head. "Wolf pairs—mates—form mate bonds. They're deep and practically unbreakable. Sometimes, they're instant like my connection to you. That kind is somewhat rare and usually pretty celebrated in the wolf world. Sometimes, they're forged over time. Wolves in the wild mate for life, and werewolves do, too. There's the occasional Casanova wolf, which is exactly what it sounds like, and there are those who don't pair off. But among those that pair, they mate for life. That was one of the reasons my dad was so angry with me—aside from the fact that biting you was a major offense—biting you also made you *mine*. Up until the last century, that's how mates staked their claims. With a solid bite.

"Aside from that, I'm the Beta in the pack. It's my job to become Alpha one day. Having a bitten mate with no prior knowledge, no blood ties, or established bloodlines makes things more complicated. A wolf's dominance over other wolves in the pack is determined by the strength of their blood. My biting you also ruined Dad's plan to have me mated off with someone more of his choosing—probably another pack Alpha's daughter to ensure our bloodline stays strong. If you stay human, it's still another complication. I won't ever be able to bond completely with anyone else. I won't ever feel the same about anyone as I feel about you."

"But he's the Alpha. Couldn't he order you to bite me as a wolf and make me part of the pack officially?" I wasn't gunning to be a permanent wolf, but I was curious.

Sam's face got blotchy red spots on it. "He did. Not to bite you again, but to make you stay a wolf."

I took in his red cheeks and felt a curl of unease in the pit of my stomach. "Then why am I still human?"

"Because I refused. I'm Beta." He heaved a sigh. "I told him if he forced me to...keep you a wolf, that I'd defy him and fight him for Alpha right then. It was the only way I knew how to ensure that you still had a choice if the toxins don't change you permanently."

He'd defied his own father for me. And Mr. Wolfe was one scary Alpha. I wasn't sure how I felt about that, but at the moment, I was thankful to still have a chance to be fully human.

"Wouldn't biting me have been so much easier?" I was grateful he hadn't but confused *why* he hadn't. He was silent, and I noticed the tips of his ears getting red. "It wasn't about biting me again, was it?" He shook his head. "Then what?"

"Sex, Megan."

My eyes bugged out of their sockets. "I beg your pardon?"

"Once a pair mates—literally—the bond is solidified in every possible way. If we were to sleep together before waiting for the next full moon, it would ensure that you stayed a wolf. My dad thought that was the best possible outcome. He wanted me to seduce you and make myself irresistible to you." He ran his hand over his hair again. "But you are not the sort of girl that is easily seduced or who crawls into bed with every guy you date. And I'm not that guy." His gaze fell to the table, not meeting my eyes. "I...it means something in the wolf world. That's something you only share with your mate. It's not something you do to manipulate a person. Anyway, I don't exactly have experience seducing women."

I wasn't sure what to say to that. He certainly kissed like he had plenty of experience.

"Are you a virgin?" The words erupted from my mouth before I could stop them. Red flooded my cheeks. His head came up, and he nodded slowly. A tendril of heat slid through me. Something else unexpected that Sam and I had in common. I felt a smile tip the corner of my mouth. For whatever reason, that knowledge made me glad. Most guys I knew were all about getting into bed with anything that had boobs and a pulse.

"Are you?"

I nodded back, and he let out a relieved breath. "That's hot."

Wolf puffed out her chest. "I was raised by grandparents from a different era. I always wanted to be like my grandma, saving that for my wedding night." I blushed darker, confessing all this to Sam. Neither one of us knew what to say after that. There was an awkward pause where we both consulted the mugs in front of us. My wheels were turning, and I snagged on one piece of information. My mug thumped down onto the table as the information took root.

"That's why your dad insisted on this marriage agreement, isn't it? It's not necessarily a wolf-human thing, or a safety issue, it's because he wanted us to have sex." I was still working through the details, anger, confusion, and growing clarity steaming through me like a kettle working up to a boil.

"Yeah." His hand ruffled over his hair again.

"But why force us into marriage? People have unmarried sex all the time. Not that I plan to, but still."

"I'm eighteen," he said simply. It dawned fully on me then.

"I'm seventeen. I'm not legal."

"You nailed it. Dad the Alpha lawyer. He likes everything neat and tidy. In our great state of Delaware, I could be sent to jail for statutory rape if we slept together. If for whatever reason we did—" He cleared his throat. "—and something went wrong or whatever, this way Dad has legal grounds to protect me and by proxy, the rest of the pack." His cheeks reddened. "It keeps the pack safe from outside scrutiny."

"And Grandpa knew. He had to sign off on everything because I'm still a minor, and he's my legal guardian. That little toad!"

"Easy. Yes, he and Rev talked it over a long time that first night while you were asleep. But I wouldn't be too hard on him. It was a hard decision for him to make. In the end, he only did it for your safety, and because, as you said, he's from a different era and our current living arrangements aren't something he'd approve of without our being married. If something did happen to him before the next full moon, you'd be legally bound to the pack—to me—and he knew that we would take care of you no matter what."

I harrumphed, thoroughly irritated with Grandpa for having done this behind my back. I took a long drink of my now-cool tea and huffed a breath out through my nose. "I'm glad you told me, Sam."

He nodded and a piece of his damp blond hair flopped across his forehead. "Me, too. But where does this leave us?"

"I don't know. I...I still want to stay human. Is pretending to date going to work? I don't want to make this more difficult for you than it already is."

He snorted. "I think that ship has sailed. If I were a regular guy without fangs and fur, would you date me?"

"Yes," I answered without hesitation. Seriously. I might even consider dating him knowing he was a werewolf.

"If we were two regular people dating, which, for all intents and purposes, we are, if you're still okay with it, would you kiss me?" I nodded, a smile tugging at one corner of my mouth despite myself. "You could prove it," he said with a wink. He tugged my hand. I got up and stood in front of him. He pulled me down onto his lap, and I squeaked in surprise. He'd never been so forward. His hands draped my waist loosely. Unsure what to do with my hands, I laid them across his shoulders, our faces only a few inches apart.

"Really, Meg. I don't want you to walk on pins and needles around me. I think that would be worse than avoiding you altogether." His brow creased, his blue eyes deep and intense, mouth turned down at the corners.

I let my eyes rove over his face. His expression changed, watching me as I raked my gaze over his features. His thumb rubbed once against the soft cotton covering my bottom rib, my skin practically igniting beneath my tank top. I knew he needed my reassurance, wanted it tangibly. I wasn't sure what I was willing to give, but I wanted him to know that he meant something to me, even if I didn't know what that was yet.

"Okay," I whispered. Slowly and carefully I lowered my face and grazed my lips across his. His arms tightened around my waist, and his chest heaved as I pulled my head back.

"Okay," he whispered back. "Meg, is it all right if I kiss you every so often? You know, not just to calm your wolf? Like, we actually are sort of dating?"

I smiled and nodded, my finger absently twirling a piece of his damp hair. The thought of Sam Wolfe wanting to kiss me made my stomach twist with anticipation. Wolf was dancing around like she was doing the cha-cha. I ignored the rational part of my brain that told me this was not a good idea.

He closed his eyes. "Meg, if you keep playing with my hair like that, I'm going to kiss you a lot sooner, rather than later."

I giggled—actually giggled—and wiggled off his lap. "We should go to bed." Once the words were out, I couldn't take them back. I peeked at Sam, smirk on his face. "You know what I mean," I stammered as my cheeks heated again.

My fingers grappled with the mugs as I snatched them from the table and took them to the sink, my face flaming. I had just set them in the sink when Sam's hands slid around my waist, turning me to face him. My stomach dropped to my toes and butterflies swarmed in my gut. Wolf let out a contented sigh. Sam's hands were warm through the thin knit of my pink tank top. No guy had ever affected me the way Sam was now.

"Meg." His voice was low. A deep rumble from his chest. My hands rested on his forearms, wanting to walk up his biceps and slide down his chest. *What?* I blinked and focused on what Sam was saying.

"Was it you or your wolf that kissed me at the theater today?"

His gaze held mine, uncertainty, desire, and curiosity flashing across his face. This was Sam. The real Sam. Not that he hadn't been real before, but tonight he'd made himself vulnerable to me. He'd leveled. And the look he was giving me now pulled at my heart, and I felt another little piece break off. Was it possible that I could be falling in love with Sam?

"It was me." The words came out soft like a warm breeze on a spring evening. He closed his eyes and his face relaxed. Without opening his eyes, he spoke.

"Meg, unless you stop me, I'm going to kiss you right now."

His eyes opened, searching my face. I didn't move, my lungs freezing.

He brought his hands up slowly and cupped my face, his lips brushing mine lightly, again with more pressure, still light, but more deliberate. The third time his lips came down I moved into him, my hands sliding up his arms as I leaned my face up, wanting more. My brain piped up that this was not a wise thing to be doing if I wanted to remain human, but I shoved the rational side of myself back down, intent on enjoying this moment.

One of Sam's hands slid back into my hair; the other trailed down my back to rest at my waist, pulling me closer. His lips. *His lips!*

It wasn't a fiery kiss of passion. It wasn't so urgent as the one at the theater. It was long and slow and deep and...intimate. I'd been kissed enough to know when a guy was kissing for his own pleasure. And I knew Sam was enjoying this, but it was more than that. This kiss was about me. The way his lips moved, the way he cradled my body against him. It was all about making me feel...loved.

I stopped thinking and let my body mold itself to the hard planes of Sam's chest, my hands wrapping around his sides. It was as if his lips were trying to speak to my very soul. Maybe they were.

For long minutes, we stood there in the kitchen kissing. It could have been an hour. I wasn't sure. There was no pressure to do more, no urgency to kiss as much territory as possible, no wandering hands.

It was the most intimate moment of my life. If I had been unsure of Sam's emotions earlier in the evening, any doubts were soundly laid to rest. Heat curled in my belly. Sam loved me. Without question.

Sam pulled back first and leaned his head against mine, his eyes closed. "Good night, Megan."

I tiptoed up and kissed his cheek. "Good night, Sam."

He smiled at me, and for the first time since this whole ordeal began, Sam's blue eyes shone.

It was rainy and overcast Monday morning. I was dying to talk to Rachel, to get my emotional bearings, using Rachel as my ever-present sounding board. There wasn't a good way to do that on the phone when the object of the conversation was always within hearing distance. However, the rest of the weekend had been more relaxed. I'd baked, and we hadn't kissed again except for a quick good-night kiss Sam had placed on my cheek last night. He was more open with me. His smile came quicker;

his touch did, too. He wasn't demanding, and he wasn't pushy, but he was consistent.

It was drizzling when we reached the school parking lot.

"I'll drop you off at the door so you don't get wet."

"Thanks," I said, genuinely pleased. I flashed him a quick smile and made to open the door. "I need to talk to Rachel. Is it okay if I catch you between classes?" I was confident enough with my wolf not to require Sam's presence every second.

He raised a blond eyebrow. "Sure. Hope it's something juicy." His lips curved into a devilish smile. My face heated and I jerked the door open, making a mad dash for the school.

Rachel was by our lockers, stuffing her English book into her backpack. "Hey, Meggie!" she chirped, wagging her eyebrows at me. Rachel was always a morning person.

"Hey back. Time to spill." I cut right to the chase. We only had about fifteen minutes before the bell would ring for first period.

"Absolutely! Library?"

I nodded, and we took off at a decent pace. "So...repeat of the theater? I need details," Rachel prompted as we neared the door.

I grabbed her hand and carefully checked the aisles as I dragged her to the far back corner. No one ever bothered to check out the reference books that weighed as much as the quarterback of our football team. Things were dusty and undisturbed back here but right next to a large window. If there hadn't been a window to the outside here, it would have been the perfect spot for making out at school. As it was, it made this an ideal spot for a private conversation.

"Beyond that. There has been a major development. Apparently, I'm Sam's *mate*."

Her eyebrows shot up her forehead like they were on fire. I quickly filled her in on the basics of the conversation. And about the kiss.

"I swear, I've never been kissed like that before. Ever. It was like...defining. Only, I'm not sure what it defined. I can tell Sam likes me. In fact, I'm pretty sure he loves me," I admitted as I bit my lip. "I think there's credence to this mate thing. It all sounds far-fetched, but I believe him." I groaned in frustration. "But I want to stay human. I can't be a wolf forever. That would be a disaster of epic proportions. I'm not even good at being a wolf. And we want to start a baking business. Go to college. I want to travel. I want to go home with Grandpa. I...I don't know how to be a wolf and still be *me*. It feels like I'd have my entire future ripped away. And not to be totally selfish, but I have dreams. None of them involve fur and three-inch canines. But...that means giving up Sam. And he's sort of grown on me," I admitted.

"Wow. That's a lot to take in. At least this way, it's out in the open. And you know how he feels. Which is totally awesome, by the way, and even better that he's an amazing kisser. So the big question is, how do you feel about Sam?"

"I have no idea. That's what you're supposed to help me figure out."

She sympathetically patted my arm. "We'll figure it out. You'll figure it out. And no matter what, you'll always have me." She gave me a cheeky grin.

"Tell me you did not entertain the thought of me staying wolf."

Rachel winked. "Come on. We'll be late." The warning bell rang in confirmation. "We can continue this after school. I'll come to the cabin, and we can do more baking. We have ground to cover for HarvestFest. Maybe we can send Sam out for more flour or something." I smiled at her as we scooted to first period.

I had trouble focusing on my schoolwork. My thoughts kept straying back to staying human, now that I knew how Sam felt. Did that make a difference in my desire to stay in skin? Should it make a difference? I honestly felt more confused than anything. Wolf didn't help. Anytime I thought about Sam, she pushed up feelings and thoughts that were best left in the dark recesses of my mind if I wanted to survive this without a permanent side of dog breath.

Fourth period came, and Sam was waiting for me, gorgeous and muscled as ever, leaning against the wall in his green flannel shirt, sleeves rolled up to his forearms. It made his eyes stand out even more and they twinkled at me as I approached.

"Get things squared away with Rachel?" he asked casually.

"Not remotely." I grimaced.

"Hey, it can't be all that bad. Can it?" A note of uncertainty crept in.

"No, no," I quickly reassured him. "I'm stuck in my own head. If that makes any sense."

"Not a lot." He bent down. "But I'd be happy to distract you." His breath tickled my ear and sent Wolf scampering around. I felt myself blush even as a grin threatened the corner of my mouth.

"You're impossible," I whispered back, trying not to enjoy his flirting so much.

"You're tempting," he retorted. His hand grazed the small of my back, ushering me into the classroom and toward our seats.

I caught a few looks as we came in together, obviously *together*. Apparently, we weren't old news yet. Or maybe we appeared *more* together now. After all, we had kissed in a pretty major sort of way in front of half the student body at the movie theater, and we were on a much deeper level of communication now. Did that show in our body language? I knew I felt a lot more connected to Sam on some level, but that made part of me want to pull away. Not to get too close—when all the other part of me wanted to do was throw myself back into his arms. I was a mess.

Chapter 33

Sam

Meg was definitely distracted. I hoped that was a good thing—like maybe she was thinking about me. I had no idea. Trying to figure out the workings of Meg's female brain was more than I had the energy for today. I got my notebook out and tried to take notes. Meg was doodling more than usual, still jotting down things here and there with her pink pen—she color-coded all her classes by ink color—but doodling little vines and hearts and scrolly loopy things. I nudged her knee under the table. She glanced up, and I winked at her. She rolled her eyes even as she grinned and turned back to her notes, vines momentarily forgotten.

Fifth period rolled around, and I walked with her to her next class on the way to mine. She didn't object when I loosely grabbed her hand, so I went a step further and twined our fingers. She smiled up at me shyly. So far, the not-really-but-maybe-we-are-sort-of-dating thing was going well.

Noise pressed in all around us, and the smells from the cafeteria—lingering eggs from breakfast and could-use-a-few-more-minutes-in-the-oven casserole for lunch, body spray, body odor, pencil lead, and old textbooks—were stronger than normal.

My legs rooted to the ground as one scent suddenly stood out from all the rest. My body jerked to attention, and each of my senses homed in on that smell.

"Sam?" Meg asked, and then her head whipped around, too.

It was wolf. The same wolf I'd smelled at the theater. I didn't know this wolf. It made me uneasy. My hackles raised.

"I smell it, but it's faint. There's too much other stuff." She tugged my sleeve as I glanced around, taking in all of the surroundings and other students milling around. I didn't see anyone I didn't know on sight, and the scent wasn't completely fresh but not more than a few hours old.

Meg tugged my hand and traffic resumed where we'd been standing. We were outside her science classroom. "Do you know them?"

"No. I don't. And that's what worries me. I don't like it. I smelled the same one at the theater when I left to go get sodas."

A tiny frown appeared between her eyebrows.

"It's strange for one to be coming through like this and not announce themselves, right?"

"Yes. We make a point to let *residents* know if we'll be in the area." I put my hand to the small of her back again, ushering her toward the classroom.

"Keep your eyes open. Wait for me after class. I'll walk you to lunch." I couldn't help that my eyes trained to her lips. "Be careful," I said quietly instead.

"I will. You, too." She squeezed my arm and went into science.

Another quick scan didn't show me anything out of the ordinary. My senses were on high alert on the way to Humanities.

I was hyper-aware of everything but my classes for the rest of the afternoon. Lunch passed peaceably. We sat together at our normal table, ate bland rice and chicken casserole, and I scanned the room about once a minute. I caught Cade between classes and quietly told him to keep a nose out but not to alarm anyone else yet.

I hadn't gotten a chance over the weekend to talk to Dad about the strange wolf scent at the theater, either. I had meant to fill him in but had been distracted by other things, namely Megan's lips. I resolved to tell him that evening. It was one thing to get a random whiff at the theater. It was another to find that the wolf had been to the school as well.

Finally, the bell rang at the end of seventh period. I had homework, thanks to my distractedness that afternoon. Meg was waiting by my locker, which brightened my mood considerably.

"Hey." She smiled.

"Hey back."

"Find out anything else?" She referenced the new wolf. "You were pretty distracted today at lunch. Are you worried?"

I shoved three textbooks into my bag and zipped it up as I replied. "Yeah. It's unusual enough in and of itself, but I don't like that whoever it is has been here at school, too. That makes it more than a coincidence. I need to make sure I tell Dad about it tonight. You ready to go?" I hitched the straps of my backpack over my biceps to my shoulders and reached for her hand.

"Yep. Rachel is planning on coming over to the cabin tonight. I forgot to mention earlier. We were hoping to get some baking and prepping done. We've got tons to do. HarvestFest is this weekend."

"Sure, that's no problem. I've got homework anyway, so I'll be out of your way."

"Sam," someone called down the hallway as we were just leaving the doorway to the freedom of the parking lot. I glanced back where Jake was jogging down the hall.

"Go ahead," Meg said. "I'll wait by the car." She smiled. "He looks concerned and probably doesn't want me listening in."

Jake did appear concerned. His brows were furrowed, his hands clenched into fists as he closed the distance between us.

"Okay," I conceded. "Be there in a minute."

"Sounds good." She flashed another smile, and I desperately wanted to give her butt a quick squeeze as she turned around but knew that would result in my untimely death, so I shoved my hands in my pockets and turned my attention to Jake.

"Jake, what's up?" My nose wrinkled as I sniffed something *foreign* on him.

Jake glanced around, his longish brown hair flipping around as he confirmed that no one else was in the immediate vicinity. A few girls chatted down the hallway and a few lockers shut further down. We were alone enough for Jake's comfort.

"Sam, we've got a serious issue." He had my full attention. "There's a new kid at school."

"Is that what I smell? Where's he from—I've never smelled anything like it."

"I know, sorry." Jake grimaced. It wasn't a bad scent, just something outside my range of sensory knowledge.

"It's fine. Just new. So why are we concerned about the new kid?"

"He's one of us. But not."

My eyes narrowed. "He's what?"

"He's a half-breed," Jake whispered, his voice barely audible.

My mind froze on that last phrase, but I didn't have time to process because there was a loud *screech* from the parking lot. "Megan!"

Chapter 34

Megan

I walked out into the cold afternoon sunshine, reveling in the slight heat on my face after being cooped up indoors. I was ready to be back at the cabin and up to my elbows in flour. Baking was such therapeutic stress relief. I selfishly hoped whatever Jake needed didn't take too long.

Picking my way across the black top, I kicked a little pebble with the toe of my leopard ballet flats, thinking again of the thoughtful gesture the shoes represented as I watched the rock skid away. It stopped about ten feet in front of a black sedan. I didn't have time to process anything else because, at that moment, the sedan roared to life and charged across the pavement straight for me.

Time stopped and sped up at the same time. Wolf took over without my permission, jerking me to the side and coiling my muscles as the car careened mere feet in front of me. I landed in a crouch and sprang from the ground to land behind the flagpole, embedded in a thick border wall of concrete. Fur rippled softly under my sweater, but I willed my bones to stay as they were as the black mass of metal screamed over the remaining feet between us.

The whine of metal on concrete set my teeth on edge and the fur poking through my arms stood on end. The car swerved at the last second and scraped a path of destruction down its shiny sleek side as it mashed up against the concrete wall I hid behind.

There was no question. That car had intended to hit me.

"Megan!" I kept my head down as exhaust fumes choked the air and the snarl of the engine shrieked out of the parking lot and down the street. My head came up, eyes dilated and more wolf than human, and only barely visualized Sam's face in front of me before he swooped strong arms around me and hauled me to his chest. My head was muffled against him, and I think he cursed before releasing me enough that my eyes could focus on him.

His face was wild and frantic. His heartbeat throbbed in the vein of his neck. His hands ran over my shoulders and down my arms, checking for injury. "Are you hurt? I should have been with you. Are you all right? Megan?" His words tumbled over themselves as his own eyes dilated dangerously large. I'd never seen him remotely out of control until now, his eyes belaying his bare emotions.

"I, I'm not hurt," I stammered, my knees shaking, Wolf still on high alert, simmering below my skin but contained for the moment now that Sam was here. I gripped his arms and stood up on my own but leaned on him. My brain was trying to catch up to what had just happened—and nearly happened—to me.

Sam pulled me to him again, kissing the side of my head, his chest going up and down like he'd sprinted the four-hundred-meter dash.

"What happened?" he murmured, his breathing starting to slow.

Jake loped up to us again before I could respond. "I'm sorry, Sam. No plates. I went as fast after them as I could on two legs. But there was a little scent, mostly exhaust though."

"Good." Sam stared hard at Jake while Jake's head cocked to the side. "Thanks. Got it."

"Want me to drop by to fill you in more on the new guy tonight?" Jake asked.

"Yeah. Let me text you first though. I need to talk to Dad." A shudder rippled through him as an expression that could have been fear flashed across his face and then disappeared.

Jake nodded and we parted ways, Sam carefully scanned the parking lot and surrounding area as he opened the car door for me.

Once he was in the driver's seat, he just sat there a minute, both hands gripping the steering wheel. His knuckles were white.

"Sam?" I asked tentatively.

He turned the full force of his blue eyes on me, and I felt my heart trip up a little at their intensity. "Are you sure you're okay?" he whispered.

I nodded. "Yeah. A little shaken up, but I'm fine. I'm not hurt."

He dragged both hands through this hair, clearly still distressed. I reached over and took his right hand in both of mine.

"I'm okay. You're okay. We're both okay," I murmured. He was starting to scare me a little bit.

"Sorry. I haven't been this close to letting the wolf out in public since Tyler Smith tried to pick a fight with me in sixth grade." He swallowed hard before glancing at me again. "Do you want to call the police?"

"Do you think we should?" I wasn't sure what the police could do at this point. I had no real proof. No license plate number, nothing other than that a black sedan tried to run me down in the parking lot.

"Normally, we'd already be on the way there. But since it was definitely a wolf driving, it might be better to handle this within the pack."

"What was Jake doing—when you asked about the scent?"

"We were using my Beta link. He sent me the scent information. It's kind of like sending me the memory of a memory. It's weaker than the real thing but still helpful."

"Can all wolves do that?"

"Only the Betas and Alphas have that sort of mental link with their pack members. Pack members can't send mental messages to each other—only the Alpha and the Beta can do that. Sometimes mates form similar links and can share basic thoughts or feelings if they concentrate hard enough and practice enough over time. Remember the day after you changed when Rachel was over? Like that—we tend to use it more, and better, than most," he finished.

"I didn't realize we used it more. But that first time you just heard my thoughts. Is that what you mean?"

He nodded. "Partly. The link allows pack members to send information to their leaders, and we can do the same, but there's—I guess you could call it a *command* feature that goes with it. Though it's rarely done, and there are rules prohibiting it. The chain of command allows the Alpha or the Beta to issue commands that a pack member is bound to follow. Technically, any wolf can command another wolf, so long as the wolf doing the commanding is more alpha than the other. Does that make sense?"

"I think so," I said, trying to wrap my brain around this new phenomenon.

"Nobody besides the Beta or the Alpha ever uses it. It's against one of our wolf laws, and we use it so infrequently that it's almost legendary when we do. When things were wilder and packs were more savage, it was helpful in controlling the pack as a whole. We like to think we're all more civilized now. Anyway, Betas and Alphas still have a link that lets them transfer information or commands to the rest of their pack. Pack members can send information to us if we're close enough to each other as well."

"Okay. I think my brain is officially overloaded. What a day. Right now, all I want to do is go bake things. Lots of things."

"I hope I get to sample?" He tried to crack a smile, but the strain lingered in his eyes.

"Of course."

Rachel beat us to the cabin, all excited to dive in and get started. She was bouncing on the balls of her feet, leaning against her car with a big box of supplies waiting at her feet. I wasn't kidding when I told Sam we had tons to do. The festival was mere days away and going wolf over the past weekend and then skipping for movies Saturday cut into our usual prep time.

"Sam, would you mind letting us work, just the two of us for a while? I hate to run you out of your space, but I'd really like to talk to her...you know...about girl stuff for a bit."

His jaw muscle clenched as he stared out the windshield and turned the car off. "No, I don't mind at all. But I'm not comfortable leaving you unprotected after this afternoon."

I frowned. I needed some time to process what happened this afternoon and have a good conversation about Sam with Rachel, without Sam in the room.

"What if I have an extra patrol run while the two of you guys are in there?"

I bit my lip. "I hate to inconvenience anyone. Besides, any new wolf will clearly know they're on someone else's land the minute they get within whiffing distance."

"Seriously. No worries. Several people owe me favors." He winked. "I need to talk to Dad anyway, so this is as good a time as any for me to let you ladies have the cabin. But I'm not okay leaving the two of you up here alone."

"Fine. But you make sure you tell any patrols to stay clear enough of the cabin that they won't overhear anything."

He grinned. "Deal. Let's get you inside so there are hot cookies when I get back."

I chuckled. "Good to know your real motives."

After Sam had called in patrols and left the cabin, we made short work of the supplies Rachel brought out, and together with what we already had at the cabin, we had enough to keep us busy for days. I laid out the small bowls for different colored frostings and filled Rachel in on the afternoon's events.

"Are you kidding?" Rachel gasped. She did a quick scan over me as she nearly dropped the pound of butter in her hands. "You're okay? You're not hurt? Did you notice anything identifiable about the scumbag?"

"Unfortunately, not. Jake ran after them, but short of shifting, he couldn't keep up long enough to catch anything useful off the car. But he did catch a sort of scent. I'm not sure how reliable it will be, mixed with exhaust fumes, but it's more than I caught. I think the adrenaline overrode everything else. In my mind is a figure wearing a black ski mask behind the wheel of a black sedan, screaming down the parking lot and trying to mash me into the pavement." I shuddered at the memory.

She put the butter on the counter and came to grab me up in a quick, fierce hug. "I'm glad you're okay. Going wolf is enough excitement for this semester. Let's leave the hit and runs for another day."

I squeeze her extra tight. "Fine by me."

"Speaking of going wolf, now that we're alone, tell me how things are really going. Catch me up to speed. These little snatches at school are just enough to keep me salivating for more." She winked and turned back to her electric mixer to put in the butter to cream with the sugar.

"Where do you want me to start?"

"Tell me more about this mate business."

"Good call." I proceeded to fill her in on all the details I had on how the mate bond worked.

"So he's head-over-heels smitten and honestly can't help himself, and you're..." She let the sentence dangle once I finished my rundown.

"I don't know. I totally have a crush on him—I mean, not only is he gorgeous and an amazing kisser, but he's the real deal. He's kind. He's thoughtful. He's respectful. He's dependable. Grandpa likes him." I snorted. "I think Grandpa wants to adopt him."

"Ha, well, technically, Sam is already Grandpa's grandson-in-law." She shot me a sly grin.

"Shut it, you little turd. And pass me that cocoa powder, would you?" She passed the jar over and waited for me to continue. "The intensity of this mate-bond thing scares me a little. In some ways, it puts this extra added pressure on me—which, I get why Sam didn't tell me about it at first, because I do feel added pressure now. I still want to stay human. But now that I know more about the mate bond, I don't want to leave Sam hurting like he will when I leave." Sadness pooled in my stomach, and my mouth turned down as my brows drew together.

Rachel's face held a deep, unreadable expression. "Say it," I prompted.

"What happens if you stay wolf?"

"I don't know. And I'm too afraid to ask."

"Do you want to talk about it more now?" she asked gently.

I sighed into the bowl of flour and cocoa I was sifting. Thinking about staying human but leaving a gaping wound in Sam's heart twisted up my insides like a washrag wrung up tight to get the last drops of water out. I wasn't sure Sam was the only one who would leave with a gaping hole. "No. Not really. The whole thing makes me uncomfortable. I don't know what I think about any of it. Everything is so jumbled in my head that nothing makes sense when I try to sort through it all."

"You've been through an incredibly traumatic event. You've only been a werewolf for barely over a week. Give things time to settle into place. Things will probably start to resolve, and then you'll wake up fully human again, and this will all be behind you."

"I suppose so. That's the wish, I guess."

"You guess?" She raised an auburn eyebrow at me as a grin hid in the corner of her mouth.

"Rachel," I droned.

"So enough of this heavy stuff. Tell me more about this amazing, defining kiss. You've been kissed a lot more than me. Girl's gotta get pointers, you know." She flashed her perfectly straight teeth at me, and I couldn't help myself from laughing.

"Come on, you've been kissed."

"Not as much as you, and clearly, I've been kissing the wrong guys, since I've never had *a moment* like you and Sam."

"It was..." I floundered for the right words as I started to mold little balls of double-chocolate-chunk cookie dough. "I don't know. He was kissing me because he wanted me to feel loved. It wasn't because he was getting anything out of it—I mean, he was, but that wasn't the purpose of the kiss. Like, I've never experienced anything remotely that intimate with a guy before. This was a whole new ball game. I didn't know kissing like that actually existed outside rom-coms."

"So different than the movie theater then?"

I felt my face heat, and not from the preheated oven in front of me. I groaned. "I can't decide if that whole thing was more embarrassing or more phenomenal."

"How about it's a bit of both, and you leave it at that." She smiled as she dumped her dough onto waxed paper to roll out. "Although, like I said at the theater, it looked pretty hot to me."

I groaned again. "It was." Rachel laughed.

Just then, a knock sounded at the door. We looked at each other, and I dusted off my hands on my apron and opened the door, surprised to find Raven standing on the stoop.

"Hey, Raven." I motioned her inside.

"Hey." She smiled back.

"What's up?"

She crossed her ankles and clasped her hands in front of her. "Well, I hope this isn't rude, but I actually have a favor to ask you guys."

I lifted my eyebrows. "If anything, I owe you the favor after you did major grocery shopping for me last week."

"Oh, that was no big deal." She waved her hand in the air in a dismissing gesture. "I actually need some volunteer hours for my résumé."

"Aren't you a junior this year?" Rachel asked as she floured her rolling pin.

"Yeah, but there's this graphic arts program that I'd love to start this summer if I get in. They love volunteer service. I do a lot of different stuff with my dad's construction company and that sort of thing but nothing really artsy. Since it's graphic design, I was hoping to have some sort of art-related volunteering on my résumé." She bit her lip. "Would it be too much to ask to maybe decorate a few cookies? If you don't like the way they turn out, that's fine. I won't be offended, and we'll leave it at that. Cade said Sam mentioned you guys were doing all kinds of stuff for the HarvestFest, and that you guys own your own LLC.?"

I glanced at Rachel who nodded enthusiastically. "We do. And actually, that would be great, if you know how to ice cookies. We're way behind, and that's one of the most time-consuming parts."

"Here," Rachel said, putting down her rolling pin and grabbing a few of the little pots of colored icing I'd made up. She put them down on the extra fold-up table we'd put out and pulled up a chair. "I've got some leaf shaped cookies that are about completely cooled. You want to take a stab at a few of them, see what you come up with? We usually try to do fall colors and a wide array of them, so they're nice and creative. They don't need to be uniform, either."

"Ooh, that sounds great. I can do uniform, too, if you have anything like that. My mom and I like to do iced sugar cookies together. Although, I confess, I only do the decorating. Mom always does the baking part." She gave a nervous chuckle. "I won't volunteer for any of the baking."

I smiled back at her. If she was a decent icer, this would be a massive time-saver. Plus, she probably had some insider information on Sam, if I could figure out how to bring it up so I didn't give away that my being a werewolf was accidental.

Raven set to work once she had all the colored icing and the icing bags, tips, and a few knives.

"So Raven, I don't know you that well. What sort of things are you into?" Rachel broke the ice as we all went back to our tasks.

"Oh, well, I do like graphic design. I like a lot of different artsy sort of things. I draw—paint sometimes."

"Really? Ever consider painting some drama sets? We're always looking for talent." Rachel grinned.

"I hadn't actually thought about that. I'm just starting cheerleading now, but maybe for the spring play? That would probably be good on the résumé, too." Her eyes twinkled. "I did tumbling and gymnastics when I was young. My best friend—well, my best human friend—" She stopped, her eyebrows drawing together. "I hope that's not offensive?"

Rachel laughed, and I smiled. "Rachel is pretty entrenched in the paranormal. And it's hard to offend her."

Raven nodded in relief. "Anyway, Aria convinced me to try out for cheerleading this year. There was another girl on the squad, but she moved right before the season started. Skylar—the team captain—is a little hard to please, but Aria thought I'd be a good fit with my background. It's been fun so far. I like that I'll be getting to go to all Cade's games."

"Yeah, Cade has played basketball forever, hasn't he?" I commented. He was the point guard for our school, and he was good. "Didn't I hear something about scouts coming to games this year?"

"That's what Coach Watson told the team. He said there would be potential opportunities for scholarships and playing some college ball. Cade is pumped about it."

"Wow. I mean, *wow*. Meg, look at what this girl can do."

I popped over to where Rachel was looking over Raven's shoulder and felt my eyes widen in surprise as I took in the cookie she'd decorated. It looked like an honest-to-goodness leaf. She had blended the colors in a way that was beyond my skill. She'd taken the slightest hint of gold dust and run it up the veins of the leaf where it reached out to touch the beautiful orange, yellow, and hints of crimson.

"Raven, forget volunteering. We'll *hire* you," Rachel exclaimed.

Raven laughed. "I'm glad you like it, but really, I need the volunteer hours."

Chapter 35

Sam

I smelled Mom's chili on the stove before I opened the door to the house. I sighed, thinking about Meg fixing dinner for us. She was a great cook. Mom was, too, but there was something about having the girl you loved cook for you. I shook my head. That wasn't why I was here. Someone had tried to kill my girl today, and I needed to know why.

"Hi, Mom," I said as the door creaked open.

"Samuel?" Mom's face broke into a huge grin. She hugged me tightly. "How are things?" She gave me a motherly look, wanting to know how things were *really* going.

"Um, they're okay. I'm not sure which way things are going to go down yet."

Her smile fell a little. "Let me know if there's anything at all I can do to help." She squeezed my shoulder, and I nodded.

"Thanks. Is Dad home? I actually need to run a few things by him."

"He's out in the garage. Do you want to go meet him out there? I think he's working on one of his cars." My dad liked to fix up old junkers in the little spare time he had.

"That's fine. Catch you later, Mom."

She smiled as she went back into the kitchen, and I went to the door leading to the garage. Oil and grease were two scents I always associated with my father. That, and paper. As a lawyer, my dad was always carrying around some sort of legal document, and when I was little, I remember he smelled like paper. As I got older, he spent more time working on his cars, and the odors of fixing up old cars became a part of his smell, too. He'd taught me the basics, but it wasn't something I really liked, so we hadn't done much of it together in the past few years.

I took a breath before opening the door. I wasn't sure what kind of terms Dad and I were on at the moment. I knew he still wasn't happy about the possibility of Meg not staying a wolf, especially since I refused to keep her a wolf myself. Not that I wouldn't love to. My ears heated at the thought. But this was pack business. He was always more rational when it came to my acting as his Beta, rather than his son. Some emotion I couldn't quite identify twinged in my middle, but I shoved the uncomfortable sensation away and opened the door.

"Dad?"

"I'm over here, Samuel," Dad called, his head stuck underneath a beat-up piece of machinery that was once probably a nice car. "Hand me that Phillips?"

I squatted down and passed over the screwdriver. A minute more and my dad slid out and sat up. "What brings you here?"

"A few things, actually. I meant to mention this earlier, but things were, uh, progressing with Meg, and I got distracted."

Dad's mouth tightened, even as his eyes brightened. He nodded for me to continue. "Progressing well?"

"Um, better than they were?" Dad grunted. "I scented a wolf at the theater on Saturday—not one of ours, and not one I've scented before. And then, today at school, I caught the same scent." Dad's brows darkened. "I assume no one has told you they're passing through?"

"No. They haven't." His lips thinned into a tighter line.

"Today, after school, another wolf tried to run Megan down in a black sedan." My chest hurt just saying it aloud. I could still feel the rattle of my heart as I ran out and saw the car racing away.

My dad paused a beat too long, and it sent concern tripping up my spine. He squinted. "You sure about that?"

"Yes. I'm sure." Why would he question me about that? Didn't he think I knew when my own mate was in mortal danger?

"An odd coincidence." He frowned. "Why Megan? You know, if you'd go ahead and get the job done, she'd be better able to protect herself."

I tried not to squirm under his baleful gaze. "I will not take that choice from her. Although, she does know what staying wolf entails now."

Dad harrumphed. "I'll look into things." He scratched his chin, his dark eyes thoughtful. "Anything else on the sedan? Driver?"

"Not much. I'll send you what Jake caught. Speaking of, there is one other thing."

"You're full of information today."

I wasn't sure if it was a compliment or not. "There's another new wolf in town. A half-breed."

"A half-breed?" Dad spluttered, shock and interest lacing his voice.

I nodded. "Jake met him today. Apparently, the half-breed approached him, scenting him in one of his classes. He'd like to meet with us. I don't have many details. I didn't even catch his name. Jake only started telling me before Megan was nearly run down."

Dad ran his hand down his face, leaving a line of grease on his cheek. His face looked older than it had a few minutes before. "All right, son. I will look into things. Meantime, check if Jake can give you any more details about this half-breed. Very unusual."

"I will."

"Go ahead and pass along that scent of the rogue wolf."

I passed him the scent memory. Dad nodded once. "I'm glad you stopped by. I needed to tell you a few things myself. Friday night, the Thornehill Alpha and some of his pack will be at HarvestFest." He paused and heaved a weary sigh. "His daughter will be there. I—we—had hoped that you and she would be potential mates." His face soured, and my belly dropped. "An alliance with their pack and our two bloodlines would ensure an Alpha stronger than we've had in generations."

My gut flipped, and a stone of emotion lodged in my throat. "Dad, I didn't intentionally bite Megan, and I can't help that she's my mate."

"I know that, son," Dad replied gruffly. "I can explain that Megan is your mate, but only if she stays a wolf and truly becomes your mate. I'm not sure how to excuse our sudden non-interest in Sarah Thornehill, because you accidentally bit a girl who may not stay a wolf beyond the next full moon."

Guilt wracked me. My mistake was already having long-term effects for the pack.

Dad continued in a gentler voice. "If Megan does not stay a wolf, Sarah would be among the top contenders for your mate," Dad said carefully. "I want you to meet her and seriously evaluate things from as objective a point as you can. It is vitally important that your blood be carried on for the benefit of the whole pack. Someday, you must sire the next Alpha."

I felt my face heat as unease slithered like a snake in the grass into my veins. I had no idea what to say to that.

"If Megan leaves you at the end of the month—"

My breath hitched painfully in my chest at Dad's words.

"—you will have to choose a new mate." Dad's voice was hard, with no trace of sympathy for the pain that would cause me if it came to that. "It will be like Megan has died. There will be no going back."

I swallowed. The mere thought was painful. "I'll meet her. But—"

"No," Dad interrupted. "No buts. You meet her, and you seriously consider it. Or you make sure Megan stays a wolf. There is nothing else at this point." He stopped, an unreadable emotion flittering across his face. "Best get on back now. Think about what I've said." He patted me once on the shoulder and popped his head back under the car. His meaning was clear. I was dismissed.

I decided to go for a quick walk to give Megan a few more minutes with Rachel and give myself a chance to calm down some, even though I had the strong urge to check on her. Dad's words had rattled me. As had his questioning of Megan's near miss. There had been something in his tone that felt wrong. I mulled it over as I set off on the sidewalk that ran around the edge of the subdivision and ended where the woods started.

Sarah Thornehill. I knew her name but had never met her. The Thornehills held a powerful pack in upstate New York. She was the daughter of parents who were both children of Alpha parents, same as me. If the two of us had kids together, our children would have incredibly powerful bloodlines—their Alpha powers would be magnified.

I shuddered at the thought of it. Wolf whined inside me. I wanted only Megan. But if my toxins weren't enough and she chose to leave, I'd be forced to choose another mate. And for the betterment of the future pack, it would most likely have to be Sarah Thornehill.

Walking until my brain numbed itself to the pain of too many heavy thoughts, I jogged back up to the cabin. Not surprisingly, Rachel's car was still parked in the gravel, but Raven's car next to it was unexpected. The lights cast a cheerful glow from the curtained windows and were like a beacon to me as dusk began to fall.

Laughter bubbled up inside as I opened the screen and hesitated to open the door. I was saved from my indecision as Megan pulled the door open, smiling at me.

"I could have been anyone, you know," I said softly, unable to help my grin from answering hers. "Wolf knew it was you," she replied, eyes going wider. "Raven's here." She whispered as she leaned in and kissed my cheek, explaining her actions even as my stomach flipped at the contact.

"Wow. That's a lot of dessert." The kitchen table was piled high with cookies, and there were boxes lined up along the back wall. Raven sat at the extra table, frosting coating her fingers and the impressively decorated cookies on cooling racks.

Megan beamed. "Raven helped speed up production, and we're almost back on track. We should be able to get everything done in time." Her body had lost its tense posture from earlier in the afternoon. Baking really was her ultimate stress relief.

"All right. I'm going to finish up this last bit of dough and pop it in the oven. I think I'll head out after that if you don't mind taking them out, Meg? I've got to get home and get on the research project for English. I'll take these," Rachel pointed at a collection of full boxes, "and make sure they get into the freezer at home."

"No problem. Wolf is going to want out soon, anyway. She's getting antsy." She turned to me, her eyes questioning.

"First month of shifts. Always fun," Raven quipped as she stood. "Is there anything else you'd like me to decorate tonight? I'd be happy to do more tomorrow?"

Raven glanced at me, and I knew she could tell I was off kilter. I appreciated her bowing out along with Rachel, though I was slightly perturbed that she could read me so easily.

"You've been so much help, Raven. I'll finish up and put everything away once it all dries," Megan replied.

It took a few more minutes, but the girls and half the baked goods were finally out the door, and I was alone with Megan. "You look like you ate one of Mrs. Crumb's prawn sandwiches," Megan said dryly. "What's wrong?"

Wolf nudged me, luxuriating in her concern, but needing her close. She moved over to me and easily melted against me as I wrapped my arms around her, my face buried in her hair. "Exhausting talk with Dad." She squeezed my waist. I took a breath. "And images of you in the parking lot stuck on repeat. I'm not sure I've ever been so scared in all my life."

"Sam," she said pulling back, her hands coming up and resting on either side of my face. "I'm all right. I'm right here. Perfectly safe and sound." She looked over my face once more, then carefully put her lips to mine, kissing me softly. She broke away far too soon, and I followed her lips and kissed her back. Harder, wanting more, guilt and desire fueling me. She pulled back again, breaking the kiss and leaving me feeling hollow. I sighed.

"There's one more thing you should probably know." Her eyebrow rose. I cleared my throat and began explaining the Thornehill Alpha's presence and the plans for his daughter.

Introductions moved quickly with the half-breed, whose name I discovered was Alexander Kypson. Jake connected us the next day at school, and on Wednesday evening, while Meg, Rachel, and Raven baked and decorated to their hearts' content, and Rev, Cade, Steve and Amalie Rivers ran border patrols, I found myself sitting in my parents' living room as Mom ushered in a tense guy about my own age and his young-looking mother.

I stood and held out my hand. "Alexander, Ms. Kypson."

"Please, just Kyp," he answered.

I nodded. "Glad you could come on short notice." I wasn't sure what else to say other than the normal niceties. It was a strange situation. There were stories of half-breeds, but I'd never actually met one until now. The legends had them as malformed beasts who were either too far gone to the wolf, or so human that they couldn't shift. Kyp looked perfectly normal. He wasn't overly large, but he was wiry and though he cleared just under six feet and wasn't heavily muscled, I'd bet he was pretty handy in a fight. I didn't know of any other half-breeds actually in existence, though I certainly didn't know all the wolves in America.

"And I'm Jennifer. No need for the Ms. And it's our pleasure," his mom answered with a nervous twist of her lips. Mom smiled in return and motioned toward the couch opposite.

"Can I get either of you anything to drink? Soda, tea, coffee?"

"No, thank you," Jennifer answered.

"I'm fine, thanks," Kyp echoed.

"Jennifer, what do you do?" Mom asked politely. "I was an RN in Kentucky, but I also have my EMT certification and am working on a crew here in Rock Falls. It's been good so far. Do you work outside the home?"

Mom beamed. "I used to be an accountant, actually. When Sam was born, we decided it was best for me to stay home full time. Once he was big enough, and he didn't really need me as much anymore, I took over the pack accounts and a host of other pack-related things, and it's been rewarding and fulfilling, so I've stuck with it."

"It's wonderful to find something you enjoy," Jennifer replied.

"And do you enjoy nursing?"

"I do. It kind of fell into my lap." She looked anxiously at Kyp, who gave her a nearly imperceptible nod. Jennifer cleared her throat. "When we found the Kentucky pack, Kyp and I were really struggling. I was young and working two jobs trying to keep a roof over our heads. The pack took us in. They offered to put me through college to earn my RN degree if I'd agree to act as their personal pack nurse. I accepted. It's been quite a ride, learning both human and wolf anatomy and reactions."

Dad walked in through the kitchen door, and I could smell the anxiety rocket off our two guests. They'd been nervous enough to meet me, but Dad brought all the Alpha with him whether he meant to or not. He gave them a quick once-over and nodded. "Welcome. I'm Dominic Wolfe. I trust you've met my wife, Mary, and my son and Beta, Sam." They bobbed their heads as we all took a seat. "I have to confess my curiosity," Dad said as he crossed his leg and rested his hands in his lap. "And if you'll forgive the bluntness, I've never met someone in your position, Alexander."

"Just Kyp, sir," he said quietly.

Dad nodded. "Why have you come here?" Dad asked, addressing Kyp.

He swallowed before speaking. "I was a part of a pack in Kentucky. They were not...what I wanted for the rest of my life."

Jennifer broke in. "I didn't know about werewolves until Kyp changed. Had no idea his father was one, had no idea they existed at all. I did the best I could when he was younger and, through sheer luck, found a pack."

"You can shift then?" I had to ask.

"I can."

"Fully?" Dad chimed in.

"Yes, sir. All fur, claws, and teeth."

Dad nodded for them to continue. Mother and son shared a quick glance before Jennifer continued. "The Kentucky pack was cruel. Now that Kyp is of an age, I was not convinced it was safe for him to remain with them."

"Did you leave the pack?"

Kyp sighed. "I did. I am currently a Rogue wolf."

I lifted my eyebrows. It was dangerous to be alone without a pack for support. It made it hard on the wolf—could even drive them feral. We were not made to be solitary creatures.

"We heard rumors of a large pack here in Delaware, did some research, and here I am," Kyp finished, not producing any details to speak of.

"You want to join our pack?" Dad said.

"Yes, sir."

"How do you know we will be any less prejudiced than your last pack?" Dad asked Kyp, reading between the lines of his story.

"I'm taking a gamble that you're cut from the same cloth your father was. If the rumors are true, then his was one of the first mixed-race packs in the country. He admitted ethnicities to your pack long before anyone else thought about mixing races among the family group packs."

Dad's eyebrows quirked, and Mom smiled at Jennifer, conveying some motherly sentiment that I didn't entirely follow. Dad tapped his chin and glanced at me. I liked Kyp. There was something about him that struck me as genuine, if guarded. He'd been hurt by his pack. That was obvious by the stiff way he carried himself and the haunted depths of his eyes. I nodded back at Dad.

"We don't allow just anyone into our pack. But neither will we turn our backs to someone who is potentially in danger or who is looking for something better. We will have a trial period and several tests that you will complete. After that, we will make a final judgement. Until then, you may consider yourself under the Wolfes' protection." Kyp's shoulders visibly relaxed, and Jennifer sighed, some of her anxiety bleeding away. "Sam will show you the ropes over the next few days. You don't need to move to the neighborhood, but you may need to come here quickly at times."

"Yes, sir," Kyp answered with more excitement.

"You two go on and start getting acquainted. Mary, would you like to show Jennifer around some? I need to make a call." Dad rose and nodded to them.

"Of course. Jennifer, are you sure I can't get you a cup of coffee?"

"Coffee would be wonderful, thank you."

Chapter 36

Megan

The rest of the week went by in a blur. Evenings and nights were consumed with baking, packing, shifting, and running. I was anxious and excited for HarvestFest tonight.

Friday's last hour of the day before early release at one fifteen was an assembly. Cade, Raven, Rachel, several of her friends from the drama club, Kyp, and Sam all sat around me, and it was weird to have the two worlds I belonged to melding together.

After the assembly, Sam and I raced back to the cabin so we could load up everything while Rachel sped to her own house and her deep freezer packed with extras of everything that could be frozen.

Wolf's ears perked up as Cade and Raven pulled in behind Sam's car in the driveway. "We thought you might be able to use a little help packing up," Cade called. I grinned.

"I figured I'd better come along, too," Raven piped up. "I would hate for Cade to accidentally smash all those pretty leaf cookies I decorated." Cade shoved her shoulder playfully, and she punched him back, scowling at him in mock irritation.

With the extra hands, we made light work of carefully loading our vehicles with enough baked goods to sustain a small country. We were crammed full. I was hopeful that this would be our best year yet. We'd done well the past three, and now that we had some notoriety as regulars at the festival, we were hoping for good things.

I was pleasantly surprised again when we pulled into the fairgrounds and found Jake, Cindy, Tammy, and Kyp waiting by the long building where we'd be setting up. Jake had some tables stacked in the bed of his truck, and Wolf wiggled in excitement. She was sharing my enjoyment of the HarvestFest.

"Hey, guys," Sam called to those waiting as I climbed out of the car. My attention snagged for a minute on the width of Sam's shoulders tapering down to a slim waist. I jerked my head around as my gaze continued their descent toward his denim-clad rear end. So not going there. Wolf smirked. Knowing my face was flushing, I dove back into the car for a few bags that held the tablecloths and some cookie stands.

"Kyp, can you grab this sign?" Rachel called from her car. Kyp moved quickly to help her take out our new vinyl sign—our pride and joy.

"Does this stand come, too?" he asked. Rachel flashed him a smile and nodded as I caught up to her.

"This is going to be the best year *ever*. Here, give me a high elbow. All our hands are full." I laughed at her words and tapped my best friend's elbow with my own.

We laughed together as everyone traipsed in behind us to help set up.

Our spot was stall twenty-seven. The building was massive, and vendors bustled about, hurrying to set up for the grand opening in two hours' time. Once everyone was set, it was a huge indoor market. It was the only thing like it in Delaware, except the State Fair. HarvestFest had started out seventy-some years ago as a small-town celebration of the season and had morphed into a three-day bonanza that brought in a decent amount of money and short-term tourism to Rock Falls. Rachel and I planned to capitalize on that. This was, essentially, our job for the year, completed in three days' worth of sales. We were also banking on our notoriety to use as a springboard to launch our own baking business wider into the surrounding area after high school. Maybe even with a physical shop.

Once stall twenty-seven was located, Sam and Cade brought in tables two at a time, and Jake and Kyp set them up for us. This was the first year we'd been on this side of the building. We had a wall to the back of us, which did limit selling space, but we were located at a decent intersection of walkways.

"How many tables do we have?" I asked, surveying the space.

"Jake has six in his truck, but we could probably find more if you need them," Sam answered as he came up beside me, his hand brushing my arm. I pursed my lips, gauging.

"What if we make a giant square? We can do two tables up the sides and two tables across the front. We'll have to put all the extra stuff in the boxes and crates on the ground, but that would maximize the selling space," Rachel commented. I nodded.

"I like that idea."

"We've got another table similar to these at the house. If I can borrow a truck, or someone wants to drive me, I'd be happy to go get it. You could put it against the wall, so you don't have to keep everything on the floor," Kyp said.

"That would be awesome," Rachel replied. I watched them a minute. They'd hit it off well. Rachel's eyes shone with excitement, and her cheeks were flushed.

"I'll run out with you in my truck. Cindy, you good here?" Jake volunteered.

"Sure. Megan, what do you want me to do?"

I handed Cindy the bag with the tablecloths. "If you want to set these out on tables, I'll go start unloading more stuff."

"I'll come help," Sam quickly offered.

"Is it okay to start setting up these stands? Do you want them specific places?" Tammy asked.

"If you can get them out of the boxes, that would be perfect." I smiled back. She was still a little uncomfortable around Sam and me since she'd let the mate business slip.

Sam snatched up my hand and interlaced our fingers as we walked out of the building, not at all bothered by Tammy's discomfort. "Is your wolf okay that I'll be meeting my former-potential-mate tonight?" Wolf stirred within me, narrowing her eyes to slits, remembering the anguish and the unexpected shift the news had brought on when Sam first told me. Sam squeezed my hand, and Wolf settled. "She's still a little testy about it."

"Sorry. This is one of the biggest gatherings of wolves for the whole year. There are a lot of potential matches made at these sorts of social events. My dad and I have met other pack leaders at HarvestFest for several years now. It's easy for all of us to meet up inconspicuously." His face darkened. "This is the first year Dad has brought up a possible mate for me though."

I squeezed his hand, unsure how to respond. All of me hated the idea of Sam with someone else, but the rational part of me realized how silly that was. If I were to stay a human, then I'd be giving up this world. That meant no Sam. So logically, someone else would have him. All of him. Wolf bared her teeth at the thought. I mentally shushed her and handed Sam a box of cookies.

"What is it?" he asked.

I guess my thoughts were written plainer on my face than I'd realized. I quickly schooled my features. "Sorry, just thinking."

Sam cocked his head to the side, looking at me, his eyes slightly narrowed. I lifted an eyebrow at him. Catching me by surprise, Sam dipped his head and put a quick kiss on my lips. "Will you have time at all tonight to wander around the festival some with me?" He switched subjects.

"It depends on how much traffic we get, I suppose. I'd love to take in some of the festival. I haven't much the past couple years since we've been manning the booth." I glanced around. The traditional archery station wasn't far off, and a giant old oak tree bordered the edge of the festivities to the right. I could smell the grease as the finishing touches were put on the few carnival-like rides. Taking a deep breath, I inhaled horse, leather, and buttery popcorn. People chattered as games and booths were set up. I did want to explore it.

"You'll have more than enough help if you want it." He winked. "Not to volunteer her, but Raven would probably be delighted to step in for you for a half hour or so while we wander around together." Turning serious again, he stopped outside the doors and lowered his voice. "My wolf will definitely want to be near you after the meetings."

"Oh. That should be fine then." I still wasn't crazy about his meetings, but I told myself that this was just the way it had to be. I was definitely looking forward to strolling around the festival with Sam. I smiled. It was the perfect romantic setting for a date.

"The table is here," Jake called as he and Kyp brought it in. They'd been gone the better part of an hour, and we'd made good use of the time in their absence. With Raven, Cindy, Tammy, Cade, and Sam to help set things up as Rachel and I directed, we were looking good. Pastries, scones, and biscotti lined one side of our square with seven different kinds of breads and rolls on the other, while we displayed our beautifully decorated cookies along with the other nine types of cookies front and center.

"Raven, you really did such a beautiful job on these cookies," I couldn't help but gush. She'd done fall leaves, scripted *HarvestFest* in practically identical lettering, and piped designs on sugar cookie rounds and had done many one-of-a-kind cookies in all sorts of colors and designs. Each one looked good enough to be in a professional confection shop.

She smiled up from putting the last touches on a three-tiered display of her unique cookies. "Thanks." Her decorating powers would certainly bring in extra income this year.

At five p.m., HarvestFest officially started, and it wasn't long after that people started trickling in. At first, it was only a few, but soon, Rachel and I were blurs of pink, purple and black in our new *Nutmeg & Crumbs* shirts .

Our new sign proudly displayed our name, *Nutmeg & Crumbs*, at a better vantage than it had in previous years, and people were taking note. Several took extra business cards.

"Meg, that man asked if we could do decorated cookies for his daughter's birthday party," Rachel said as she grabbed a bag from under the back table.

"Seriously? That's awesome. Tell him yes," I told her as I counted change out. "We'll do them ourselves or rope Raven into doing a few more if we have to."

Rachel grinned and swiped an errant red curl out of her face.

"Hi," I greeted our next customer warmly, confidence properly boosted. "How can I help you? Are you looking for anything in particular?"

"I must have some of this hazelnut, dark chocolate biscotti. I got some of it here last year, and I have not been able to find any that's tasted better since," an elderly woman enthused. "Wherever did you find your recipe?"

Memory bloomed warm in my chest. "It was my grandma's. She was the one that taught me to bake. We do custom orders anytime," I offered.

"Well, she certainly did a good job. You don't sell any coffee here, do you?"

"Sadly, we don't," I replied, a light bulb going off in my head as I bundled up the indicated ten biscotti into a bag. "But let me give you one of these almond and apricot biscotti to try. The white chocolate on them is a bit sweeter than the hazelnut ones, but the apricots give it a nice zest."

The white-haired woman beamed at me and looked greedily at the freebie biscotti I put into her bag. She patted my hand as she deposited her cash. "I'm just so thrilled that you young people are taking such an interest in baking. I'll be sure to drop back by tomorrow if I make it in again."

"Thanks so much! Enjoy your biscotti." I smiled as she trundled down the aisle.

"Rachel." I gasped in a spare minute between customers. "We need to get coffee in here, like, yesterday. The percolator at the cabin holds a ton."

Rachel's eyes glowed. "Why have we not done this before?"

"Probably because we haven't ever had a plug at our booth. Look." I pointed to the back wall. Sure enough, there was a blessed outlet, just waiting for a percolator. We looked at each other and nodded quickly.

Before we could get plans any further solidified, Sam sauntered down the aisle toward me, eyes light but face drawn. His gaze softened when it landed on me, but I knew he must be getting ready to go to the meeting. Where Sarah Thornehill would be waiting. Wolf bristled, and I shushed her and took a big inhale through my nose.

"Hey," he called with a smile. "How goes the booth?"

"Fabulous," Rachel enthused.

"Can I talk to you a sec?" Sam asked me.

"Sure, you can talk to Megan," Rachel replied with a wink. "Kyp, can you come help while Sam and Megan take a minute?" Kyp, who had come up behind Sam, looked like the proverbial deer in the headlights for a second but then blinked and his expression relaxed.

"Yeah. What do you need me to do?"

Rachel launched into a quick rundown of things while Sam took my hand and led me a few stalls down and into a sort of alcove where we were more secluded. "Meetings start in a few minutes. You okay?" he asked, taking both my hands in his.

Wolf growled inside but didn't try to lurch her way out. She'd come to terms with things, even though she wasn't happy. I was trying to be rational and realized that this was probably a good thing for Sam since he'd have to move on once I returned to permanent skin. The thought soured in my belly.

"She's fine. I'm fine," I whispered, not sure if I was lying.

"Okay." He blew out a breath. "Kiss me?" I grinned. "Maybe it's *my* wolf that wants the reassurance." He gave a nervous chuckle.

I took perverse pleasure in the fact that for the first time, it wasn't my wolf that needed calming. I reached up and kissed him. His lips moved against mine, and I could feel his uncertainty. I pulled back and hugged him tight, putting one more tiny kiss right on his earlobe.

He drew in a shuddering breath. "More of that later, I think."

I laughed as he walked me back to the booth. Rachel and Kyp were thoroughly enjoying themselves if their expressions were to be trusted. Raven and Cade had come up and were chatting with them during a lull of customers.

"You ready?" Cade asked Sam once we were within conversational distance. Cade was going as Sam's second.

"How can I help you guys? What do you need?" Raven asked Rachel. Sam gave my hand one more squeeze, and he and Cade took off. Sam's shoulders were tight, and unease slithered into my belly.

"What time is it?" I said aloud as I glanced at my watch. "It's about seven. HarvestFest shuts down at ten." I glanced up as I answered myself. "Raven, how long do you think it would take to get back to the cabin, get the percolator and coffee stuff, and get back here?"

"Ooh! Coffee is a fantastic idea. But we don't need to go as far as the cabin. I happen to know that Dominic rented out one of the fair booths for the weekend, and they brought a huge percolator and all the stuff. The only thing is that we'll have to wait for tonight's meeting to be over. The formal stuff will probably take about an hour or so, but after that, we should be able to use it. It would take at least that long to get everything from the cabin."

"Perfect," Rachel chimed. "We can bring the one at the cabin tomorrow so they can have the other one back."

With that settled, I ignored Wolf's pacing, wondered what Sam was doing, and then focused on our customers. Things were picking up again as people were looking for after-dinner treats, and Raven and Kyp stuck around. There were quite a few students from school and several pack members that swung by, and it helped pass the time.

Chapter 37

Sam

I wiped my palms on my jeans, more nervous for this meeting than I probably should have been. I couldn't help the sinking trepidation that made my legs drag like lead. Should Megan not remain a wolf, my most likely future stood behind the doors in front of us.

"Deep breath, dude." Cade nudged me, sensing my unease.

"If things don't work..." I trailed off, and he looked at me sympathetically.

"I know. Let's just get through the meeting. It might be horrendous, and there'll be no question of you two matching up." He tried to sound hopeful. I forced a laugh.

"Yeah. She probably has three eyes and horns." Cade rolled his eyes and opened the door.

Sarah Thornehill did not have three eyes or horns. She was there, front and center, seated between Dad and Mr. Thornehill, other wolves from both packs in the background. She was beautiful—light blonde hair that barely met her shoulders, eyes green like celery, and pale skin with a gentle upturned nose. She was stunning, but I felt nothing beyond a polite curiosity and an objective opinion about her looks. Wolf even recoiled, and a twisted part of me was relieved that there was no pull of attraction to her. I swallowed as I noted Cade's inhale beside me. Dad's eyes followed me closely, and I carefully schooled my features to look polite, but blank.

"Samuel, come meet Sarah Thornehill." They all stood. "You already know her father, Austin." I nodded respectfully at him and turned to Sarah.

"Hi, Sarah." I smiled.

"Nice to meet you, Sam." Her voice had a lyric quality.

I scented her neck at a polite distance, and she did the same. Rain-washed spring. But not the sunshine and roses I wanted. "This is Cade Rivers, my son's second," Dad continued with introductions.

"Nice to meet you both," Cade said before exchanging scents with both of them. Was it my imagination, or was there interest in Cade's eyes?

We all sat, and the other wolves from both packs settled themselves in their own conversations around the room. There were other social meetings going on in our private room, but ours was the only political and mate-related meeting to my knowledge.

"Samuel, your dad tells me you're a fine young man," Mr. Thornehill opened. I felt my ears turn red. What had Dad said? I glanced over at him. His eyes were warm, but the rest of him sat stern, as unmovable as stone.

I cleared my throat. "Thank you," I said, unsure what else to say.

"There's been an unexpected event since we last spoke. I probably should have called but knew that we had other business to attend to," Dad intervened. "Without beating around the bush, Sam has met his mate." Dad's turn to clear his throat.

Mr. Thornehill's eyebrows shot up. "Well, in that case, congratulations." He reached out and shook my hand. Sarah said nothing, her face unreadable, but her shoulders sagged a fraction of an inch. I wasn't sure if it was relief or disappointment. "I have to say, I was hoping you and Sarah would hit it off." He looped an arm around his daughter's shoulders. "But finding your mate is a rare and beautiful thing." He smiled genuinely, and Wolf slowly let his shoulders relax.

"Thank you. We're very happy," I stammered, knowing I was elated, not sure where Megan stood, but also unsure what else to say.

"With that in mind, how would you like to proceed?" Dad asked, all business again. No time for trivial emotional mess.

"Even though we won't be making an alliance with a mating ceremony," Mr. Thornehill said as I caught Dad's thick swallow.

Guilt fluttered in my gut. I shoved it away. Megan had to stay wolf. What would Dad tell the Thornehills if Megan walked away in skin? That their potential son-in-law broke one of the cardinal rules—an offense that would possibly ruin any alliance with the Thornehill pack? That she had died? That I was untethered?

Ice lodged in my spine as a horrible thought took root. If Megan were dead, then I—the pack—would be literally freed of the encumberment I'd caused. I forced myself to breathe through my nose at a normal rate. Flashes of Megan crouched behind the concrete barrier wall as the black sedan screeched away crashed through my brain, and I blinked. Cade subtly elbowed me, and with some effort, I focused in on the conversation once more.

"I still think a formal alliance between our packs could benefit us both." Dad nodded at Mr. Thornehill's words. A frown creased between the blond man's eyebrows. "There's been talk." His voice lowered with the gravity of the words he was about to utter. "Talk of an uprising."

An uprising? Wolf raised his head and perked both ears forward. This was the first I'd heard of such a thing.

"An uprising of *wolves*?" Dad clarified, shock evident in his voice.

Mr. Thornehill nodded gravely. "There are rumors of a growing unrest among some of our population that think humans should no longer be our equals."

Dad's eyes widened and his nostrils flared. "This cannot be." Icy tendrils started winding through my veins. I felt Cade tense beside me and noted the worry etched on Sarah's forehead. "Wolves are meant to protect and serve. Not to rule," Dad continued in a voice that carried his authority.

"Our sentiments as well," Mr. Thornehill agreed with another nod. "We will keep our noses to the ground up north. I trust you and your pack will do the same. Should something arise, it would be in everyone's best interest to quash things quickly and quietly. Together, if necessary."

"Agreed."

The icy tendrils wove their way around my heart. If it got out that werewolves existed, that some were trying to take over the human population—rewrite the entire system of government in the United States—mass pandemonium and witch hunts that put Salem to shame would sweep the nation. It would destroy not only the werewolf population but essentially thrust America into a dark age. No one would trust their neighbor, discrimination, enslavement, murder on a Hitleresque scale, nothing was beyond the realm of possibility.

"Mind you, I've only heard rumors. I've no concrete proof of anything," Mr. Thornehill was saying, "but I felt it wise to inform you."

"We appreciate that," Dad said as he encompassed me in his gaze. I nodded my agreement.

The rest of the meeting took a lighter tone as we discussed more trivial matters and outlined the key players in our packs, and how communications should work as we felt it would be in everyone's best interest for our packs to become more acquainted. While the shock of the uprising rumors faded, I still felt a slither of unease. Whether it was lingering nerves or worry over what would happen with Megan, I wasn't sure. My senses stayed heightened.

About eight PM, the formal side of things wrapped up, and we stood. "Shall we continue pack acquaintances here tomorrow or meet more informally?" Dad asked the Thornehills as he sipped the last of his coffee.

"I think having our ranking pack members meet here briefly and then interspersed throughout the festival might be the most unobtrusive." He glanced at Sarah, and she nodded. "Sarah, why don't you go on with Sam and Cade and meet a few other pack youth while we finish things up here?"

"Of course," she replied, turning a polite smile on us. I hoped Megan wouldn't be opposed to meeting Sarah, and that her wolf wouldn't overreact. My own wolf was ready to be next to Megan again. I needed the reassurance that she was still mine—and I was still hers.

Chapter 38

Megan

After another busy hour, there was finally a lull. There were still plenty of browsers, but not as many die-hard purchasers wandering the stalls. People had finished with desserts and the urge for a late-night snack hadn't hit yet. We had a little bit of a breather for now.

"So Kyp, how are you liking Rock Falls?" Rachel opened.

"It's nice. It's good to have some new scenery. Mom is an EMT, and she said her crew is really friendly."

"That's awesome. Are your classes going well?"

"They're all right. About the same as they were in Kentucky." He smiled ruefully and dragged a hand through his dark brown hair. It had a slight reddish cast to it. "Have you guys ever considered opening up your own bakery at some point?" Kyp directed the conversation away from him as Rachel took a swig from her water bottle, and I munched on a cherry Danish.

We looked at each other. "Yes!" we said together.

"We're hoping to open up our own bakery business—something bigger than HarvestFest—after graduation," Rachel chimed.

"We've got some notoriety already from doing HarvestFest the past few years, and we've done several party cakes and different dessert catering things," I offered.

"I think we could do well with an online bakery at first," Rachel said.

"And the community college over in Circleville has several business classes we plan to take to work through more of the logistical side of things." Wolf nudged me. That was close to home.

Kyp chuckled. "Well, if tonight is any indication, you guys shouldn't have trouble drumming up business."

"Ah, thanks." Rachel's eyes lit up.

I nodded in agreement. Tonight's success had blown away previous years. And there was still tomorrow and Sunday. It was a comforting thought to dream about baking for a living. Flour up to my elbows, replicating Grandma Elsie's recipes, making special orders, and taking good care of our customers.

"I hope it works the way we've envisioned it," I said. I bit my lip as Wolf nudged me again. Community college was near Sam.

"It will. These are amazing," Raven commented as she took a bite of a double-fudge chocolate-chip cookie that made me think again of Sam.

"Well, I'm pretty sure some of tonight's success lies in your awesome decorating skills. You may have to come work for us," Rachel told Raven with a wink.

Just then, I caught sight of the shaggy head that made my heart stutter. Then I caught sight of the gorgeous, leggy blonde beside him, and my heart stopped altogether. The Danish turned to ash in my mouth, and Wolf jerked, howling to be let out.

"Look at me, don't look at her." The words were the softest breath of sound, and I ripped my eyes away and looked into Kyp's brown ones. He was far more observant than I had given him credit for. I breathed hard through my nose, clenched my fists, and forced myself and Wolf to calm down. I thought of Sam's smile, the way his eyes twinkled, then remembered his kiss at the movie theater, the kiss we shared in the kitchen that night. Wolf stopped howling but did not retreat. I shivered and took the water bottle Kyp handed me.

Half the bottle was gone in one gulp, but I had myself mostly under control when Sam, Cade, and the gorgeous girl who could only be Sarah Thornehill, sidled up to our booth. Sam wasted no time, came right in, and slid his hands around me, planting a kiss on my lips in front of everyone. Wolf immediately calmed at his touch, and I only just resisted the urge to thoroughly make out with him right there to stake my claim.

When he pulled his head up, his eyes searched mine for a second longer, then he took my hand. "Megan, this is Sarah. Sarah, this is *Megan*." He put emphasis on my name that warmed me. His tone said *she is mine*. Part of me squirmed at the emphasis and attention, while Wolf, and not an insignificant human part of me, relished it.

Sarah beamed, genuine pleasure lighting up her face and her pale green eyes. "It's nice to meet you. I'm really glad you and Sam found each other."

I gave her a tentative grin. "Thanks. It has definitely been an adventure," I said. Sam snorted beside me.

"Are they done with the big percolator in the meeting room now?" Raven asked.

"Probably. They were finishing up a few things," Cade answered.

"Good. Would you come help me bring it down here?"

Cade rubbed the toe of his shoe on the ground, hesitating.

"Rachel, can I steal Megan for a few more minutes?" Sam cut in before Cade replied.

"I'll stick around if it would be helpful," Kyp said.

"Be my guest." Rachel smiled. "We'll get coffee sorted while you're out." She winked at me, and I rolled my eyes as my lips twisted up.

"Thanks. You definitely get a break when we get back," I told her.

Sam tipped his head to the exit, and I grabbed my purse and my jacket, threading my arms through the sleeves as we headed for the door.

"See you guys," he called as I waved.

"I feel a little guilty leaving Rachel at the booth."

"I don't think she minded too much. Although, I *am* being selfish. I want to walk around the festival with you. And possibly find a dark corner and make out," he finished with a roguish look.

I laughed. "Riiiiight... So. That was Sarah. How was the meeting?"

His expression fell. "The mate business went better than expected, but there are some rumors circulating up north that are concerning."

"Concerning how?" I asked as we exited the building. The night was clear, cold, and shining with stars and hundreds of sparkling lights strung up on poles throughout the festival lanes. My breath plumed in front of me, a frosty mist that dissipated as we walked. The sounds of fun, general merriment, and aromas of tempting food swirled around while a loud cheer went up from the archery stalls directly to the left along the back perimeter of the festival grounds. He took my hand, and we meandered toward the archery games and the giant old oak tree wound in shadows.

"Probably best not to talk about it out in the open. I promise I'll tell you on the way home, though."

Heat curled in my belly at the word *home*. Our home together. I shook my head. It wouldn't be my home forever. I had to keep that in mind. It was getting harder to pretend we weren't really together.

Footsteps thudded behind us, and we turned to find Cade jogging up. He flipped his black hair out of his face. "Sam, Beta Babe," he teased in greeting. I grinned back at him but noticed Sam was tense beside me. "So uh, I was wondering..." Cade was suddenly tongue-tied. "Since you won't be, um, pursuing Sarah, is she—" He cleared his throat. "Is she fair game?"

Laughter burst from Sam's chest, some of the tenseness fading, his arms regaining some looseness. The old oak tree towered behind us, a breeze rustling the leaves like they were laughing with him. "As far as I'm concerned, she's completely up for grabs. Although, you may want to have a chat with her dad. If you think it's going to get serious, you may want to have a chat with my dad, too. He takes the Alpha bloodlines very seriously," he finished softly so there was no chance of being overheard, even though there wasn't anyone close to us this far back by the perimeter.

Sam cocked his ear slightly to the side, his eyebrows drawing together. Then several things happened at once.

Cade opened his mouth to respond as Sam's eyes enlarged to momentarily show his wolf's irises. Sam ripped his hand from mine and shoved me hard. I hit the dirt with enough force to crack my teeth and bruise my jaw. There was a whirring *thunk*. Sam grunted, and then something wet was running over my hand as Sam's body fell across mine. Wolf rose to the surface, my senses on high alert, still confused and unsure what was happening as pain radiated down my jaw and neck.

"Cade, *go*!" Rolls of icy power crashed over me as Sam commanded Cade. I'd never heard a command issued, and the raw intensity of the power behind his words both thrilled and terrified me. Cade wheeled around and sprinted toward the archery stalls. I struggled to rise, but Sam's body covered mine and offered no give.

"Megan, don't move," he gritted out between clenched teeth. Panic bloomed in my chest, and my hands trembled where they were trapped beneath me. Something was wrong. So, so wrong. From the corner of my eye, I saw Sam looking in all directions, his body still completely covering me. My hand and arm were sticky wet and the tang of blood suddenly saturated my nose, flooding me with a fresh wave of panic. Wolf assessed us, concluding we were uninjured aside from a few bruises. So much blood. *Sam*.

"Sam?" The terrified whimper left my mouth as Wolf thrashed to get out, to protect Sam.

"Be still. I'm all right." Pain laced his words. Wolf listened, stilling but whining. Panic bled through my pores. "On my mark, I want you to get up and stay behind me. We're moving toward the building. Keep to the shadows." He waited a moment. "Now."

He jerked us both to our feet, his body a human shield between me and the archery station. Glancing around wildly looking for the threat, I stumbled and sucked in a breath when I saw the arrow protruding from the ground a few feet from where we'd been.

"Sam, where are you hit?" My voice came out an octave higher than normal.

"Just my arm. I'm okay." His eyes never left off scanning the crowd. Miraculously the festival carried on around us, oblivious to the near-death experience we'd just encountered. My body started to shake uncontrollably as Sam guided us quickly nearer the main building.

At the last minute, he dodged into the row of cars parked not far from the entrance and away from the streams of people.

"Get in my car," he ordered, clicking the unlock button. He opened the door and all but shoved me in before racing to his side and locking the doors behind us.

He leaned his head against the headrest for a minute, closing his eyes as his chest heaved for breath. I couldn't move, couldn't think for a full minute in the silence before Wolf burst through the shock and moved me into motion.

"Sam." I gasped. "Show me your arm."

"Are you hurt?" He looked at me fully, eyes dilated dangerously large again.

"I'm fine. I'm a little bruised, but I can already feel it healing."

He grimaced.

"Show me your arm," I repeated.

He grunted in pain. "It's my left arm. Can you help me out of my jacket? I called Cade back. He didn't find the shooter, and there was no panic. No screams, so no one saw what happened. No witnesses." The pain and frustration were evident in his voice.

Gingerly, I reached up and tugged the right sleeve of his jacket. His back arched and he groaned. An agonizing noise that sent my heart lurching up in my throat and brought tears to my eyes. With his right arm out, he maneuvered his left sleeve off.

"Your shirt is soaked with blood." My voice quivered. "Here." I grabbed at the towel in the backseat that had been wrapped between layers of cookies earlier. "Use this on your arm."

"Cade's here," Sam replied so I wouldn't startle as Cade's dark head came into view. He grunted again as he hit the unlock button and put the towel over the river of blood on his arm as Cade slid into the back seat.

"Whoa, Sam, that needs stitches," Cade said without preamble as Sam covered his wound with the towel. Cade's face was ashen in the festival light filtering in.

"I know," Sam gritted. "For right now, this stays between us. No one else is to know anything."

Chapter 39

Sam

I was woozy from the pain in my arm and possibly blood loss. My body was healing, but it was a fairly deep gash and needed some professional attention.

"You need to get your arm looked at now," Cade pressed. I could feel his fear and guilt that he hadn't caught the perpetrator.

I closed my eyes a second and tried to think past the slamming of my heart and the throbbing in my arm.

"Okay. Someone hand me a phone. Mine is in my left pocket, and I can't get to it."

Megan whipped her phone out. "911?" she questioned.

I shook my head and gritted my teeth as the movement pulled at the torn muscles down my bicep. "No. I don't want this going any further than the three of us for as long as possible."

"What are you thinking?" Cade asked.

My brain was spinning ninety miles an hour going through scenarios and calculations of the best course of action. "Later. Arm first. Meg, dial for me. Hold it up for me and put it on speaker. I'm all bloody." I rattled off Kyp's number to her and was thankful he picked up on the second ring.

"Hello?" the speaker voice was tinny and muffled with the noise inside the building. "Kyp. It's Sam. I need a favor."

"Sam? What's wrong? You sound...off."

"Yeah. Is your mom working the festival shift right now?"

"She should be. Is someone hurt?"

"Yes. Please call her and have her bring her med kit to the back entrance of the building. Cade will meet her there and tell her where to go. Tell her to hurry and come alone, and don't say anything to anyone else. Tell Rachel that I got sick, and Megan is taking me home early, and that she'll call her later. Consider this your first pack test. Got it?"

"Got it. Human injury?"

"Wolf," I croaked.

"Dialing now." He hung up, and my head fell back against the headrest again.

"Cade, I want you to go wait by the entrance. When Jennifer gets there, bring her here, but do a sweep to check for anything out of the ordinary. If anything is even remotely off, even if it's someone from our own pack, abort. Take her back into the building."

Two sharp intakes of breath met my words. "What do you mean?" Cade's voice was steely.

"I have to be sure," I murmured. I was so tired.

"Sure of what?" Megan's strangled whisper broke the shroud of silence in the car.

"Sure that you're safe."

Cade cursed under his breath. "I think that's her. Hang on, Sam. Don't pass out."

"I'm hanging." I flexed my arm, and a wave of fresh pain and nausea traveled through my system, the pain sharpening my senses again, keeping me alert.

"Sam," Meg whispered again. I knew she was battling shock, but she was holding it together. She rested her hand on my thigh.

My heart was still slamming in my chest. That arrow had been meant for Megan. Two attempts on her life. My brain twisted through the fog of blood loss and adrenaline to snatches of conversations. If Megan stayed human. If she stayed wolf. Her blood didn't carry the Alpha gene. If she were dead, the impediment she brought to me, and therefore the pack, would be gone.

No. I couldn't—wouldn't—think it. But it was there. The suspicion had taken root. Could my own father be capable of murder?

Five agonizing minutes later, Cade and Jennifer Kypson were outside the door of my car. "Keep watch." I ground out the words with a nod of thanks at Cade. Jennifer got out a flashlight and knelt at once to better examine my arm.

"Sam, this is a doozie." Her face impassive, she fished something out of the bag slung over her shoulder with one hand and opened her med kit with the other. "Here. Eat this. It's a special blend of things that I make up for Kyp to help speed up the healing process and dull the pain. Wolf-friendly." I bit down on the proffered food. It tasted like chewy oats and had a distinct bitter edge to it that I identified as willow bark. "Hi, I'm Jennifer, Kyp's mom. What's your name?" she asked Megan.

"Megan," came the strangled reply.

"All right. Megan, I'm going to need your help. Can you come over here and hold this flashlight up?"

"Of course." Meg got stiffly out of the car and obediently held the flashlight as Jennifer cut the rest of my sleeve off.

"Right," Jennifer said calmly. "Let me get this cleaned off, and we'll check out the damage." She worked quickly with a bottle of water, gauze, and iodine. "Well, your deep tissues are already starting to knit themselves back together, but I think we had better stitch this up to give it a little nudge." She spoke soothingly, and her voice and assurance calmed some of the storm raging in my chest. The willow bark started to take the edge off the sharpest of the pain and allowed me to breathe easier.

Jennifer made quick work getting the sutures ready. The needle bit my flesh, and I flinched.

Megan moaned. "Oh, I'm sorry, but I can't watch that." The flashlight quivered as she turned her head away. "Move my hand where you need the light."

"Megan, are you good?" Jennifer asked, concern evident in her voice.

"Fine. Just keeping my eyes shut."

The stitches didn't take long, and Jennifer covered them with antibiotic ointment and gauze and taped it in place. "Try to avoid getting it wet if you can tonight and tomorrow. Tape a plastic bag over it in the shower. At the rate you're healing, I'm guessing you'll be tender for a few days but probably mostly healed up by the morning." She hesitated. "I'm not trying to cause problems, but is there anyone else we should tell about this?" She bit her lip and fear radiated in her eyes for having spoken, and I briefly wondered what her life had been like with the Kentucky pack.

"Not at this point. Thank you, Jennifer. I won't forget this."

She nodded, relieved. "Will you be coming back to HarvestFest tomorrow?"

I glanced at Megan. "If you think you can, I think we need to act like everything is as normal as possible. Are you up to coming tomorrow?"

"If you'll be coming with me." My heart warmed at her confidence in me, though I was still terrified for her safety. There were too many unanswered questions. But until I had answers, I didn't want anyone getting spooked.

"I'm on duty for the morning shift. Either come find me or let me know, and I'll come to you. I want to check those stitches tomorrow." Jennifer shifted, her knee popping.

"We can do that. Thanks again. Really." My jaw clenched, and even that motion sent a ripple of pain shooting down my arm.

Jennifer nodded as she put the last of her supplies back into her kit. "I'll see you tomorrow then."

"What's the plan now, Sam?" Cade asked, his back to me, still scanning the surrounding area.

I sighed. Megan crouched beside me, taking my bloodied hand in hers. "Megan, are you okay to drive us back to the cabin?"

"Yes. I've had a few years scared off my life, but I think I'm okay to drive."

"Cade, can you go back in, support the story that I'm violently ill from some festival food—obviously nothing from our favorite bakers"—I attempted to crack a joke—"but act normal. Keep your ears open."

"All right. Stay safe. Meet at your place in the morning to drive down, or meet here?"

"We'll meet you here," Megan cut in. "That's what we would have done. If you want things to be as normal as possible, that's what we should do."

"Megan's right. We'll meet you here at seven thirty. Keep your guard up."

Cade's dark hair flopped over his forehead as he nodded, the seriousness of the situation not lost.

The ride home was tense. I kept looking in the mirrors every few minutes to be sure we weren't being followed.

"What were the rumors from up north?" Megan asked as she pulled out of town and onto the road that would take us to the forest and the cabin.

"There's been talk of a sort of wolf rebellion."

"Rebellion? Against what?"

"Essentially against our long-held traditions and rules. Austin Thornehill said he'd heard rumors—only rumors—that there are some wolves that want to overthrow the humans. Rewrite history and set werewolves up as some sort of demigods or something."

Megan was quiet a minute. "Could...could that actually happen?"

"No. We won't allow it."

"But, theoretically, if enough wolves got together and tried, could it happen?"

"It would take some serious masterminding. The human population has always far outnumbered the werewolf population, but fear is a powerful weapon. With wolves placed at the right spots, there could be some sort of overthrow attempt, though I doubt it would get far. The real damage would be the fear, distrust, and absolute chaos it would leave behind. Neighbor would turn on neighbor. There would be a hunt for wolves that would probably bring our populations dangerously low and cause the deaths of countless other innocents." I shuddered. Too much death and near death tonight.

We rode in silence, each lost in thought, processing.

"You know, I...I'd probably be dead if it weren't for you tonight." Tears rimmed her eyes. She glanced over at me as she parked the car in front of the cabin. The porch light shined merrily in its spot, unconcerned, and untouched with the heaviness of the night.

"Megan." My heart clenched all over again. *I'd die for you, rather than live without you.* The words echoed in my head but wouldn't exit my mouth.

"I don't know what to say. Thank you is so inadequate. My brain is all mush trying to make sense of it. I can't understand the why? Why is someone trying to kill me?"

"I don't know," I answered, suspicion clouding my thoughts. "Let's go inside so I can hug you properly and get this shirt off. The blood is drying all stiff against my side. Let me get out first and be sure no one else is around though."

She bit her lip but did as I asked.

I rolled over again for the fourteenth time, trying to get comfortable. I couldn't help it. Every time I tried to close my eyes, that arrow imbedded in Megan's heart instead of the ground. My brain knew that Megan was safe. She was fine, sleeping in the bed across the room from me. But that wasn't enough to fully convince me.

She sighed into the dark room, and I knew I needed to see her—check on her again before having any remote possibility of falling to sleep.

The bed springs bunched. Their metallic noise was muffled by the layers of blankets as I swung my legs over the edge of the bed.

My bare feet made no noise as I padded over to Meg's bed. To my surprise, I could make out little glints of light reflecting in her eyes. She was awake. "Sam?" she said sleepily. My heart lurched, and my throat constricted.

"I—" How did I tell her what I really meant? "Can I hold you?" The broken whisper struggled past my lips. I brought my hands up in surrender, wincing as it tugged my bicep painfully. "I swear I won't try anything. I just...need to be close to you for a little bit. I'll get up when I get sleepy. No sharing the bed all night."

I ached with the need to physically be near her, to assure myself that she was here, that she was all right.

She didn't say a word, simply pulled back the blankets beside her in invitation. Breath left my lungs in a whoosh. I crawled over her quickly and settled, pulling the blanket back up over both of us. My body curled around her, pulling her as close to me as I could. My injured arm was on top, her shoulders snugged up next to me. I finally felt like I could breathe again with her body nestled against me.

We lay there for long minutes. Eventually, the heat from her body and the comfort of having her near started to make me drowsy. I knew I'd have to get up to keep my promise, but it was the last thing I wanted to do.

With significant effort, I shifted, pulling away to get up. Meg grasped my hand.

Stay.

Always, I replied in her mind. Knowing that I had been given an extraordinary gift, my body quickly found the right place again. Megan held my hand still, tucking it under her cheek. I dropped a kiss on the curve of her neck and buried my head into the pillow next to her hair. She wiggled back, fitting her body more securely next to mine. Her heartbeat thumped through her back against my chest, and the steady rise and fall of her breathing settled me. She squeezed my fingers lightly.

Maybe I wasn't the only one that needed holding.

Chapter 40

Megan

I woke relishing Sam's body pressed against my back. I'd fallen asleep with him spooning me, cradling me against his body, and it felt surprisingly *right* to wake up the same way. He'd kept his word and tried to leave before he fell asleep, but I had been selfish. I wanted to feel him next to me. He made me feel safe. After a second attempt on my life, I needed to feel safe. But he made me feel things that were *not* safe, too. He must have realized I was awake because his hand moved slowly from its tucked position under my head and slowly traced my arm down to my hand. His fingers curled around mine, and I felt his heartbeat pick up a notch, his chest still pressed against my back.

I turned enough so I could crane my head, and his face swam into view. He faced me, his head on the pillow, blue eyes blazing with a fire that took my breath away. While his actions were slow and sweet, his eyes were not. They were wild and fevered.

Before I could say or do anything, he reached up and slowly brushed an errant piece of hair off my forehead. His eyes trained to my lips, and my mouth was suddenly drier than stale bread.

Instead of leaning over and kissing me as I expected—and wanted—his whole body moved, leaving my side cold in its wake. His body slowly grazed mine as he moved to hover over me, supported on his knees and elbows, heat radiating from his body, but not actually touching me.

My eyes went wide, and the breath froze in my lungs as his gaze raked over my face, and he leaned forward.

His nose skimmed my collarbone, up the side of the pulse pounding in my neck to the back side of my ear, scenting me. With the lightest of kisses right behind my jaw, he was gone. The bathroom door shut, and I laid there, *alarmingly* aware. My breath came in ragged gasps, my heart drummed, and my whole body tingled.

Oh...my...word.

Human. I want to stay human, I told myself as convincingly as I could while refusing to acknowledge how badly I wanted to feel Sam's body against mine.

"Coffee. I need coffee," my voice croaked. I forced myself to move, declining to dwell anymore on the scene that had just taken place in my bed. My face flushed as I thought about it. I turned my head once more to where Sam had laid, his scent still wrapped around the pillow. I inhaled before I could think better of it, his smell sending the wolf into ecstasy.

Chapter 41

Sam

Meg had a cup of hot chocolate waiting for me on the counter and a large pot of coffee brewed by the time I exited the shower. The gesture warmed me more than the hot shower had, especially since the first half had been intentionally cold, and I found my eyes straying to her bed, the covers still rumpled, where I'd nearly lost my mind when I woke up with my arms still wrapped around her.

"How's your arm?" Meg's question jerked me back to the present. Her eyes skittered to my chest, bare since I still had a plastic bag taped over my arm and hadn't put my shirt on over it. I watched with satisfaction as her cheeks heated. Pushing it, I waited until she met my eyes again, a grin teasing my mouth, letting her know I'd caught her staring. She rolled her eyes and her flush darkened.

"Like what you see?"

"I don't know. Let's take the bag off and look," she retorted.

I smiled, sat down at the table, and held my arm out to her. She helped me peel the tape off around the plastic bag and then she gingerly peeled back the layer of gauze stained with iodine and blood. A wide, red, ropy scar with protruding stitches stood out starkly from the flesh of my bicep.

"Well, that arm is never going to look the same," I mentioned as I flexed the muscle. It had healed together well. There wasn't much pain, and I could tell the muscles had healed properly. I didn't really care about the scar itself.

"It gives you character." Meg smiled. I realized she was flirting with me. Her hand was still wrapped around my arm below my scar. My eyes trailed to her lips as her gaze flew over my bare shoulders. Her lips parted and for the first time, desire flashed across her face. My blood roared in my ears as I slowly angled my head to kiss her.

A familiar fantasy theme song blared from her phone two feet away on the tabletop, yanking us out of what could have been one of the best moments of my life.

"That's Rachel," Meg stammered, heat flooding her cheeks again.

"That's Rachel," I repeated dryly and moved to finish getting dressed.

Meg and Rachel chatted while I found a short-sleeved shirt that covered about half of the new scar on my arm. Over that, I put a dark gray quarter-zip sweater. The skin pulled some as I moved my arms up over my head, and for a minute, I was tempted to play it up and see what happened if I asked Megan to help me. I sighed, biting the inside of my cheek. Last night had bonded us together more firmly than anything else had yet. There was something about two people surviving a major scare that had a way of knitting them together.

The corners of my mouth tugged down as I thought about the festival today. I was going to have to go to Dad's meet and greet for part of the morning. If I didn't, he'd be mad, and if he was involved—ice lodged in the pit of my stomach at the thought—it would make him suspicious. I didn't want to widen the circle of knowledge any larger than it already was. Cade was supposed to be there with me as my second. I wasn't sure who else I trusted at this point. It was a horrible, hollow feeling to question the trust of the pack I'd grown up with, embraced, and was poised to lead someday.

Bitter emotion rose in my throat. I choked it back down and wracked my brain for a solution. Maybe I was asking the wrong question. It wasn't so much who I trusted, but who loved Megan, rather than had cause to remove her from the picture?

One person came to mind. Rev. He had been a part of Megan's life since she was born, and I was pretty sure that loyalty to her went every bit as deep as his loyalty to my father. Rev would not condone or take part in an act that hurt Megan. I didn't think he was above killing for the just cause—much like an officer of the law would be—Rev was, in many ways, an officer of the pack. He'd find a peaceful solution if at all possible. And it had been Rev that offered the way out for Megan if she stayed human.

"Rachel is significantly freaked out and angrier than she's ever been." Megan cut into my thoughts. "Only with the reading between the lines that she's done. She surmised you weren't sick."

"I can't say I blame her. I'm not exactly thrilled either," I said.

"So what's the plan today?" she asked, her eyes serious as she bit her lip.

"How do you feel about Rev?"

"What do you mean?"

"I need someone we both trust while I'm at the meet and greet this morning. I don't think there's any way I can get out of it and not look suspicious. Cade will have to be with me, too, so I can't leave him with you either."

"I trust Rev."

I looked her in the eye. There was no wavering, only confidence.

"All right. I'm calling him now. I'm only giving him sketchy details though, until I have more information."

She nodded. "Sam, I'm scared."

"Me, too," I whispered as I enfolded her in a tight hug.

I hadn't liked it, but I'd left Rev at the booth with Meg. She and Rachel were scurrying around, and I could tell the daylight hours and the business of the festival was distracting Meg enough that she was more or less enjoying herself, despite the cloud of terrifying uncertainty hanging over us. Jennifer had removed my stitches first thing without anyone else being the wiser. I ran into Kyp not long after that, and he was going to do a few rounds of patrols around and in the long building. I wasn't entirely sure I trusted him, but he had no motive to hurt Meg and only got to Rock Falls a few days before the sedan tried to crush Megan into the pavement. I suppressed a shudder. I was going to have to confront Dad. Soon. I couldn't let this sit. I wasn't sure I had the luxury of time.

"Sam, you look angry," Cade said quietly as we made our way to the enclosed space where we'd had our meetings last night.

I blew out a hard breath. "Right. Blank face." Concern flashed over Cade's face. "I'm fine. My arm is healing well. Just...thinking about a conversation I need to have."

"You want backup?"

I smiled at my friend. "Yes. But I have to do this alone. Thanks." He nodded, and we pushed through the door.

Sarah and Mr. Thornehill were there along with most of their top-ranking pack members. Most of our top pack members were present, sans Rev, though my attention was riveted on my father. Nothing looked out of the ordinary. He even cracked a grin at a joke the man next to him shared. Mom flitted around in the background and smiled at me as I walked in. I waved back, never letting Dad leave my periphery. He caught my eye, nodded once, and went back to his conversation. It felt like the casual gathering stretched on and on. When I couldn't stand it anymore, I used the link and checked in with Megan.

Are you okay?

The slight pause dragged on for eternity.

I'm fine. All is good here. I'm saving you a double-fudge chocolate-chunk cookie.

That drew a smile to my lips. Forty-five minutes later, most everyone had trickled out. The pressure built in my chest. I slowly approached my father, my palms sweating, Wolf pacing and tightly wound. "Dad, I'd like to speak with you. Alone."

His eyebrows raised, uncertainty quickly crossing his features and sending my stomach plummeting to my toes. Wolf rose up, ready to act quickly. I didn't think it would come to an actual fight between us, but if it did, I had to come out on top for Megan's sake. I swallowed, my mouth like cotton. I looked at Cade. We nodded to each other once, and he left, making his way back to Megan.

"Give me a few minutes," Dad replied. With a few discreet murmurs, the room completely cleared. The door snicked shut behind the last wolf. We were alone. I felt the vein in my neck pulsate visibly.

"What is it, Samuel?" Dad turned fully to face me and for a moment, my courage fled completely. His features were stern, commanding. Every inch the Alpha.

Afraid my voice would crack if I tried to use it, I shrugged out of my sweater and pulled up the sleeve of my shirt to fully expose my still-healing scar. Dad's eyes widened, and his mouth fell open. "Last night someone shot an arrow at Megan from the archery station. I was able to get her out of the way in time." My teeth clenched as Dad's face drained of color. For a long minute, neither of us said anything. "This is the second time someone has tried to kill my mate." Deep breath. Courage. "I have to know if you were behind it. Did you call for her death?"

Dad visibly started, his skin paling further as he stared, then blinked slowly at me. "You think I was behind it?" His voice was quiet—almost childlike.

"I don't *want* to think you had anything to do with it," I replied. My muscles were tense. Wolf was ready to spring at any sign of aggression.

"Samuel, I swear to you both as your Alpha and your father, I would not do, and have not done, any such thing." My chest ached at his words. There was no lie in them. Dad wilted into a chair. "Why would you think *I* tried to kill her?"

I swallowed thickly as my dread slowly started to dissolve. "If Megan were dead, it would solve all the problems I created when I bit her. I would have no living mate. I'd be free to make a more political match.

It saves face since I broke one of the big rules. You can hardly look at me without getting angry about it." Tears pricked my eyes. Mortified, I blinked them back.

Dad steepled his hands in front of his mouth as he looked at me, quiet for a long moment. "Oh, Samuel. When did I stop being a good father to you?" His voice was broken; anguish leaked out with his words.

I felt like I'd been punched. There was suddenly no air in the room.

"The day I became your Beta." The words strangled themselves past the fist of emotion closing on my windpipe.

To my shock, a tear leaked out of the corner of my father's eye. I'd never seen my father cry—only rarely ever seen him show any kind of vulnerability. "I'm sorry," he whispered brokenly.

Relief and hope burst from my chest in a wild rush that left me dizzy.

"I'm sorry," he said again as another tear followed the first. He stood and closed the distance between us. He looked me in the eye, and I realized that I no longer looked up to him. We were eye to eye. This giant of a man was now my equal, in stature, height, and possibly something more. Slowly his arms came up and drew me to his massive chest. He hugged me. Hard. Hugged me like I was six years old again and I'd run to him after he'd come home from work. My arms came up around him, and I hugged him back.

"I love you, son. I've always been proud of you. I *am* proud of you." He drew back to see my face. Something sweet bloomed inside my chest at his words. "A pack is only as strong as its Alpha and Beta. Our pack is not as strong as I thought. But we can fix that. More importantly, you are my son. Somewhere along the line I lost sight of that. I want you to know that I'm sorry, and that I want to fix this rift between us."

I couldn't speak. Instead, I hugged him back, a sob breaking loose from deep inside me. Chains broke free around a dark place I hadn't realized I held trapped inside. Feelings of inadequacy shriveled up like mist burned away under a hot sun, replaced by something whole and healthy. We held each other for a long time, words unnecessary as the bond between father and son began to repair itself after years askew.

Finally, we released each other, both of us swiping an unmanly tear or two. Dad cleared his throat, but I spoke first. "So who is trying to kill Megan?"

Thunder and lightning shuddered across my father's face. "Someone is trying to tear this pack apart from the inside. *We* will find out who and deal with them." My father had never looked so lethal or sounded so protective. My heart beat steadily in my chest, hope kindled, and relief fresh that my dad, my Alpha, was behind me completely. That we'd face this thing head on and face it together. It was a new beginning for us both, and I planned to grab it with both hands.

Chapter 42

Megan

We survived the rest of Saturday and into Sunday. The festival ended at three, and an hour later, Rachel and I were packed up and headed for naps. We'd made a killing and decided we'd meet up later to tally final profits. It was a good but emotional two days with thoughts of murder floating through my head. I felt the need to stop and check my surroundings frequently. I felt watched, and not just by Sam and the other wolves I knew he had making rounds for suspicious activity. I worried for Sam. Someone had me in their crosshairs, but it had been Sam who had taken my metaphorical bullet. It made me feel equally safe and guilty.

Dominic had even stopped by and purchased a hefty order of cookies, rolls, and bread. He went so far as to compliment our ingenuity and our products. He was changed. There was a new air of purpose about him.

Once Sam and I were back at the cabin Sunday afternoon, he told me to go take a nap and he'd take care of bringing in the boxes. His arm was doing fine, and I was so worn out that I collapsed.

I woke up an hour and a half later to Sam sitting on my bed, lightly running his fingers down my cheek. "Mom and Dad would like us to come down to dinner tonight. You up for it?"

I stretched, a groan escaping. I was still pooped, but I wasn't sure dinner was optional. I wasn't thrilled about sharing a meal with Dominic Wolfe, either, although Sam was now more at ease with his dad than ever before. Their conversation Saturday morning must have righted several wrongs between them, and for that I was deeply thankful. Wolf gave a good stretch and nudged me. She was as tired as I was because she wasn't even asking to be let out. She was content and sleepy.

"I guess *yes* is the correct response?"

Sam grimaced. "Really. I think Dad has changed or at least is trying to change." He caught my hands and pulled me up to sitting.

"I'm still wiped. Will they care if I come in a sweatshirt?"

"Not at all. I'm pretty sure this is an apology dinner, not a formal event." He winked at me. "I'd like it if you wore one of *my* sweatshirts…" He trailed off, his eyebrows waggling suggestively. I rolled my eyes but couldn't stop the grin that surfaced along with a few errant butterflies in my stomach.

"I'm glad you both came down for dinner," Dominic began without much preamble as he passed the steaming dish of Swiss steak. He was wearing one of his classic flannel plaid shirts and jeans, but his face held an openness that I'd never observed before. I wasn't sure if it made me more relaxed or more nervous. "Megan"—he turned his full attention to me, and Wolf backed up, ready to cower—"it has been brought to my attention that I haven't made your first weeks as a werewolf very welcoming, nor have I made your entrance into our family very pleasant. I'd like to apologize and tell you that despite the unusual circumstances that brought you here, you *are* welcome, and you *are* a part of our family now. Even if you don't stay here forever, you will always have a place of safety should you need one." His eyes were serious, and I knew he meant every word he said. I was speechless.

"Thank you," I managed to whisper around the emotion lodged in my throat. Wolf shook out her coat and lay down adoringly, basking in her Alpha's acceptance. Heat bloomed across my shoulders, and I snuck a look at Sam. He was smiling at me, pride clearly written over his face. He squeezed my knee under the table.

Dominic nodded. "Mary, would you please pass the noodles?" The moment was over, but I still held that acceptance close to my chest. I *belonged* here. At least, part of me did. The Alpha of the pack just confirmed it in no uncertain terms. But where would I fit once I was fully human again? Wolf whined.

It was completely dark by the time we drove back up to the cabin. I was quiet, reflective. Sam didn't break the silence but let me process, loosely holding my hand on the console. It had been a full few days. The festival, the second attempt on my life, waking up next to Sam, dinner, and complete acceptance by Dominic Wolfe.

"What are you thinking?" Sam finally spoke as he locked the cabin door behind us.

I sank down onto the couch and wrapped my arms around my legs. "I'm not really sure. So much has happened the past few days, and I'm not sure what to think of any of it."

He sank down on the cushions next to me. "Dad is on board now. We'll find out who tried to hurt you." His forehead creased as his eyebrows drew down before he met my eyes. "I will do everything in my power to make sure you're safe."

"I know." I believed him. He would do anything to keep me safe. The thought heated me to my toes but also made me question myself. What was I willing to give to save Sam? If it came down to it?

We decided to put a movie on since neither of us had much motivation to do anything else. Even Wolf was too tired to run. I tried to call her up to make sure there weren't any unscheduled shifts, but she was mostly unresponsive. She raised her head and tried to stand but flopped back down to the ground in an exhausted heap. I knew exactly how she felt.

I zipped through the shower, and once I was in my pajamas, I snuggled back on the couch, Sam's arm around my shoulders, a blanket over my lap.

The movie distracted me from everything, and when it was over, it was time for bed. School would come early in the morning.

"Night, Megan," Sam said quietly, with a soft kiss to my lips. I struggled to smile back through my fatigue. I was asleep within minutes of my head hitting the pillow.

Shadows clawed at my throat as a faceless figure hunted me, growing closer with each second. Panic enveloped me, and the scream that tried to escape my mouth was shoved back into my lungs as the menacing figure reached inky fingers to my neck. Blinding white lights burst behind my eyes as I felt the life draining from me. Wolf jerked pathetically inside me, unable to free herself. The lights flitted away as darkness stole the breath from my body.

I jerked awake, gasping and sputtering, a cold sweat on my forehead and heart pounding. Safe. I needed to feel safe.

"Megan?" Sam said sleepily from the other side of the room.

Without another thought, I grabbed my pillow and scooted across the room to Sam's bed. "Will you hold me again?" I whispered as tears threatened over the pounding in my chest.

His arms reached for me, and I slid in next to him and pulled his covers up to my chin as his arms enfolded me. Snow and pine enveloped me, and I breathed him in with a shudder, the nightmare still at the front of my brain. He kissed the top of my head and rested his chin against the same spot. "I've got you. You're safe," he whispered. I shivered and buried my face in his chest.

I woke slowly. Part of me knew it was still early, but I was thoroughly scattered, my thoughts like bits of cloud blown away in a stiff wind. I stretched and thought I must have rolled over next to the wall as my front moved against something solid. I heard Sam's quick intake of breath and felt the warmth of his hand seep into my skin between my shoulder blades. My eyes flew open, thoughts centering as his blue eyes materialized in front of me. He looked down at me, propped up on one elbow, eyes fierce with emotions, his arm wrapped around me. Heat curled in my belly and spread throughout the rest of me, my face flushing in embarrassment, as I realized the solid thing I'd been stretching against was Sam's tightly muscled body.

His gaze raked over my face, his hand sliding down my back, over the curve of my waist to rest on my hip. I felt his breath on my face, felt his heartbeat beneath my fingertips, felt mine accelerate to match. Blue eyes drank me in, desire, pain, restraint, and something wild flashed across his face. He searched my eyes, and my lips parted. Immediately, his gaze was drawn to my mouth, and then, for the first time I'd ever seen him do it, his eyes dipped below my face to my chest, which was pressed tightly to his and exposing more cleavage than normal. Heat sizzled through me when he didn't immediately look away. He swallowed hard, his hand gripping my hip like a vise. When his eyes met mine again, he looked anguished, his breathing coming harder. My fist curled into his shirt, want coursing through me with enough force to scare me.

His head dipped slowly toward mine, my face tilting up for his kiss. Wolf was nearly panting, anticipating his touch.

Surprise ripped the moment away as a sharp knock sounded at the door. Sam growled low in his chest, and grabbed me roughly to him, not even room for air between us, and crushed his lips to mine in a kiss that was both quick and searing and left me breathless with my heart hammering in my ears before he rolled out of bed and stalked to the door.

Chapter 43

Sam

I was going to kill whoever was on the other side of that door. I yanked the door open to the startled face of my father who took in my dilated eyes and rumpled hair. I probably reeked of pheromones. His face turned stricken, and color rose in his cheeks as his eyes widened in surprise. Any other time, it would have been amusing. Not this time.

"I can come back," he stuttered. I glanced back in the cabin. Megan was up and knotting her bathrobe. I heaved a sigh and ignored the urge to adjust my pajama bottoms and held the door so my dad could come in.

"I..." He cleared his throat, uncharacteristically uncomfortable. "I'm sorry to barge in, but I felt like this shouldn't wait."

I gestured toward the table. Megan filled the coffee pot, and Dad sat as she put grounds into the filter.

"I didn't open yesterday's mail until late last night. There was a letter waiting there with some interesting information," Dad started. It had better be life-altering information. Meg joined us at the table, and I resisted the urge to pull her into my lap. "There was a business card for a Victor Atwood with a phone number and a message to call regardless of the hour."

"Atwood? I wonder if there's any relation to Shelby from school?" Meg voiced.

"I doubt it—Victor Atwood is the Alpha of a pack that wants to settle in this area."

"Oh, Shelby isn't a wolf," she replied.

"He wants to *settle* near here? How big is his pack?" I demanded, hackles rising at the thought of another Alpha moving into our territory.

"I'm not sure of his pack numbers, but he said he'd like to meet to attempt to work out a peaceable agreement."

"Did he say why he wants to settle here?" My full attention was now on this matter.

"I believe his family is from this area, so he feels it's somewhat ancestral, though it must have been many generations removed. The Wolfes have been here for over three hundred years."

I scowled. "Do you think he's interested in joining packs?" It wasn't unheard of for packs to join up, but it didn't happen often, and it required one Alpha to surrender to the other so there was only one Alpha over the whole pack.

"It's possible. We didn't talk overly long. Just long enough to solidify a meeting. The meeting is tentatively set for Wednesday, but I wanted to check with you that the time works."

I was momentarily stunned. It was unlike Dad to be so considerate of my schedule. Typically, in Alpha fashion, he made the plans, and everyone else followed them. His expression remained open, and I knew he was making his best effort to make good on his promise to build a bridge to stem the gap in our relationship. I smiled.

"Wednesday is good." Then I sobered. "But I want to be sure that Meg has full protection. We still don't know who is behind the attacks."

Dad nodded. "I thought of that." He glanced at Meg. "Would you feel safe if you were with Mary, Rev, and Cade?"

Megan glanced at me, and I nodded back. Of the pack, those were the three people I trusted most with Megan's life.

"Yes. If Sam agrees," she said. My confidence soared with her sureness in me.

"I agree those are the best to make a protection detail right now."

"Wednesday evening then?" Dad asked.

"Fine. I'll bring Megan down to the house and meet you there?" I offered with another glance at Meg to be sure she was comfortable with the plans. She nodded, and Dad smiled at both of us. Two smiles in fifteen minutes—real smiles.

"All right. Again, sorry it's so early. I have to get into the city today for a client. I've got my cell on me. Also, I set Steve Rivers on the trail of young Kypson to check him out more fully."

"You know, I like him. I think he could be a good addition to our pack."

"I hope so. He needs a home."

Dad clapped me on the shoulder and nodded toward Megan.

"You two have a good day. Don't be late for school."

I glanced at the clock on the wall as I shut the door behind him. Six forty-five. We had plenty of time not to be late. Heat raced to my cheeks again as I found Meg and our eyes met. She quickly cleared her throat and turned to pour a cup of coffee. Sighing, I went to gather my things for the shower.

Chapter 44

Megan

I felt off. Not quite sick, but just...off. Maybe it was the nightmares, the adrenaline, and Sam's kiss this morning, or being up too early and too much caffeine. Maybe Mary cooked with something I wasn't used to last night. Wolf was still lethargic at best. I went ahead and skipped a big breakfast, opting for a piece of dry toast in case it turned out to be something more sinister. The morning passed in a blur, and by lunch, I wasn't any better. Wolf was acting strangely, too. The bell was a few minutes away, and I raised my hand. "Yes, Miss Carmichael?"

"May I use the restroom?"

The teacher nodded. I was a model student and never asked to leave class for any reason. I felt justified today. I gathered my things and trudged out the door to the bathroom.

Meet you in the cafeteria. Heading to the bathroom. I sent to Sam through our link. He didn't immediately respond, but I didn't worry much about it as the bell rang, and I was closing in on the hallway to the bathroom and students flooded out of classrooms.

Wolf was wobbly legged as I staggered past a few girls at the sinks and into a bathroom stall just in time to throw up in the black and white porcelain toilet. I spit the nasty taste out of my mouth and flushed it down, wiping my mouth on the back of my hand. Wolf lay down, her eyes closed, her fur dull and dingy, not glossy and shining as usual. Clearly there was something wrong with us.

I didn't feel ill, just unsettled. Just...off. And obviously I ate something weird that didn't agree with us. Shaking my head, I exited the stall and found two curious pairs of eyes belonging to two cheerleaders watching me, and Shelby Atwood staring at me from her view in the mirror.

Skylar, the captain of the cheer squad—the one Raven had said was hard to please, glanced at her red-haired friend and smirked.

"Morning sickness?" she shot at me before they giggled and left the bathroom. I was too shocked to say anything. Shelby whirled around and looked at me, an unreadable mask on her face.

"Are you pregnant?" she asked bluntly. My head snapped back, and Wolf looked up, snorting in disdain.

"Of course, I'm not pregnant," I retorted. "But either way, it's not any of your business."

Her lip rose in a silent snarl before she turned on her heel and stalked out of the bathroom. Belatedly, I remembered her fawning attention to Sam at the movie theater. Oops. I guessed that wondering if the object of your crush had impregnated his girlfriend could make a person irritable. I sighed as I methodically washed and dried my hands and rinsed my mouth out. I really hoped that my new nonexistent pregnancy wasn't going to be the latest gossip headline. I blushed thinking about it.

I was not that sort of girl. I thought most people *knew* I was not that sort of girl. I hoped my previous reputation was upheld even though I'd been dating Sam and from all accounts we were pretty into each other.

Leaving the bathroom, my phone vibrated. From Sam.

> Where are you???

Frowning, I quickly texted back.

> In the bathroom. Didn't you hear me?

> Wait there. Coming.

I huffed a little breath and adjusted my backpack and shoved my phone back into my pocket. Sam's head broke through the sea of people thronging to the cafeteria. The look on his face was intense, and my anxiety rose.

I moved to meet him, and he grabbed my hand, weaving us through the hallway to an exit that led out to the courtyard. It was cold, so there was next to nobody there. "I about had a heart attack when you weren't waiting for me," he said urgently, voice pitched low.

My forehead creased as I crossed my arms against the cold. "I *told* you I was going to the bathroom and would meet you at the cafeteria."

He blinked. "When?"

Icy fingers slithered into my belly. "Right before I left class."

"I never heard you. Did you not *hear* me—after the bell?"

I shivered and the icy fingers gripped me harder. "No," I whispered. "I didn't hear you at all."

Sam's expression fell, and the color emptied from his face. He scrubbed his free hand down his jaw as his hand holding mine squeezed once.

"Okay," he breathed.

"Sam, what's wrong?" Panic tinged my voice.

He looked at me hard, sorrow bleeding from his eyes. "How's your wolf?"

I gulped and shook my head. "I just threw up. She's not very responsive." The words forced themselves between my teeth as the icy hand clenching my gut grew claws and buried them in my midsection. Sucking in a lung-full of frigid air, I took a minute to try and process what I knew was the most likely culprit. The werewolf toxins were leaving my system. Humanity was winning.

I shook my head, denying the possibility. "I think it was something I ate. I'm sure after a nice run tonight, she'll be back in tip-top shape. She's probably needing a good stretch. She's been holed up for a few days. Remember? I was too tired to shift last night..." I drifted off, recognizing my own rambling.

"Probably so." Sam's voice was hollow. "Do you want to try to eat something and stick it out, or are you feeling too sick?"

"Maybe some soda and crackers? I have a test this afternoon that I'd rather not miss." I had felt worse and made it through a day of school. And the distraction from what might actually be happening inside me would be good. This was a good thing. This was my body telling me that I would have permanent skin, not fur. It was what I had wanted all along.

Wasn't it?

Chapter 45

Sam

*S*he couldn't hear me. And I couldn't hear her. Wolf was tearing me up from the inside, and I relished the pain as it kept me grounded enough that I couldn't fly into a thousand pieces. This was it. The beginning of the end. I clenched my fists and forced a swallow past the despair fighting its way up my throat. I was close. She was close. I knew it. But could she be close enough? Could she choose me? If we had time, I thought she could—would. But time was running out. Faster than ever.

I don't remember much of the rest of the day. I was strung halfway out of my mind with worry over who might be after Megan and what might happen to her, especially since I couldn't hear her thoughts regularly now, and what would happen to us, to the pack, to me, if she continued her way to returning human.

Dusk came early as it did this time of year. I was both eager with anticipation and loaded with dread. Anxiously I waited for Meg to come out of the bathroom in her robe so we could shift and enjoy some crisp fall air as the evening chill descended.

"Ready?" Meg asked as she clicked off the bathroom light behind her.

"I am. Weather should be good for a run. It's cold enough your breath fogs. Wolf always enjoys this time of year. I bet yours will, too." I tried not to roll my eyes at the way the end of my little speech came out higher than the beginning. I was nervous. I was anxious. Meg offered me a tight smile of her own.

Opening the door for her, we went down the steps. A few others were coming in the distance and figured it would be best to shift now without everyone as audience.

I nodded at her and in seconds was in my wolf form, silently urging her to take her animal form beside me. I blinked as I watched her forehead crease in concentration. There was a gentle ripple under her skin but no fur. Nothing broke the smooth flesh over her arms. She glanced at me, fear hiding in the depths of her eyes. A whine escaped my throat. I couldn't help it. She closed her eyes and spread her fingers, willing them to change. Nothing happened. Not even the ripple. Her eyes opened wide, fear morphing into terror and shock.

"Sam, I...I *can't*," she breathed.

My heart hurt so bad it might have been torn out of my chest. I shifted back.

"Go wait inside. Give me a few minutes to let people know we aren't coming." Her head bobbed; her eyes still wide in her pale face.

I gathered my tattered emotions around me and braced myself to look nonchalant and as if my entire world weren't coming apart with every breath I took.

Chapter 46

Megan

I closed the cabin door behind me, my fist shoved in my abdomen as I leaned against the polished wood. I sucked in a few ragged breaths and tried again to call up Wolf. She was there, moving sluggishly inside, but all attempts to bring her out, to shift our forms, were in vain. She whined, and I think a similar noise escaped my throat. Night fell outside. With only the light on the end table by Sam's bed to offer defiance against the darkness, long shadows cast themselves over the floor.

On autopilot, I slipped out of the robe and into my tank top and pajama bottoms. My mind was a swirl of worry, anguish, and confusion. I tried to bring to life the excitement I should have been experiencing at the revelation that I was morphing back into my human self. All human. No more split personality, no more coexisting wolf, no more hidden life...which would bring no more Sam. I swallowed thickly as I leaned my back against the kitchen counter.

The door opened, and a gust of air whooshed into the room, bringing in the crispness of the autumn night. Sam shut the door, and his stare burned into me. Something primal and unspoken flashed across his gaze, ratcheting up my own emotional turmoil. The kitchen counter pressed into my back as I leaned against it for support, gripping my hands against it like a lifeline. My heart was pounding in my ears, my chest rapidly going up and down. Anxiety rolled off me. My fingers twitched as my stomach heaved. I wanted Sam to hold me.

Without breaking eye contact, Sam snatched a pair of his sweatpants off the back of a kitchen chair. He turned quickly and slid them on under the heavy gray robe. As he turned, he let the robe slide off, and there he stood bare chested across the room, his eyes locked on my face.

I stayed rooted to the spot, unwilling to let my body betray the shred of rational thought left in my head. Part of me—my wolf—was in agony that I hadn't been able to shift. My brain said this was confirmation I would stay human. Why did those two thoughts conflict so badly? Wasn't this what I wanted? Sam moved slowly across the kitchen. I knew his gaze was riveted on my face even though my own stayed staring straight ahead.

Another step. Another. He was in my space. My eyes closed against the onslaught of emotions his nearness brought. I tried to swallow. His body hovered on my left, close enough that heat radiated off him but not touching me. Slowly he leaned his face down to mine, resting his forehead and nose against the side of my cheek, his arms bracing himself against the counter behind me.

His scent wrapped around me, the now-familiar tang of wolf, pine, outdoors, and *Sam* teasing my nose, calling to my wolf. She rose within me, pushing for release. I wanted to give it to her, to shift. I *wanted* to be a wolf in that moment more than ever. But I couldn't. My body wouldn't obey. My bones wouldn't change their shape; my fur wouldn't ripple along my arms, silky and soft.

I felt his inhale and knew he was scenting me, something that was now so much more intimate than a simple handshake.

He swallowed. "Megan," he whispered, his voice breaking. Tears pricked at the back of my eye lids, still screwed shut. I could practically taste the emotions in that one word. What he'd meant was, *don't leave me.*

His lips brushed across my cheek, once, twice, trailing white fire everywhere they touched. A choked noise clawed its way from my throat as his lips touched the corner of my jaw. With that noise, every wall between us came down.

I turned toward him even as he took one more step so that he was in front of me, pushing his body against mine, harder against the counter. His lips were on mine, tinged with desperation, tongue probing, finding no resistance as my mouth opened for him.

It was a far cry from the gentle kisses we'd shared in this kitchen that night after the movie. This kiss was hard and rough, wild and wanting. His hands gripped my waist, roaming from my hips to my sides and up my back, his body a lean, chiseled line of coiled muscle pressing against me. My hands gripped his biceps, tracing the ropy scar left by the arrow meant for me, then tracked up his shoulders and fisted into his hair, pulling his head from my mouth to my throat, gasping as his lips touched my skin.

My wolf rose within me, pushing me, fueling my already-heightened desire. Need seared through me. His lips broke away from the curve of my neck as he groaned. One hand gripped my hip, nearly too low to be decent, while his other stalked the curve of my spine, my shirt riding up at the hem, as he cupped the back of my head and his lips crushed mine.

I couldn't stop the noises that rose up in my throat, but it didn't matter. Sam kissed me harder, in a way I didn't know was possible. Each kiss set my soul on fire. How could I have lived without this? How *would* I live without *him*?

My hands dragged down the front of his chest, feeling the hard planes of his muscles. I wasn't the only one making noises now. His hands were hot fury, barely contained, as he grasped me even closer to him. They palmed my shoulder blades, his tongue sliding in and out of my mouth sending my senses reeling. I felt his thighs press up against mine. The counter was cutting into me in several places, but I couldn't bring myself to care. My back arched farther, Sam's body following me. His hands began their descent down my arched back and to my sides. Without uttering a word, I knew he was going to slide his hands all the way down to my waist, pick me up, and put me up on the counter. Butterflies swarmed in my belly but were quickly overcome by the lava coursing through my veins. I wanted Sam. Wanted him like I'd never wanted anything.

Images of what would be if we kept going sliced into my brain alongside the euphoria Sam's touch brought. I was about thirty seconds away from throwing all caution to the wind and giving Sam exactly what I knew he wanted, what *I* wanted in that moment, when his hands, still sliding down my sides to my waist, found the raised hemline of my shirt, his hand landing on my bare skin.

I had never allowed a boy to touch any skin normally covered by a shirt and a pair of shorts. Sam's hand on my naked flesh sent pinwheels of fire dancing over the spot. His tongue darted into my mouth again as his hand slid up under my shirt, caressing my side, his fingers reverently tracing their way up my body.

My lips broke away from his as I gasped from both shock and want at the feel of his hand on my skin.

With a sound not quite human and not quite animal, Sam ripped his hand away. Shreds of sweatpants *poofed* around me, and Sam stood before me, a great silver-white wolf. His tongue was lolling out the side of his mouth, his sides heaving. Deep blue eyes found mine, and he whined once before turning and practically running into the bathroom.

I don't know how long I stood there, my own chest heaving, looking at the closed bathroom door. A few minutes ticked by, and I heard the shower start. My hand came to my mouth, gingerly touching my kiss-swollen lips.

What had I done?

What had we almost done?

If Sam hadn't stopped himself, I wasn't sure I would have. I stood there, still frozen to the tile floor, just pondering that fact. What was wrong with me? If we had gone any further, there wouldn't have been any going back. I'd be a wolf forever. I'd be mated to Sam forever. I was only seventeen! I wasn't ready for that sort of commitment.

My head fell into my hands. I didn't want to cry, but I felt the tears brimming over anyway. I was so confused. Half of me knew that it was best to remain human, unencumbered, unattached, unmarried, and unmated. But, the other half, and shockingly enough, not all of it my disappearing wolf half, wondered, seriously wondered, would it be worth it?

This was too much. My head was going to explode.

I couldn't figure this out on my own.

About twenty minutes after the wolf went in, Sam came quietly out of the bathroom. His wet hair made dark splotches on his light blue T-shirt. It stretched across his shoulders, straining a little over his biceps, pink scar still poking out from under his left sleeve. I felt my face flush as I met his gaze.

His eyes were dark in the pale light, his eyebrows drawn together, his mouth a grim line. He ran a hand through his damp hair, scattering more droplets down onto his shirt. His mouth opened, shut, then opened again. "Megan, I'm so sorry." His voice was hoarse.

Those were not the words I was expecting.

Before I could reply, he raised his hand and cut me off. He snagged a chair from the table and slumped into it like a man defeated by the world. "When we first started this, you gave me a list of things that were not okay. I told you I was good with your boundaries because I respected you—do respect you. I crossed the line tonight. I broke my word, disrespected you, and you probably hate me now. I'm so sorry."

I gaped at him. This was probably not the best time to tell him that I had been seconds shy of happily following him down that path.

"I don't hate you, Sam. I could never hate you." I put as much conviction into the words as possible. As for the other things, well, what he said was true, but I was as much at fault as he was, probably more so. "And I'm sorry, too. I wasn't exactly putting the brakes on. But your apology really means a lot." And it did.

Aside from my grandpa, I'd never met a man who kept his word as religiously as Sam did, and I could tell it bothered him like nothing else that he'd broken his word to me. I wanted to go to him, wrap my arms around him, comfort him. But in light of what we'd just done—and nearly done—I thought it would be wiser to keep my distance for the moment, though part of me railed at the decision. If I was going to stay human, I *had* to keep my distance. But if I stayed human that meant giving up Sam.

"Will you be able to trust me again?" His eyes pleaded with mine.

"Sam, of course I trust you." I wasn't sure I trusted *myself* with him though. There was a long pause. "Sam?"

"Yeah?"

"I think I need to talk to my grandpa after school tomorrow. Alone."

"Okay. We'll go over as soon as school is over. I...I'm going to head on to bed now. Good night." With one last sparing look at me, he got up and shuffled to his bed across the cabin.

He did not try to kiss me goodnight.

Sam and I got ready the next morning making a lot less eye contact than usual, and there were no good morning hugs or kisses. I missed them but didn't have the guts to initiate. I called Grandpa to let him know we'd be swinging by after school. Tammy rode to town with us that morning. Her dad's truck died, and he needed to use her car. I was relieved that Tammy kept a noncommittal conversation going and remained oblivious to the tension radiating between Sam and me. The bus stop that would take her to campus was about two minutes from school, and I was thankful it was only two minutes of awkward silence.

Rachel was not so oblivious when I met her outside first period.

"I'll see you," Sam said with the lightest brush of his fingers against my arm. The first touch since last night. I smiled, my face feeling tight.

"Whoa, did you guys have a fight?" Rachel asked as soon as Sam's broad shoulders were down the hallway. I hoped there was enough other noise with kids going to class and slamming lockers that he wouldn't be able to overhear. I ushered her into the classroom anyway.

"No...we didn't fight. I don't think?" My forehead crinkled.

"And that means?" Rachel prompted. I glanced at the clock. Five minutes was so not enough time to bring her up to speed. Most of me wanted to spill all the details, but a small part of me wanted to keep that kiss to myself. It was a lot of things, but above all it was intimate.

"We kissed last night." Rachel waggled her eyebrows and brought her head closer to mine so I could dish. "I mean, we *really* kissed."

"Like he grabbed your boobs while you kissed?" she whisper-shrieked.

I pinched the bridge of my nose and screwed my eyes shut. "No! But...like...if he'd tried, I don't think I would have stopped him," I wailed, miserable and confused.

Rachel's mouth hung open, totally slack-jawed. "You're in love with him, aren't you?"

I stared into the green eyes of my best friend. "I don't know."

Rachel arched an auburn eyebrow.

"Maybe," I amended. "I'm going over to talk to Grandpa after school. I need his opinion. Obviously not on boob grabbing or kissing, but...you know...maybe being in love. It's not like this is just being in love with the guy you're dating. Things are a lot more complicated than that."

"They are, but love is complicated. What's a little fur in the mix?" Rachel winked at me and patted my hand as the bell rang. "You talk to Grandpa. He'll tell you what to do. And then tell me every single detail. And we are so not done discussing that kiss, either."

I smiled in spite of myself. Rachel was the best friend a girl could hope for.

School dragged on the rest of the day. Sam met me after each class, and we sat next to each other in the classes we had together and at lunch, but things were strained between us. I think he was still feeling guilty or ashamed, and I was confused and suddenly didn't know how I was supposed to act around him. And then there was my silent wolf. I know Rachel noticed everything, but I'm not sure who else did. No one else commented on our behavior, so I assumed nobody else really cared that much, or they didn't notice at all.

The last bell of the day rang, and I trudged to my locker, thrilled that I'd gotten all of my homework done in sixth period where we'd had a sub and a movie. I glanced up as I was getting near and saw Sam waiting for me. The breath caught in my chest as I looked at him leaning there against the wall of metal. He hadn't noticed me yet, and I took a moment to really look at him. His strong profile with his straight nose, shaggy blond hair, those piercing blue eyes. His mouth was still a straight line, not its usual friendly curve, and not set in that special smile that he reserved for me, either. The air left me in a whoosh like I'd been sucker punched. What if I never saw that smile ever again? Would he find someone else to give it to? He said he'd never feel about anyone else the way he felt for me, but were those just words? Would someone else get that secret look that used to be mine? I felt all empty inside. I was a mess.

Sam turned his head then, and his eyes did light up a little as he took me in, and though he grinned, it wasn't that secret twist of his lips that only belonged to me. "Hey, good rest of your day?" he asked casually as I jammed books into my locker.

"Okay, how about yours?" I asked, knowing the spark wasn't in my eyes. I felt sad. Sam picked up on it right away.

"What's wrong?"

I closed my eyes. "A lot of things. But I'm not sure I'm ready to talk about it yet."

Sam's eyes were sad now, too. "All right. Let's head on over to your grandpa's. Tammy's riding back with Raven."

We made awkward small talk for the seven minutes it took to get to my old house. Funny. When had I started to consider it my "old" house?

Sam killed the engine. "I'll walk you to the door, say hello, then go hang out at the park. Give me a call when you're ready for me to come get you."

Before thinking better of it, I put my hand on his arm. "Thanks, Sam." I meant it. For so many different things. He covered my hand with his free one.

"You're welcome."

I noticed that the door had been freshly painted and wondered if someone in the pack had come over to help out while I was away. Probably one of the wolves running patrols noticed and took the initiative. Gratitude warmed my heart even while a pang of melancholy came with it. I hadn't been here to help. And because of the need to have this house I'd lived in nearly my whole life protected from the unknown.

My knuckles hit the frame three times before I opened the door, and we walked in.

"Grandpa? We're here," I called out.

"In the kitchen, Meggie-Girl. Sam, you come on back, too," Grandpa said.

"I can't stay today, Mr. Carmichael, but I wanted to make sure Meg got in, and I wanted to say hello." Sam shook Grandpa's hand. Grandpa clapped him on the back.

"Well, that's all right. I'll get some quality time in with my girl." He beamed at me, and his eyes twinkled. I missed seeing those twinkly eyes every day.

"Meg, call me when you're ready." Sam's eyes ever so briefly tracked to my lips but then flitted back up to my eyes. He brushed his fingers along my arm again and then was gone.

"Meggie-Girl, I've missed you." Grandpa looped an arm around my shoulders, and I wrapped both mine around his waist.

"Not as much as I've missed you," I countered.

"Here now. I've just got the tea off. Go pour us a few mugs."

"Grandpa, I need to talk to you. About serious stuff."

His white brows rose up his forehead. "Well. Why don't you bring that tea into the living room while I go and get situated. It takes these old bones a while to get places these days."

I poured the fragrant tea—orange spice, our preferred blend—into two of our favorite mugs and brought them to the living room, setting Grandpa's on the end table next to his recliner and taking a seat across from him on the love seat.

"What's on your mind, Meggie?"

I bit my lip, unsure where to start. I took a sip of my tea, scalded my tongue, and put it back down. Grandpa waited patiently, blowing the steam from his teacup.

"I...um...I think I'm in love with Sam," I finally blurted, heat rushing to my face as the words left my mouth.

Grandpa's eyebrows rose to new heights. "Is that so? You sure could have fooled me with that chilly sendoff between you two."

I blushed darker and picked at the fuzzy brown corduroy of the love seat. "Well, things are a little awkward at the moment. We...we kissed last night." I snuck a look up and Grandpa's mustache was twitching, a sure sign of his amusement. I scowled at him.

"Don't get your dander up, girl. I remember being young and in love, and I certainly enjoyed kissing your grandma. Go on. Why did that make things awkward? Surely that hasn't been the first kiss you two have shared?"

He asked so matter-of-factly and then gingerly took a sip of his tea. I sighed. This was going to get even more awkward before it was over.

"Well, we, um, yes...we've kissed a few times. But not like we kissed last night."

Grandpa's face was suddenly much more serious. *Serves him right for teasing me*, I thought. "I'm listening," he prompted.

"First of all, nothing wildly improper happened," I stammered, "but, things went a little further than we intended, I guess." I was sure my cheeks were redder than the cherries Grandma had embroidered on the couch's throw pillows.

Grandpa wasn't laughing now. "Go on," he urged.

"And, well—" I clenched my eyes shut and took a deep breath and decided to have out with it. "His hand slipped up my shirt just a little bit, and then he changed into his wolf, presumably to keep himself from doing anything else." I said the whole thing with my eyes shut.

Grandpa took a sip of tea, and I cracked my eyes open. "I always knew I liked that young man." The twinkle was back in his eyes.

"Grandpa." I resisted the urge to roll my eyes. "Anyway, he knew that he broke one of my rules, I guess you could say, and things have been really awkward. He apologized and everything. But, while we were kissing, I think I realized that I might want to be with Sam. But then I keep trying to tell myself how impossible that is. I'm seventeen. *Seventeen*! For Pete's sake! I'm not old enough to be married, to stay with one guy for the rest of my life. What about college? What if I go off and meet someone that I fall in love with and end up not loving Sam as much as the new guy? What happens then? I'm stuck with Sam. For life. What if I wake up and find out that I'm miserable, or worse, that I make him miserable? Grandpa, I can't stay with Sam. I mean, at least, not now. But if I wait, and I stay human, and it's looking like I will, I won't *be able* to be with him."

I took a breath and then a gulp of my tea while Grandpa looked on. He knew I wasn't finished yet.

"And then, last night—about staying human—I...I couldn't shift. The change wouldn't come, no matter what I tried. I felt so lost, so..." I shrugged helplessly. "I don't even know the right words. But it didn't feel good like I thought it would. I've always wanted to stay human—had no desire to be a werewolf—and last night appears to be confirmation that I'm not going to stay a wolf. But in the end...that means I give up Sam. Who, for the moment, I'm totally infatuated with. Maybe even in love with." I plopped my forehead into my hands and waited for Grandpa to collect his pearls of wisdom to share with me.

"Meggie-Girl, do you know how old your grandma and I were when we married?"

I glanced up at him. I should know this, but as I wracked my brain, I realized I didn't. I shook my head, ashamed I didn't know the answer to such a simple question. It didn't bother Grandpa though. He carried on.

"I had just turned eighteen, and your grandma was sixteen."

My mouth fell open. Grandma had been younger than me when she married Grandpa? I knew they had married young, but I guess I never sat down and figured out the math.

"She was the prettiest girl I'd ever laid eyes on," he said it with a sigh and a smile. "I was getting ready to ship off to war, and I wanted her to be mine for keeps before I left. Lucky for me, she agreed with me. And so did her parents, though I'm not sure what they ever saw in me to let me have their daughter."

"How did you know she was the right one?"

He smiled, full of wisdom and knowing. "Meggie, I'm going to tell you something that a lot of the world hasn't figured out about love. It's what made my marriage to your grandma so long, enduring, and wonderful."

I was hanging onto his every word. This was why I knew I needed to talk to Grandpa.

"Love is a choice."

I blinked. That was it?

"Listen to what I'm saying, sweetheart. *Love is a choice*. When I got back from the war, I was a different man than when I left. I was harder, older, rougher, broken. But your Grandma Elsie, that marvelous woman, she *chose* to love me through that difficult time. It wasn't easy for her. It wasn't easy for me. It would have been a lot easier for each of us to go find someone new to love, to be with, someone with whom to start fresh. But your grandma and me, we made a vow before God and to each other. We were married. Marriage is a lifetime commitment. And in such a relationship, if it's successful, each person *chooses* to love the other. Each and every day. The grass is always the greenest where it's watered. You may feel in love now, and I think you are in love with Sam Wolfe, but you won't *feel* in love every day. And on those days, the harder days, you make a choice to love that person anyway." He sat back in his chair and took another drink of his tea. I let his words sink in.

"So you're saying it's not about whether or not I find someone else I love more later," I mused out loud.

"If you go into a relationship with the attitude that there might be someone else out there that's better, then you're bound to find that someone. Every single time. Because you're not looking at your spouse. You've always got one eye on the prowl. You don't do that in marriage. You choose only to see each other in that way."

I sank back into the corduroy cushions. *Love is a choice.* "My choice would come with fur, fangs, and midnight runs." I sighed. "Why couldn't Sam be a normal guy?"

"Sam *is* a normal guy. He just has another side that most don't. Tell me, Meggie. What would you actually have to give up if you stayed with Sam and became a werewolf permanently?"

"I beg your pardon?" I stammered. Did my grandpa just encourage me to stay a wolf?

"Think about it. What would you actually give up if you stayed a wolf?"

I did think about it then. I had always assumed that being a werewolf would limit and change everything I'd ever planned to do, but as I sat there and really thought about it, I couldn't come up with a single answer.

"You can still go to college, get that business degree, and open your bakery. You want to open it here in Rock Falls or in a neighboring town anyway." He gazed at me fondly. "You could still travel, visit the world. With Sam at your side. The only thing that might change in the long run is your time frame."

"I guess I haven't thought this through as much as I thought I had," I confessed.

"Oh, Meggie-Girl, none of us ever do." His face dissolved into his wrinkles as he gave me one of his big smiles. "For what it's worth," he sobered again, "I would feel better, knowing that you're well-protected by the pack and by Sam in particular since you'll never be able to be fully rid of this world now that you're aware. You'll never not know that werewolves exist. You'll always be looking over your shoulder, always wondering. You won't be able to pick them out after the blood fades, if you will. And, not to be morbid, but I won't live forever. My days are numbered. I'm old, Meggie-Girl. I'll stick around for you as long as I possibly can, but even love is not enough to keep a person alive forever."

My heart was heavy with sadness and bursting with love all at the same time. I loved this man so much.

"I love you, Grandpa," I whispered.

"I love you, too, Meggie-Girl." His face dissolved into happy wrinkles again.

"I still don't know what to do."

"You'll figure it out."

"Sam said that because I'm his mate, he'll always love me. Do you think it's only because he bit me? Do you think he really loves me just because I'm me?" I asked timidly.

"I think Sam has been fond of you for a very long time. And I think if you weren't wolves and he hadn't bitten you and you were two friends at school, he'd have pursued more with you."

"How do you know so much, Grandpa?" I asked, a small grin hiding at the corner of my mouth. His words warmed me.

"Because I was once a young man in love. I know the look." He winked at me. "If that's it, go call your young man. You all can stay to supper."

Chapter 47

Sam

I pulled into the park a few blocks away from Mr. Carmichael's house. The engine was shut off, but I still sat there, my thumb rubbing over the leather on my steering wheel. I'd really screwed things up this time. Possibly as bad as I had when I bit Megan.

Last night's kiss had been unbelievable, incredible, mind blowing, and I'd completely messed it up. I couldn't even think about it without getting turned on again and then cringing as I remembered the way her skin felt beneath my fingers. I should never have done that. I'd had no intention of doing it in the first place. Megan had specifically said no hands on skin. Well, my hands had been on her skin. And it had felt so good.

The look on her face was seared into my brain. Her hazel eyes wide, mouth slightly opened, jerked away from mine as I crossed the line. My head thudded against the back of my headrest. I was torn up inside between the emotions our kiss had brought up and the wrenching pain that Meg was pulling away from her wolf.

Wind whipped through the remaining leaves on the trees bordering the creek at the back end of the park. I got out, intent on letting the air cool my blazing emotions. I pulled my jacket tighter around. The temperature was dropping. This was the perfect time of year for a run in fur, wind whistling over my ruff, bringing the smells of the season with it. The perfect time to run with my mate. Who didn't look like she was going to be my mate for much longer.

Dirt flew into the breeze as I scuffed the toes of my boot through a dry patch on the ground. Megan hadn't been able to shift. I knew in my gut what that meant. She wasn't going to stay a wolf. My toxins hadn't been enough in human form. Strangely, it made me feel impotent, like I was less of a man and less of a wolf because of it. It didn't help that Megan didn't want to stay a wolf. Didn't want to stay with me. That hurt most of all.

I was in love with Megan. I was reasonably sure she'd grown to care for me, maybe even deeply. But it wasn't enough. She didn't love me enough to stay. My heart twisted painfully in my chest. I'd known it was going to get mangled from the moment we kissed at the movie theater. It was a bloody, mangled mess right now. I drew in a frigid breath, holding the cold air in my lungs, wishing the pain would dissolve.

The park bench where I sat overlooked the creek. The musk of the wolves that had patrolled by here recently was still traceable. The water rippled gently over rounded stones and between clumps of larger rocks. It was peaceful. I let my mind wander as I watched the water. I couldn't help but track to thoughts of Megan. The way she'd looked in the moonlight that first time as her wolf. The moment I knew she was my mate. I thought of her laugh, her smile, and the way her eyes twinkled, a lot like Mr. Carmichael's I realized.

My memories of Megan kept playing over in my head, twisting my heart up more while I tried to come to terms with things. I wondered what she was talking to Mr. Carmichael about. Was she begging him to intervene somehow? I sat for nearly an hour, just being still by the creek, sifting through my own thoughts.

My pocket buzzed and startled me. It was Megan. Heat rushed over me at her name on the screen. "Sam?"

"Hey, you ready for me to come back by?"

"Yes. Also, do you mind if we stay for dinner? I think Grandpa could use the company. And I'll make pasta Alfredo."

"As if I need to be bribed to eat your cooking." I couldn't stop the grin that came with it. She laughed, and it didn't sound strained. That was good.

"All right. See you in a few minutes. And, Sam?"

"Yeah?"

"Thank you. For giving me time with Grandpa."

"Of course."

Five minutes later, I was parked in Mr. Carmichael's driveway. Megan was fairly upbeat on the phone. I was more curious than ever but doing my best not to get my hopes up. She would leave me. That would be the end of it. I knocked on the door, and Megan answered.

Her smile reached her eyes. She looked at peace. They must have had some conversation. I wasn't sure how to act. Things had been so awkward all day.

"Hey," she said softly.

I smiled back, strained. "Hey, yourself." She shut the door behind me and then looked at me, hesitating. I cocked my head to the side, not sure what she was thinking, not sure what to expect. She bit the corner of her lip and then braced one arm against my chest and reached up on tiptoe to kiss my cheek. I gulped as a mad stampede of bulls charged around my stomach. Not what I was expecting at all, but I'd take it.

"Good conversation then?" I managed.

She grinned. "Definitely. Come on. You can play Grandpa a game of checkers in the kitchen while I fix dinner."

The moon was edging its way up the sky as we drove back to the cabin. Megan was thoughtful, but the tension had ebbed from her shoulders. She was relaxed, her chin propped in her hand, staring out the window as we left the edges of town and entered the stretch of lonely highway back toward the forest.

"So..." I began, "do I get details of today's conversation with Grandpa?" I was dying of curiosity.

Meg blinked and looked over at me. One corner of her mouth tipped up. She looked down at my hand on the console, hesitated a second, and then slid hers over mine. My heart immediately galloped in my chest, and I flipped my hand over, lacing our fingers together.

"We talked about a lot of stuff. Being a wolf, being human...kissing."

I grimaced. "You told your grandpa what I did, didn't you?" I cringed at what Mr. Carmichael must think of me, though he'd given no indication of his displeasure as he beat me at checkers or later during dinner.

"What *we* did," she replied. "It came up in conversation."

"And?"

"And it gave me a lot to think about."

And she was done elaborating. I guess it couldn't have been all bad. *She* was holding *my* hand. I gave it a gentle squeeze but let the conversation drop. She'd tell me more if she wanted me to know. I hoped she wanted me to know.

She still couldn't shift when she tried once we were back at the cabin.

"She's still in there, but she can't get out," Megan's voice broke. Her tears didn't fall, but she wasn't happy that her wolf was trapped inside. "Do you need to let yours out for a while? Don't feel like you can't if you need to," she offered with the slightest wobble in her voice. My heart broke all over again. I hesitated a moment, but then carefully held my arms out for a hug. When she stepped inside the circle of my arms without reserve, I tightened them around her.

"I'm fine. I'd rather be in here with you," I whispered to her hair.

She sighed against my chest. "I think I'm going to turn in." It was nine o'clock. Early, but Meg usually liked to be in bed by ten.

"All right." I wondered if she'd end up in my bed again. I doubted it but couldn't help the hope that surfaced. I'd just as happily accept an invitation to hers. I was desperate to be with her—to be hers for keeps. She pulled back and looked at me—really looked at me. I suddenly felt naked as her eyes searched over my face. Vulnerability crawled across my features and I let it show. Everything I was feeling—the hurt, confusion, my love for her—I let her see it. She smoothed a piece of hair off my forehead, and I stayed still as a statue.

She came up on tiptoe, and I held my breath as she pressed a soft kiss to my lips. My eyes slid closed as I branded the touch of them into my memory. She pulled back as her hands slid down my arms as she moved away. Cold air rushed to fill the void she left.

"Good night, Sam."

If she had nightmares, they were silent. I remained alone.

Chapter 48

Megan

Wednesday morning wasn't as stilted as Tuesday. It was still a little awkward, but the tension was no longer palpable. I threw up again before we left the cabin.

I caught myself staring at Sam that afternoon in class. I knew he knew I was staring, but he just let me after a quick glance in my direction to be sure I was okay. I stared to the point where I was jerked from my reverie to sudden mortification when Mrs. Oliver called on me.

"Megan, I'd like to see you for a minute after class."

I had no idea what she had said prior to her calling my name. My face flamed, and I nodded then quickly ducked my head back to my open textbook and my forgotten notebook. Sam squeezed my knee under the table, and I felt all the embarrassment and confusion bubble up again.

"I'll meet you in the hallway," Sam whispered as the bell rang. I nodded again and gathered my books before trudging to the front of the room where Mrs. Oliver waited by her desk. Her face was concerned as she stood and leaned a hip against her desk.

"Megan, I'm sorry if I embarrassed you calling your name out. You were looking pretty dazed, and that's not like you. I wanted to be sure you're okay. I know you and Sam have been dating...and you guys appear serious. *Really* serious. Please don't take this the wrong way, but does your grandpa know how serious you two are?"

I looked into the concerned eyes of my teacher and couldn't help the snort that escaped. I wasn't trying to be irreverent or disrespectful. If it had been anyone besides Mrs. Oliver, I would have been tempted to roll my eyes and head to my next class, but I knew Mrs. Oliver genuinely cared.

"You seem to be so aware of each other. The way people do when they've been married for years and know each other's habits and routines. But you don't look very happy today. And you spent half the class staring at Sam. Everything okay? Did something happen?"

My lips curved up in spite of my world galloping toward a black hole of crazy. "Mrs. Oliver, I appreciate that you're concerned. I do. Sam and I *are* dating. We're working through some things. Nothing like that has happened. And yes, my grandpa knows. He's actually encouraging me to date Sam."

Her eyebrows were still trying to meet, but the rest of her face relaxed. "All right. I'm glad about that. If you need to talk, I'm available."

"Thanks, Mrs. Oliver. It's nice to know you're looking out for me." And it was. I meant it. She had no idea what was going on, but it was nice that she noticed and cared enough to ask. And it was interesting that Sam and I reminded her of an old married couple...

Sam smiled sadly when I exited the classroom. He took my hand and steered me toward my last class of the day. I knew he'd heard everything Mrs. Oliver had said, and he was giving me space to comment or let it go. The ball was in my court. The ball was entirely in my court.

Chapter 49

Sam

"You have everything you need?" I asked Megan as Dad and I were poised to head out to our meeting with Victor Atwood.

"I'm good. I've got my homework. Cade said he brought a few action movies." She rolled her eyes good-naturedly.

I chuckled. "We shouldn't be too long." I let myself sweep a few fingers over her cheek before tucking some hair behind her ear.

"Okay. Be safe."

"I'll do my best." With a quick grin, I bent toward her, but hesitated, not sure if we were still kissing or not. She didn't make me wonder but reached up and kissed me on the lips. Not super quick, and not lingering, but warm and...promising? I searched her face for further clues, but she only smiled.

"I'll see you when you get back."

I squeezed her fingers, then we headed out of the kitchen to the living room where the others waited.

"I'm going to introduce her to some proper zombie horror," Cade announced.

"I'm going to prepare my sermon in the other room," Rev quipped dryly while Mom laughed.

"We should only be a couple hours or so, I'd think," Dad said to Mom. "See you in a bit." Dad kissed Mom quickly and then we were out the door and into Dad's old truck.

I wouldn't be surprised if we got early snow overnight—one of the reasons for the truck. The temperature had dropped even lower and hovered in the low thirties.

"How are things going with Megan?" Dad asked as we rolled past the *Come back to Rock Falls* sign heading out of town. We were going to meet Atwood one town over at a restaurant run by Jerry and Lisa Grassey, a couple from our pack.

I sighed. My chest was heavy. "I don't think I have enough time to convince her to stay. I know she cares about me, but I don't know that it's enough." It was liberating to say this to my father. I wasn't scared of his anger or his disapproval anymore. I was still wary of them, but I didn't fear them.

"I'm sorry, son."

"I know it messes up a lot of things. I'm sorry, too." Dread threaded its fingers through me. Both at losing Megan and trying to navigate the muddy pack waters that would follow.

"We'll figure it out. I'm sorry you'll have to go through the pain of her leaving." Dad's voice dipped low like it did when he was feeling deep things.

"Is there anything else I can do to keep her a wolf?" It was an empty hope, I knew.

Dad shook his head. "If there is, neither Rev nor I have found it. I've had him searching through all the old accounts for anything that might help."

"Really? I didn't know that."

One of Dad's cheeks lifted in a lopsided grin. "I know I'm gruff and probably not as gentle as I should be. And I haven't treated you as I should, but I've never wanted you to be in pain. There's still a little time. Work your magic."

"Thanks, Dad."

We rode on in companionable silence for another fifteen minutes when Wolf suddenly came alert and the hair on the back of my neck rose.

"Dad?"

"I know. I feel it, too," Dad said, voice tight and knuckles white on the steering wheel. We both scanned the darkening landscape around the truck. Much like all the area outside town, there was a small open space between the road and the forest that lurked on all sides. It was impossible to glimpse much beyond a few feet into the darkened underbrush as we sped by.

"There's a service road up there." I squinted where he indicated about thirty feet ahead, searching for the cause of the raised hackles. "Is that a—"

Dad didn't finish his sentence but cursed instead as a black truck obliterated gravel beneath its tires, spinning out of the service road, and like a predator lying in wait, turned and rocketed straight for us. Dad spun the wheel, trying to move us between the looming vehicle and the ditch. I glanced behind us and my heart pounded. Another truck crushed the pavement and was gaining ground by the second.

We jerked and bounced as Dad whipped the truck through the ditch on the left side of the road. The black truck in front of us screamed down the pavement, eating it like fire.

"Sam!" Dad shouted. I braced for impact as Dad's arm flew out in front of me as meager protection. The black truck slammed into the front corner of the truck as the gray truck behind us careened into the side of the truck bed. My head smacked against the window, and I felt something sharp stab my side. My vision swam, and everything went black. I reached blindly for Dad, but the blackness took me before I found him.

Chapter 50

Megan

The zombie horror movie that Cade had brought was ridiculous. It was some foreign film from some decade past.

"Do you really watch this for enjoyment?" I asked while cringing at the bad special effects.

Cade laughed. "Not really. It's more something to pass the time. I enjoy the evolution of the horror film. This is some classic bad."

"Obviously." I smiled then glanced back down at my English paper. We were supposed to turn them in tomorrow. Mine was probably as good as it was going to get. I'd been working on homework off and on while Cade played the movie and tinkered with his own homework. He glanced over.

"I'd offer to look over your paper, but I don't have the same appreciation of the Oxford comma that Sam does." He grinned.

"That's okay. He actually already went over it earlier this week. I'm just a perfectionist when it comes to my grades." I sighed. It was a miracle that I still had A's, though a few had sunk to A minuses, after the past few weeks with their various distractions.

"So what do you want to do after high school?"

I pursed my lips. "Before all of this happened"—I gestured around and Cade nodded, getting my drift—"Rachel and I planned to set up a delivery bakery sort of thing. You know, run it out of one of our kitchens. Kind of an online delivery service for bread and cookies and stuff. We want to turn it into an actual bakery after that. We're wanting to take some business classes while running the online stuff and getting more notoriety. But it will probably depend some on what happens—" I cut off and looked sharply at Cade, realizing I may have overstepped myself.

"If you stay wolf or not?" he finished quietly, his steady eyes locked on mine, sympathy lingering in their depths.

I nodded, emotion roiling up my throat again. "Sorry. Touchy subject."

We were quiet a minute as some guy lopped off a zombie's head with a samurai sword.

"You know Sam is in love with you, don't you?" he said. I looked up at him. "He's been pretty much in love with you for years. I'm not trying to make you feel bad or guilty; I thought you should know that he loved you a long time before he bit you."

My heart thumped in my chest. I didn't know how to respond to the echo of Grandpa's words. "Cade, I couldn't shift last night." It was out of my mouth before I even consciously thought it.

He whistled between his teeth. His expression was dead serious. "Well, that explains Sam's mood then."

I worried my lower lip. "I hate this. I hate wanting to be human and still missing the wolf. I am so confused that I can't even hear my own thoughts inside my head. I want to be with Sam, but am torn because I'm so young, and I'm terrified I'm going to make the wrong decision or for the wrong reasons. It's like the world is sitting on my shoulders, and I'm cracking under its weight." I blinked rapidly to chase the threatening tears away.

"Megan," Cade started and then hesitated. "You don't owe Sam Wolfe a single thing." He took a breath. "Unless you love him. Then maybe you owe yourself something."

Chapter 51

Sam

I sneezed myself awake into a splitting headache. The pain bobbed behind my eyes as something fibrous tickled my nose. I held my breath to keep from sneezing again and possibly losing my eyeballs with the force of the pounding. I was groggy. So groggy. I slit my eyes open and found swampy darkness. My nose tickled again. I moved my head and my face hit rough material. I yanked my eyes fully open and was met with darkness. Two seconds more and the rough weave of fabric came into focus.

A crash sounded somewhere to my right and with startling clarity, memories of the wreck flooded my brain. I gasped for air and fought to stay upright, seated on something cold and hard, hands tied behind my back, my body propped against what felt like rough boards. There was a bag over my head.

Dad? I tried using the link. Nothing. Immediately I started wiggling my wrists in their restraints.

I stretched out with my ears, feeling my senses slowly returning to me. I still felt disoriented and out of joint. I didn't think it should be taking me this long to heal from wreck injuries that appeared to be mostly superficial. My side still hurt, but it was tender, not a raging pain. Adrenaline rushed my system as I considered the possibility that they had drugged me. Whoever *they* were.

Voices sounded from my right where the crash had originated. My ears, normally tuned to perceive minute sounds at great distances, felt stuffed with cotton. I could hear the voices but could not distinguish the words. It made my skin feel itchy and my heart picked up. I relied heavily on my hearing. Could I even shift? Had I been given some sort of suppressant?

I searched out Wolf; he was there, but dormant. I couldn't rouse him. Panic clawed its way down my limbs, and I took a deep breath. I'd never been without my wolf.

Sam? The faintest echo of sound in my brain.

Dad! Where are you?

...here...but...you?

His voice in my head was patchy, but I was thankful it was working at all. I felt the ropes start to give.

"Alert then, are we?" A voice like oil came from the right. I hadn't heard the person approach, and the sensory deprivation left me cold in its wake. Stilling my hands, I looked up. Wolf tried to raise his head, recognizing the threat, but was paralyzed.

The hood was jerked off and the force of it knocked my head back into the rough planks, spangling stars across my vision. My stomach heaved with the impact, my vision blurring again.

A scent wafted through the air, light, and nearly untraceable, but enough for me to recognize. It was the wolf from the theater. "Sorry to make you wait, but we're not ready for you." He glanced at my bound state, then turned on his heel and walked back out the door. My swimming vision took in a man a little older than me. Slicked black hair, not overly broad shoulders, and then he disappeared through the door. Chains clinked.

I blinked and took in my surroundings as I squinted one eye to keep the throbbing at bay. I nearly had enough room to get my left hand out.

Sam...where... Relief shot through me as Dad's voice broke through like a radio suddenly finding a signal.

Dad? I'm in some sort of outbuilding. Concrete floor, old wood planking on the walls. Where are you?

There was a muffled grunt from the other side of the wall.

Dad? Are you against a wall? I bumped my elbow behind me against the old wood.

There was an answering thump. *You...all right?*

I think they may have drugged me. Senses are dulled but are slowly coming back. Are you okay?

Drugged...can't...free? Can you get free?

You...when...I'll...and then...

Dad, I can't hear you. Say again.

I'll...you...feet?

Chains rustled again, farther away and behind me. There was a familiar human snarl. It *was* Dad on the other side of this rotting plank wall. My ears tingled as I strained to hear what was happening opposite my side of the thin wall.

"Your son is awake." More muffled words. "...wait and the discomfort." Shuffling sounds distorted the next words. "...further instructions for you shortly." Footsteps, then rattling chains again.

There's...window...side.

There's a tiny window way up, but I can't reach it human, and I'd be too big as a wolf. Plus, I'm tied. I can't get to my wolf.

Megan...waiting...

Megan. It sent another jolt of adrenaline flooding my body and brought my working senses into sharp relief. The wolf who checked on me had been the wolf at the theater. At the school. What if he was tasked with getting me out of the way so whoever made an attempt on Megan's life could have access to finish the job? Terror clamped a vice around my windpipe, and I struggled to suck in air.

Sam? Pull it together...will...must. Dad's voice was starting to come clearer, but before I could formulate a coherent thought back to him, the chains on his side rattled again.

"He'll see you now."

"Not without my son," came Dad's steely reply right behind my head through the planking separating us.

Heavy footfalls vibrated through the floor. The low voice came again, close to the wall. "Only because *he* wants to see you both. It has nothing to do with what you want or not, I'm afraid."

Even as their exchange was going on, the chains on my door loosened and an unfamiliar man entered. This one was blond. He was all angles, and his face was perfectly blank. I wasn't sure I'd ever seen a face so devoid of emotion.

He jerked his head toward the door, and I struggled to get to my feet. It was hard with my hands behind my back, with Wolf MIA, and only half my senses at my disposal. My limbs felt like gelatin and to my disgrace, my legs nearly gave way under my weight once I was upright. The blond man waited, face still impassive, until I limped over to him at the door. He indicated with his thumb that I should go first. I shuffled past him into cold night air that whipped around and bit into my cheeks. The cold brought some clarity with it, and the lingering haze in my brain started to clear, leaving a light mist of grogginess behind.

As quickly as I could, I scanned the surroundings. Nothing immediate to give me our location. We were in the forest. Deep in the forest by the looks of the underbrush that hadn't been cleared away from the path that led away from the building.

I turned as Dad was led up the trail. He was in bad shape. He limped heavily and favored his right side. I wondered if he'd been banged up in the crash. My breathing sped up as his captor nearly dragged him up the track. Dad faltered and stumbled heavily, crashing to the ground. "Dad!"

The blond man grunted and jerked my arm to keep me where I was.

Sam, go now!

An Alpha's command. Without another thought, Wolf nudged my feet and propelled me clumsily into my captor, ploughing into him in my attempts to coordinate myself, but mercifully knocking him off balance enough for me to crash into the underbrush. Shock rippled over my skin as Dad snarled and then the ripping of flesh and the crack of bone sounded in the night. His wolf was out. At least part of his heavy limping had to have been a ruse. I stumbled farther into the woods as there was more ripping flesh, the patter of blood hitting the ground, the tang of its smell waking Wolf more. He pushed for release, and I quickly gave in. Or at least tried to. Not yet. Frustration I'd never known fired through my muscles, pumping them forward as the sounds of the fight rose in my ears. The thud of bodies on the dirt, rolling, crashing against the building, snarling, ripping, blooding, all boiling in my brain.

I wanted to go back and fight, but I knew that if I didn't escape, neither of us had a good chance of leaving alive. Not after the welcome we'd received. Plus, my Alpha had *commanded* that I go. I jerked my hands against the rope, and my left hand came free. I pumped my arms, leaping over a root at the last minute. I was so stupid clumsy in my skin in these woods. Cursing under my breath I shook my head, trying desperately to clear whatever drug they'd injected into me. Terror filled me at the sounds of additional voices and the ripping of skin into fur. I was never going to make it anywhere unless I had my wolf.

The cracking of dry leaves was the first indication of pursuit. With my enhanced hearing still out of commission, I had only weak, human senses. Fear rose up my throat as my legs stumbled over yet another root. A growl sounded close behind me, and my heart tripped double time as I kept going. Into the dark. Into the woods. Hurtling into the underbrush, and finally catching my foot on a patch of dried vines.

I fell hard on my shoulder, rolled, and looked up into the face of a giant slavering wolf flying through the air. With a grunt, I twisted out of the way, but only just. The big brown wolf landed right where I'd fallen. Scrambling to gain purchase on anything to try to get away, I crab-walked backward. The wolf snarled and gnashed its jaws. The glint went out of its eyes, its face falling strangely slack, then it opened its heavy jaws and clamped them over the calf of my right leg.

Teeth punctured my soft flesh, ripping into the muscles of my leg. Blood welled up and dripped out of the beast's mouth. I screamed, the pain and fear coming over me like a smothering blanket of smoke, choking me with its acrid fingers. The wolf growled and shook my leg sending fresh waves of agony rippling through me.

Purely by chance, my flailing hand landed on a fallen branch. Gripping it with all the strength I could muster, I flung the branch against the side of the creature's head.

The wolf howled and let go of my leg. I grunted as the teeth dislodged and a fresh wave of blood soaked into the ground. I struggled backward as the wolf shook his head, his eyes clearing. He whined, then the mask dropped back over its face. Its eyes became vacant once more, his lips curled back in an ugly growl.

I raised the branch over my head, and before the wolf could move, I smashed it down right between his eyes.

With a whimper, it slumped to the ground. I didn't wait to see if it was down or only stunned. I gripped the branch and struggled to my feet. I limped as fast as I could, biting down and ignoring the pain throbbing up my leg with each movement. I continued moving as long as I could until I felt the slightest stirrings of rippling beneath my skin.

Risking it, I stopped against a tree, bent over, my head between my knees and concentrated. I put my full energy on finding my wolf, my other half, the part of me I'd never been without until tonight. With a heave and the most tenuous tethers of mind and body holding us together, I shifted. It was agonizingly slow and painful, pushing past the drugs. I clenched my teeth to keep from crying out as the sweet agony swept over me and left me breathless. With a final shake, I left my skin behind, and Wolf emerged.

My senses instantly heightened, though still not to their full effect. I glanced around, forcing the panic back.

Black night seeped around me in a dark oily haze, inky fingers snagging their way into my fur and threatening to choke me. My head pounded, and each breath I took sent an axe to the base of my skull and sent pain throbbing over the top of my head and shooting up my leg. I inhaled anyway, gathering information. I fought to keep from heaving for air after my mad sprint on legs, leaving a horrific bloody trail behind me.

I caught scent of the faintest trace of highway asphalt and motor oil. Scooping up my ripped shirt in my mouth and leaving the rest of my tattered clothes, I turned my course accordingly and ran for all I was worth.

With the change, my leg had begun healing. I knew I was still leaving a blood trail. This was bad. Very bad. I was amazed that no one had caught me yet. The wind was cold and slapped my face. The night pressed in around me, making shadows twist and writhe from their secret hiding places. My wolf had every sense on as high alert as possible, straining to hear anything that might give away a predator—a fellow wolf—one bent on killing me. Wind whistled through the underbrush, gusting against my ruff, blasting information into my nostrils. My brain processed as I moved as quickly and as stealthily as I could. Once I hit the highway, I knew I'd be an easy target for humans, but I hoped that there I'd face less threat from those hunting me.

Taking another risk, I shifted back to my skin. Panting and in pain, I knelt for two seconds gasping air like a fish out of water. I picked up my torn shirt where I'd dropped it when I shifted back and made quick work of wrapping it around my punctured leg. I wasn't sure how well it would hold once I turned back into a wolf, but it would be better than nothing. Wolf came out easier this time, though it was still painful. Most of my shirt had stayed bound around my leg, stanching the worst of things. I hoped it would help at least slow my blood trail.

The stink of oil, burned rubber, and blacktop slammed into me with the next gust of wind, and I veered east, following my canine senses and letting Wolf have his head. Another ten minutes of snaking my way around bushes and decaying logs brought me to open ground, in clear sight of the highway.

A howl raised not far from my left. With a jolt of speed that only a burst of panicked adrenaline could produce, I sped across the cleared ground, paralleling the highway. Another howl answered. This one slightly farther behind the first. They were not my wolves. These were the *dogs* who had my dad. Who had taken me. I clenched my teeth together to keep the feral growl from ripping through my lips. No sense in making any more noise than necessary. I was strong and a good fighter, but right now I didn't have enough in me to do battle. Not by myself. Not injured and drugged as I was. There. The sign for Rock Falls. I was one mile outside town. We'd been approximately ten miles out, and I prayed I'd be able to find the spot again. I should at least be able to follow my own blood trail back. I put on speed that neither Wolf nor I knew I had. I had to get to safety—to make sure Megan was still secure—and to assemble the pack to take back our Alpha.

Chapter 52

Megan

"Something doesn't feel right." Nothing was wrong, but something felt off.

"What doesn't feel right?" Cade asked as he flipped the TV off where credits of the zombie movie were scrolling up.

I drew my eyebrows together. "I can't explain what it is. Something just doesn't feel right." My phone was on the coffee table, and I snatched it up, dialing Sam's number.

My blood chilled in my veins.

"What?" Cade pressed.

"It went straight to voicemail." I looked at him, fear squeezing its hand around my stomach. "He always picks up if it's me. He'd never turn his phone off. Not now that our link isn't working," I admitted in a whisper.

Cade's eyebrows shot up to his hairline. "Mary!" He jumped off the couch and headed into the kitchen.

I took several deep breaths trying to calm myself as I heard Cade, Mary, and Rev speaking in the kitchen. Dread pooled in my gut and looking down, I realized my knuckles were white. I forced myself to unclench my hands and dialed Sam's number again. Voicemail.

"Sam, where are you?" I whispered into the room.

Sam? Can you hear me? I tried our link. Nothing. Just a black hole that swallowed my words and offered nothing.

"Megan, come with me." Mary's voice was stern and offered no room for disagreement. Phone still in hand, I followed her to the stairs. She opened the door to the closet under the staircase. "Do you see that ring there in the wall?" She pointed.

I nodded as I made out the barely visible outline of a metal ring embedded in the dark closet wall.

"If you give that a tug, a door will open in the floor. If anything happens and you're in danger, you go down there. There's food and water for several days." She looked hard at me and my eyes went wide as my mouth went dry.

"What's going on?"

"I don't know. But we're preparing for all possibilities." Mary was clearly taking charge.

"You feel it, too, don't you?"

She looked me in the eye, hers sad and uncertain. "Yes."

"Dad is assembling the fighters." Cade's blue eyes were shining. Both from fear and anticipation.

"The chain is started. Families are being notified to put their safe measures in place," Rev said as he joined us in the living room.

I jumped as my phone rang with an unknown number. "Hello?" I nearly shouted as my trembling hand held my phone to my ear.

He groaned on the other line. "You're safe. Okay."

"*Sam*! What's wrong?" I couldn't get any more out before he cut me off.

"Are you still at the house?"

"Of course."

"Put me on speaker and get everyone else in the room."

"We're all here," I told him as we huddled around the phone.

"We were ambushed. I'm at the phone in the back of Druzy's Bar at the edge of town. Someone needs to come pick me up. My leg is hurt, and I've got wolves on my trail. They drugged me and not all my senses are working. I can't use the all call. Get Jennifer Kypson and have her meet me at the house. I may need stitches again. Tell her to bring stuff for blood collection, too. Assemble the fighters. They still have Dad, and we have to go after him."

"Sam," Mary started, catching her lip between her teeth as terror slid across her face.

"I know." He heaved a breath. "I'm moving toward home. I don't want to stay in one place. I don't know if they'll follow me inside city limits, but they might. I don't know what they want." There was blood in my mouth as I realized I'd been chewing the inside of my cheek. "I'm moving east. I'm going wolf, so whoever comes needs to be looking for fur, not skin."

"I'll come right now," Rev offered.

"No. Stay with Megan. Have Jake and his dad come if you can. They're closest to this side of town. Tell Jake to bring a robe. I want everyone going in pairs. No one goes anywhere alone."

"Calling Jake now," Cade said and stepped away from the group.

"Mom, I'm sorry. We'll get Dad back."

"Oh, Sammy, I know. Be careful." Mary's chin trembled, but her voice was strong.

"Megan? Be safe. Okay? Don't leave the house."

"I won't. Please, please be careful." My whisper strangled itself from my throat.

"I will. I'll be back soon." And the phone clicked off.

I was numb. My brain was trying to work through the information it had been given, but the cogs and wheels weren't turning fast enough. Terror bloomed in my belly and spread like poison to my limbs making them heavy and sluggish.

"Megan, breathe," Rev said as he put an arm around my shoulders and led me back to the couch. "He'll be all right. We'll get this all sorted, and things will be fine," he comforted.

I wanted Grandpa. What I really wanted was Sam, but in his absence, I wanted my grandfather's arms around me, his orange tea and spice smell cocooning me. I shivered. I texted Grandpa and Rachel what I knew. And then I waited. There was nothing I could do but wait.

Wolves began to arrive. Some in animal form, some in skin. The animals blended into the darkness, flashes of green glowing eyes giving away their shadowed forms as they collected. Waiting. Waiting for their Beta to return. Waiting for news of their Alpha.

I searched for Wolf inside me. She was there, her concern ratcheting my own up higher so that I felt tied in knots. She paced, and though I secretly went into the kitchen by myself to try to let her out, I couldn't. We were agreed and of the same mind at last, but we could not change.

Nearly thirty minutes after Sam called, there were tires on pavement that came all the way up the drive. Racing to the window, I jerked the curtains so hard I nearly brought the rod down. Jake's familiar truck and then Sam's shaggy head in the front seat had my breath leaving me in a rush. "Mary! He's here!"

Mary was already dashing to the door, but I beat her through it and ran to Sam, launching myself at him, remembering he said he was hurt only at the last minute. It didn't matter. He leaned his weight against the truck and nearly lifted me from my feet as he buried his head in my neck and my arms locked around his shoulders.

"Where are you hurt?"

"Just let me hold you a second," he mumbled into my hair. I melted against him, my heart hammering as my fingers felt hard muscle beneath them, assuring myself that he was here.

Headlights danced across the front of the house as a beat-up white sports car pulled into the drive. Sam released me but kept his hand around mine, cinching his gray robe tighter with the other. Mary leaned in and pulled Sam close. "I'm sorry, Mom."

"No, Sammy. This is not your fault."

Jennifer got out of the car, and Kyp followed out the passenger side. I realized that the gathered pack members had converged and had formed a semicircle around us. Jennifer and Kyp approached tentatively.

"Let them through." Sam turned to address the rest of the pack. "Thank you all for coming so quickly. Your Alpha and your Beta were ambushed tonight by some of Victor Atwood's pack. I don't know why, but they clearly meant to hurt us. They still have Dad. We are going to get him back. Steve, Corwin, Jonathan, Rev, please come into the house. We're going to form a plan, and we're going to move quickly. The rest of you, stay close. I was drugged, and not all my senses are fully functioning. As soon as the all call is working properly, expect to move out." He nodded at Jennifer who hesitantly moved up the walkway to the house. Sam put his arm around my shoulders and leaned on me more than I expected.

"Bad?" I whispered.

He nodded and grimaced as we limped together to the door.

Chapter 53

Sam

It was a strange combination of feelings as we moved up the walkway. The terror of the abduction, the relief that Megan was safe, the pain still shooting up my leg, and the weight of responsibility all pressed in on me. I squeezed Megan's shoulder and leaned on her probably more than I should have, but I was so tired. Adrenaline flooded my system while the stress and pain urged me to give in and shut my eyes.

"Do you have any idea what they might have drugged you with?" Jennifer asked quietly as she came up beside us.

I shook my head. "No. I don't. But it's dulled all my wolf senses, and it took a while for me to be able to call the wolf out. I couldn't shift." I shivered, remembering the panic of not being able to access such a vital part of myself. Megan squeezed my hand.

She nodded. "Suppressant. Kyp, run back to the car and grab the black duffel out of the back seat, please."

"Do you know what it is?" Megan opened the door.

"Not one hundred percent, but I have a good idea. The pack in Kentucky used a suppressant as a form of discipline." Jennifer frowned.

"No wonder you left," I muttered under my breath. What kind of Alpha would encourage, let alone allow, such a torture?

Steve Rivers, Corwin Banks, and Jonathan Stone followed us in along with Cade, Mom, and Rev. I dropped to the couch and pulled Meg down with me as the rest filed into the room and found spots.

"Leg?" Jennifer guessed.

"Right one."

She glanced around then moved the coffee table over a few feet. "Can you prop your leg up?"

Wincing, I put it on the table. She moved the robe back and there was a collective inhale as everyone saw the bloody, mangled mess of my leg. It was healing, but it looked nasty. Blood still oozed in places and there was a thick, dried crust of blood, dirt, and forest bits stuck all down my calf where my makeshift bandage had slipped.

"I need a cookie sheet, a couple big containers of water and some towels, and a trash bag, or we need to move into the bathroom and use the tub," Jennifer said.

"Guys, get water in here. We need to strategize now, and we won't all fit in the bathroom." I gave a rare order. I was acting Alpha, and I found my instinct to give orders to get things done was coming more naturally than I expected. There was a scramble of bodies as everyone in the room moved at once to get tubs, water, and towels. Only Meg stayed still beside me.

Kyp knocked twice on the door and then opened it, bringing the large duffel in with him. "How you doing?" he asked as he put the bag down beside the couch. His eyes widened as he took in my leg.

"Been better. Our pack is usually safer than this. Still want to join?" I smiled, but there was more truth in my words than my tone let on.

"Absolutely." There was no hesitation and his eyes held conviction. "What do you need right now?"

"Right now, we need to get my dad back and get whatever they put in my system, out." The last bit came out on a growl. Now that I was home, safe for the moment, I was intensely frustrated with my situation.

"You were drugged?"

"Your mom said she thought it was a suppressant, whatever that means?"

"There are a couple types floating around, but there's a pretty easy compound made from wolfsbane and aspirin that will keep the wolf silent."

"Wolfsbane? Are you serious?"

"I guess that's not a myth?" Megan asked.

Kyp cracked a wry grin. "Not a myth. Hurts like the devil. Right here, behind the eyes." He pointed with two of his fingers to his own face. I thought of the pounding headache I had when I'd come to with the bag over my face—the headache still lingering, like a giant hand squeezing my scalp and poking my eyeballs from the inside. I thought it had been from the wreck, but maybe it was the drugs?

Jennifer came through from the kitchen with Mom's best cookie tray. Quickly, she knelt and arranged a few instruments, gauze, and iodine as the rest came back in carrying water in pots and Tupperware and a large metal basin that Mom kept for large pack gatherings.

"First things first. Is there anything to get this drug out of my system sooner than to let it run its course?" I asked Jennifer as she wet a towel.

"I have something that will lessen the effects if they gave you wolfsbane. But if they gave you something else, then there's nothing I have that will help." I hissed as the water hit my broken skin.

"Will it do anything if it's not wolfsbane, and I take it anyway?"

Jennifer glanced at Kyp. "It might make you tingle weirdly in your paws and make you clumsy, but I didn't have any other effects. But I'm only half wolf." He cleared his throat. "I don't know if it would be different for you."

There were some inhalations as Kyp's revelation went around the room. Not everyone was privy yet to Kyp's bloodlines.

"I'll take it anyway. Take a blood sample first, though. I want to know what this is," I told Jennifer. She nodded, then rummaged in the black duffel. "Also, Mom, would you grab some human pain killers? Are those okay to take?" I asked Jennifer. She nodded and continued to wash the gunk off my wounds.

"Where did they take you?" Jonathan, a man approaching forty with distinguished salt-and-pepper hair, asked.

"I'm not sure. It was about ten miles outside town at least. I have a general idea, and I think we can work with it. They ran us off the road, then I think they drugged us and took us to a little ramshackle dump in the middle of the deep woods. I didn't recognize anything, but the good and bad news is that there is a large blood trail we can follow back.

"I don't know how many they have, and I don't know if they will have moved Dad, which is why I think we should mobilize as quickly as possible. Any trails would be fresh tonight. If it rains, we're sunk. They will have to transport him at least part of the way on foot. There is no road going in or out past their building. It was a path."

Jennifer handed me a white square of something that looked like baking soda covered cardboard about the size of a quarter. I raised an eyebrow.

"It tastes terrible, but it works on the wolfsbane," Kyp offered. I chucked it in my mouth, chewing and swallowing as quickly as I could before the fizzy, burning solution could stay on my tongue. As Jennifer began assessing each puncture and cleaning them out, we began to plan.

Chapter 54

Megan

Plans to go and take back Dominic swirled around the room. It was clear that the men Sam had called in with him had experience in this sort of thing, although in my weeks as a wolf, I had not heard of the pack ever needing to take aggressive action. Wolf paced weakly inside me. She knew how desperately the pack needed its Alpha, but I was scared silly at the thought of Sam going back out there and fighting against the wolves who had kidnapped him, then ripped his leg into ribbons. My heart beat painfully against my ribs as I listened while they formulated plans. Sam's leg was healing but healing slowly. It wasn't bleeding anymore, but there were still deep holes. Jennifer wrapped it securely after cleaning it out and packing some sort of green goop into it that would help it heal and keep out infection.

By the time she was finished, the men and Mary had formed a plan. They were going to take part of the pack and scout their way back through the woods. Sam knew the general location of where he'd been, so half their numbers would circle through the woods and head to the general location of the shack, scouting as they went. The strongest fighters would move forward, spread out like a net, and converge on the shack from the front, following Sam's blood trail.

It sounded sketchy to me, but I kept my mouth shut. I knew nothing of battle strategy, wolf fighting, or scouting blood trails in the middle of the night. I just knew I wanted Sam safe. With me. Terror and dread sat heavily in my stomach, weighting me down to the couch. I gripped Sam's hand like a lifeline. I couldn't accept anything other than that he would be back with me in a few hours.

"Cade, Meg, come with me for a minute," Sam said as he limped toward the stairs, testing his leg. It was better, but not great. His all call still wasn't fully functional. It was patchy, and he was growing more frustrated by the minute.

He led us upstairs to his room and shut the door behind us. "Cade, I want you to stay with Megan."

"What? No way, you need me out there watching your back. No offense, Megan." He turned to me, indignation still flashing in his eyes. I agreed. I wanted Sam to have every asset possible with him.

I opened my mouth to say as much, but Sam spoke first. "You know there is no one else I'd rather have guarding my back. But there is also no one I trust more than you. I can't focus on getting Dad back if I'm worried that Megan is unprotected. She has something to do with this. Someone has tried to kill her twice. Will you stay here and be her protection detail?"

Cade's mouth thinned into a line. "You know I will."

The relief that washed over Sam was visible. "Thank you. I don't know how many Atwood has, so we need all available fighters. I don't like leaving the two of you alone."

"We'll be fine. At the first hint of anything amiss, we'll head to the vault." He referenced the room Mary had shown us. "It bolts from the inside and short of an atomic bomb, there's no getting in there."

Obviously, Cade had been down there before. I was a little disturbed that there was a potential need for such a room.

Sam nodded. "Okay. Go ahead and grab what you need. Meg and I will be down in a minute."

Cade's dark head nodded. His blue eyes were shadowy with concern. The door closed quietly behind him. There was the shuffle of people getting ready to leave below, but for the moment, only the two of us existed in his room. The two of us and my terror. He took my hands gently as he stared into my eyes. My stomach clenched. His face was serious. His eyes were deep pools of steady water. He'd become more a man in the last few hours than in all his years prior.

"Megan," he started, then stopped. He shrugged. "I'm not sure what else to say."

I shook my head, unable to speak over the emotion clawing its way up my throat. I untangled my hands from his and wrapped my arms around his neck, pressing myself against him tightly. Immediately his arms encased me.

"Please, please be careful. Come back to me." *I'm petrified that you won't*, my brain added.

"Always," he whispered before putting his lips on mine. He kissed me deeply. It was tinged with regret, and as he moved his lips against mine once before pulling away, I tasted the slightest hint of goodbye.

I stared at him, shook my head, and kissed him back. *You have to come back.*

He pulled away again, gently, but it still left me cold.

He nodded once and was out the door. *I love you*, echoed in my brain.

Sam? I called back trying our link. Nothing. Nothing but the black void.

Chapter 55

Sam

Night was always blackest a few hours before dawn, or so the saying went. It was midnight. And this black was tangible, blanketing everything, smothering us in its darkness. The temperature was dropping, and a few flakes of snow swirled around us as we crept in our net-like formation to the shack. My blood trail might as well have been a neon beacon signaling the path. My gut twisted as the wildlife around us quit chittering. The nocturnal creatures of the forest were absent. As were the wolves who had held me prisoner hours before.

It's too quiet. Anyone see or hear anything? I sent to the pack. Every pack member of majority would hear me, so the entire adult pack would be able to receive my all call directives. Cade, and Megan by proxy, would be in the loop, which gave me some comfort.

Nothing on our side, but agreed that it's too quiet, came Jonathan's reply. He was leading the pack from the back. He'd been an army Ranger and had experience with battle.

We continued, senses on high alert, finding nothing of note. When the building was in view I crouched down and waited, watching. Everything was still. No movement, no anything.

Dad? I tried. No response. I wasn't surprised as I assumed they'd given him a heavy round of drugs or worse, beat him into unconsciousness after he created such a spectacular diversion that allowed my escape.

Mal, I called one of the younger wolves who was probably the fastest runner we had with us, *move forward. Stay low to the ground but move closer. Try to scent if our Alpha is still there. Run if anything feels off.* I kept my instructions on the all call so no one was surprised when Mal moved forward. She inched along, nose to the ground, eyes and ears alert. She made it all the way to the door of the cabin. At once her ears went flat, and she backed up rapidly.

Someone's in there! she called, right as the door burst open and a wolf the size of Goliath came bounding out. He was huge, brindled, and had drool slinging off his canines as he charged Mal.

Before she even had a chance to back up more than three paces, he was on her, jaws snapping. Mal yipped, but before the brindled wolf could get at her, Jonathan charged from the bush, his teeth sinking into the big wolf's throat. There was thrashing and whimpering, but it only lasted a moment as the big wolf went down hard, immobilized by Jonathan's teeth.

Is he dead? I asked from my spot in the brush, heart thrumming, leg throbbing, anxiety well over the healthy limit.

No. I bit a pressure point. He'll be down for a while. Jonathan sniffed the air again. *No one else is here. They must have expected a solo or small party rescue.*

Cautiously, I moved toward the cabin, my wolves following my lead. *Mal, you okay?*

I'm not hurt.

Fan out. Find out what you can. I put my nose to the ground and immediately picked up Dad's scent. The others soon had it, too.

We need to keep our numbers concealed, Jonathan suggested.

Taking his experienced advice, I gave the order and we melted back into the wood. I alone stayed on the path. I walked boldly, despite my fear and trepidation.

We heard the voices before we could see them, and I knew they sensed us at the same time.

"They're here!" someone called. Immediately, we could pick up the noises of underbrush crunching, growls working their way out of chests. The stench of motor oil and gas hung in the air. This was the transport spot. Dad might be up ahead! *Go!*

As one, we moved through the underbrush nearer the enemy pack. As planned for this scenario, Jonathan's group stayed behind, letting my group take the lead.

A small clearing came into view and a dozen wolves were on the ground, teeth bared, hackles raised. Like a gun sounding the start of a race, they lunged toward us, and we met them in equal force. Though Wolf pushed to enter the fray, jaws open, I tried to stay back on the fringe of the clearing. It was important that I wasn't heavily engaged because I was the only one who could do the all call. Without my voice, my pack couldn't move as one. We couldn't be effective.

The enemy pack knew this, too. Immediately, a brown wolf sized me up as he came at me. Jaws wide, teeth glinting in the weak moonlight that filtered down through the canopy on the fringe of the clearing. We met in midair, paws swiping heavily. My right paw found purchase on the wolf's neck, batting him down while his teeth snapped harmlessly at the air. It took less than a second for him to right himself and even less time to ascertain my injured leg.

Using the bulk of his muscled body, he knocked into me, sending all my weight on my injured leg. An involuntary yelp escaped, and I used the momentum to move into a roll that put me beside the wolf's back legs. I wasted no time in biting down, much in the same way my own leg had been bitten earlier. Blood filled my mouth, and Wolf reveled in the power of the taste. I shook my head hard, and the wolf came down, whimpering as I locked my jaws in place. With another shake of my head and twist around to miss his swinging front paws. I cracked the wolf's leg against the ground and felt the wet snap between my teeth.

The wolf howled, and I let go, knowing the wolf wasn't an immediate threat now. Where that wolf had been, a large black one now took its place, slavering in front of me with eyes narrowed to slits and trained on my throat. My leg throbbed, but I didn't have time to dwell on that or on the battle going on around me. All of my part of the pack was engaged with enemy wolves, and in my quick glance, several from Jonathan's group were coming in to swell our numbers.

Are we outnumbered? I shouted the all call, meaning to send the thought to Jonathan.

Nearly. Wait! Dominic! He's in that truck.

Get him! It was all I had time for as the black wolf launched and was on me. Talking to Jonathan had distracted me enough to provide the opening the black wolf needed.

Snarls, screams, and blood filled the black night, and my head swam with the sensation of teeth nicking the flesh of my shoulder. I winced, growling in pain and frustration, and circled the black wolf, his eyes still on my throat.

Shots rang out, and several startled yips and howls ripped through the air. I cringed involuntarily, but quickly squared my shoulders as the black wolf rammed into my chest, nearly sending me flying head over tail. I let the momentum move me back and, quicker than lightning, bit my teeth down into the black wolf's ruff. I didn't get much flesh, mostly fur and hide, but it was enough to keep him from reaching my throat with his ugly canines. He struggled beneath me, and I fought to maintain my grip on him.

More gunfire sounded around the clearing.

Three down over here!

Wolf down!

We need to move out! Corwin's voice echoed last.

I could feel the tension, knew our time was running out. Panic gripped my gut, and my mind was divided, trying to manage the black wolf trying to kill me, and direct the wolves trying to get my dad out of the truck.

Jonathan, do you have him? I all but screamed.

One more minute! They have him tied in here!

Can you drive him out?

The black wolf growled and shoved the whole weight of his body upward, catching me under the chin. The force of his upward lunge sent me sprawling. The moment seemed to play in slow motion as I stared at a wolf lunging over me for the second time that night. I braced for impact, trying to roll out of the way before claws and teeth cut into me, when a black-red fireball of fur leaped from the shadows and caught the wolf midleap, right before it landed squarely on me. The mass of black-red fur and black wolf snarled and bit and clawed and fought. Shaking my head to clear it, I went to join in and finish the black wolf when another shot rang out and the world went black.

Chapter 56

Megan

I paced. Cade paced. We paced opposite each other, crossing paths in the middle of the living room. For the seventh time, I broke my pacing and went again to the window. "Is he saying anything at all?" It was killing me not to have my link with Sam in place. I had been horrified to have him in my head at first, but now I wished he was there more than anything.

"No. They might not even be there yet."

"I'm going to go text Rachel. I'm literally going to lose my mind if I do this anymore."

"Where are you going?"

"To get my phone. I left it on Sam's dresser, I think." I hadn't been worried about having it on me since there was no chance Sam would call while going out full wolf stealth mode. I shivered. I had texted Rachel and Grandpa earlier and given them the barest of updates but had then gotten preoccupied with the finishing up things that needed to be done before the pack fighters left.

There were a few messages on my phone. One from Grandpa telling me to hang in there and that he loved me.

I typed back quickly.

> Love you, too! No news yet.

One from a friend in Chemistry wanting to borrow notes. I scoffed. I was so distracted these days that I doubted any notes I took would be worth copying.

The last was from Rachel.

> Hear anything yet??? Need me to come over?

I punched her entry to call her, rather than text, figuring it might help pass the time.

"What have you heard? Is everyone okay?" she jumped in after the first ring.

I groaned. "No, I haven't heard anything. Please, distract me from myself, because I'm seriously going insane worrying." I ran a hand through my hair, bit my lip, then flopped backward onto Sam's bed. It still smelled faintly of him, even though he hadn't slept in this bed in weeks.

"How shall I distract you? Um...I think we've finally settled on a spring musical. Want me to blab your ear off about that?"

"Definitely." I fingered the blanket. It had a soft, worn texture, and the weave of it under my fingers along with the faded traces of Sam's scent soothed some of my frazzled nerves.

"It's *The Elf King and His Horse, Tremaine*."

"That sounds...interesting."

Rachel laughed. "Trust me, it's better than the title implies. It's actually a comedy about a teenage guy who writes fantasy stories that come to life in his dreams. Some of the song numbers are hilarious. I think Luke is going to try out for Tremaine. He will be a riot."

"And who will you be auditioning for?" Rachel took her role as co-president of the Drama Club very seriously.

"I think I'm actually going to focus on directing this year. I want to do more behind the stage things. I love acting, and I love singing, but I want to do something different. I want to have my hands all over this play—you know, mold it like a lump of dough or something."

I smiled. "You'll be a wonderful director. Does Garrett agree that you will be the best director?" I referenced Rachel's co-president.

"Fortunately. Garrett wants to be the main character. He'll do a nice job if he'll let me boss him around." I could hear the grin in her voice.

"Absolutely."

"So we got another email about a personalized cookie order. You know the guy at HarvestFest? He booked cookies for his daughter's birthday, and apparently his wife spread our name around her work, and her boss would like us to cater desserts for a retirement party for someone in the office."

My fingers drifted over the blanket in soft, soothing circles. Sam. I closed my eyes. *Sam.*

"Megan?"

"Sorry... I only caught about half of that."

"Would it help to talk about Sam? About what's going on?"

"I don't know. Maybe?"

"Tell me your biggest fear."

"That he won't come back," I strangled the words out.

"Oh, Meggie. He's going to come back. You have to think that way."

"Who knew being a wolf was so unbelievably complicated?"

"Well, skin can be complicated, too?"

"Not like this."

"No second thoughts? You want your skin back?"

"Life would be so much less complicated in skin."

"But complicated might suit you after all?"

A noise in the hallway caught my attention and sent my heart up to my throat before I could answer. Cade tapped on the door, and I brought my hand over my pounding chest.

"He's started using the all call. I'm hearing a few things," Cade said, his eyes unreadable.

"Rachel, I've got to go. To the ends of the earth!" And then I was incredibly rude and hung up before she could reply. "What did he say? I need to know everything."

He walked over and joined me on the bed so that we sat side by side on the edge. "They're at the shack. He's sending Mal to check it out. She's fast. Really fast." His head jerked.

"What?" I nearly screamed.

"Mal got attacked." His breathing came heavier, and I thought I might faint dead away from the anxiety eating me alive inside. "It's okay. Jonathan got the beast. Man. He was huge."

"How is Sam?"

"He's fine. He wasn't even in the fight. Keep your shirt on."

I scowled at him. "Easy for you to say. You know everything he's saying. I'm totally cut off over here."

"Okay. They've found Dominic's scent. Sam is taking the path and everyone else is moving parallel, hidden in the forest." He was quiet, and I hardly dared to breathe for several agonizing minutes. "Oh no."

"*What?*" I was nearly out of my skin with worry, but unfortunately not any closer to being in my fur.

"They're under attack." Cade got up and paced the room. His hand was in his hair, pulling at it. I chewed three fingernails down to the quick.

"What's happening?" I whispered.

"I'm not sure. I think Sam is fighting. No, he's definitely fighting. He's hurt. Ah! I can feel it radiating through the link, though I don't think he meant to send anything. Still nothing from Dominic. They must have him drugged still."

My knee bounced, and two more nails disintegrated under my teeth.

"They found him. Jonathan is going after Dominic. Sam, Sam!" Cade shouted into the room. A cold sweat broke out on my forehead, and I stood, no longer able to stay seated.

"It's gone." Cade's voice was hoarse, his eyes vacant.

"What do you mean, it's gone?" I echoed. Dread carved a path from my belly to my extremities.

"Sam, the link, it...it's gone."

A sob hiccupped out of my mouth, and I collapsed to the floor on shaking legs. I wrapped my arms around my knees and stared, unblinking, refusing to acknowledge the fear, the fury, the dread, the agony all fighting to break free and rage inside me. Cade sank down beside me. We sat there together in silence, both stunned, refusing to believe our worst fears, surviving on the hope that Sam was still alive.

Chapter 57

Sam

Everything hurt. My eyeballs, my ears, my neck, my shoulders, my back, my butt, my legs, my arms, my feet. I tried to roll over, get my bearings but groaned at the effort.

"Easy. You'll come to in a few minutes. Just slow down." Jennifer's voice.

"Jennifer?" I croaked.

"I'm here. You've had a nasty shot of suppressant, plus a few new punctures." She might as well have *tsked* for all her tone hid.

"What happened? Where is the pack? My dad?"

"Let me get Jonathan for you." I felt the pressure of her fingers at my shoulder lift, and I cracked my eyes against the searing brightness. I didn't recognize the room. It was little, and I realized it was actually fairly dimly lit.

It was a living room. Clean, but with old furnishings. Drapes were drawn across the windows, and lamps gave the room its light. I was still squinting when I recognized Jake laid out on the couch. Fear lurched into my throat until I took in his even breathing, his chest going up and down. I swallowed and tried to use my link.

Jonathan? No response. My head flopped back down to the table painfully. I realized this must be someone's kitchen table. I was lying on it. The strangeness of the situation struck me, and I nearly laughed but stopped before I made my head throb any worse.

"Sam," Jonathan said as he came into the room. He stood next to the table and looked down at me.

"What happened? Did we get Dad?"

Jonathan cracked a smile. "The mission was a success. Your first battle was a success." His smile fell, and his face turned grim. "Dominic still has some pretty bad cuts and bruises and a few breaks, but he'll heal. Do you remember what happened?"

Relief washed over me, making me lightheaded. I closed my eyes for a second before answering. "I remember I was about finished, and then some wolf I didn't know bullied the black wolf out of the way. I don't remember anything after that."

"Well, the wolf you didn't know was none other than young Kypson, here." He motioned with his hand, and I winced as I craned my neck while Kyp walk into the room. His shoulders were tight, his head down.

"Kyp?" I asked, more curious than anything. I hadn't given him permission to come. He wasn't officially a part of the pack, although Jennifer's ability to work medically with her knowledge of wolves was a valuable asset, even if Kyp turned out to be horrible.

"I know I shouldn't have come. I'm sorry. I...I wasn't ordered *not* to come. I was only trying to help." His eyes flashed up to me, and he whispered the last part. "Please don't send me back to the Kentucky pack."

Surprise rippled through me. "I think you probably saved my life tonight. That means I owe you one." I grimaced when a wave of nausea roiled through me. "Loyalty isn't something we forget in this pack. But next time, follow orders." I closed my eyes against the pain in my head.

"They used a much stronger dose this time. That's what made you black out. I think they were aiming to hit me—they were shooting guns packed with suppressant-filled bullets. They were trying to *kill* you, not wound you with suppressants," Kyp explained.

My dry mouth became even drier at the thought. Tonight had been a narrow miss. "How long have I been out?"

"A few hours. Your new bite is starting to heal, but the drug appears to be slowing everything down," Jonathan supplied.

"Dad?"

"Is recovering down the hall. We'll get you up and around to see him soon."

"Has anyone called Cade or Megan to check on them?"

Jonathan looked sheepish. "Sorry. We were busy getting the wounded here and treating them."

"Hand me a phone, and then I want all the details. Who is hurt, where we even are, all that. But first I need to know that Megan is safe."

Kyp fished his phone from his pocket and handed it to me. My fingers felt fat and clumsy as I dialed Megan's number. No answer. Panic bloomed in my gut. Desperation moved my uncoordinated fingers faster as I dialed Cade.

"Hello?" The voice on the other end was hard, cold, flat.

"Cade?"

"*Sam*? What happened to you? Yes—it's Sam, he's alive," he shouted in the background. "I'm putting you on speaker."

"Meg? Cade?" Guilt welled up—they thought I was dead?

"Sam?" There were tears in Megan's voice, and I winced again. "I, we couldn't hear you. Everything just stopped."

Everything clicked into place then. When the drug-bullet had blasted me into unconsciousness, the all call had gone out again, leaving the rest of the pack in the dark. "I'm all right. Or at least I will be. I've been drugged again, but otherwise, I'm good."

We spoke a few more minutes, reassuring each other that things were fine and that as far as I knew, things were under control. When I hung up, I was exhausted but still had things I needed to do. "Okay, where are we? Literally and figuratively?" I asked as I rubbed my temple with the heel of my hand.

"You're at our house," Jennifer supplied as she handed me two of the same squares I'd eaten earlier and a couple of regular pain killers.

"We've got eleven that were shot, but all are recovering. Everyone who was shot got hit with those hollow bullets filled with poison," Jonathan said as Corwin and Rev moved into the room. Corwin moved slowly like an old man, though he was only in his sixties, which wasn't all that old for a wolf.

"I think they meant to capture, not to kill," Rev offered as Corwin moved Jake's legs over and sat down on the couch. "Except you. I agree, they were trying to kill you."

I sat up, wincing as pain flashed all over my body, but I stayed upright. "And Dad?"

"He's still asleep. They beat him pretty bad, but he's healing. It will take him awhile with as many injuries as he's got," Jennifer supplied.

"I want to see him soon," I said, not sure I could walk on my own yet. All considered, it wasn't a bad outcome. We'd got Dad back and hadn't lost anyone. We knew a little more about Atwood's pack, but still not how many or why he attacked us. But that would come. For the moment, sleep was the only thing I could think about.

The day was spent sleeping off the effects of the fight and the drugs. Dad came to and was prouder than I'd ever seen him. It filled me with a sweet sort of heat. Wolf and I both relished his approval. We hugged for a long time there in Kyp's bedroom where Dad had been laid out on the bed. His arm and at least one rib were broken, and his face was black and blue along with several other patches of his body.

I woke from a nap about six o'clock, finally feeling whole. I was still fuzzy around the edges, but I knew the drug was about out of my system, thanks to Jennifer's little miracle biscuits. I showered and threw on some borrowed clothes. I called Cade, eager to be home. Needing Megan with me.

"Sam?"

"I think things are about wrapped up here. We're going to go ahead and move Dad home. The drug is about gone, and I'm ready to be home, too. Can you go ahead and take Megan up to the cabin? We should only be a little while longer here. There are extra patrols running, so it should be safe enough for you guys to move, but I want you to stay with her until I get there."

"Will do. Sam, about that." He huffed a breath, and I could picture him tugging his dark hair. Apprehension bubbled up in my belly.

"About what?"

His voice dropped. "She was talking to Rachel last night—right before the attack. She was talking about going back to her human skin and things being much less complicated. I...I think she might have made her decision. I didn't want to tell you but thought it might be best for you to be prepared."

The high I'd been riding burst. My limbs got heavy, and I felt like sinking into the floor.

"Okay." I swallowed. "I appreciate you telling me. Don't say anything to Megan, okay?"

"Sure," Cade said, his voice somber.

By full dark, I was exhausted but still riding the tide of adrenaline that had spiked again getting everyone moved out, and I was anxious to get back to Meg. I knew she was in good hands with Cade, but I knew I wouldn't relax until I saw her again. I was desperate to enjoy the remaining time I had with her before the next full moon. My heart sank as I thought about it. She'd be gone from me then. I had days at the most to convince her to stay with me. Forever. It was a lot to ask.

The cabin came into view, looking cheery because Meg was waiting inside. The door creaked as I opened it, as if waiting for my return had taken too long. Cade was waiting right inside the door, knowing I wouldn't be long after I called, and assuming correctly that I'd want time alone with Megan.

"Dude. Don't ever scare me like that again," he said as he pulled me in for a tight hug and slap on the back. I gave him a quick squeeze across the shoulders in return.

"I'll do my best. But it looks like we'll be having bigger problems with these wolves down the line," I said, my mouth a tight line as I thought about it.

He looked me in the eye, nodded solemnly and gave me one more slap on my freshly healed shoulder, then walked out the door without another word. I closed the door and wriggled out of my jacket before manning up and looking at Meg. I couldn't stand to be away from her but couldn't stand the torture of being near her only to lose her either. Her eyes were wide in her face, her expression unreadable as she stood by the sink. Hands clasped under her chin, she watched me like a hawk.

My mouth dried. I cleared my throat. "Megan?"

Her chin wobbled. "I thought I lost you." Her strangled whisper filled the air between us. Before I had a chance to formulate an answer, she launched herself across the small room and collided into me.

My arms came around her as she pressed her lips to mine, shocking me speechless. Her arms wrapped around my shoulders, her body pressing into me, her lips aggressive against my mouth. Fire ignited every cell, and I kissed her back. My hands slid to her waist, and I heard myself groaning as her tongue swept my mouth. Sweet mercy, I was going to explode. Our mouths worked together, knowing part of this dance, eager to learn more. With her body tight against me, I could feel her curves, and it about drove me to my knees. A quick twist, and I rotated us around so that I pressed her back against the door, my lips claiming her mouth, moving to her neck and hovering there when she gasped. Her hands slid down my chest, fisting into my shirt as I kissed her collarbone and back to her throat.

I wanted her so bad, and my self-control was waning fast. I knew I was in serious trouble when she kissed me full on the mouth and her hands trailed down over my shirt, muscles beneath taut with emotion, to rest at the top of my jeans, her hands pulling me even closer. Wolf pushed me. I wanted her to be my mate. To stay with me. To love me. Wolf urged me again and I wasn't sure if I could keep kissing her like this without going too far. But I wasn't sure I had it in me to pull myself back.

"Sam." Her breathless voice had me needing a cold shower. I pressed against her as my lips traced their way down her jaw.

She groaned as my hands gripped her sides, and her head tipped to the side as I kissed behind her ear. "Sam, stop."

No. *No!* Wolf lunged forward, my body pressing against hers once more, committing every curve to memory as I felt a tremor shake through me. I screwed my eyes shut as I felt tears prick the back of them. This was it. It was the final rejection. Her decision was made. I wasn't enough for her. She was leaving. Pain shattered my chest as I yanked my face and hands away from her body, bracing both my arms and my head against the door with her still enclosed in my arms but no longer pressed up against me.

My breathing was jagged, and I tried to drag a deeper breath in but felt choked as her rejection washed over me in great crashing waves that threatened to take me under and never let me surface. "Sam," she whispered. I couldn't look at her. Everything hurt. My heart was being ripped out and crushed, and I couldn't look at her without flying to pieces. Wolf howled something primal inside me, and I think a whimper may have escaped. I was pathetic. I couldn't even face rejection like a man. Shame, anger, and loss burned in the back of my throat.

"Sam, look at me." Her soft breath on my cheek was agony. I shook my head, sure that one look at the pity in her eyes would be my complete undoing.

Her lips were soft on my cheek, and I felt myself crumbling. "Megan, *please.*" My voice was raw. Did she have no idea what she was doing to me?

"Look at me," she repeated softly. Her fingers grazed my face, tracing up the light stubble on my jaw and to my cheek, turning my face to her.

I was powerless to stop her. At last, I opened my anguished eyes and looked at her. Her gaze was kind, sympathetic, but mercifully held no pity. Something else flashed in their depths, but I couldn't read it. "Sam, I'm in love with you."

My blood froze, and all thought processes stopped.

She what?

My mouth fell open, moving, though no words came out. She continued.

"I *choose* to love you," she whispered, her own eyes filling with tears. "I didn't want any of this at first, but it happened. And in the midst of it all, I found a family, I found a second half of myself I didn't know I had, and I found *you*. I was scared that I'd lose myself in the wolf, and never be me again, but then Wolf and I made peace, and in the end, I'd have to give up *you* if I want to stay human. And that's too high a price. I love you. And even though I don't think I fully feel the mate bond like you do, with my own free will, I will choose to love you each day from here on out. You and no one else."

Sparks edged my vision, and my heart started pumping again, galloping in my chest where it was momentarily frozen.

"Megan." My voice grated against the emotion lodged in my throat. "Are you sure?" I could have eaten my own tongue as the words left my mouth. "This is forever. And...and we'd have to—" I swallowed, hating myself for thinking it, let alone saying it. I wanted her more than anything. Every fiber of man and wolf screamed at me to take what she was offering and bind her to me forever before she could change her mind. But I couldn't. I loved her. And as bad as I wanted her, we'd both hate me for eternity if I made any of this decision for her.

I found my voice again before my courage deserted me and I let my body make the decision. "If we do this—and I want to in every possible way—there will be no going back. The full moon isn't for a few more days. There's still a chance you could be human. If you give yourself to me right now, the wolf bond will be sealed. There will be no returning to a different life. You'll be bound to me forever, woman, wife, and wolf."

My mouth was dry. I had no words left. Just a desperate, wild hope that teetered on the brink of the black abyss of despair.

Her eyes met mine and she smiled. "I'm sure."

A rush of air left my lungs and left me lightheaded. I couldn't stop myself then, my lips came down on hers in a kiss that was gentle but held the promise of more to come.

"I love you, Megan. So much," I murmured against her lips.

"I love you, too."

"Mm, one more thing," I said as I regretfully pulled back. Meg arched an eyebrow at me, apparently not liking my lips' absence any more than I did. I winked at her. She would like this. I loped over to the top drawer of my dresser and pulled out what George Carmichael had given me weeks ago. It burned against my palm. When I got back to Megan, I hesitated. I wasn't sure how I should do this. Plunging ahead, I dropped to one knee.

"Megan..." I took her hand as her mouth fell open. "Will you," I stuttered, "stay married to me?" I held out her grandmother's ring.

Her smile nearly split her face. "Yes. Yes, yes, *yes*!"

I slipped the ring on her finger and scooped her up in a hug. It was mutual when we turned our heads and our lips met once more. It was a kiss full of promise. A kiss that quickly deepened into something much more. Her hands slid up my shirt, over the ridges of my stomach and up to my chest. I blissfully let mine wander, and a few minutes later we stumbled to the bed where we tumbled down together.

It was awkward and beautiful. Neither of us knew what we were doing, and that was the awkwardness and the beauty of it. I was hers, and she was mine.

Afterward, we lay together in the dark, content, still wrapped up in each other's arms. Sleep came easy.

Chapter 58

Megan

The first hints of Friday sunlight peeked through the blinds and hit my eyes. I started to stretch and then smiled as I felt Sam's arms still around me. Wolf nudged me. We were of one mind. She was here, and I knew without doubt that I could shift at will. She rubbed her head against me and gave me a wolfy grin.

Sam stirred, his hand lightly squeezing my bare skin. He sighed in appreciation as his eyes cracked open. "Morning, Mrs. Wolfe."

I giggled. "My name hasn't been officially changed yet."

"All in good time," he replied, his fingers caressing my side. We lay still for a minute, and last night started replaying through my mind. With a sudden jerk, I bolted upright, clutching the blankets to my chest.

"Oh no." I gasped. "Oh no, oh no, oh no!" I wailed into the blanket, my stomach writhing with anxiety.

"What? Megan, what's wrong?"

My face flamed, and I could hardly bring myself to look at him. He propped himself up on his elbow, concern covering his face. My eyes darted to his face and away and then back. "Last night. We didn't...I'm not...you didn't. Oh, crap. Sam, what if I get pregnant?"

His face relaxed, and I wanted to slug him. "You won't."

My eyebrows probably disappeared into my hairline. "Seriously? It only takes once. *Once.* You know how many times Camilla Kovos had sex? Uh huh. Once." Camilla was a sophomore and seven months pregnant.

"No, I'm not saying that. You won't get pregnant this time. Not from last night."

I gave him a scathing look. "Is there some wolf protocol that has built in birth control?"

He chuckled. "No. But if you were, you know, ready to have a baby, I'd be able to smell it."

My jaw swung open, and I turned horrified eyes on him. My brain raced a mile a minute. "You can smell if I'm...what, *in heat*?" the words screeched out of my mouth.

He collapsed back onto his pillow, a laugh working its way up from his belly. "Well, I never thought of it that way, but yeah. I guess so." His blue eyes twinkled at me before I pulled the covers up over my head.

"This is so mortifying," I mumbled. My whole body flushed with embarrassment. He sobered beside me and tugged the blanket back from my face.

"Seriously, Meg." His eyes were intense and vulnerable. "Do...do you regret it?" he asked softly.

I looked at Sam beside me. He looked at me pleadingly, unsure of himself. Love swelled in my chest as I searched his face and looked in his blue eyes.

"Not even a tiny little bit," I answered as I leaned over to kiss him.

I called Grandpa on the way to school. "Just now getting to school, Meggie-Girl?"

"We're running a bit late today." I felt myself blush. "Um, I decided to stay a wolf. To stay with Sam." Sam squeezed my knee, his cheek lifting as he kept his eyes on the road.

"I'm so pleased to hear it, sweetheart. Sam is a fine young man. He'll do right by you. Your Grandma Elsie would be proud of you, too."

"Thanks, Grandpa."

"I love you, Meggie-Girl. Swing by when you have the chance. I have a wedding present for you, now that it's official."

I giggled. "Okay. I love you."

"Love you, too, Megan Elizabeth."

I finally ran into Rachel before lunch. She took one look at me and her jaw nearly came unhinged. "You did it. You *did* it. You did *it*. *You* did it!" her voice, starting in a hushed whisper was getting louder as her eyes got wider.

"And I'd prefer the entire student body not know about it," I whispered as I dragged her down the hallway where students had dispersed. She gaped at me, words completely failing her now. I'd never seen Rachel so speechless—not even when I shifted into a wolf for the first time in front of her.

"Was it good?"

Laughter burst from my throat. That would be her first question. "It wasn't like what you always think it will be—I mean, it was kind of romantic—a little frantic, but also kind of awkward. It was..." I shrugged, searching for the right word. "...*sacred*," I finished, serious again. "And it sealed the deal. Not just, you know, *that*."

Rachel nodded knowingly. "You chose him."

"I did. I do. He's worth it."

She smirked. "Should I say congratulations?" Her nose wrinkled as a smile formed. My answering one felt too large for my face.

"I'll take congratulations. But let's get in line. I'm hungry."

"Work up an appetite, did you?" she said snidely as she poked my ribs.

"Shut up. Seriously. I could eat a horse."

The day ended on a high. I floated through every class. Wolf was with me. She would be forever. But more importantly, I'd be with Sam forever. The thought made me giddy. I was his as much as he was mine. A sappy sigh escaped as I rounded the corner to the gym. Sam was there, blue eyes twinkling at me, a secret, sly smile stretching across the whole lower half of his face.

Skipping, I went over to him, and he bent down and kissed me quick. The bell was about to ring, and he still needed to get himself to class. "Have fun in gym, *Mrs. Wolfe*." His breathy whisper in my ear made me giggle, and I felt Wolf stretch herself out, preening for Sam. I winked at him and turned to go through the door. A squeak escaped as he gave me a quick squeeze on my backside before sauntering off down the hall.

I continued to float into the girls' locker room. It was practically deserted. I glanced over at the bulletin board for the sports calendar and realized that the girls' basketball team left early today for a game over in Centerville. That meant our gym class was going to have about seven people in it, and I knew at least three of them were out, because they hadn't been in my earlier classes. With a smile still plastered to my face, fairly oblivious to the rest of the world, I went toward the lockers at the far side of the room where it opened up to the left into showers and a few rows of long benches.

"Oh! Shelby, you scared me." I gasped as my peripheral caught her reflection in the mirror inside my locker. I glanced over to find her staring at me, her eyes radiating hate like I'd never encountered. "Shelby? What's wrong?"

She stood, the muscles in her arms bunching as her hands twisted into fists. Her nostrils flared, and I felt the hair on the back of my neck stand on end. She raised her chin and inhaled, her lip curling in disgust. "He was supposed to be mine. How many times do I have to try to kill you?

Why won't you just *die*?" She hissed the words. I had no time to process her meaning as her face suddenly melted, her jaw jutting out and canines protruding from her gums. Her eyes sank into her head and were pushed out to the sides as ears struggled through her hair. Black fur rippled along her arms as claws swelled from her fingers.

My mind completely blanked in shock. The moment I registered that Shelby Atwood was indeed a werewolf, Wolf took over, and I shifted within two seconds, teeth bared, hackles raised, a dangerous growl sliding through my teeth.

Shelby's shift was arrested, and she morphed back into her skin, her clothes still intact. "No! How can you—" Her eyes went from feral to fearful, and her mouth parted, a shocked gasp escaping. Her pounding heartbeat reached my ears as we stared each other down. Wolf growled again, and Shelby turned and fled through the emergency door at the back of the locker room.

Immediately, the alarm blared to life, and I looked around, realizing my clothes were in a heap of ripped pieces, and I was standing as a giant wolf in the girls' locker room. Shifting back as quickly as I'd become a wolf, I snatched the towel out of my locker and shoved the remnants of my clothes back in right as Coach Theobald came dashing in, her hair coming loose from her ponytail and frazzling around her face.

"What happened?" she asked as she swiped an errant piece from her eyes.

"I'm not sure. Shelby just took off out the door. No idea what happened." I hoped I sounded normal and that my voice didn't waver as the lie slipped off my tongue.

Coach Theobald groaned. "I'll go page the office. Also, don't worry about suiting up. Use today as a study hall," she said over her shoulder as she jogged back to her office outside the locker room.

I heaved a breath as I looked down at my blue towel clutched tightly around me. That had been far too close. *Sam. We need to go. Shelby Atwood is a* werewolf. *Can you get us excused from class?*

What? Are you hurt? What happened?

She shifted on me—she wanted to hurt me. Wolf came out to play, and Shelby ran out the emergency exit. I need to find some clothes. I'll be ready in five.

Already have Dad calling in to excuse us both.

Can your dad do that? Have me excused?

His name was added to your school file as an emergency contact when we got married.

I rolled my eyes, annoyed that this, too, had been done behind my back, but happy for it now.

Megan? Are you safe?

Yeah. I'll fill you in more once we're on the way.

How could Shelby hide that she's a wolf for the two years she's lived here? I'd bet every hair on my hide that she's related to Victor.

I'd like to sink my teeth into his worthless hide.

I wrinkled my nose as I shook out my used gym clothes. I didn't have anything else at hand, but at least I had a sports bra. I looked again. Ugh. I had no spare underwear.

"Megan," Coach Theobald called.

"Yeah, Coach?"

"You've been paged up to the office. Sounds like you're leaving early."

"I'll be right there."

I jammed on my wrinkled, T-shirt that could have smelled fresher and mesh shorts and hurriedly plunged every scrap of my ruined clothes into my bag to take home. I didn't need any more raised questions. It was a miracle no one wandered in while Shelby and I had had our fur on.

I texted Rachel on my way to meet Sam.

> Stay away from Shelby Atwood! She's one of them.

> ?!?!?!?!

Her reply was swift. Hope she didn't get caught texting in class.

> Call me on your way home.

OK!

Dominic blasted out the door of his house the second Sam's tires hit the driveway. His eyes were wild, his hair unkempt. His face still held traces of the previous night's activities, his arm was in a sling, and he held it protectively across his middle where his ribs still ached. "You're not hurt?" were the first words out of his mouth as he looked us both up and down.

"We're fine," Sam answered for us. "But how could Shelby Atwood live here, mingle with us *for two years*, and keep her wolf side to herself?" He slammed his car door shut.

Even novice as I was, I understood the ramifications of this. If we couldn't pick out each other, our world just got a lot more dangerous. Especially with wolves like Victor Atwood roaming free.

"Let's get inside. There's more. I heard from the patrol." Dominic ushered us gingerly inside and limped in behind us. He sniffed.

"Megan?" he asked, startled. I blushed to the roots of my hair. Sam laughed.

"Um, so Megan is going to stay an official member of the pack." Sam grinned as he looped an arm across my shoulders.

"Ha!" Dominic Wolfe laughed so loudly I jumped. "I'm thrilled. Truly." He smiled down at me in what could only be called a fatherly fashion. An answering grin tugged my lips upward.

Mary had put a tray of cookies on the table and was getting the milk out of the fridge. She thunked it down and ran to us, overhearing Dominic. Her eyes lit up as we entered, and she ran to embrace us both.

"Welcome home," she whispered as she released us. My heart warmed. I *was* home.

Sam snagged a cookie, offered me one, and then sat at the table. "What did the patrol find?"

Dominic shocked us both. "Amalie Rivers and Jonathan Stone caught a wolf from Victor's pack today."

I felt my eyes nearly leave their sockets as my mouth swung open.

"How? Where?" The questions tumbled from my lips.

"He was at the border of our land, but it was right at the entrance to the heavy forest." He looked at Sam. "It was the spot right by the big boulder."

Sam's head tipped back. "My favorite spot to enter and exit the woods. My scent, and Megan's too, would have been all over that spot particularly."

"Mine would be at least a few days old, though," I added.

"I'm still not ruling it out. Someone has tried to hurt you twice. They've succeeded in capturing me once. Dad, too. It's clear they're after one or both of us or maybe all three of us," Sam responded.

A shiver slipped down my spine. Sam was right. Somehow, we were connected to some manic plan. To what end though? Kill us both? To what purpose? I thought of Shelby today in the locker room.

"Shelby said something today. Right before she shifted. She snarled and said, 'He was supposed to be mine. How many times do I have to try to kill you? Why won't you just die?' I think she's behind, or at least knows more than she should, about the attempts on my life and maybe the abduction. What if she was behind the car and the arrow? To get you? To get me out of the way? That sounds completely crazy out loud. And she can't have masterminded your abduction. There's no way she has that kind of power or resources at her disposal."

"She's a wolf. She's not thinking in human terms. She's thinking in mate terms. I think it's the first solid lead we've had on any of it," Dominic admitted gruffly. "We need to find her. She knows things we do not. In the meantime, son, I think it best we go and have a chat with our guest. He's the same wolf you scented at the theater and at your school."

Sam's eyebrows rose. "Maybe some answers at last."

Chapter 59

Sam

Dad and I went to the shed behind the garage a little while later. Megan stayed in the house with Mom when Amalie Rivers dropped by.

Snarls and sobs echoed inside the small space, and Dad and I looked at each other in confusion. We listened for a minute as the man's crying continued, only to be broken by snarls and the clink of chains.

Opening the door, Dad flooded the small space with cold gray afternoon light. The man stopped jerking and sat still in the chair, his arms chained in manacles he wouldn't be able to escape as man or wolf. The manacles were chained to a heavy ring embedded in the concrete floor. There was enough slack that the man could sit comfortably, even scratch his ears if he had an itch, but not so much slack that he was any danger to us, standing right inside the door. The time-regulated space heater buzzed back to life, throwing some heat into the otherwise chilly room.

Without speaking, Dad opened a bottle of water and handed it to the man. Conflicting emotions roiled across his face. Hate, fear, longing, and that curious blank stare the wolf who bit me had exhibited. After a charged moment, the man raised trembling hands, accepted the bottle, and drank greedily.

Dad stepped back. "Care to tell us what you were doing on our land?"

The man's lip curled. "I didn't know it was yours," he muttered, a snarl touching his words.

"Does your nose not work?" Dad asked in typically blunt, sarcastic fashion.

"Victor owns this land. This is all his."

"Victor Atwood would have to be three hundred and fifty years old to own this land, because that's how long ago the Wolfes settled here. This is generational family land. I'm afraid your Mr. Atwood is mistaken."

The man snorted.

"What's your name?" I asked.

"You don't need my name."

Dad sighed. "How about we get down to business. Why did you kidnap us?"

"You're just pawns in his game. We all are."

Dad and I shared a glance. My skin began to crawl at the despair in the man's voice.

"What is his game?" I asked quietly.

His eyes stared at me. Haunted and desolate. "He's going to kill me anyway."

"Then you might as well tell us what's going on, and maybe we can protect you from him," Dad offered an olive branch.

The man closed his eyes and breathed deeply through his nose. "Nobody can protect themselves against Victor. Not once he's got his claws into you. I don't know a lot. Victor is very secretive, and I'm no one of consequence in the pack. But he wants a large pack. The largest pack anyone has had in centuries."

"Why?" I asked, at least getting an inkling of why my pack was shot at with wolfsbane bullets and not real ones. Maybe his sole purpose was to assimilate.

"He can control us. His pack." He shuddered. I glanced at Dad.

"Use command?" Dad clarified.

He shook his head. "More than that."

Dad cocked his head, the light catching on a particularly nasty purple bruise. "He can control you how?"

The man's lip quivered, and he tapped his head. "In here," he whispered.

"Do you know how?" Dad pressed, concern and the slightest hint of fear rippling over his marred face.

The man shook his head. "I just know he does."

"Why were you at the theater and at the school?" I asked, unable to keep the questions silent anymore.

"I'm a scout. I followed several wolf trails. I watched. Waited. Reported back." He glanced at the ground.

"And?" I prompted.

He shrugged again. "That's it. I told Victor numbers and locations, just like he told me to."

"Do you know anything else that might be useful?" Dad pressed.

He shrugged a piece of dark hair out of his face. He was younger than I first thought. Probably only a few years older than me. "I'm not sure what else to say. I'm a lackey," he said with a bitter twist of his lips.

"A lackey he trusted enough with our abduction," Dad hinted.

"A lackey far enough down on the food chain that is easily controlled and manipulated." The bitterness was outright. "Were you serious? Earlier, when you said you might be able to protect me?" His voice was raw and vulnerable. A fissure cracked in the man's armor.

"I have some friends up north. I don't think it's safe for you to remain here, and you'd have to officially leave Victor's pack, of course."

"I'm not sure I can. Victor's control goes pretty deep. I joined his pack when I was a boy."

"Do you want our help or not?"

"Jordan. My name is Jordan. And yes. I want your help."

Dad nodded stiffly. "We'll work on leaving the pack after a while. I will need to make some calls."

Jordan's face sagged in relief and exhaustion. "Thank you," he whispered.

"What do you know about Shelby Atwood?"

Jordan jerked in his chair. "Shelby? She's crazy. Like should-be-institutionalized crazy."

I leaned forward. "Tell me everything you know about her."

Jordan glanced at me then Dad, confusion on his face. "I'm not sure what you want to know. She's Victor's daughter. He dotes on her. She's nearly as manipulative as he is, but she doesn't have mind control the way Victor does. I try to stay far, far away from her. She's cruel. Like Victor."

"Has she ever mentioned the names Megan or Sam?"

Jordan thought for a minute. "Like I said, I try to keep away from her, but she did say something about removing an obstacle. I got the feeling there was another wolf encroaching on a mate she wanted." Jordan looked up. "You?"

"Possibly," I conceded. "How is she able to keep her wolf secret? She's lived here for two years, and I've never smelled wolf on her."

"She doesn't always live with the pack. I'm not sure who or where her mom is, or where Shelby goes. I'm not sure how exactly she keeps her wolf secret. I know she had a surgery a few years back. She smelled properly wolf before then. I'm guessing that she had some sort of operation that tampered with her scent somehow. I have no idea how that would even be possible."

"Who operated?"

"I know it wasn't done in a hospital, and we don't have any doctors in our pack."

I had an idea who might be able to tell me more. "Dad, I'm going to go make a call. Yeah?"

"Sure." He turned to our prisoner. "Jordan, I'm going to go make a few of my own calls. I'll bring you out some food soon but know this. If anything you have told us today has been anything less than the truth, or if you have intentionally misled us in any way, I will kill you myself." Dad's voice was deathly low by the end, and even I had goose bumps.

I didn't doubt that my father would take this man out in the woods and that he'd never be seen again. I barely suppressed a shudder, thinking that only last week I wondered if he'd tried to kill Megan.

Moving back to the house I found the ladies sitting at the table, chatting happily over cups of tea and cookies. It was such a contrast from out in the shed, speaking with a man who had successfully kidnapped me, to this cheery, warm room full of female energy and soft laughter.

"Find out anything?" Meg asked as she glanced up. A shy blush spread over her cheeks, and I grinned like a stupid fool before clearing my throat.

"We did, actually. A few things. I'm going to head back up to the cabin and make a few calls. Are you ready to go?"

"Sure. Thanks for the cookies and conversation." We said our goodbyes and climbed into my car.

"So what did you find out?" Meg asked as she looped her fingers through mine.

I smiled and squeezed our twined hands. "I need to call Jennifer when we get home. I think she may have a few additional answers or theories." I quickly filled her in on what Jordan had told us and by the time I parked, she was up to speed.

"That's terrifying. To have your mind controlled? How is that even possible? You can't do that, can you? I mean, you can command someone in your own pack, but could you actually control someone beyond that?" she asked as I flipped the deadbolt.

Shaking my head, I pulled my phone out and put it on the table. "I don't know how to do anything beyond the command. Judging by Dad's face, I don't think he does either. And it is scary. If he can control his whole pack, and he has a large pack, he could essentially make them do whatever he wanted. Rob banks, steal cars...kill people." We were thoroughly sober at that thought.

"What about Shelby?"

"I think she did want me—I think she's most likely behind the attempts on your life, too. I don't know if she acted alone or with Victor's help." I shuddered and pulled her into a hug which she readily returned. "Let's call Jennifer. She may have some ideas."

Meg nodded and sat down at the table. Sitting opposite, I dialed and put it on speaker.

"Hello, this is Jennifer." Her voice was cheerful.

"Jennifer, it's Sam. Again. Megan is here, too."

"What can I do for you?"

"I'm hoping you might have some information for me."

"I'll certainly give it my best shot."

"Do you know anything about a surgery that could remove all scent traces of a werewolf?"

Jennifer inhaled sharply. "I haven't been privy to it myself, but Kyp and I heard about something similar while we were in Kentucky. It wasn't someone from our pack, but someone a pack member knew by association. The story circulated because it was so unusual. Anyway, there was a young wolf who was diagnosed with cancer in her glands. Now, because werewolves have extra glands, this was additionally concerning. The way we heard, she underwent a surgery and had her scent glands removed as well as her additional wolf glands. It fixed the cancer but removed all traces of her wolf scent." She paused. "It also drove her mad. Legitimately crazy."

I raised my eyebrows. "So this has been done before. When?"

"According to the gossip spreading around the Kentucky pack, it was probably close to five years ago."

"Crazy how?" Megan asked.

"She really went off the deep end after a few years. I think it started with delusions and probably some vivid hallucinations, or even altering her brain chemistry to the point that she felt and saw things that weren't real. By the end, she'd lost her powers of speech and would only scream and howl. She'd shift at will and couldn't control her body. I don't know if it was the removal of the glands, or if it was the cancer that was actually the root cause."

"It's possible that there is another wolf in our midst that has had her glands removed. At least, she has no wolf scent. She hid in plain sight for over two years."

"Wow. That's a long time to go undetected. Let me know if there's anything else I can do to help."

"I appreciate it. Tell Kyp I said hi. I'm thinking you both have passed the wolf tests with flying colors. I'll be speaking to Dad about his officially joining the pack."

There were tears in her voice. "You don't know what that means to me. Or what it will mean to him. Thank you."

Chapter 60

Megan

We joined Dominic and Mary again for dinner at the main house.

"I've called Austin Thornehill. He's agreed that he'll take Jordan into his pack for protection for the time being. And we're going to have a strategy meeting tomorrow. It's obvious that Victor Atwood is a threat. I'll be sending out some more scouting parties this week, and we're going to get as much information as we can and then assess what needs to happen. Austin has pledged his help," Dominic shared around a mouthful of mashed potatoes.

"I wish we knew what it was Atwood actually wanted," Sam added.

"I agree." Dominic nodded.

I swallowed a bite of delicious pot roast. "We're assuming Shelby is behind the attacks on me—do you think she was doing it on her own, or for Victor?" I asked.

"I'd like to know that, too," Dominic said.

"I think one of our chief concerns needs to be finding Shelby. She can't roam free. If she did have her glands removed like the wolf Jennifer heard about, Shelby could be literally losing her mind—doing all kinds of irrational things and planning another attempt. I won't have that," Sam said.

I nodded, heat curling in my belly, and I squeezed Sam's thigh under the table. He rubbed his leg against mine.

Mary dished out another carrot onto her plate. "Dom, do you think the pack will be safe enough, going in numbers? No one going anywhere alone?" Mary asked.

"Short of putting everyone on pack arrest, what else can we do right now? We don't have enough information. That's the first order of business."

A knock sounded at the door, and Dominic got up to answer it. His arm was still in its sling, and his face was still multicolored. "Austin, I didn't expect you to come yourself. Please come in. We're just having dinner. Mary, grab another plate," Dominic called back.

"I'm sorry to have come at an awkward hour. With things the way they are, I thought it might be best if we met in person and that I transport Jordan myself," Austin said as they came through the living room to the kitchen.

"Please sit down and join us," Mary said as she put another plate and silverware at the table by Sam. We all stood and leaned over to politely scent each other before Austin Thornehill sat down to a large helping of roast and vegetables.

"I appreciate this," he said with a smile. "Part of why I came myself, is that I wanted to assess the prisoner before taking him back. I am open to taking him with me, but only if I don't get any sort of duplicitous reading off him. I won't take a threat back to my pack."

"Completely understandable. I made him no guarantees," Dominic agreed.

Chapter 61

Sam

Austin Thornehill wasted no time, and immediately following dinner, he and Dad went out to chat with Jordan. I was invited, and while part of me wanted to go, my body was still recovering from the attack I'd led two days ago, and I was still reveling in the fact that Meg and I would be together. Forever—as long as that was.

With a promise that Dad would give me and Meg details later, he sent us on back to the cabin with a wink. "Go enjoy *your mate*," he'd said. And I planned to.

Megan and I both flopped down onto the bed once we reached the cabin. I grabbed her hand as we lay there, tired, happy, and content just to revel in her presence.

"What do you think Victor is planning?" Megan asked as we stared at the ceiling.

"I think he may be the one that Austin heard rumors about. I think he's probably after power. And a lot of it."

"Shelby?"

"Crazy."

She snorted. "Obviously." She rolled to face me. "I'm glad I'm here, and not her."

"Me, too. You're definitely better looking. And I'm certain you're a better cook," I teased. She smiled.

"What would you think if Rachel and I started a business together? Like a bakery-upon-request type thing we'd operate out of the kitchen?"

"I think we might want to consider making the kitchen bigger," I replied.

"We could make do." She squeezed my fingers.

"No, I'm serious. We could expand the kitchen. I think we ought to add an actual bedroom on, too. I mean, we're married. We're going to be living here together." I grinned at the thought. "I'd like to spend a significant amount of time with you. In our bedroom."

She laughed. "Are you being serious? About adding on to the cabin?"

"Steve Rivers has his own construction company. I've got plenty in YouTube ad money stashed away for that."

"Let's do it."

"Let's do it. You and Rachel can hash out plans for your bake-on-demand business."

Her smile stretched all the way across her face. "Sam, I love you."

"I love you," I whispered back as the glow in my chest spread throughout the rest of me. The glow spread to her as our lips touched, igniting a fire that soon consumed us together.

Early the next morning my phone beeped. I scrubbed a hand across my face and glanced at the text. Megan stirred beside me. "What is it?" she asked groggily.

"Dad and Austin are going to help Jordan initiate a break with Atwood. I think I should be there for this."

"Okay. I'll come, too."

I kissed her on the forehead, and we threw on clothes and headed back down to Mom and Dad's house. We got there right as gray dawn light was being pushed aside with the pink and yellow fingers of the sun.

A scream ripped through the air as we shut the car doors. Anxiety kicked through my veins, and Megan grabbed my hand as we hurried to the door. Jordan was slumped on the carpet of the living room floor with Dad and Austin hovering on either side, and Mom standing in the back of the room. Jordan gripped his head, sobbing unabashedly. He groaned and leaned over so that his head rested on the floor. His back heaved with his erratic panting.

"Is he okay?" Megan asked cautiously as we stood inside the doorway, afraid to move farther into the room.

"It's done. He's Rogue," Austin answered.

"He's officially gone from Victor's pack," I explained quietly. Megan's lips thinned.

Jordan groaned as he tried to sit up. "He'll come, and he'll bring everything he has." Jordan gripped his head. Dad gripped his shoulder. I gripped Megan's hand.

War was coming to Rock Falls.

Acknowledgments

Pater, gratias ago tibi, quia donum verba.
Husband, thank you for the gift of time.
Mom, Dad, Landon, Grandma—thank you for all your prayers, support, and cheerleading.
Karen, this book wouldn't have happened without you.
Tami, you're the best Fan Club President east of the Mississippi.
Lacey, your friendship and creativity have been invaluable.
Sarah, thanks for saying what you honestly thought about the book. Your insights made it better.
To the most amazing beta readers in the world—Ayra, Robin, and Bonnie. You guys are the best.
And my AV kids who sparked the ideas in the first place.

And to the Q&F Team who stepped in at a moment's notice. You have my undying gratitude.

About the Author

 Writing books full of murder, mayhem, sometimes magic, and always kissing, AJ (also writing as April J. Skelly) is an author, reader, and lover of all things fantasy, medieval, and fairy-tale-romance. And werewolves. She has a serious soft spot for them. As an avid life-long reader and a former high school English teacher, she's always been fascinated with the written word. She lives with her husband, children, and many imaginary friends who often find their way into her stories. They all drink copious amounts of tea together and stay up reading far later than they should.

You can read more about her stories, shenanigans, random factoids, and new books at www.ajskelly.com

IF YOU LIKED

FIRST SHIFT

CONSIDER CHECKING OUT MORE QUILL & FLAME PUBLISHING HOUSE TITLES

HEAT WITHOUT THE SCORCH

Quill & Flame
PUBLISHING HOUSE

WWW.QUILLANDFLAME.COM

www.ingramcontent.com/pod-product-compliance
Lightning Source LLC
LaVergne TN
LVHW012032070526
838202LV00056B/5475